Spook Squad

For Laith!

Jordan Castillo Price
GRL 2013

Spook Squad

A PSYCOP NOVEL

JORDAN CASTILLO PRICE

jcpbooks.com

First published in print in the United States
in 2013 by JCP Books.
www.jcpbooks.com

This book is a work of fiction. The characters, incidents, and dialogue are drawn from the author's imagination and are not to be construed as real. Any resemblance to actual events or persons, living or dead, is entirely coincidental.

Spook Squad: A PsyCop Novel. Copyright © 2013 by Jordan Castillo Price. All rights reserved. No part of this book may be used or reproduced in any manner whatsoever without written permission except in the case of brief quotations embodied in critical articles and reviews.

First Edition

ISBN-13 978-1-935540-65-6

ACKNOWLEDGMENTS

Writing a book is a collaborative effort. Since this is a story about teamwork, this book is dedicated to my team.

There would be no PsyCop 7 without Dev Bentham and Clare London, who held my hand through the entire writing process and kept me motivated when I was going through the "scrap the whole project and go get a day job" phase.

I appreciate my mother going out of her way to do a read-through even though she had a bunch of home repairs that needed doing. I'm told there were days her TV was never turned on at all!

Special thanks to Andy Slayde and Cindi Sulken for helping me keep the series events from contradicting themselves, and making sure I made sense.

I'm also grateful for the generosity of Sonia Ballesteros Rey for her Spanish advice, and Sey and Andre for their assistance with Marie St. Savon's writings.

David Warner was invaluable for troubleshooting points of legalese where I could have potentially sounded ridiculous.

All residual ridiculousness and errors are, of course, my own.

CHAPTER 1

I OFTEN WONDER WHAT I might have done with my life if I'd never become a cop. There was this kid who sat behind me in fifth grade. His name is long gone from my patchy memory, but I do recollect two things about him. One, he annoyed the hell out of me by wiggling his foot against the leg of my chair all day long. And two, he knew exactly what he wanted to be when he grew up: a garbageman. Not in an ironic kind of way, either. Careers in sanitation fascinated him. He drew pictures of garbage trucks like other kids drew rocket ships or unicorns. On trash day, he would set his alarm early so he'd be waiting there in the alley to get a glimpse of his heroes. If you gave him a box, he wouldn't make something useful out of it like a car or a teleporter. He'd make a dumpster.

When I hear the pneumatic wheeze of a garbage truck's air brakes, I occasionally think of this kid, whatever his name was. I wonder if he ever did manage to live the dream, or if his parents talked him into being an accountant, or maybe a doctor.

At one point in my prepubescent life, I had aspirations of joining the military. Not because I'm pro war, and certainly not because I'm good at following orders. I suspect my subconscious was grooving on the idea of being dumped into the plastic bag with a few dozen other little green army men and losing myself in a tangle of arms, legs and rifles.

Real life being as disappointing as it often is, my chosen career (or the career that chose me) turned out to be a continual display of territoriality and machismo rather than teamwork. Other than my partner, Bob Zigler, I've never really grown comfortable with anyone at the precinct. The feeling is mutual. Sometimes the evidence of exclusion is subtle, like when conversation ebbs as I cross the threshold. Sometimes it's overt, like finding every last pen gone from my desk when the fully stocked supply room is a hell of a lot closer to everything else, and Zig's desk is untouched.

It says something about how awkward things were that I preferred being at a crime scene to reporting back to the station and dealing with all the other cops. This aversion to groups probably started early. I grew up in group foster care with a rotating stream of snotty kids—troubled kids, I know now. I'm sure they acted like they did not because they were inherently jerks, but because they'd been starved, beaten, and molested, or at the very least, neglected. Sure, we had toys, but they were nasty second hand toys. Naked dolls. Games with missing parts. Dirty plastic action figures with the paint rubbed off.

One thing I don't remember attempting to play with is a jigsaw puzzle. I'm sure we must have had them, probably with a good handful of pieces missing from each one. But I couldn't dredge up any specific memory of putting together puzzles.

Maybe eventually I'd get the hang of it, although probably not tonight. It was already past six—and while I'd been focused on my project, the cannery had grown dim.

"I'm home," Lisa called from the foyer. My heart did a little relief-flip every time I heard her say that. Even now. All these months after we coaxed her out of the greedy clutches of PsyTrain.

"I'm in here." My voice was phlegmy from staring so hard I'd forgotten to swallow.

Lisa tracked in melted snow and frowned down at the dining room table. "You're not done with that thing yet?"

To be fair, it might be my first jigsaw puzzle…as far as I knew. "I didn't realize there was a time limit."

"That's not what I mean." Lisa tousled my hair and went back to hang up her coat. "Me and Jacob gave up after the first hour. But you're still at it. Thought you said those guys aren't your type."

Judging by the box lid, the puzzle seemed like it should have been fun. It featured male dancers with bare chests, bulging muscles, sparkly bowlers, clingy slacks, bow ties fastened around bare necks, and ginormous baskets. Yeah, not my type. But kitschy and stupid in a way I could appreciate. Figuring out which tab fit into which hole was a welcome distraction from the way I'd spent my day: figuring out which vehicle must be covered in minute traces of a distressed murder victim's blood.

Cops need a solid chunk of time to unwind when they clock off. I hadn't been actively searching for something to deaden my brain after work. It just happened to be there. Jacob's gym pals had presented him with the goofy gift at his private retirement party—the one that guys on the force weren't privy to—along with a card that read, *We're puzzled that you're retiring. Don't go soft on us!*

Lots of people were puzzled. Not me, though. I knew exactly which carrot Regional Director Con Dreyfuss had dangled in front of Jacob to get him to join the FPMP, and more importantly, which stick he'd subtly suggested might beat Grandma Marks to death.

I tried and rejected yet another piece. "They're all skin-toned or black." Maybe I should have started with something easier, like a bouquet of differently-colored flowers. As it was, I'd been staring at one particular dancer, a guy with a dorky come-hither look on his face, for the better part of an hour. There was a big puzzle-shaped hole in his gut where his six pack should have been. You'd think I could spot a set of washboard abs without much problem. But with masses of spray-tanned skin cut into jigsaw pieces, the body parts eventually started to blend.

Lisa turned on an overhead light and joined me at the dining room table. The puzzle and I had been monopolizing the tabletop for a while now, but none of us actually ate there anyway, since meals happened on the coffee table and TV trays. Usually the big table was home to books and newspapers. Now the books were on the floor and the papers in the recycle bin…and somehow, inadvertently, I'd ended up with a new hobby.

All it took was a critical need to unwind and a major life change in my partner that neither of us had seen coming.

Lisa and I sat together and stared down at the die-cut cardboard pieces, and eventually she found a piece of someone's thigh and clicked it into place. And then a smoky bit of background. And then an oiled shoulder. All the while, I continued searching for my abs. Then she found three nondistinctive gray background pieces, one after the other. Click, click, click. "Are you using the sí-no?" I finally asked.

She looked up, startled. "No. Why would I…?" She laughed and cuffed me on the arm. "That would take all the fun out of it."

Right. Fun.

I was trying to finesse a not-quite-right bellybutton into position when the doorbell made us both jump. Since the cannery's bell was meant to be heard over the drone and clang of heavy equipment, its chime wasn't exactly what you'd call melodic. You don't want to be caught holding a hot cup of coffee when it goes off.

I collected my sidearm before I answered, not because I'm a paranoid nutcase, but because I'm a realist. Since I wasn't expecting anybody, I'd need to be prepared for the possibility that some whacked-out anti-Psych had decided to visit—with a shotgun. But it turned out this time my caution was unnecessary. Yes, my visitor was scary. But at least her gun was holstered.

"Is Jacob here?" Carolyn asked.

"Uh, no. He's…" I glanced at my watch. Nearly seven. Ideally he'd be home by now, but no big surprise that he wasn't. "Not yet."

"I figured. I didn't see his car out there."

Oh. Here I thought she'd been looking for him—not looking to avoid him. I stepped aside and let her in.

"So he left some stuff in my car." Carolyn began dropping things on the catch-all table beside the front door. A leather-bound notebook, some fancy pens, an MP3 player. I considered mentioning that maybe she should stay awhile, since Jacob would be really glad to see her. Unfortunately, I sensed her reply might be phenomenally awkward, given that she can't whitewash the truth like the rest of us can. She'd probably considered mailing his effects—I know the idea would have crossed *my* mind—but that would seem too weird. Easiest to engineer the drop-off while Jacob was at work. She seemed eager to rid herself of his things and then bail, but when Lisa drew up beside me to see what was going on, Carolyn paused, cocked her head, and looked Lisa up and down. "Are you just visiting," Carolyn asked, "or do you still live here?"

"For now," Lisa began, while in my panic I talked over her and said, "It's really not a problem. We have plenty of room." Because I'd been through too damn much to get Lisa back, and I wanted to keep her right where I could see her. I didn't want Carolyn fucking that up with any inconvenient truth. "All kinds of room."

Carolyn looked pointedly around the foyer, then said, "Room, but not many walls. That's not exactly an ideal situation for three adults."

Now, Lisa and I may not possess the type of talent where we could feed thoughts back and forth without other people being any the wiser. But we can read each others' body language like a front page headline. Lisa shifted forward slightly. So did I.

As if that wouldn't just pique Carolyn's curiosity.

Hey, I said Lisa and I were in synch. Not that we were adept at steering a conversation. Carolyn strode past us like we'd just told her there were warm brownies in the living room that needed eating. Lisa and I turned away from each other. I shrugged. She sighed.

"How long have you…?" Carolyn's voice seemed overloud against the hardwood and brick. "Whose idea was this?"

We followed her into the main room and shot guilty glances at the big blue dome-shaped tent in the corner. Yes, it's not something you see every day. But if it worked for the three of us, who was Carolyn to make us feel like a bunch of weirdos?

I'm not even sure who'd suggested the tent. Just that after Lisa spent a few weeks on our couch, there'd been an edge to the "I should probably find my own place" discussion that sounded pretty serious to me. And Jacob's tent was going to waste rolled up in the basement.

And if you have a room big enough to hold a living room set, a dining room set, and an entertainment center with space left over for a four-person tent…why shouldn't you pitch it? "It's just a privacy thing," I said. "Not a fashion statement."

Carolyn glanced up at the loft, where we'd be able to see down over a room divider with ease, and then looked me over to see if I was being truthful. Apparently she was satisfied; she didn't challenge me on it. But she did subject Lisa to additional scrutiny. "Are you running from something, is that what this is? Or did something happen in California that nobody's talking about? Because the three of you troop out there, and when you get back, suddenly you're playing living room adventurer and my partner hands in his—" she broke off and turned away with her hand clasped against her mouth, and I realized with a sudden and awkward certainty that I was about to see hard-assed Carolyn Brinkman cry.

"I'm not running," Lisa said. Unlike me, she wasn't moved to awkwardness the minute anyone teared up. But exactly like me, she'd seen way too much weird shit at PsyTrain to sleep without a nightlight…and she didn't like to discuss the big, fat, ectoplasmic mess any more than I did. "And I'm not bothering anyone either. If Victor don't want me here, he'll say so."

"I do want you here."

"So don't be judging me." Lisa punctuated her statement with a ghetto-tastic side-to-side head move that made me realize I was seriously outclassed in the current discussion.

"Is that what you think this is about?" Carolyn snapped back. "I'm not *judging* you—I'm worried. You lost your PsyCop badge, you skipped out on PsyTrain, and you're sleeping in a tent in your ex-partner's living room. Does that sound healthy to you?"

"I'm no quitter," Lisa said—and she was even bringing out the big ammo now, the no-finger, which she proceeded to wag in Carolyn's face, bangle bracelets jingling. "Don't you ever call me a quitter."

"I'm not—"

"I got suspended helping you people. And PsyTrain is none of your business."

Although Carolyn was about as white bread as a person can be, Lisa's "talk to the hand" posture didn't daunt her. In fact, instead of backing off, she took an even closer look. "How many carats are those diamonds?" she said.

Since Carolyn doesn't do her shopping at SaverPlus like Lisa and I do, she doesn't realize that the best one can hope for at the second floor jewelry counter is rhinestones and crystal. Lisa's idea of adornment is big plastic sunglasses and a little diary-type key she wears around her neck. She buys her bling from spinner racks, not glass cases. Even so, she backed off from Carolyn, startled—and she took her hand and its bangle bracelets with her. But instead of educating Carolyn on the ways of the budget conscious shopper, she said, "What does it matter to you?"

"Four carats? Five?"

Carats? Right. I was fully aware that Lisa had answered the question with a question to dodge Carolyn's built-in polygraph—but before I could ponder why she would suddenly feel defensive about wearing costume jewelry when everyone knew it was fake, the front door banged open.

Jacob. Great timing.

"Carolyn?" He dashed into the living room as if he was in danger of missing her—as if he didn't stand between her and the only escape route. "I just left you another message."

Carolyn turned and looked at him coolly, though an unshed tear still glittered in her eye. "I know."

His shoulders sagged, though so imperceptibly I was probably the only one who'd noticed. His impeccable suit, his carefully honed physique, even his ramrod posture, everything about Jacob was rigid, controlled perfection. A man of steel…but not inside. I've never wanted to be an empath—too damn confusing—but at that moment I could have really used the insight, 'cos it was a real struggle to figure out how emotions had tanked so fast. Here Lisa and I were contentedly fitting pieces of half-naked cardboard men together, and before I knew it, the atmosphere was soupy with anger, frustration, resentment and hurt. The stupid part was, we were all on the same damn side.

"Look," Jacob told Carolyn. "What I've been trying to get you to hear is, there's no reason we can't keep working together."

"Other than the fact that you retired."

"Come on, think about it. You'd help a lot more people if you would—"

"No, Jacob. I wouldn't. I wouldn't help more people, I'd help a different kind of people. If I followed you to the Federal Psychic Monitoring Program, I'd be looking out for Psychs—and it would be a hell of a lot more dangerous than what I'm doing now."

"You don't know that."

"Yes, I do. The majority of my perps are single guys, acting alone. Once we find them, once they're charged and arraigned, they're not my problem anymore. You're dealing with big, organized groups. They've got money behind them, they've got widespread religious support, and worse than that, they've got their fears that one day all the NPs will wake up in a slave state where they do nothing but bow down and serve their evil psychic overlords."

I don't know how she got that sentence out in a single breath, and I think she didn't either. She stopped and blinked, and then the thought occurred to me that Carolyn didn't really have much of a knack for hyperbole, thanks to her talent keeping tabs on her truthfulness. And then I realized she wasn't exaggerating.

That's how Carolyn actually thought the Non-Psychs saw us. And it scared the crap out of her.

"My daughters aren't even in high school yet. They need their mom." She dropped her gaze to the floor. "I can't work with you. Not at the FPMP."

"If there is a threat out there, don't you want the best Psychs in the world on your team? Besides, you're overestimating your opponent. They're not nearly as organized as all that. Tell her, Vic."

How was I supposed to make Carolyn feel better when I'd just answered my door with a Glock in my hand? "Uh, I don't know. Safety in numbers?" It was the best I could do, at least to Carolyn's face.

"More like a bigger target," she said.

This was so not the way I'd hoped Jacob's reunion with Carolyn would play out. I said, "Listen, it's late. We're all tired. I can order us some pizzas and maybe once we eat, we'll all be thinking straight."

"Actually," Jacob said, "I need to put in a couple of hours at the firing range. Night training. You want to come with? I can make a call, see if there's room—"

"I've just put in a ten-hour day," Carolyn snapped. "Now I'm going home. To my family."

Jacob looked to Lisa and me to see if either of us would tag along. I could definitely use the practice, especially at night. The Fifth Precinct requires one firearms session a year. That's right: one. Since I'm not an overachiever, initially I didn't put in any extra time on my own. Not until I failed my first recertification—and you only need to hit seventy percent of the targets to pass that thing.

I should have jumped at the chance…but I didn't want the FPMP to think I was easy.

Jacob looked to Lisa. She said, "Actually, I already have plans." She gave a sheepish shrug. "Sorry."

Carolyn didn't call her out on these purported "plans," so they must have existed. The awkwardness between the four of us was thick enough to cut with a spork, but at least Lisa was no longer going Jerry Springer Baby Momma on Carolyn, and Jacob wasn't tooting the Federal Psychic Monitoring Program's horn. I gave the ropy muscles at the back of my neck a couple of squeezes, said, "Well, I guess I'll go see if Crash wants pizza," and turned to retrieve my phone from my overcoat.

"Vic," Jacob said. I tensed, because I really thought I'd successfully weaseled my way out of that awkward conversation without resorting to an untruth, but I didn't bolt when he reached toward me. I was prepared for a caress, or maybe a hug, some sort of attempt to entice me to stay and keep trying to convince the girls we were all still one big, happy family. But instead he just plucked something off the back of my shirt and handed it to me.

It was a puzzle piece with a tacky smear of jelly on the back of it. I turned it photo-side up. Fake tan flesh-tone—and it looked suspiciously like a set of washboard abs.

CHAPTER 2

PARKING SUCKED BY STICKS AND STONES, but that was nothing new. On the first floor of Crash's building, huge sheets of plywood covered the place where the palm reader's front window used to be…now *that* was new. I found a spot on a side street and sprinted toward the store with my cooling pizza. At the front door, I paused briefly to consider the board-up job, then toed some sparkly chunks lodged in the crack of the sidewalk to see if they were rock salt or broken glass. Hard to tell, especially while I was balancing a large double-cheese veggie supreme in my hands. I went upstairs before the cheese could congeal any more than it already had.

Thanks to a formidable boiler system, the temperature in Crash's building is subtropical, even in the dead of winter. Although it was below freezing outside, Crash answered his door in bare feet, holey jeans and a skimpy white T-shirt at least two sizes too small. The shirt was gray with age and half-hearted washings, and it clung to him like a second skin. Next to the dull T-shirt, the ink on his arms looked twice as vivid. I don't think he'd been aiming for that specific effect. It looked more like he'd just grabbed the first clothes he laid his hands on. Instead of standing in its usual careful spikes, his peroxide blond hair was damp, finger-combed back, showing dark, wet roots.

"Aren't you a sight for sore eyes?" he said. He acted like he was talking to me, but I suspected he was addressing the pizza. Business hours were over, so he locked the door behind me, whisked the pizza over to the cash register and plunked it down on the plexi countertop.

He doesn't have much by way of furniture. Even if he owned a table, there'd be nowhere to put it. There are four tiny roomlets behind the shop:

a cramped office, a galley kitchen, a closet of a bedroom, and a bathroom where you can hardly turn around to pee. It was easier to just hang out in the shop where we had some elbow room. I enjoyed Sticks and Stones that way, after-hours dim with a couple of lit candles flickering behind the register and the scent of sandalwood and myrrh lingering in the air. It felt safe from prying eyes—psychic eyes.

It usually felt safe from your garden-variety mayhem too, tucked away on the second floor, out of harm's reach. But not tonight. "What happened to the windows downstairs?"

"Smash and grab. Not that Lydia had anything to grab—the storefront is basically a waiting room with a lot of black curtains and some cheesy esoteric symbols on the walls to get her clients in the mood for their readings. They trashed her big neon palm reader sign, too. I loved that thing…I hope she can replace it."

"Won't insurance cover that?"

"Dunno. Maybe she can't afford to carry any. One thing's for sure, my insurance bill got shuffled to the top of the stack this month."

Crash handed me a folding chair and I set it up on the customer side of the counter while he delved back through the beaded curtain. "I'm out of pop," he called from the kitchen, "but I can make iced tea."

"Don't worry about it. Water's fine." I had thought about picking up a 2-liter at the pizzeria but it seemed like too much trouble to carry. I opened the box and peeked at the pizza. There was a bit of slideage going on. I nudged the cheese back into place as best I could, closed the box, and licked the grease off my fingers before he came back with the drinks.

Crash set down a stack of McDonald's paper napkins and a pair of coffee mugs filled with water, then whisked open the box. "All the toppings. You sure know how to spoil a guy." By now, the pizza was at that temperature where you might end up with an empty triangle of saucy crust if you pulled it the wrong way. But he finessed out the perfect amount of cheese and toppings…then ate it as if he hadn't seen food for days.

Maybe it had been a while since he'd been shopping. Or maybe he needed to choose between groceries and insurance. I wondered how little I could eat without seeming too obvious, and I wished I'd had the foresight to not only add soda, but breadsticks to my order.

"So Carolyn seems pretty pissed off," I ventured.

"The operative word there is *seems*. She can't pretend something's not bothering her when it is. It's actually pretty refreshing…once you get used to it."

"Jacob's trying to lure her over to the dark side."

"Oh? And what—you're jealous it's not you he's wooing?"

I choked on a mushroom, coughed it up into my mouth, swallowed it again and said, "Right…I'm jealous."

"Don't be that way. Here's what I'm saying: it's obvious the pigs and the feds should both be plying you with cocaine and handjobs to try and buy your allegiance. But Jacob hasn't messengered you any offers yet, has he? How long has it been?"

I'm not sure if Crash realizes how hard-hitting his flattery can be. I'm not even sure he was trying to flatter me. "Couple of months."

"A couple of months." He looked at me sagely and tapped his tongue stud against the backs of his teeth. "And no one's offered you so much as a quick stroke or a tasty bump? C'mon, it's so obvious. They're scared you'll take off in the opposite direction if they so much as lean toward approaching you."

"The FPMP doesn't need to sweet talk me. I owe them an exorcism."

"True. But still, F-Pimp hasn't sent out anyone to break your kneecaps and collect the debt."

"I don't see what they'd want with me in the long-term anyhow. Once they're clean, they'll stay clean." Presuming they stopped killing people in their offices, anyway.

"You're smart to keep your distance, if you ask me. You're a better fit for the police."

"I…am?"

"Sure. As much as my left-wing, bleeding heart, painfully liberal Buddhist philosophy requires that I razz the cops every chance I get, it's obvious that when you work, you're in the zone."

I'd never thought much about it. Then again, police work was the only sort of job I'd ever done…despite my own personal and philosophical aversion to the force.

"Today, for example," Crash said. "What did you do today?"

"You might not want to hear about it while you're eating."

"I've got a cast-iron stomach. Try me."

I thought I'd stared hard enough at the dumb jigsaw puzzle to numb the day out of my brain, but apparently I hadn't. As soon as Crash asked, everything rushed back. The victim's ghost. The vehicle. The fucking bully of a husband who had his wide-eyed-innocent look down pat. The homicide had been given up for hopeless, but my chat with the dead woman had obtained the search warrant to seize his blood-riddled 4x4. The evidence wasn't fresh and gory, though it was extensive, dried to invisibility on a black paint job that lit up like a disco ball with a few spritzes of luminol and a pass of black light. As bloody homicides go, since the evidence was old and dry, it was one of the less gruesome scenes. It's not just blood that sticks in my mind, though. The thought of what atrocities one human being can commit on another was the part that haunted me.

Crash's appetite wasn't visibly dampened. "If that's not an example of being in the zone," he said, "I don't know what is."

I'd never considered the idea that I had a "zone." I can't say it felt good, exactly, though it did feel satisfying. But before I could get too carried away with myself by reveling in the thought, a sharp knock on the front door startled me back to everyday reality. Crash went very still, listening. Or maybe feeling. Softly, I said, "You're not expecting anyone, I take it."

He shook his head as a guy on the other side of the door called, "Hello? Hello, are you there? I saw lights on from the alley."

"A friend?" I guessed.

Crash cocked his head and focused on the voice. "Doesn't sound familiar."

If it was a casual hookup looking for a repeat of the action, I couldn't blame the guy for trying. Except if I were to drop by some casual lay's shop in hopes of scoring, I'd at least attempt to sound a bit more…flirty.

And I don't have a flirtatious bone in my body.

The knocking turned into banging. "Hello? I really need to—look, I tried to get here earlier but the buses run so bad in the snow."

I looked to Crash to see if he recognized the voice yet. He shook his head.

More banging, and then the guy yelled, "Your store's hours fucking suck."

Crash's eyebrows shot up toward the dark roots at his hairline. "Sometimes the whole non-violence discipline feels incredibly limiting."

"You want me to…?"

"No, you're my guest, not my bodyguard. Keep eating." He rounded the counter and headed for the door. "I'm happy to provide a refresher-course in manners."

Right, as if I was going to just sit there and keep stuffing pizza in my face while he dealt with this guy. For all we knew, this was the same creep who'd robbed the downstairs neighbor, coming back for round two. As I grabbed the entire stack of napkins and began buffing the grease off my fingers in anticipation of drawing my sidearm, a calm and familiar voice said, "Let Curtis handle it."

Not that I didn't value Miss Mattie's opinion…but I kept de-greasing anyway.

"You care 'bout him, I know, but he still a man. You can't fight his fights for him. When you let people make their own choices, you show them your respect."

Darkened store, agitated customer, recent robbery—whatever cop-sense I'd developed over the years was shrilling "danger" at its highest volume. I crept up the aisle, right hand ready…and then I saw the guy who'd preempted my dinner wasn't brandishing an ice pick or a chain-wrapped baseball bat. He had a can of incense in his hand. "I need to return this."

Crash flipped on the overhead lights. They flickered to life, and my ominous sense of foreboding ebbed. He took the can from the guy, shook it a few times, and said, "It didn't light?"

"It lit…but it was wood, mostly wood." He was a normal-looking guy, but normal-looking guys can carry a switchblade or a pistol in their pocket just as easily as an obvious thug. I kept my eye on his body language, his aggression. Now that he had six feet of tattooed Crash up in his face, he was nowhere near as cocky as he'd been on the other side of the door.

Crash is assertive, but he's not aggressive. He doesn't maneuver like a cop—he steers situations with words. "That's characteristic of this type of self-lighting incense. Anything you get in a canister will be tinted sandalwood infused with oils and resins. The wood is what keeps it burning without charcoal."

"But it's awful. All the different types smell the same, like wood."

I spied movement out of the corner of my eye. Miss Mattie was fanning herself with her paper St. Anthony fan beside me. I wondered if her fanning had anything to do with the hissing radiators or if, since she was non-physical, it was simply habit. "That man is just here for an argument," she said. "And Curtis happy to give it to him."

Taking into consideration the posture, the gestures…I'd have to agree. Since I'm the type of person who avoids arguments rather than feeding off them, I wandered back to the counter. "Is he okay?" I said under my breath. "In general, I mean. He's not…starving or anything. Is he?"

When Miss Mattie didn't answer, I thought maybe she'd disappeared. She hadn't, though. She was gazing off into eternity, gently fanning her broad face. Finally, she said, "Curtis grew up with money. Big house, out in the suburbs. Only child. Two parents working, jobs that pay good… jobs they hate. His daddy dropped over dead the day after he turned fifty. His momma fightin' an ulcer."

I tried to picture Mattie in this well-to-do suburban scene, and couldn't quite see how she'd fit in. "And you were their neighbor?"

"That's just how his momma explained it to him." She snapped her fan shut. "I cleaned their house."

"Oh." If that was a mental shift for me, I couldn't imagine what Crash would make of it. I sure as hell wasn't going to be the one to break the news.

Miss Mattie disappeared as the argumentative guy's voice carried up the aisles. "Aren't you going to offer me a refund?"

"I might have, if you didn't barge in here after closing—"

"I told you, the bus—"

"And on top of that, it's almost gone. How bad could it have been if you used it up?"

"The can was half-empty to begin with. The contents settle. Open a new one and you'll see."

How long was this guy gonna carry on? I swallowed the last of my water, then delved through the beaded curtain to the inner sanctum for a refill. Okay, and maybe to snoop while Crash was occupied, so I could reassure myself that I wouldn't swing by and find he'd starved to death because I hadn't thought to bring bread sticks.

The fridge looked pretty sparse. There were condiments on the door, soy sauce and chili paste, and jars of who-knows-what covered in colorful Asian characters. An egg carton with ten eggs left. Numerous packets of McDonald's ketchup and Taco Bell salsa. I tried not to imagine him living on fast food condiments, but I didn't see any way to drop off some vegetables without coming off as incredibly condescending. The freezer, in which you could usually find some microwave vegetarian dinners and a big bottle of vodka, now contained nothing but a two-inch layer of frost and a few trays of ice cubes. A package of marked down Halloween cookies, crumbled as if someone had stepped on them, sat on the countertop. The cupboards held a canister of generic oatmeal, a bag of dried lentils, and a stack of ramen noodles as long as my arm. I'd endured the occasional all-ramen menu when I was first sprung from Camp Hell. I hadn't ended up with diabetes or scurvy, and actually, I didn't mind the taste. Were they still ten for a dollar? Maybe, in the local bodegas. Nowadays, I wouldn't dare bring any home for fear of an all-night lecture on the dangers of sodium. I closed the cupboard door before I got caught rifling through Crash's stuff, refilled my water from the tap, and made my way back through the piles of books, recycling and dirty clothes to the store.

Crash and the disgruntled customer were now standing in front of the incense display. "You're gonna have to upgrade to charcoal and resin. If you don't like that wood smell, it's the only way."

"You're probably just trying to get me to buy an expensive incense holder."

"Absolutely not—a heavy ceramic ash tray will work just fine. If you don't wanna buy a new one, wash an old one in salt water and say your favorite cleansing ritual over it first." The guy grumbled a reply, and Crash said, "Tell you what. Try some of the primo stuff, and I'll throw in your first roll of charcoal, free."

"Free" must have been the magic word. The guy picked out his incense and Crash rang him up around the now-cold pizza. He even had the decency to look slightly chagrined for interrupting our dinner. Once we heard his footsteps recede down the stairwell, I said, "How much did that encounter net you?"

"Pff. Maybe five bucks. Plus the satisfaction that I didn't give him a refund for the used up thing he was trying to return."

"And the charcoal?"

"Costs me a quarter."

He was a savvy salesman and he knew how to handle a customer, but it seemed like a hell of a lot of effort for a measly $4.75. Especially when he was living on ketchup packets. I didn't want to come right out and say it—he hadn't asked for my financial advice, after all, and Miss Mattie's assertion that too much interference would emasculate him was fresh in my mind. I cared about him, though. I couldn't just say nothing. I closed the box on the cold pizza and said, "Retail seems like a tough business."

"You're telling me."

"I'll bet you'd be good at marketing." This wasn't necessarily a hundred percent accurate. His flyers were artsy, but also cryptic and vaguely disturbing. Although maybe, for the right sort of customer, that sensibility would be a bonus. Truthfully, I added, "You seem to enjoy it."

"As a full-time gig? I dunno. I'd need to go back to school. Plus I'd end up having to deal with a lot of corporate dickwads."

"And how are they any worse than tonight's charmer?"

Crash pulled a pack of gum out of his pocket and offered me a stick. I shook my head, no. He unwrapped a piece and said thoughtfully, "Maybe I'd be good at marketing, maybe I wouldn't. It doesn't much matter. This store is my world. It's my life. It's who I am. I'm my own boss, and I make my own rules. I couldn't close up shop any more than you could turn in your badge and start taking orders from F-Pimp."

CHAPTER 3

TROUBLE SHARED IS TROUBLE HALVED—THAT'S how the saying goes, anyway. Unfortunately, describing the bloody truck to Crash brought back the day I'd been working so hard to forget. The ghost was so young, maybe Lisa's age, not even thirty, and she was still hung up on the guy who'd stabbed her…twelve times, by my count…three of them in the neck. The only reason she'd told me it was him was to ask me—to *beg* me—to help her understand why he'd done it.

And unfortunately, I had no good answer for that.

A Valium might take the edge off my thoughts, but it wouldn't do anywhere near as good a job at dulling the day's memories as a Seconal would. Too bad I was fresh out of reds. They're a hell of a lot harder to score than Valium.

Since the objective was to knock myself out completely, I turned to over-the-counter sleeping pills instead. Slumber came not on a gentle wave of barbiturate euphoria, but with a sickening lurch. Still, it was better than seeing the victim every time I closed my eyes, her stabbed throat working as she wailed her husband's name.

Jacob got back from the range while I was dead to the world. I surfaced from the tar pit of chemically-induced sleep to the feel of a tongue sliding over the nape of my neck, a hard-on prodding the back of my thigh, and the faintest ballistic whiff of metal. I'm always up for a nightcap. Too bad my drugged body was so sluggish, so numb, it felt like it wasn't even mine.

"Can't," I managed to say. "Tired."

Jacob settled against me and allowed his hand to drift from my crotch to my thigh, stroking absently while he ground his head into the pillows searching for just the right spot.

I checked to see if my body might rally and rouse itself for a quickie, but moving wasn't just difficult. It was nearly painful. "Jerk off on me," I slurred.

He exhaled a silent laugh. "It'll keep." As he breathed a lingering kiss into my neck, he pushed his knee into the crook of my legs, and now it was perfect, with all of our hills and valleys pressed together, like a puzzle piece that's just snapped into place. "It's not nearly as fun without you in on the action."

That was probably for the best, otherwise I could be replaced with a porno.

"I couldn't stop thinking about how angry Carolyn was tonight," he said softly. "We used to train together. It was weird without her."

I made a sympathetic noise.

"She would've been crazy about this range, all the latest stuff—indoor, outdoor, simulators, the works…but I don't think it matters. It's as if joining the FPMP would be like picking sides, Psych versus NP. And she'd rather not be a Psych at all."

Imagine that.

He said, "I used to understand why you'd rather just get rid of it. If there was some kind of switch you could flip—a procedure, a surgery, whatever. I could see you doing it, even if it was permanent, and even if it meant you'd be out of a job. Maybe it would be easier, not having to see all of it, all at once. All the 'stuff' most people don't need to see. But after PsyTrain, seeing what little I did…now I know ignoring it won't make it go away. Trying to switch off psychic ability is like turning off the lights when a burglar's in the house so you don't have to look at him."

What he didn't understand, and what I couldn't articulate with over-the-counter lethargy surging through my veins, was that I totally agreed that knowing was better than ignorance. Yet, the analogy fell apart if you drilled down too far. The burglar wasn't just swinging by to relieve me of some valuables and then hustle off to the pawn shop. He lived with me…and then he followed me to work. And to the store. And the diner.

And anywhere else I might care to go. There's bound to be a saturation point, a point at which I give up and say, *Fine, take what you want. You will anyway, and I'm sick of the sight of your ugly face.*

Jacob said, "Carolyn was right about one thing—I did make a difference to more people on the force. But it's not a numbers game, not when it's about us: you, Crash, Lisa, Carolyn too. Our families. All of us." Sleep was dragging me into its leaden embrace, but just as I teetered at the brink, he added, "Now it's personal."

The next morning, I woke to the sound of the downstairs toilet flushing. Jacob's side of the bed was cool. He'd already left—he put in some long hours as a Fed—so I knew it was Lisa puttering around down there. I felt relieved. And then a bit guilty, but mostly relieved, because if Carolyn's relentless truth had been hard for me to hear, it must have been way worse for Lisa. She must've come in pretty late, so I was surprised to find her watching the coffee drip when I came downstairs to shower. Jacob had stopped drinking his customary jumbo-sized cup. I'm guessing our home coffee tasted like swill compared to the stuff at the FPMP. Out of habit, though, we always brewed a full pot, then ended up staring at it, wishing it would hurry up and happen already. Her eyes looked strange. She'd been wearing makeup the night before, and the smudginess around her eyelashes made her look a lot girlier than usual, and a bit younger, too.

"How's Crash?" she asked me.

"Broke."

Lisa frowned. "Okay, I think I need a haircut." We both watched the dripping slow down, and finally she couldn't take it anymore and snatched out the pot. A long stream of coffee dribbled onto the heating element with a burnt-smelling hiss. "So, you're still doing that exorcism for Agent Dreyfuss, right?"

And here's where I would pay for being dead to the world when Jacob got home from the range. "Now he's got you on the bandwagon too?" I asked. She gave me a wide-eyed look, and I said, "I hope he didn't wake you up just to tell you to give me a push. I know he's gotta work there, but it's not like anything dead can touch him." Lisa still looked kind of blank, so I added, "Since he's a Superstiff."

"Oh, right, Jacob. He's Teflon. But when I ask the sí-no if you should do the exorcism, it gives me a yes. I don't usually ask the sí-no if something 'should' happen. Too subjective. But, you know how you just talk to yourself sometimes." Did I know? Heck yeah—for every word I spoke I probably thought a zillion more. Although when I talked to myself, my answer wasn't apt to be correct, not like Lisa's. "So," she said, "you should go do the exorcism. Soon."

I'd be better off all around discharging my debt to Dreyfuss. It was a shame to burn a sí-no to confirm something that obvious. "Fine." I dumped half the pot into my travel mug, then put the carafe back on the caramelized burner. "I'll give him a call." Then I pawed through the drawer in hopes of finding some of those individual caffeine shots I pocket from the coffee kiosk in the minimart. The sleeping pills had left me wuzzy and slow, and even my double-strong home brew needed help to clear the cobwebs and ready me for a delightful day of paperwork at the Fifth Precinct.

So far that season there'd been one sizeable snowfall that "stuck," and one instance of plowing. The Fifth Precinct parking lot had a short ridge of leftover snow around the perimeter that was crunchy from the temperature easing up over freezing than dipping below again. The rim of dirty white was gray with pollution and studded with gravel. That morning, as I found the least desirable parking spot was the only one left for me to take, the spot that abutted the old snow on the driver side, I suspected the gravel was the only thing that kept my feet from shooting out from under me and leaving me sprawled on the ice. My phone rang—Zigler's ringtone—and I realized my partner's beloved Impala wasn't in the lot. Once I had two feet on dry ground, I answered.

"I'm going out of town for a few days," he told me. "Funeral."

Great. I never knew what to say when someone died. Plus, with the people who knew me well enough, it seemed like something especially insightful was expected from me. "I'm sorry for your loss." That was so generic I might as well have said nothing. I added, "Make sure you get a copy of the death certificate so you can get your paid leave. It took Maurice three months to get his benefits when his brother-in-law died because of some screwup with the paperwork."

"It's not family," Zigler added quickly. "It's an old family friend...so I'll just take some personal days. But...thanks."

He sounded pretty stressed. "Take care of yourself," I told him.

Not having a partner changed my day dramatically. If I was in the middle of an investigation I could commandeer some temporary help, but we'd finished gathering evidence on the bloody truck the day before. I considered calling in "sick." But Betty, my boss' secretary, chose that moment to adjust the blinds beside her desk. She looked out the window and spotted me standing there in the parking lot waffling about going back home, and waved to me cheerfully. I waved back, quelled a sigh, and headed in.

Since police work is probably ninety percent administrative bullshit, there were reports that needed filing, and the bloodmobile we'd discovered yesterday wasn't going to make its way through the system itself. While I'm as capable of filling in the blanks as the next guy, there's a certain art to choosing the right words. When faced with the big, empty spot where the narrative should go, I didn't have the faintest idea where to begin.

After I tried a half dozen times to start my first sentence, I decided to pull some of Zig's old reports and get the ball rolling, figuring I could use his language while I tweaked the particulars to match up with our incident. I dug up the paperwork from a similar case we'd done in August: man bludgeons girlfriend to death, I stumble across her repeater, forensics has a field day. Not that the incident report said anything like that. The cop-speak is so dry it's practically encrypted.

```
          **ONGOING HOMICIDE INVESTIGATION**
At 14:15 on August 20, PsyCop Unit arrived at Irving
Park with warrant to search premises. PC-M5 noted
disturbance in rear hallway.
```

That was me, PC-M5. Catchy nickname for PsyCop, Medium, fifth-level…at least as far as anybody knew. And to say I "noted" the victim's repeater getting her face smashed in with what turned out to be a giant ceramic dog dish was another understated bit of code. Later on in the report, PC-NP (that would be Bob Zigler: PsyCop, Non Psychic) questioned the subject, who gave him some flimsy story about their doberman mangling a raccoon in the back hall. I guess it didn't occur to the murderer that our labs can tell the difference between raccoon blood traces and human DNA.

I'd read through the report a few times, gut twisting, before I paused to remind myself that I had been trying to pull the language from it. Nothing more. Maybe, I figured, what I needed was something older, something that wouldn't hit me quite so hard. I flipped through a few more reports. Ninety year old man versus home invaders armed with baseball bats. Honor student mowed down in a drive-by. A guy who knifed his brother for having an affair with his wife…an affair that turned out to be entirely fabricated by a neighbor with too much time on her hands and a mean streak a mile wide.

Delving farther back into the files wasn't helping. Not at all.

It took me until lunchtime to cobble together a stilted accounting of the bloody vehicle PC-M5 "noted," even though the narrative was barely three paragraphs long. There's a certain tone you need to aim for, tedious and technical, something that will stand up in court. I took care to make sure my language was just right. No sense in coming this far and having issues later on down the line due to poor word choice.

Lunch without Zig was duller than the prose on an incident report. Although I knew the rationale behind pairing a Psych and a Stiff didn't apply to the two of us since Zig was actually an NP, work just wasn't the same without him. Together, we were the dreaded Spook Squad. Alone, I was just a guy who sucked at typing. I finished my burger in five minutes, then stared out the diner window for half an hour while visions of bloodied ghosts and repeaters danced through my head.

Normally, I wouldn't dream of trying to score while I was on duty. Now, though, I had the image of the dog dish repeater overlaying the pathetic throat-stabbed ghost. Although I'd just stuffed a giant burger down my maw, I still felt like I was starving…and the only thing that would satisfy my gnawing hunger was a little red pill. I swung by the greasy gin mill where the stepbrother of an ex-friend, a guy with connections, could usually be found nursing a beer anytime after noon. He didn't often have reds—they're really hard to find—but on my lucky days, he did.

Although I'd buttoned my overcoat to cover my suit, I still worried I projected the air of law enforcement by virtue of being on the clock. I slumped my shoulders, hoping that changing my posture would make it less likely that someone would tear open my coat, rip the badge out of my pocket, and exclaim, *You were a cop all along!*

Instead, a bartender who I vaguely recognized, a graying Caucasian guy who probably appeared to be ten years older than he actually was, looked up from where he was clearing lunch dishes from a table. He glanced my way and said, "He's not here."

I paused there in the doorway and processed the information. A few lunchtime patrons were finishing their fries. A couple of all-day drinkers were watching ESPN with their stale popcorn and beer. None of them paid any attention to me.

"They caught him driving with a suspended license," the bartender said. "He's in lockup."

"When…?"

"Yesterday." The bartender rounded the bar and emptied the plastic baskets in the trash behind it.

Can he make bail? I didn't ask, since I knew full well that bailing out my dealer was a profoundly stupid idea. Especially if I wasn't even sure he was holding.

There was a time a few years back when the manufacture of Seconal was stopped—but then, to the delight of all the insomniacs who swear by it, the precious red pills started rolling off the production line again. Unfortunately, now they're classified as Schedule II controlled substances (like morphine and honest-to-God *opium*) that most doctors refuse to prescribe. All the doctors I know, anyway.

It took deep pockets and deeper connections to obtain. Extremely deep connections…like the type of connections who can tap your phone without a subpoena and haul you to Santa Barbara in a Learjet.

I wasn't sure if Jacob got a lunch break or not—I pointedly avoid asking what he actually does all day—but when I called from my car, I didn't really expect him to pick up. "What's up?" he said. Casually. Kind of.

I sighed until there was no air left in me, then re-settled my holster against my ribs and said, "I'm gonna come handle that salting."

"Now?"

I watched the gin mill's door for another moment, as if any time now my guy would come shuffling up to take his post at the dark table in the corner…but a sinking feeling told me that chances of scoring from my usual source were pretty much nil. "Now."

CHAPTER 4

THE LAST TIME I VISITED the FPMP offices, I'd been in the custody of a fake Fifth Precinct cop who was really on Con Dreyfuss' payroll. This time, I went there alone. The building is so deliberately low-key that I'd taken extra precautions to ensure I could spot it again. Still, I wouldn't have been all that surprised if I ended up driving around the North Loop in circles without seeing it. My deliberate attention paid off, and once I counted the lamp posts, I spotted the parking garage and pulled in. The orange and white striped barrier arm raised to allow me access. I told myself it was probably just a camera-activated mechanism that does the same for everybody. Then again, when I tried a few elevator buttons at random, only one of them lit up for me. So maybe not.

It let off on the top floor with the very expensive lobby full of muted colors, pricy artwork and classy uplighting. Plus the desk with the secretary assassin behind it. Laura was wearing a pinstripe suit today, and her jet black hair was pulled back in a slick, low ponytail. Severe dark-rimmed glasses, same as I remembered. Her earrings were tiny diamonds, though I imagined that she didn't wear them because she liked them, but because she was too detail-oriented to go around with the piercings empty. "Detective Bayne," she said, looking right at me—right in the eye—as if I hadn't seen her skulking around the site of Roger Burke's shooting. As if we hadn't had an actual conversation right there in front of the prison where she'd put a bullet in his face. "Agent Dreyfuss is just finishing a phone call. There's coffee and tea in the lounge. If you haven't eaten, I can order—"

"I had lunch." I should know. The sight of Laura caused that burger to churn. I was unwilling to show weakness, though. When you need to fly under the radar, both ends of the spectrum—from aggressive loudmouthed jerk to wimpy doormat—attract unwanted attention. I usually aim for a middling attitude of non-threatening disinterest since I pull it off pretty well, but there's a big difference between calm and weak. Calm people made eye contact. And so I held it like it was no biggie. None at all.

Laura looked away first. "Make yourself comfortable. Let me know if you need anything."

I needed plenty of things, but I kept that to myself. It went with the whole unflappable demeanor I was trying to present. Before I moved out of her line of sight (barring any security cameras, which most certainly were trained on me) I snuck one more look at her. She typed, a flurry of clicks, then slipped her hand under her desk. I figured her to be activating some sort of mega-spycam, but she came up with an orange jellybean instead. She tucked it into her mouth, barely breaking stride, and resumed typing.

There's more to winning a standoff than staring the longest. Clearly I was dealing with a pro. As I sidled into the lounge, I contemplated that I might very well be in over my head dealing with the FPMP on their home turf. Originally I thought I should be the one to infiltrate the organization, but now I had to wonder if Jacob had been the better choice after all. He doesn't need to pretend to be unflappable. He really is. Or at least he's scads better at coming off that way.

I was contemplating the framed magazine covers on the walls featuring the world's most famous Psychs: Jean Dixon, Uri Geller, Marie Saint Savon, when I was joined by someone just as talented, one Con Dreyfuss. Maybe he'd have a place up on that wall too, someday. Then again, he didn't exactly broadcast the level of his clairvoyance, so maybe not. His white-guy corkscrew 'fro was back in a ponytail and he wore a baggy Bob Marley T-shirt over a pair of faded jeans. His huge platinum watch was the lovechild of Cartier and NASA. "Well, well, well. What a pleasant surprise," he said. "To what do I owe the pleasure?"

"What do you think?" *Be nice. The man's got the goods. Or if not, he can get them.* "I'm here to take care of the…matter…we agreed to." There. That sounded civil.

"How'd you manage to fit me into your busy schedule before Christmas?"

"You've got eyes all over my workplace. You tell me." I took a breath and regrouped before I said anything more I'd regret. He'd always needed me a hell of a lot more than I needed him—that's what I'd been telling myself. I didn't like it when the tables were turned. "Do you want your exorcism or not?"

"After seeing you in action at PsyTrain?" He rubbed his hands together in eagerness that might or might not have been exaggerated. "I can hardly wait."

I noticed a small hum as Dreyfuss trooped me through the series of doors and halls that led to his office. Magnetic locks. I guess no one was taking chances with any uninvited guests who managed to get past the secretary without a bullet in their back. He pulled out a key and unlocked the door—then slid a magnetic card through a reader as well. All this rigmarole for the few seconds it took to gather me from the lounge.

The office wasn't exactly like I remembered it. He'd added a leather sofa, re-positioned the desk and installed a couple more monitors on his computer—all of them now running a flying toaster screensaver. The repeaters were still there, though: the spin-around who'd taken three bullets, the guy crumpling to the floor by the bathroom, and the ducking guy who'd been shot in the throat. It felt like deja vu. They were exactly the same, but me? I'd changed. During my previous encounter with the Gunshot Trio, I'd figured them for permanent fixtures. Now I was confident I could send them packing with a sprinkle of salt…and a big dose of white light.

And once I did that, I'd have nothing left to barter.

"I still have company," Dreyfuss said, "judging by the look on your face."

I nodded. No sense in denying it, not if I wanted him to want something from me.

He said, "I had a feeling I might. Richie says a prayer for them every week. I guess no one's listening."

"Not necessarily." While it would be to my advantage to make Richie seem inept so I could maneuver myself into a better bargaining position, I'd seen him fade a repeater, the guy in the boardroom who'd shot himself. "Richie has ability. It's just that some things are more…advanced."

As my honesty spoke for me in a way that any enticement I might dream up never could, it occurred to me that I really did have plenty to offer beyond scrubbing these more stubborn repeaters. I lined Dreyfuss up in my peripheral vision and said, "Like taking care of Jennifer Chance."

I expected him to deny having her silenced, but instead he went silent himself. I thought he might deny all knowledge of her—after all, we'd only spoken about her in the astral, so he probably didn't remember any of it. But when he finally did speak, he said, "Is she here?"

With a big pull of white light, I walked a slow circuit of the office and double-checked the swanky private bathroom. Other than the three repeaters, everything was clean. "Not right now."

"But you've seen her."

"I've sensed—"

"Sonofabitch, you have." He chewed off a cuticle with absent ferocity and blotted the blood on his T-shirt. "Is she hanging around a particular area?"

I'd seen her in the boardroom as well as Dreyfuss' office. "I don't think so."

"Can she leave the building?"

"I don't know."

"Can she hide herself from you?"

I didn't know that either. I shrugged.

"In other words," he said, "she could be here right now."

"I don't think so."

Dreyfuss wasn't willing to take that chance. He grabbed a hoodie off the back of his chair, pulled on the world's ugliest knit hat, and said, "Come on, Detective. Let's take a walk."

I haven't known enough sentient ghosts to have a good idea of how far they can roam, but they do seem to have ties to the place they died. Unless they attached themselves to their murderer…in which case, all the walking in the world wouldn't help Dreyfuss.

The neighborhood was an inhospitable place surrounded by highway ramps and viaducts, with old brick commercial buildings abutting newer, uglier structures of corrugated metal. We were the only pedestrians in sight as we walked to the main drag at a brisk pace, in silence. When we turned the corner onto Grand, the feeling of stark isolation eased. I saw a bus shelter with some college kids goofing around inside. A cafe. A gym.

Dreyfuss approached a flower shop that looked so decrepit I wondered if it was some kind of front. At least until he opened the door and a greenish chemical odor hit me. It was hot and humid, and the moisture in the air carried the unfamiliar smells deep into my lungs. If it was a front, the set dressers were doing a really bang-up job.

"Okay, now we can talk." Dreyfuss cut his eyes to the lintel we'd just passed beneath. Above the door, an aloe vera leaf dangled from a length of red yarn: a warding charm. "This is a safe place."

I walked around the floor and checked all the nooks and crannies just to be sure. The pale girl behind the counter talking on her cell phone in Polish paused to watch me comb through her store. When she cut her eyes to Dreyfuss, he gave her a little nod. On his payroll, no doubt. I filed the interaction away for future reference.

He browsed a shelf of ceramic figurines, not because he was particularly interested in big-eyed puppies or smiling frogs. From that vantage point he could keep his eye on the door and window without being seen. I planted myself beside him and said, "You knew Dr. Chance was still there?"

"Apparently I wasn't the only one." I expected him to look at least a bit chagrined about killing her…but he didn't. Actually, he seemed annoyed. With me. "When we were trying to work the GhosTV at PsyTrain, you never asked me to hit her up for the instruction manual, so I figured you knew she was dead. But seeing her at the office and keeping your mouth shut about it was seriously uncool. It never occurred to you to tip me off?"

"What's the worst thing she can do? Make a cold spot?"

"Come on, genius, think. All the intel we keep at the FPMP—do you really want that falling into the wrong hands? Hire a low level medium amped up on psyactives, and a sufficiently motivated ghost could waltz in, look around, and go tell them all our psychic friends' deepest secrets."

Maybe Dreyfuss should have thought of that before he killed someone in his building. "Isn't it ironic that you, of all people, are worried about falling under a psychic microscope?"

"Oh, the irony's not lost on me," he said. "But the worst part is, if someone working against us scared up a GhosTV, between the technology and the drugs, a pretty good performance could be coaxed out of a medium who barely registers on the richter scale."

Then why the hell did he leave one with me? I shot him a look, and he said, "Either you'll master it, or you'll build a bonfire with it. Either way, I know you'd never list it on eBay. Of course, if you did happen to figure out how to get reception on that damn thing, maybe I could scoop up the potential viewing audience before anyone else got a chance to snag them."

His trust in me was touching. If only I could leverage that trust to get a few reds off him. "I never agreed to be your GhosTV trainer. Just to exorcise the guys in your office."

"Guys. Multiple. How many are we talking?"

I tried not to look too pleased about admitting how crowded it was. "I sense three."

"What about Dr. Chance? You can't just let her hang around. If she's there, you take care of her, too."

"If she happens to be there." I implied with my tone that she probably wouldn't.

"Either you're busting my balls just to get a rise out of me, or you're after something more." He looked me up and down, then turned to a shelf of small potted cactuses and began browsing them intently. "Agent Marks is here of his own accord, you know. If I fire him just to get you to cooperate, it'll only come back to bite you in the ass."

I hadn't realized Jacob's career might be on the table. I'd only been angling for some Seconal. Now that he'd mentioned it, I couldn't help but toy with the idea of freeing Jacob from the evil clutches of F-Pimp. Holding that power in my hot little hands was seductive. The thing was, I'd just witnessed Jacob defending the damn place to Carolyn. He *enjoyed* being a federal agent. I wasn't about to take that away from him.

Before I outmaneuvered myself and ended up doing something I'd regret, I came right out and said, "I need a prescription."

He paused with his fingertip poised against a cactus spike. "Okay, then. Let's negotiate. What're we talking?"

"Seconal."

He gave a low whistle. "They don't subject PsyCops to random drug testing. If you're having trouble sleeping, why don't you just…?" He made a puff-puff pot smoking gesture.

I glared at him as I considered whether I was willing to walk away from the whole thing—give him the one exorcism, take a barbell to the GhosTV, and be done with him and his ugly hat once and for all. If Jacob weren't involved, maybe I would. But I didn't want things to go sour for Jacob at the FPMP just because of me.

Dreyfuss sighed. "Just sayin'. I could hook you up with some killer bud, no problem. But reds? They're a bitch."

"Is that a 'no'?"

"I can't get you an honest-to-God prescription without setting off a billion alarms. But as for scoring you some pills…you're lucky I've got friends south of the border." He pulled out his pillbox, flipped it open, and extracted a single red pill, which he held up to the light between thumb and forefinger. "Go home. Get a good night's sleep. And I'll clear my schedule so tomorrow we can give my office a good going-over."

One fucking pill? One? I held out my hand, unwilling to give him the satisfaction of snatching it from his grasp. Although when he placed the little red capsule in my palm, I'd say he looked pretty damn satisfied.

I parted ways with Con Dreyfuss when he picked out a fuzzy-haired cactus and brought it up to the register. Although I was on high alert from our sparring, when I turned the corner of the underground garage and found someone tinkering around in the general area where I'd left my car, I tried to keep calm and tell myself it was nothing. Someone doing something completely innocuous. Opening their trunk. Putting a bumper sticker on their car. But as I neared and saw it was indeed my car they were messing with, possibilities flooded my brain ranging from tracking devices to car bombs. Until I saw who it was, anyway.

"Hey, Richie."

He jumped up and spun around, goggle-eyed, then broke into a smile when he registered who I was. "Hardcore Vic!" He wiped his hand on his overcoat, then reached his squatty hand out for a handshake. A freshly-wiped hand is unappealing to me since it draws attention to whatever was just on it, so I would've rather kept my hands to myself. Plus his fingernails were too long, with grayish crescents beneath the whites that looked less like fresh dirt and more like a couple weeks of neglect. But I was such a dickhead to Richie back in the day when the two of us were "classmates" at Camp Hell, now I felt the need to be extra-specially nice to him. So I shook.

"Can you believe this piece-of-shit beater?" he asked. I glanced at my trunk. He'd written WASH ME in the film of road salt.

Awkward. "Yeah, uh, that's mine."

He stared at me for a moment, then said with absolutely no shame, "You know the hubcaps aren't really metal, don't you? They're plastic."

"Right."

"You should get a Lexus. That's a good car."

"I'll keep it in mind."

"I got my new one already—next year's model, heh-heh, before it's even out."

I tried to look suitably impressed.

"It gots a heated steering wheel. Heated mirrors, too." He crossed over to a numbered parking spot much closer to the elevator and pointed at a sedan. "Cool color, huh? Fire agate pearl."

It was brown.

"You're gonna work here," he said, "right? So you'll get to pick out your Lexus in a year, too."

"Probably not. I'm pretty attached to the Fifth Precinct."

"That's not what Agent Dreyfuss says."

Oh, really? "What does Agent Dreyfuss say?"

"That you'll get sick of pushing pencils eventually. Heh-heh." He thought about what he'd just said, then added, "What does that mean?"

CHAPTER 5

DID I CARE WHAT CONSTANTINE DREYFUSS thought of me? No. Why should I? At least I did an honest day's work. I didn't pretend I was all "regular guy" and then go around in an ugly knit hat putting out hits on people and flying airplanes and commanding a squadron of Psychs. Not that Jacob and Richie constituted a squadron all by themselves. Undoubtedly there were more people with special brain chemistry at the FPMP.

Maybe it wasn't all secret-agency and slick, but police work needed to be done, damn it. Even though from the minute I heard my first punk song I'd thought it was cool to make fun of cops, after a dozen years on the force—seeing what I've seen and knowing what I know—I can say with certainty that if you think cops are dicks, wait 'til you deal with a hardened sociopathic criminal. Then wait 'til you realize there's plenty more where he came from.

Lisa's car was there when I got home, so I was surprised when I opened the front door to a slide of junk mail. Since she's home more than Jacob or me, she tends to do most of the picking up. I'm not too bad about creating messes, but there'd be trails of Jacob's clothes and books and miscellaneous stuff all over the house if we didn't go around behind him and gather up the flotsam.

"I'm home," I called out, as slippery catalogs evaded my grasp and spread themselves farther into the vestibule. I stacked them more assertively, and wondered if it would be okay for me to talk about the cop-subject with Lisa, or if that would be like complaining about the price of your heating bill to someone camped out in a homeless shelter.

"You're home early." Lisa had a jacket on, and a purse slung over her shoulder.

"Another date?" I said, before I considered whether we really needed to go into it. She raised her eyebrows high, and I realized she wasn't wearing any makeup, so probably not. "Uh…sorry…what I meant was, when do I get to meet the lucky guy?"

"It's a little weird." She glanced back over her shoulder. "You know. The tent and everything."

"Right," I said. When I really wanted to say, *No, it's not weird, it's fine. Anyone good enough for you wouldn't dare think any less of you because of the tent. And if this jerk does…* "We could always meet at a restaurant."

Catalogs slid, despite my attempt to keep hold of them. A particularly slick publication with a big brown Lexus on the cover landed on my shoes. I shifted the mail and picked it up. It was addressed to Jacob. Surprise, surprise. I huffed in annoyance and dropped all the mail back on the floor.

Lisa stepped around the pile. "I'm just going to get that haircut we talked about."

"Not short," I said, and oh my God, since when had I developed the compulsion to micromanage her life?

"Not short. Just a trim."

It was probably for the best that I didn't use her as a sounding board to go off on the value of police work. All she'd ever wanted to be was a cop, and now she was a PsyTrain dropout living in a tent in her ex-partner's living room.

The door shut behind Lisa, and I was left on my own to ponder the weight of my decisions, the meaning of life, the big stack of mail on the floor, and the single Seconal pill. I could practically feel it sliding down my throat, but if Dreyfuss was doling them out one at a time, I knew better than to swallow it and leave myself without. Instead, I dug through Jacob's stash of vitamins until I found some enzymes that came in capsule form. I unscrewed the capsule, tipped the powder down the drain, and blew the remaining enzyme dust out of the empty halves. Then I opened the red over a sheet of tin foil and split the powder between the two capsules with a butter knife, careful to capture every last bit of powder. I swallowed the adulterated vitamin to ensure no one else took it upon themselves to eat a strange pill they found on the kitchen counter. Not that either of the people I lived with would actually do that. Not after Lisa's first and only Auracel incident, anyway.

The relaxed euphoria didn't set in immediately, but knowing it would soon was enough to take the edge off. While I waited for the barbs to kick in, I decided I might as well have a look at the car catalog to weigh in on my preferences early, so we didn't end up with a big brown sedan with a shiny new tracking device in it parked out front once Jacob reached his one-year FPMP anniversary. There'd be no way around the tracking device, of course. I suspected they were already in our phones anyhow. But the thought of riding around in a brown car was depressing.

Since the goofy puzzle was still monopolizing the dining room table, I took the catalog pile to the couch, kicked off my shoes, propped my feet on the coffee table and began flipping through the stack. As I was thumbing through to the Lexus catalog, I spotted a magazine sticking out from behind it, a thin wisp of a periodical called Inner Eye that caters to Psychs and psychic wannabes. Usually I just throw it on the pile in Jacob's office—not only is it addressed to him, but I've always found it to be bone dry, mostly filler and conjecture. The current issue's headline stopped me in my tracks, though. *Murderer Walks Free.* And then I got hung up on the cover photo—because I knew that fuckhead.

It was the human scum who'd pummeled his girlfriend to death with a dog dish.

One of the pages tore as I jerked it open to find the lead article. It was eight pages long. I read it through fast—once, twice—and then slow, lingering over the phrases "convicted with psychic-gathered evidence" and "judge with a record of anti-psychic bias" and "acquittal." And just for good measure, "victim's family is devastated."

I was reading through for maybe the twelfth time when Jacob got home. He led with, "What's this I heard about you coming back to the FPMP tomorrow? All you owed Dreyfuss was an exorcism, right? He didn't talk you into anything else. Did he?" He sat down beside me. "Vic?"

While I did register that he was speaking to me, I was currently occupied with the fact that my reality had just tilted on its axis. Not because of anything supernatural, either.

Once Jacob realized how livid I was, he did try to talk me down, but he was subtle about it. He'd actually ratcheted down my pissed-offedness significantly by the time Lisa came home. I realized, vaguely, that her hair looked nice, loose around her shoulders. But mostly I was as devastated as the victim's family. Because I hand the system a murder scene swimming with evidence and a perp so obviously guilty his own mother would convict him—and he's acquitted?

"The last case I worked on," I said to Lisa, "guy's truck covered in blood evidence. Does he get convicted?"

"I don't know. That's the future, it hasn't happened yet."

"But is there a chance he'll get off? The sí-no must be able to see that."

"Maybe there's a chance, but there's usually some kind of chance for anything you can think of. You'll go crazy wondering about every possible way it can turn out."

"A good chance?"

No answer. I didn't need to do any wondering to piss myself off all over again, that was for sure. "Why bother?" I snapped. "Why bother bringing in these lowlifes at all if the only consequence is a few months in lockup while they wait for their acquittals?"

"You can't think about it that way," Jacob said. "You did your part. You're not responsible for what happened after that."

Holy shit. "I never said I was—although you've got to admit, the fact that I gathered the evidence with my ability did seem to be the deciding factor."

They tried to convince me it was a fluke, that the system needed people who cared, people like me. That the use of PsyCops' testimonies was so new and so radical it had a long way to go, but it would never gain legitimacy unless judges and juries got used to admitting psychic evidence. Maybe it was true, and someone had to be the poor schlub whose work was systematically destroyed just to allow the idiots in the courtroom to begin reaching outside their comfort zone. But did that someone really need to be me?

Going back to working on my jigsaw puzzle didn't feel worthwhile, not in comparison to the puzzle of my life that needed sorting through. I couldn't see flipping on the TV, either. Prime time features bad guys who get what they deserve in the long run, and my cynicism cup would surely runneth over if I had to bear witness to fictional karma in action. So what was left to do? Jacob put food in front of me and I ate it, but I didn't taste a thing. And then I swallowed the remaining half of my Seconal and headed upstairs, ignoring all the well-meaning inquiries as to whether I was okay. I could have told them tomorrow was another day, or it would all come out in the wash, or he who laughs last, laughs best—but I've never been much for platitudes, and I figured my inner circle wasn't either.

I was staring at the pressed metal ceiling, counting the number of diamonds across (twenty-four and a half, same as always) when Jacob joined me. He lay on his side, facing me, with his elbow planted and his head propped on his fist. "I'd be pissed off too," he said.

"Forensics found a fragment of the dish stuck to a bloody fucking hair under the baseboard," I said. "How can anyone with a brain manage an acquittal out of that—just because I told them where to look?"

Jacob didn't bother answering. We both knew it was bullshit.

"So how do they treat the evidence you find for the Feds?" I asked. Then I realized I had no idea what he actually did with himself once he left the cannery. For all I knew he was a glorified bodyguard, or, God forbid, a pencil-pusher. "Assuming you're an investigator."

"I am."

I counted to twenty-four and a half, then flipped onto my side to face him. I'd figured him to be bubbling over with eagerness to sell me on his spiffy new job, so the reticence seemed telling…though I don't know what, exactly, it told me.

He searched my eyes, and said, "I can't really say how they'll treat my evidence. I haven't found anything."

"In two months?" He would have put away at least a few scumbag rapists by now if he was still on the force. "Couldn't you ask Lisa a few questions to move things along?"

"I have."

"And?"

"She can't see anything. It's like the signal is blocked."

Although Jacob wasn't the only True Stiff in the world, that seemed pretty damn inconvenient. "At some point you give up, tuck away the file and start something new, right? How much longer does Dreyfuss expect you to dig?"

Jacob shrugged. He seemed awfully unconcerned to me, given that he cares enough about everything for everybody. Some small part of me must have been wondering why he wasn't more frustrated about his lack of results, because I almost missed it when a sinew in his jaw shifted.

And then I realized his nonchalance was all a front.

I tested the waters with, "Maybe all that matters to you is keeping an eye on the FPMP."

He clenched his jaw again.

Maybe not.

"I could talk to Lisa for you," I suggested. "She might sí-no with me a little longer—"

"I thought you didn't want anything to do with the FPMP," he said, and he was right. I didn't. "So don't worry about it. It's my problem."

Of course, by saying that, he basically ensured that I'd worry about it. Plus, picking at the edges of Jacob's investigation was infinitely more appealing than contemplating the futility of my own job. "Maybe the sí-no could point you at someone who'd be able to help you."

"We've hashed through it already. It's not working. Not for this."

"Then maybe they need to let it go and let you move on to something fresh. Some things take time to unravel."

Jacob rolled over and showed me the back of his head.

I kept talking. "They'll shift the investigation to the back burner eventually, right?"

"Not anytime soon."

"It just seems like such a waste."

Since I wasn't letting it go, Jacob sighed and rolled to face me again. "The agency's whole mission is to keep Psychs from getting picked off. And here an ex-FPMP Stiff was gunned down on a crowded street in broad daylight."

How had that managed to evade the news? And the water cooler talk? "Recently?"

"Last February."

Whatever I'd had for dinner churned in my stomach as my body put together what Jacob was saying before my brain did. "Here, in Chicago?" I asked stupidly.

"Right in front of the Metropolitan Correctional Center."

Maybe my brain had been searching its databases for the appropriate film clip. It played that delightful bit of memory now: the gray drizzle, the traffic, the SUV sideview that nailed me in the shoulder. The gunfire, the panic, the churn of the crowd. The red hole in Roger Burke's forehead.

It also played the pantomime his spirit did before it got sucked into hell—the one where he'd implicated Dreyfuss' secretary in the shooting.

Jacob had been watching me for a good long while before he said, "The statement you gave the investigators was pretty straightforward. You didn't mention seeing anything other than the physical."

And because I hadn't been willing to go into Roger's ghost-charades, I hadn't mentioned seeing Laura at the scene, either. I groaned into a sitting position and scrubbed at my face with my hands. One Seconal was totally not cutting it. "You're working on a case for two months where I was an eye witness, and you tell me now?"

"I was hoping you weren't directly involved."

"Well, I didn't shoot him."

Jacob kept his tone deliberately bland. "We recovered the bullet. It was a 9mm round, but not from a Glock. A Glock's firing pin leaves a square impression, which eliminates your service weapon."

Jeez. Good thing I only had one gun to my name.

"Is there a reason I should have run it by you?" he asked. Smoothly. Calmly.

As if I didn't see right through him like a decade-old repeater. "What does Lisa say?"

"That you know more than you put in the deposition." Fantastic. They had actually discussed this already—although Jacob could have presumed as much with no help at all from the sí-no. Then he added, "But not that you know who pulled the trigger."

Hold on a minute.

Didn't I?

CHAPTER 6

"Laura Kim?" Jacob almost laughed, but then his expression hung, not quite smiling, as a dozen emotions played across his face, all of them some subtle flavor of confusion and disbelief. "You're joking. Right?"

"You know me better than that."

"But…" Jacob's mouth worked. I'd never seen him so gobsmacked. "Laura *Kim*?"

"Was she there on some other official business?"

"I had no idea she was there at all. Are you sure it was her?"

Yes, I am able to tell one Asian person from another. I answered with a look.

"But it doesn't make any sense," he said. "I was just at the firing range with her—she picks bull's eye targets instead of human-shaped outlines. That's how uncomfortable she is with shooting at a human being."

Too bad he hadn't known…maybe he could have grabbed one of her casings. I read the thought on his expression, and just as quickly I saw him counter it. Snagging a casing wouldn't do any good, since he didn't have any casings from the scene in evidence, only a slug. He'd need a slug for comparison, and the bullets that pierced the bull's eye targets last night would be sunk deep in ballistic rubber mulch. Good luck finding it among five tons of additional used lead.

"She's the nicest person you'd ever meet, Vic. A real sweetheart. I can't believe she'd…you *saw* it?"

"Not directly. Burke's ghost told me it was her."

"You talked to the…? My God, that's huge. What did it say?"

"Nothing—he was a good twenty yards away." There was no

sugar-coating it, I supposed. "But he gestured to me. He made Chinese-eyes. And a gun-shooting motion. And then he disappeared."

"She's Korean," Jacob murmured. "Not Chinese."

He wanted more, I could tell. A plausible reason, for instance. A more likely suspect. Something that could potentially make sense. We both searched for inspiration in the tin ceiling, and finally I said, "He could have been lying. He'd love to make a fool out of me."

"Isn't it your theory that naming the killer is usually the whole reason a murder victim sticks around? If that's the case, why would he go against the flow just for the sake of pointing you in the wrong direction—especially if he wasn't going to be around to revel in the fallout?"

I'd never been able to pin down Roger Burke while he was alive, so I wasn't exactly shocked that I couldn't make heads or tails of him now that he was dead. Since the most definitive answer we could possibly get was right downstairs, I figured I might as well go see what the sí-no thought of our predicament.

The overhead lights were off, but a reading lamp was glowing inside the tent, throwing Lisa's silhouette against the blue nylon. Her hair was still softly loose. I caught a snatch of conversation, and then a pause—talking on her phone, judging by the tilt of her head and the angle of her arm. Low laughter. More talk. Spanish, I realized as I cleared the bottom step. Which was good. Because it would be creepy to stand outside her tent and eavesdrop.

Most of my Spanish vocabulary consists of phrases like *I didn't know that car was stolen*, or *I was home watching TV during the shooting*, or *That's not blood, it's molé sauce*. Given her tone, I was pretty confident Lisa wasn't in the midst of that type of discussion. I stood for just a moment and let the lilt and cadence sink in, and enjoyed the fact that she sounded happy. Really happy.

I imagined a Hispanic guy on the other end of that phone call. Maybe thirty-ish. Earnest looking. Good hair. Someone her family would approve of—hell, someone I would approve of. Maybe a cop. Or maybe something less brutal, like a teacher, or a social worker, or a fireman. My question could wait, I decided. It had gone unanswered since February, after all. I was just about to turn and head back upstairs when Jacob came thundering down after me, so loud he couldn't have made more noise if he'd been trying.

Lisa's silhouette stood and unzipped the tent flap, and then the nylon peeled down and she wasn't a silhouette anymore. Her fight-or-flight response is just as well tuned as mine is, and Jacob's "herd of buffalo" impression on the stairs had triggered her alarm. "Hold on," she said into her phone. Then, to me, "What?"

Jacob wobbled to a stop behind me, taking in the tent flap, the phone, Lisa. He's as skittish as I am about her leaving, and while they're obviously close, there's more awkwardness between the two of them than there is between Lisa and me. Once you get to know me, I'm pretty predictable. Not Jacob. For years Jacob has lived by the adage, if you can't say anything nice, don't say anything at all…and if you've gotta lie, do it by omission. But thanks to the sí-no, he can't even think a dissenting thought without Lisa knowing about it by asking herself a few quick questions. He walks on eggshells around her now. Not that it really helps. "It can wait," he said. "We didn't mean to…it can wait."

Lisa looked us both over, then said, "I gotta go," into the phone. A small pause, then, "*No, llegarás a mañana.*" I knew *mañana* meant tomorrow, but had no context for the rest of the phrase. Probably something mundane, like "see ya." I considered looking it up later in my Spanish-English dictionary, but knew my chances of remembering it more than thirty seconds without writing it down were slim. She disconnected, then said in a voice more exasperated than curious, "It's no big deal. What?"

Jacob said, "When Roger Burke was shot in front of the prison, Vic says he saw Laura Kim—"

Lisa looked startled. "He did."

"I already said that." Why was this such a difficult concept for Jacob to grasp? I recognized Laura, and I'd seen her there. "Laura Kim was in a bus shelter across the street. She talked to me, told me I shouldn't be there. I got away from her, and then I heard the shot. I wouldn't have pegged her right away—I figured she was just a secretary, you know? And with all the skyscrapers, you couldn't tell where the noise had come from, it was like an echo chamber. But once he was dead, Roger indicated she was the shooter." I don't use the word "indicate" in common conversation, but I was fresh from reading all those carefully worded reports. Indicating, noting. Careful words for when reality sounds completely whacked.

Lisa's eyes tracked back and forth like she was watching a tennis game play on the front of my shirt. After the first second or two, I realized that she hadn't said yes.

And she hadn't said no, either.

I held my breath. Jacob held his. The distant sound of a motorcycle engine peaked and ebbed. The radiators hissed. The refrigerator motor kicked in and settled into a low hum. "Vic saw her," Lisa repeated, puzzled. "But it won't tell me if she shot him."

"See?" I said. "She was there."

Lisa looked troubled. "Actually…I don't know about that. Only that you saw her."

"Okay," Jacob said, "that's fine, that's good—it's something to work with." He grabbed a pen off the coffee table and started pawing around for something to write on. "All we need to do is narrow down a better question."

He was looking so hard for a piece of paper that he didn't see the look on Lisa's face, or the fact that she was shaking her head. But I did. "I'm not helping you investigate Laura Kim," she said.

Jacob paused his search for paper. "Why not?"

"Don't you know? She's Constantine's ex-wife." Holy shit…Laura was *way* out of that weirdo's league. "It wouldn't make any sense for Laura to do it. Maybe they're not married, but they're still close—they trust each other with everything. If she was the shooter, either she went behind Con's back and…" she shook her head. "No. Or Con knew and…no, he didn't know."

Jacob said, "That's good, it means he didn't put me on the case just to keep me busy."

"No…and that's it, I'm done. That's all I'm going to look at. We've been through it back and forth, up and down."

Jacob said, "But not with Laura—"

"It's like one of those Magic Eye pictures where you're supposed to see something else in the pattern. If I don't see it, and I try to force myself, it's not going to come. Especially not if I'm upset about it. The sí-no won't show me the main thing you want to know, and the harder I try to see it, the more you grill me about it, the muddier it gets."

Jacob looked startled. "Why are you upset? I'm not grilling you."

"What does it matter to you if she used to be Mrs. Dreyfuss?" I asked. "Since when do you care what either of them think?"

"You two weren't the only ones who came out to Santa Barbara to help me when I was in a bind. Con was there too."

"Oh sure," I scoffed, "out of the kindness of his heart."

Lisa gave me a warning look. "I'll ruin my own credibility if I go around accusing people that close to him, especially if the sí-no isn't clear and I could be completely wrong."

She zipped up her tent while Jacob stared at her like a drunk who'd missed last call by ten seconds. I took him by the elbow and steered him toward the stairs. Lisa might be unwilling to play the psychic game tonight, at least not with us. Still, I had no doubt she was sí-noing herself to sleep, whether she would admit it to Jacob or not. As someone who's accustomed to having a handle on things, she must've been irked by her talent's non-responsiveness. I was sure she'd keep picking at it. And when she came up with something definitive, we'd be the first ones to know.

CHAPTER 7

THE BUNDLE OF TWIGS THAT hung above our front door was stale and cobwebby, since Crash's monthly cleansing ritual was coming up any day now. Even so, Jacob and I bent together, whispering a few last minute plans beneath it. He put two fingers to my forearm—a little reminder we'd developed to keep one another from getting carried away when talking plainly wasn't safe—but that was fine. I'd be able to get my point across while keeping what I said uselessly vague. "Don't worry. I can do this."

He pressed his forehead into my temple. "Just…be careful."

"Believe me, I know how to bullshit. I've been practicing my whole life." With the sí-no holding out on us, somebody needed to start scrutinizing Laura Kim. Since I didn't really know her, it would sound less fishy if I was the one to ask the questions…even though it was killing Jacob to turn over this critical piece of his investigation to anyone else. Even me. In my fantasies, I would come up with a question that bowled her over to the point where she readily admitted exactly what she'd been doing that day, then signed an affidavit to seal the deal. But since Laura was no slouch in the brains department, it was doubtful I'd stun her with my clever interrogation skills.

We'd cooked up a plan that had seemed plausible when it was whispered beneath the comforter in the dead of night. Now, though, I was getting cold feet. Jacob climbed into the big black Crown Vic and pulled away, and there was nothing else I could do other than follow through.

I took my own car, once I'd smeared off the words WASH ME with a handful of gray snow. My unimpressive compact was a critical part of our plan. I fidgeted in my seat all the way there, and followed Jacob into the underground parking garage with a death-grip on my steering wheel. He pulled into a numbered spot, and I slotted my car into visitor parking and cut the engine.

Pulling the keys from the ignition was so automatic for me, I did so despite the fact that I'd been planning to deliberately lock them in. As I put them back, I tried to recall ever having locked my keys anywhere and came up blank. Maybe the part of my brain that's responsible for lock awareness was more highly developed than your average Joe's. Probably so—the sight of the keyring dangling from the ignition made me uneasy. But according to Jacob, this would be the best way for me to get Laura Kim alone. So I opened my door, powered the locks down, made a silent apology to my keys, and slammed the door shut behind me.

Jacob and I got on the elevator, and I said, "Shit, I left my keys behind." I thought it sounded reasonably natural.

"Check your pockets," Jacob said, which we hadn't planned, and damn if it didn't sound even twice as natural as my remark. He was good.

I patted them all down, locating a couple of aspirin, a few packets of salt, a small flashlight, and a breath spray container Zigler had refilled with Florida Water. "Not here."

The elevator sighed open and we strolled out into the classy FPMP lobby. "Vic locked his keys in his car," Jacob announced to Laura—again deviating from the script. It was supposed to have been me admitting my negligence, but somehow, this flowed. "Can you pop the door?"

"Onboard navigation will open it for you," she said. "I can make a call."

"It's an older car," I said.

"Is there a car alarm?"

"No." I'd figured my Fraternal Order of Police window decal was deterrent enough. So far I'd been correct. Either that or it was obvious there was nothing in there worth stealing. "As cars go, it's pretty low-tech."

"I can take a look, but if it's not the right kind of lock, it won't work." Laura took off her headset, routed her multi-line phone somewhere else, then opened up a desk drawer and fished out a long piece of metal.

Jacob caught my eye and held it for a fraction of a beat, then said, "Call me if you need anything," before he keycarded himself away.

And then it was just Laura and me and the slim jim. And the awkwardness. Yeah. That was pretty present, too. Riffing with Jacob had felt pretty good. But now I was alone, and I realized that I actually had no desire to be there, and the thought of being alone with Laura wasn't exactly heartening. Without my sympathetic Jacob audience to play to, I realized I was actually fairly rusty at bullshitting.

The elevator doors were a dull, brushed metal that only reflected us back as fuzzy blobs of light and dark, but I was probably a head taller than her. We were both wearing black, with black hair and pale skin. I could make out her glasses frames as a dark smear. My reflection had a spot of red where the knot of my tie was. We rode down without a word, unless you counted the screaming in my head that said, *Make conversation! Say something! Anything!* "So. You're the resident locksmith?"

"I guess I'm pretty handy."

As I wondered whether that was supposed to have a double meaning, the doors opened onto the garage level. I then began to doubt the intelligence of placing myself with someone I suspected to be an assassin in a deserted underground parking facility. It hadn't struck me as particularly creepy when I'd convinced Jacob to let me try it—but that was then. And Jacob was upstairs somewhere now. When Laura left the elevator ahead of me, I unbuttoned my overcoat and my jacket, and shrugged back the right side. Given her training, Laura could probably shoot circles around me, even if she didn't practice on human-shaped targets. Still, I felt better knowing I could draw if I had to.

There were no windows, just wall-mounted lights every few yards. The concrete looked white and fresh, and the framing was painted yellow. Still, there was an underground oppressiveness to the garage that no amount of lighting and paint could illuminate, and a chill that settled on my skin where sweat prickled at the back of my neck. I cuffed it away and followed my subject, only slightly behind, so it didn't seem too obvious. Either she didn't notice, or didn't care. Probably she was just trying to make sure I knew she was on to me by deliberately ignoring my tension.

She paused a few steps away from the elevator and said, "Where's your...oh." The other vehicles were sedans and SUVs. Mine was a compact. The others were garage-kept, and they'd seen the inside of a car wash within the past week. While I'd managed to rub Richie's message off my trunk, there was still a salt coating that speckled my car without obscuring the shopping cart dent on the rear passenger door. My little Ford stood out like a sore thumb...a cheap thumb covered in salt. "I should be able to pop it," she said.

She moved to a rear door, the dented door, then said, "Are you sure you don't want to call a locksmith? A car door's got all kinds of wires in it, and there's always a chance to mess up—"

"You've done this before, though?"

"More times than I can count."

What was the encore, hiding in the back seat and introducing a well-placed bullet to the unsuspecting driver? I stood several steps away while she peeled back the weather stripping and slid the tool in. "You've gotta take your time," she said. "When you finally do grab the lock, you can tell by the way it feels." I checked her side. Was she packing? It didn't look like it, not unless she had a really, really small firearm under her fitted suit.

"Sorry to pull you away from your..." I let it hang, hoping she'd fill in the blank with her job title.

"No problem. I don't mind."

I so sucked at covert questioning. I gathered myself for another try. "When you're not popping locks, what is it you do?"

She laughed. It sounded a bit self-conscious. Maybe I made her as nervous as she made me, which was never a good sign. That's what they always say about things like bees and stray dogs, right before you end up in a world of pain. "Agent Dreyfuss calls me The Fixer. Because I can fix just about anything."

Anything at all...like the Roger Burke situation? Hoping she might be circling around to an explanation, I said, "Like what?"

"I think I found the spot." She paused in her lock-fishing and did a few shoulder rolls, then looked me in the eye. "Things like stopping a movement to have Psychs disqualified for state college aid. You wouldn't have heard about it—we nipped that one early. Things like locating partners and allies in the business community willing to provide us with additional monitoring. Things like checking out our personnel."

She dropped her gaze as she said that last item. Since I was on the FPMP hire-list, I could only presume it meant she knew every last thing about me. In other words, the balance of power here was way more skewed than I'd thought. I did my best impression of "comfortable" by aiming for a light tone. "As job titles go, it's got a better ring to it than PC-M5."

Maybe she had perused all my un-private records, but she didn't know me well enough to see that I was faking comfort. She laughed nervously. "It is pretty catchy. Too bad all my official paperwork says *Operations Coordinator*." She turned back to the car door while a million grisly variations of *fixing* things flashed before my mind's eye. "I think it was…okay, there. Right there." Pull, click, and the rear door was open. "You can reach into the front to hit the power-lock. You've got longer arms."

Why couldn't a person unlock a whole car from the rear doors? Not everyone kept small children in the back seat. Some of us consumers would have preferred to open up the vehicle without exposing our backs to the person who'd just helped us break in. I solved this dilemma by facing her the whole time I stretched over the passenger seat rather than making my back a target. Luckily I did have long arms and I got the car open in a few awkward flails. I then hopped in the front door and grabbed my keys from the ignition.

As I battened down the car, I was relieved our little lockpicking stunt was over. Unfortunately, it hadn't really told me anything at all about the elusive Operations Coordinator—other than the fact that I'd now need to check my back seat every time I got in my car to make sure she wasn't hiding there with the ice scrapers and poorly folded maps. All my careful maneuvering, and I'd managed to come up with a job title, one that Jacob could have easily supplied. Super. I attempted to pry out just a little bit more. "So does everyone pack a slim jim…or is exclusive to The Fixer?"

She held up the narrow strip of metal. "This isn't exactly standard issue." She began to walk toward the elevator, while I hung back to buy a bit of time. She was clearly baffled by my body language. We pause-walked to the doors, completely out of synch, and finally she needed to reach across me to push the call button. I did my best not to flinch visibly. The doors slid open. We climbed in, the doors closed, and we faced our blurry reflections. The elevator began to rise. "So, what is standard issue?" It would've been smooth, if I'd said it maybe five seconds sooner. As it stood, it came off as a non-sequitur.

"What?"

"Weapons. Does everyone have matching sidearms?"

"No…not exactly. Most of our field agents go with a Sig P229. Ex law enforcement tend toward Glocks."

"And you carry…?"

"Only if I'm assigned to a sensitive location." I'd been aiming for a make, but she took the question in a different way entirely—whether she packed any heat at all. Like it didn't occur to her that Jacob had told me she was at the range. Like I didn't know a shot had likely come from her general direction that day in front of the prison. "Most days I work here. I'm really more effective if I have access to my secure computer and all my databases and files."

"And your slim jim."

She gave an edgy laugh and said, "The car I had in grad school was such a beater. The hinges on the driver-side door were rusted through, so I couldn't open it without the whole door falling off—which it did on Maxwell Street, you know, when they used to have that big Sunday flea market? Someone actually tried to buy it from me, too, like I was going to drive home without a door. Once I wired that back on, my key broke off in the passenger door lock. Slim jim and I got to know each other really well that year."

"Wow. My first used car smelled like hard-boiled eggs. I hate to think why."

She appeared to relax, just a bit. "Can I ask you something?"

Hopefully it wasn't why I was so interested in her gun. "Sure."

"Is Con going to have you sweep the fifth floor?"

So. She'd dropped the *Agent Dreyfuss*. Not that I knew what it indicated. "He might."

"I hope he does." She gave a shudder. "How can he stand it? That feeling, you know, like someone's watching you."

Hard to say if ghosts were her entire problem in that regard. After all, the ex-husband who now signed her paycheck was a remote viewer. Did she know? Or was that fact a strategically placed glimpse good ol' Dreyfuss revealed to make me feel like a special snowflake? The elevator stopped and I steeled myself to exit, but then I realized we were only on the fourth floor—and that someone was getting on. Someone who'd recently written WASH ME on my beleaguered little car.

"Hardcore Vic!" Richie grabbed my hand and pumped it up and down as if we hadn't seen each other in years. He wore brown loafers, brown wool pants, and a nubby brown cardigan over a beige permanent press shirt that was buttoned wrong, so one side of the collar rode higher than the other. The top of his head, of which I had a great view, was nice and shiny. His hand was moist. Once he was done giving me the big handshake, he swung around to Laura and said, "There you are. I've been trying to call you for like *ten minutes*." Then he swung back to me—and Stefan's Camp Hell impression of him swinging around to look at people when he spoke came to mind, which made me feel like a dick. Because of course that classy boyfriend and I had laughed ourselves inside out over the way Einstein couldn't talk to someone without lining them up with his whole body. "What're *you guys* doing?" Richie demanded, insinuating hanky panky between Laura and me with the subtlety of an eight-year-old.

"I was helping Detective Bayne unlock his car," she said placidly. Not like it cost her any effort, either. I wondered how often she dealt with Richie. My guilt over the way I'd mocked and antagonized him would undoubtedly wear thin at some point, and his unbridled stupidity would begin to annoy me. But Laura seemed to have a good supply of patience.

"What a piece of junk," Richie declared. "Maybe when Agent Marks gets his Lexus, he'll sell you his Crown Vic cheap."

"Your concern over my vehicle is touching."

"Them are like cop cars," he explained. While no one ever accused me of being the king of grammar, ouch. "And you'd have the same name… Vic, driving a Crown Vic. Heh-heh."

Laura smiled politely at the witticism. The elevator disgorged us onto the fifth floor none too soon. We made our way to the wide sweep of the big modern desk, and Richie planted his elbows on it, sprawling as if he was about to order a two-for-one drink special at happy hour. "So them guys never installed my new TV last night," he told Laura.

"Was there a structural issue with your wall?"

"Nuh uh. They just didn't show up."

"Okay, I'll call."

"'Cos I need my TV."

"Right. I'll reschedule."

"I can't miss that show. You know. The one I watch."

"Understandable."

"It's just sitting there in the box. I mean, what good is it in the box?"

I was wondering how long he could sustain an argument with someone who kept agreeing with him when Laura nudged him toward the finish line with, "What time should I have the installers come—seven?"

"Uh, yeah, okay. I should be home by seven. It's all-you-can-eat wing night at The Blue Room."

"Got it. Seven."

Maybe I learned more about Laura Kim from that little exchange than I had the whole episode in the parking garage. While it was my experience that technicians supplied a broad window of arrival and then showed up whenever the hell they damn well pleased, The Fixer's quiet confidence led me to believe she could make seven o'clock happen. She did it with the same cool confidence she'd just employed to get Richie to stop complaining about the installers, although whether he'd be there to let them in, or whether he'd still be anointing two-ply paper napkins with ranch dressing, chicken fat and hot sauce at that time would be anyone's guess.

Once Laura fixed her headset in place, tapped a few buttons and listened, she said to me, "Agent Dreyfuss would like to see you in his office. I'll walk you there."

"Let me," Richie said. "I got a question for him. An important one."

A look flickered across her face. Was that a small calculation? Weighing the pros and cons of setting me loose with only Richie to wrangle me—or determining the most non-invasive way to keep Richie in line? She pressed a button, paused, and said, "Agent Duff would like a word."

Who?

She listened, then told Richie, "Go ahead."

CHAPTER 8

NOT THAT I'D BEEN UNDER the impression Richie's last name was actually Einstein, but the realization that I never even knew his damn surname was pretty disturbing. Almost as disturbing as hearing him called by the title *Agent*, which, I gotta admit, looks pretty slick in front of Jacob's name. Not so much preceding Richie's.

He knocked on the door, which gave a faint electronic click, then elbowed me aside and bounded in as if we were racing toward a box of donuts with only one cruller. "So I met these guys at karaoke," he told Dreyfuss, "and they really want to come see the Bears with me on Thanksgiving."

"How many guys are we talking?"

"Two. Uh…three."

"That's a total of thirty-two guests."

Richie thought about it. Then he started counting on his fingers. Then he got lost somewhere around eight while the repeater beside him took a bullet to the throat. "Well, there's my bowling team, that's four. Plus my neighbors Bernie and Meg…."

Once I got over the idea of Einstein singing karaoke, I attempted to wrap my head around the cost of comping thirty-two people at Soldier Field—especially on Thanksgiving Day. That game had sold out two hours after the tickets became available…not that it would prevent Dreyfuss from scoring more. Just that the thought of him being willing to do so was interesting, to say the least.

"I don't know if we can swing that many behind the fifty-yard line," Dreyfuss said. "You're sure you don't want a skybox instead?"

"It's only three more seats."

"Free booze, Richie. People love an ice cold keg. Think how much fun it'll be in your exclusive box—climate-controlled bliss. Shrimp cocktail and caviar. Sexy bartenders. Hell, I can even get you lap dances if that's what you're into."

"Not in front of my *neighbors*." Richie flushed pink. "How about pizza? Will there be pizza there?"

"I think that could be arranged."

Richie considered the offer, then swung around to fully face me. "Hardcore Vic—did you want to come?"

The thought of watching Richie's bowling team scarfing down some fat, oozing deep-dish while sexy bartenders rode their groins was mildly amusing, but it wasn't the way I wanted to spend Thanksgiving. It would probably be funny for about ten minutes…and then I'd start thinking about the way we all had to chip in five bucks the last time someone made a pizza run back at the precinct, and how there'd been nothing left but a few crusts by the time I got to the break room. "Jacob and I already—"

"Agent Marks can come too," Richie added.

"We already have plans." We hadn't discussed whether we'd be heading up to Wisconsin or not, but I wanted to leave the day open in case we did. Even if that meant turning down all the shrimp cocktail I cared to eat.

"There'll be pizza."

"I heard. But, you know. Family stuff."

Richie seemed puzzled by that excuse, but Dreyfuss adroitly steered the conversation away from my personal life. "Speaking of Agent Marks, would you mind getting him for me, Richie?"

"Sure," he said. "No problem." I guess it didn't occur to Richie to wonder why Dreyfuss didn't pick up the phone and buzz him.

After the door sighed shut with a gentle magnetic click, I asked, "So how much is Richie's Amazing Thanksgiving Adventure setting you back?"

"About half as much as it would have if he'd insisted on the fifty-yard line seats."

If I tried to get a single pair of tickets from Sergeant Warwick, even up in the nosebleed section, he'd tell me to go beat them out of a scalper myself. "Deep pockets."

"Money is only money—the treasury prints more of it every day. The seats behind the bench, however, have strings attached I'd just as soon not pull. I'd rather juggle my budget than burn favors."

Money, favors, connections, all of it was worth something. Seconal required all of the above, and I'd be blissed out for the rest of my life on the amount of reds he could score for the cost of a skybox. Heck, I'd do a tap dance for the handful of reds in his pocket, but I didn't let on. Seemed to me I was nowhere near as demanding as Richie, and I provided a lot more value in return for my fee.

I paced the room. The three repeaters looked the same as they had the day before. "Chance isn't here," I said.

"Of course not."

I rubbed the back of my neck, turning to catch Triple-Shot in my peripheral vision. The first bullet took him in the thigh. I glanced away before I saw a replay of the other two rounds, disgusted. Salting the dead junkie shooting up in the corner of the convenience store was one thing. The poor saps working the cash register had nothing to do with his death. Dreyfuss, though? "If you don't like working in a haunted office, you should've thought of that before you had the guys killed."

"You think it's a pain in the ass to score tickets?" he said. "Try covering up a shooting. I think you know me well enough by now to see it's not my style."

"I like to keep an open mind."

"You don't believe me? Ask 'em yourself—who put them here, me or the old guard? I'll just stand here and pretend you're floating a rhetorical question."

The ducking throat-shot repeater pitched backwards. It would be a hell of a load off my mind if I *could* ask them. Sure, they might lie. But usually they didn't, not about their killers. They were just repeaters, though. They had nothing to say…verbally, at least.

I stared at the spot where the victim landed, then knelt and touched the berber. The texture looked different where his blood pooled, though when the blood disappeared, the texture moved, shifting until it blended with the rest of the rug. So the carpeting had been replaced since the shooting. I scanned the current carpet. It had been there a while; I could detect a subtle hint of wear between the door and the old position of Dreyfuss' desk. But the pile was expensive and didn't give much away. Plus Dreyfuss had been Regional Director for a few years now, so carpet wear was nothing much to go by.

I glanced up at Triple-Shot. While I didn't think I'd suddenly find a date and time of death stamped on his forehead, it would've been nice. It also would've been nice to notice he was in a leisure suit with a great big collar, or a power-suit with giant shoulder pads. But menswear doesn't exactly have major fashion swings every decade, so there weren't any clues in his wardrobe, either. I thought maybe I could date the hair of the guy by the bathroom, but it turned out he just had high widow's peaks.

Dreyfuss' voice startled me. "Maybe you don't need to ask anything…maybe you communicate with them telepathically."

"Who said I was communicating?"

"You, my friend, are a riddle wrapped in a mystery inside a polyester blend."

I refused to let him bait me.

"Still, your body language tells me they're not much of a threat…unlike a certain someone who can apparently come and go as they please." He glanced at the tiny cactus on his credenza to remind me of our flower shop chat about Dr. Chance, then lowered his voice and said, "It's refreshing that I don't need to tell you how to play the game. You know nothing. You see nothing. You're operating under the vaguest impressions. Fine. But if you should happen to 'sense' something important, it's in both of our best interest that you tell me about it—not like the major sighting you decided to keep to yourself. Got it?"

"If her whereabouts are that important to you, maybe you should have the guy who just got the skybox find her."

"We both know that's not happening—so what's your point?"

"I don't appreciate having my payment doled out one pill at a time."

"Get rid of the problem and I'll set you up. Gladly."

I was about to pin down the specifics of getting "set up" when Jacob and Mr. Skybox himself joined us. "Sorry I took so long," Jacob said. "I was right in the middle of something." As the words left his mouth, I realized that he'd probably intuited Dreyfuss' reason for sending Richie to fetch him, and stalled the poor guy to buy us some time alone. Jacob must be in his glory. He no longer had a partner who'd pipe up, "No you weren't!" and spoil his truth-bending.

By way of greeting, Dreyfuss asked Jacob, "Any luck getting the Metropolitan Correctional Center to play nice with your investigation?"

"Not yet. Your contact hasn't called me back."

"Well, keep chipping away at him. He owes me a favor." Dreyfuss turned to me. "Let's focus on our home turf—which parts of the building are first in line for Operation Cactus?"

"The conference room I searched the last time I was here." And if Dr. Chance wasn't waiting for me there, then what? "The last…physical site, too." In other words, wherever it was he'd ordered her gunned down.

"Any supplies we should get you?"

I had my salt and my Florida Water. I shook my head.

"Agent Marks will show you around," Dreyfuss said.

Jacob said, "The conference room, that's by personnel, right?"

In his best "duh" voice, Richie told him, "Totally different floor."

"And the other location," Jacob asked. "The subbasement?"

"Fourth floor guest suite C," Dreyfuss supplied.

"Someone really needs to get you a map," Richie said. "How long have you been here, two months?"

Jacob gave a shrug—and as I saw the minuscule movement, I realized his "I'm lost" act was yet another ruse. He knew full well where everything was. He'd probably plotted out the entire building within a week. But why set me up to have Richie as my tour guide instead of him?

About a million reasons why. My relationship with Richie spanned nearly two decades. Sure, most of that time consisted of a few years when we were in our early twenties, and the majority of *that* time I spent ruthlessly mocking him. He seemed to have made out well enough in the end to let bygones be bygones. Or maybe, despite my shitty attitude back then, I'd been the closest thing he had to a friend.

Not only did Richie seem to enjoy my company, but he'd been working at the FPMP for years. While Jacob could certainly show me around, he wouldn't have a feel for the history of the place, especially the dirty little secrets I wasn't supposed to know.

And not only did Richie like me…but he wasn't bright enough to censor himself in my presence. Especially if he was trying to impress me with how much he knew.

If only I could get him to stop talking about cars.

"I'll probably have better luck scoping things out with Richie," I said. "Jacob's vibe might send something into hiding." This was patently untrue, of course. Jacob's Stiffness didn't act as any kind of ghost-deterrent—they just couldn't sneak inside his skin.

Fortunately, Dreyfuss didn't know that. "Whaddaya say, Richard? Can you make the time in your schedule to show Detective Bayne around?"

Most people given additional work would have hemmed and hawed about how they'd need to shuffle their responsibilities so they could milk something out of Dreyfuss for taking on an extra task, but Richie immediately said, "Sure! No problem." Then again, he'd just been handed a skybox on Thanksgiving. Maybe it was simpler that way, to give and take in an exuberant display of trust without holding any collateral in reserve. But I couldn't see adopting that methodology myself.

We turned to go and Jacob filed out of the room first. As he brushed past me, we locked eyes. For someone as inscrutable as he can be, the micro-expressions he manages to slip through are beyond intense. The way I'd flowed with his lead? He approved. His eyes were two dark points of fierceness, and he'd sucked in his cheeks for a split second to make his supermodel cheekbones jut in a way that left me weak-kneed. That look promised to take me and use me and make me beg for mercy…then leave me wrung out and hung up to dry. He slipped through the door, and the devastating look was gone.

I moved to follow, and Dreyfuss said to me, "If you do make contact, act fast and do what it takes. She's no dummy. If she figures out what you're trying to do, you might not get another chance. No pun intended."

Although most of the ghost-zapping I do consists of erasing repeaters, moving Jennifer Chance along wouldn't be the first exorcism of a sentient ghost I'd performed. I'd escorted out about a dozen spirits with personalities since the day I released the Fire Ghost from her spectral dog chain. Those spirits had been victims, though. I'd nudged them out of the rut where they lingered around wallowing in their deaths, figuring I should help them move on to something better. Although Dr. Chance technically qualified as a victim, something about the way I'd been deployed made me feel less like an assistant and more like an assassin.

Maybe I had more in common with Laura Kim than a history with lousy used cars.

Richie and I arrived at our first location, the conference room. I caught a whiff of spice on the air, which confused me because herbal props were used in earth magic and Hoodoo, and Richie was more of a holy water and frankincense guy. Then again, it smelled suspiciously like tandoori.

"You want me to have the power cut so we can concentrate?" Richie said.

I really didn't feel like blundering around in the dark if I could avoid it. "Let's hold off for now. You haven't sensed any activity here lately, have you?"

"Just the quarterly budget meeting. Heh-heh."

I laughed unconvincingly and scrutinized the spot where the repeater who'd blown his own brains out used to be. Suicide guy wasn't there anymore. But seeing that expanse of table and the subtly textured wall behind it—a wall that had probably been entirely replaced to get rid of the trace evidence—I couldn't help but wonder. Why did that guy pull the trigger? Maybe he saw it as a better option than submitting to interrogation. Or maybe there'd been another set of hands in play that I couldn't see, as their owner wasn't dead yet—a kind of macabre grown-up version of "Why are you hitting yourself?"

Or maybe there was a high-level telekinetic pulling the victim's strings.

I shuddered.

"Do you feel a cold spot?" Richie said. He got up in my comfort zone. "I don't think I do."

"No, it's just…it's nothing. It's clean."

Richie marched around the table. His stride was weirdly balanced, heavy, graceless. When he completed his circuit, he stood in place, swung his arms parallel to one another and looked at me expectantly. Given my aversion to being locked up, I wasn't exactly eager to see the "guest suites." But since Dr. Chance wasn't in either of the places I'd seen her before, I supposed her holding tank was the next logical place to look. My discomfort grew to something closer to fear as we neared the super-high-security area, passing first through a keycard slider, then a manually locked door with two very large and capable hard-eyed men in plain black suits keeping tabs on it. Richie spoke to them with as much obnoxious entitlement as he had Laura. "We need room number, uh… d'you remember what it was, Vic?"

"Suite C," I said. My voice sounded rusty.

One of the grim agents turned back to a computer monitor. The other was watching me, and though I didn't know why I'd caught his eye, I'm guessing it wasn't because he was hoping I'd be free for dinner. He was a few years younger than me, buff and capable, and while the level of his personal grooming pinged my gaydar, the rest of his body language definitely didn't. His hair was cropped even closer than Jacob's, practically bald. He was tanner than the rest of us white guys, as if he'd just come back from a Florida vacation, and his pale gray eyes were striking against the tan. It was possible he knew who I was, and who Jacob was, and exactly who we were in relation to one another. Probably, some thicknecks back at the Fifth knew too, but it wasn't openly acknowledged. Here, though?

I wasn't sure. Being out on the job was new to me, and I wanted to make sure I handled it right. Since I didn't want to seem like I was cruising him, I looked away first.

He left the other agent at the computer and led us to a hallway that contained four staggered doors and no windows. It didn't look like a prison, or a hospital, or even the strip search rooms at O'Hare airport. It looked like a nice apartment building or maybe a classy motel, albeit a motel with incredibly robust locks on every door.

Back at the flower shop, I'd said Jennifer Chance couldn't really do anything other than make a cold spot, and for most people, that was true. Because of my talent, my subtle bodies were a lot looser in my physical skin than most people's. Disgruntled ghosts sometimes grab at me, as if I don't notice them trying to sneak in—and Jennifer Chance was the poster child for disgruntlement.

I sucked white light as we walked down the short hallway to the second door on the right, opening myself wide like a fireplug at the scene of a big blaze, encouraging my connection with whatever cosmic psychic energy fuels my ability to load me up, pronto. And then I channeled all of that bright white energy into a psychic bodysuit to protect me from being penetrated, by Chance, or by any other potential ghostly trespassers.

You think walking and chewing gum is hard? Try walking and sucking white light. My vision went wobbly and I listed toward Richie. He shouldered me into place and said, "Walk much? Heh-heh."

We paused in front of the door, which didn't look nearly as ominous as I thought it should. The agent used a key card as well as a metal key to open the suite. "You want the door open," he asked Richie, "or shut?"

"Open," I answered, before Richie could volunteer to have us sealed into this place, the one where Dr. Chance met her end…because before, seeing her in the boardroom or in Dreyfuss' can, I could have dodged her. Or maybe not, since she was noncorporeal and wasn't hindered by slippery shoes or poor aerobic capacity, but at least I maintained the illusion that I could at least try. Locked in a room, though? No thanks.

Richie strode right on in. I hung back in the doorway. The bald guy stood at the ready in the hall.

It was a plain room, no sharp corners. The curvilinear edges gave it a sixties mod feel. If there'd been any windows, it might have felt like executive quarters for temporary staff. Its appearance was completely at odds with what I'd expected, which involved fire pits, manacles hanging from the ceiling, and whatever gear they use to waterboard terrorists at Gitmo.

"Here it is," Richie said, again swinging his arms in tandem, front, back. Front, back. "I don't feel nothing."

I peered around. There was a built in bed, a built in desk, and a toilet in a discreet nook in the corner. Not entirely private, but better than a communal jailhouse crapper. The soothing colors and lines were not only modern, but they'd show off a ghost as effectively as my old white-on-white apartment…if there'd been a ghost to show.

I took three steps in and helped myself to a few cleansing breaths. Then I channeled some of that protective white light into my vision. I know it's not really my eyeballs and optic nerves that perceive the spirit plane—but maybe that ability lives close enough to the visual part of my brain that the distinction is moot. I sucked light, and I peered.

Nothing.

"This was Jennifer Chance's room?" I asked Richie.

"Who?"

I was about to throw my hands up and say, "For heaven sakes!" when I saw the agent in the hall was watching me. He gave a single small nod.

I wondered if he'd been the one to press a gun to her forehead and pull the trigger. I broke eye contact and turned away. "What is it you think we're doing right now?" I asked Richie.

He pondered the question, then said, "Looking for ghosts?"

"And who usually gets locked up in these rooms?"

"I dunno."

"If you had to guess…."

"People." He sounded like the subject bored him. "I dunno." He galumph-walked around the room staring fixedly at the wall.

Was he better at keeping secrets than I thought, or was he floating on a bigger cloud of blissful ignorance than yours truly? "You've never heard of Jennifer Chance?"

"Nuh uh."

"And you don't know what these rooms are for."

"Don't know. Don't care."

I shouldn't have been surprised about his thought process, or lack thereof—and yet, somehow, I was. Maybe I'd expected him to learn a few things over the years. Maybe he had—he'd figured out how to milk a skybox from the Regional Director of the FPMP, after all. But deep down inside, he was the same old Einstein.

Maybe Richie's ignorance wasn't the thing that was bugging me. Maybe it was the parallel I couldn't stop drawing between him and me.

At least I could say this for myself: I did care. I did want to know if Con Dreyfuss had ordered those guys in his office to be put down, or if someone else really was responsible for the trigger-pull. I did want to know if Jennifer Chance was still a danger to anyone.

I did want to know if all the years I'd sunk into the police department were nothing more than busywork.

"It's time for lunch," Richie said. "You don't want to miss lunch."

Could I even bring myself to eat? I supposed if I cared as much about the truth as I was telling myself, I would need to. Every moment I could spend at the FPMP was another chance at finding the puzzle piece that would click everything around it into place.

The lunch room was as quiet and subdued as the rest of the building. I suppose I'd imagined some kind of cafeteria, a grid of bright white plastic tables with black-suited federal agents all lined up in rows. They'd be wearing sunglasses and bluetooth earpieces. And none of them would be talking.

The reality was nowhere near as freakish. The room had windows, and even though they overlooked a tangle of train tracks and a switching station, it was still a welcome view. There were a few round tables covered in white cloths where relatively normal-looking men and women ate in small groups. They were wearing dark suits, but they weren't all overlarge thirtysomething Caucasian men. You'd peg them for corporate drones if you didn't know better. A sideboard held chafing dishes and a small assortment of bottled waters and juices on ice. A serious young man in an immaculate chef jacket stood next to it, stirring one of the dishes so it couldn't skin over.

Richie charged up to the food, jammed his face against the open dish, then snatched the spoon from the cook and started stirring the dish like he was digging for gold. "Where's the meat?" He stirred harder, and I caught a subtle whiff of herb and butter. "It's all vegetables. Who eats this crap?"

I resisted the urge to apologize to the kid in the chef coat. He was probably used to it. Although I hinted that some people ate vegetables by making a point of taking the vegetarian entree, my choice sailed over Richie's head as he filled his plate with sirloin tips in gravy. He then launched into a detailed and grandiose criticism of the Bears' quarterbacking strategy that made me wish he'd suck a mouthful of steak down the wrong pipe and choke on it a few minutes to give me some small reprieve. While I considered the likelihood of me successfully vaulting over the empty chair beside me to get away from the never-ending football talk, the Regional Director sat himself down in it, blocking my escape. "Judging by the look on your face," Con said, "I'm guessing this morning was a bust."

"You could say that," I answered.

"I take it you didn't stay for lunch to soak up the ambiance." He glanced out the window at a freight train trundling past. "You're probably itching to get the hell out of here and be done with us. Willing to stay and do a floor-by-floor scan?"

"It does seem like the next logical step."

"Okay. Good." He drank down half his bottled water in a few long swallows. "I'll need to get you an escort with more clearance."

CHAPTER 9

WHAT A RELIEF. NOT ONLY was it growing painfully obvious that Richie knew nothing, but he was getting on my very last nerve. Once the grown-ups were done talking, Richie began his analysis of the Bears' offense versus the Colts' defense while Dreyfuss tooled around on his smartphone and I tried to determine what was on my plate. Evidently, I'm better at naming herbs and spices in a botanica than I am in an entree.

I was poking at something green trying to determine if it was spinach or kale when Dreyfuss motioned someone over. I recognized the bald head and the striking eyes immediately—the guy from the holding cells.

"You've met Jack Bly?" Dreyfuss said.

"Not…formally."

"This is Detective Victor Bayne," Dreyfuss supplied.

"The PsyCop," Bly said.

I wasn't quite sure where to look since Bly was watching me so hard. Hopefully he wasn't gearing up for some kind of pissing match. "The PsyCop," I confirmed, and went back to my spinach, or maybe kale.

"Are they out of steak?" Richie asked. I saw that Bly had picked the vegetarian entree too. "They'll make more if you tell them to."

Bly turned his unflinching gaze to Richie and said, "I like chard."

Richie couldn't fathom that other people might want to drive some other model of car, or spend Thanksgiving somewhere else, or eat a different meal, so he looked like he'd just been slapped with a rubber hose. When he recovered, he gave out a tentative, "Heh-heh."

As we finished our food to an account of next year's draft order and an opinionated assessment of a handful of free agents, Dreyfuss asked me, "Will you be requiring Agent Duff's services this afternoon as well? Or shall I leave you in Agent Bly's capable hands?"

Obviously he was trying to manipulate me into doing one of those two things, but given the likelihood of multi-reverse psychology, I was at a loss as to which option he was gunning for. "Richie doesn't need to come along," I decided, not because I was trying to thwart Dreyfuss, but because I'd grown profoundly weary of the subject of football.

My experience of the FPMP wasn't quite the same with Bly as my babysitter. Sure, it was a lot more peaceful. If he had any strong opinions about the Bears' defense, he kept them to himself. Something about him set me on edge, though. While he seemed knowledgeable about the building, and while he did answer whatever questions I asked, there was a subtle knowing in his eyes that made it seem like he was holding back a lot more than he was saying. Plus, I had the sense that he was watching me too closely, kind of like the fake cops Dreyfuss had planted at my precinct.

Fine. I'd keep one eye on him, one on the tour…and another on potential spirit activity. Luckily, the facility didn't require much attention. An office is an office—and we saw plenty of offices. No spirits, though. No repeaters, and no sentient ghosts, either. Once we'd exhausted the offices, we took a walk through the parking garage. Plenty of Lexuses. No ghosts.

I supposed it was possible Dr. Chance had moved along sometime in the past few months. I wouldn't know for sure until I asked Lisa. Although it might be for nothing, poking around all the dark corners of the FPMP had made me feel less antsy about Jacob spending his days here. Unless you were worried about developing a nasty case of carpal tunnel syndrome, there was really nothing to be scared of at the FPMP headquarters beyond the surveillance we already endured as a known Psych and Stiff.

The elevator released a herd of dark-suited agents who dispersed to their respective Lexuses. Good thing the headlights flashed when they tapped their key fobs, otherwise they'd be roaming around down there all night trying to determine which Lexus was whose. One by one, they rolled toward the exit. As we watched the cars begin to file out, Bly actually initiated conversation. "So, how do you like being a PsyCop?"

"If Dreyfuss recruited you to extol the virtues of the FPMP," I said, "it's not gonna work."

"Nope." Bly cracked a smile, the first one I'd seen on him all day, and gave a dismissive laugh. "Just curious."

The last thing I felt like doing was chatting, especially with him. If I had been feeling chatty, I would have made a quip about being unaware that there were actual set work hours here since Jacob had been putting in ten and twelve hour days. I didn't need some stranger to be privy to that very personal bit of information, though. Especially one who seemed to want to know me a lot more than I wanted to know him.

I understood that trying to figure out who killed Roger Burke was the type of task Jacob wouldn't be able to drop until he found an answer. Maybe now that I'd introduced good ol' Roger's final "statement," Jacob would be that much closer to his big discovery. What I hoped was that he'd find out Roger was lying; it wouldn't be news to anyone that my ex-partner wasn't exactly trustworthy. Or maybe he'd find that Laura Kim was some kind of double-agent…a very convincing double agent who did a damn good impression of a thirty-something office worker.

What I was worried he'd discover, though, was that Con Dreyfuss had put out that hit himself, and then saddled Jacob with the case to distract him while I was lured into the FPMP fold. And that Dreyfuss had concocted some kind of whammy to cover his tracks so the sí-no couldn't expose his machinations.

As I imagined the smoldering look in Jacob's eyes, the look that resulted from all that thinking and deducing and knowing, the man himself stepped out of the elevator and veered in the direction of the black Crown Vic. Then he noticed me standing there with Bly, since nothing slips by him. He course-corrected and headed toward the corner of the parking garage, the spot where we stood to watch the agents, one by one, head home.

Jacob approached. Bly said, "Agent Marks?" and offered his hand. "Agent Bly."

Trying to get a read off Jacob was futile. I made an attempt anyway, since I was curious if he'd turned up any new info while I was touring a bunch of boring office space. I came up with nothing. His expression, his posture, his voice, everything about him was placidly neutral. Though he did seem to spend an extra nanosecond sizing up Bly. "Just about wrapping things up?" he asked me, which meant he was ready to leave—on time, even—and that he also had some juicy news, too. I could hardly wait to get home and—

"We've seen everything but the lab," Bly said.

I paused with my weight shifted in the direction of my car.

"You're not going to take off before you check out the lab," Bly said, "right?"

Crap. If I'd known there was a lab on premises, I would have looked at it first, before I wasted my time poking through archives and personnel.

"Mind if I join you?" Jacob put in smoothly.

Bly gave the laminated badge clipped to Jacob's lapel a quick glance. Just checking, or looking for a reason to turn Jacob away? Hard to say, but apparently he was satisfied with whatever clearance level he found there. "The more, the merrier. Let's go."

It's bad enough that we head underground. Add to that the thickness of the steel doors and the creepy wheezing sound they make when they close. Top it off with a scientist who's *way* too happy to meet me. Now you've got a good idea of how comfortable I felt in the FPMP lab.

"My name is Kudryasvstev," our host said in a lilting Russian accent, "so everyone calls me Dr. K." This scientist didn't look much older than Jacob, but he exuded an unflappable, worldly, hard-earned jocularity. Nothing would shock this guy. Nothing would slip past his notice, either. The whole time, he'd be content to observe the proceedings, rocking on the balls of his feet with his belly thrust forward, hands jammed into the pockets of his lab coat, and an enigmatic gaptoothed smile on his broad Slavic face. A smile that was currently turned on me. "And you…are the PsyCop."

I dry-swallowed. "That would be me."

"Thirteen years," he said. I almost corrected him and said *twelve* when I realized he was right. Why did he know more about me than I did? "That's a long time."

"Not necessarily." Although lately, I'd been feeling every last minute of it.

"Long enough," Dr. K said. "Especially in the field of Psych. It's like aeronautics in the thirties, or computers in the eighties. Psychic research is the most compelling science of the twenty-first century, and it's evolving every single day."

He led us through a warren of white linoleum cabinetry and stainless steel countertops in which every bin, door and drawer was labeled—seriously labeled. It looked like someone with clinical OCD had been handed a label-maker and turned loose on the science department. *Pipettes. Burettes. Bulbs. Forceps. Clamps.* "So what is it you're testing?" I asked.

"The results are classified," Dr. K said. "But generally speaking, we're trying to figure out the specific mechanism of how Psych works. How much is genetic? How much is environmental? How common is it, really? And how can it be augmented?"

I bit back a disdainful snort. Augmentation? That was rich. All the Psychs I knew would be happier to get fitted with an off-switch.

We delved deeper into the lab. The coffee supply bins in the corner were clearly marked as *regular, decaf* and *tea…sugar, sugar substitutes* and *creamer. Cups. Napkins. Stirrers*, too. I supposed I should find that encouraging. If there was any medical hardware I wanted to steer clear of, it would be easy enough to identify. Even to an amateur like me.

"Is there anything in particular you need to see?" Dr. K asked. Jacob and Bly had dropped back a bit, and now that Dr. K was alone with me, he seemed more likely to chat. I wondered how I ever got anything done without Jacob to wrangle people for me. "I can't give you the data…but I can show you around."

"Well, just walk me through. I'll, uh, know it if I see it." I wasn't sure how likely it would be to find ghosts in the lab, but when I thought about it too hard, Camp Hell memories of the marathon session with a dead woman's wig made my throat flutter. Because how else do you put a medium through their paces in a laboratory setting, if not by torturing them with relics from the dearly departed?

Or maybe there'd been an accident, like some unfortunate science geek who'd blown themselves up, or gotten too close for comfort with an electrical current. Or maybe a test subject took some psyactives that disagreed with them. Or maybe the science team sacrificed people to create a spot that was likely to be haunted…although if they did, I presumed they labeled it properly.

What I found instead was a bored-looking guy with a couple of electrodes stuck to his temples staring at a houseplant. He was in a room with plexi walls, white plastic table and chairs, fluorescent lighting, and not much else. "Plant communicator?" I asked.

"We've never had one of those," Dr. K said with amusement that seemed fairly genuine, answering my question in a kinda-sorta indirect way. "This isn't about Phil—we already know his abilities and limits. But, that?" Dr. K gestured, and a good twenty yards away, behind a bank of bland-looking computers, I noted a cabinet of exposed electronics that included a TV tube with horizontal bars of static rolling past. A GhosTV, or at least the guts of one. I shuddered. "I take it you've seen something like it before—so I'm not telling you anything you don't already know."

Although Dr. K knew exactly who I was, and exactly what I knew about GhosTVs, I had no plans of divulging my most valuable secrets to him within ten minutes of making his acquaintance. I answered with a noncommittal shrug.

"We're determining if the equipment affects Phil's performance."

Given that I didn't know which flavor of Psych this Phil guy was supposed to be, I wouldn't know if a GhosTV would affect him or not. Besides, who's to say the damn thing was tuned to the right channel, anyway? I glanced back over my shoulder to see if Jacob had burst out in his telltale red Psy-veins, but he and Bly had hung too far back for me to tell. At first they looked pretty embroiled in whatever conversation they were having, but then I realized it was a kind of macho standoff that neither of them was willing to back away from. If testosterone was amplified by a GhosTV, they would have been surrounded by a big, thick cloud of it.

I gestured toward the controls. "Can I get a closer look?"

"Go ahead—just don't change the settings."

I approached the GhosTV, with its wiring and circuitry all on display. Positioning my back so that it shielded the gesture from the scientist, I gave my hand a quick wave. My spread fingers left brief tracers. The TV was working, all right. I glanced back toward Jacob, but he and Bly had edged their conversation out into the hallway. Hopefully Jacob was finding out something worthwhile. I sure wasn't. With a GhosTV playing the medium channel, any spirits in the vicinity would be lit up like spectral beacons for me. But there was nobody home except me, Dr. K, and Phil the plant guy.

I noted the settings. They looked like the same ones we'd used at PsyTrain to ramp up my talent. Although mediums did get extra juice from the broadcast, I wasn't the only one affected. A lot of other Psychs who'd been straining to go astral finally crossed the threshold that day. But if plants had subtle bodies in the astral too, and if those subtle bodies could be manipulated, I had no idea.

I walked up to the plexi. It was like a two-way mirror, but without the telltale distortion. The guy inside the box ignored me, but he seemed to be doing it of his own free will. I stared at the plant. No tracers, then again, I only saw the evidence of subtle bodies when things were in motion. Since I didn't want to taint the results by adding my energy to it, I didn't linger. At least, I didn't mean to. When I looked beyond the plant, I realized that Phil had a pulsing ray of light emanating from his solar plexus—and I couldn't help but give that light beam some extra attention. It was aimed at the plant. Since I hadn't seen anything like it at PsyTrain, it was possible I was viewing a real, live telekinetic in action. Or inaction, as the case may be, since he did look phenomenally disinterested.

"Let's leave Phil to his task," Dr. K said, and steered me away from the plexi with a solicitous hand on my upper arm. I flinched away from his touch. My discomfort over touching makes me easy to steer. We delved deeper into the lab, where there were other test subjects in other plexi rooms. A woman wrote things on slips of paper in one. A man sequenced a series of cards in another. None of the subjects appeared sleep-deprived or drugged. There were no gurneys or hospital gowns, no I.V. drips or restraints. Even so, I felt a panic attack with Camp Hell written all over it waiting to overtake me.

By the time we found ourselves among the big equipment storage, I was ready to leave. More label-maker excess here. *Centrifuge. Geiger counter. EKG. Defibrillator.* All the wires and electrodes were starting to freak me out. Shock treatment—did I know what it felt like, firsthand? Possibly. It seemed like one of those things I would block out. And now I'd wonder about it all night, maybe all week.

I'd seen enough. "I'm done."

Dr. K paused in front of a door labeled *Cold Storage* and said, "You sure you don't want to—?"

"I'm done," I repeated.

CHAPTER 10

NOW I SAW HOW EASY it was to get carried away and end up lingering at the FPMP well into the night. By the time I fled the lab, the fifth floor was locked down and Dreyfuss was gone—and with him, my payment. I climbed into my dented Ford Taurus and pulled out of the parking garage with Jacob right behind me. We were separated in traffic when I re-routed myself past the gin mill. I'd been trying to tell myself I was better off with Dreyfuss owing me something for a change, in this case a dose of Seconal for the day's work, but that logic didn't ring true. What I needed was my own stockpile, not promises and debts. I idled past, scanning both sides of the street. My dealer's car was conspicuously absent. Figuring he was still stuck in the system—and doing my best to avoid wondering if it was Dreyfuss keeping him there—I swallowed past the itch in my throat and headed home.

I caught up to Jacob on the front stoop unlocking our door. The cannery was dark, and Lisa's car was gone. We were alone. Sort of. If you didn't count whatever surveillance was pointed in our direction. So much to talk about, and no privacy to do it in. We stepped into the foyer, and he flipped me around and mashed me against the wall before I could even hang up my overcoat.

"I thought we'd never get out of there," he said against the side of my neck.

Maybe he was trying to convey factual information disguised as sweet talk. Or maybe he was trying to get a rise out of me. If anything could distract me from my lack of decent drugs, it was those whiskers dragging across the second-most sensitive part of my body. I'm such a sucker for the neck, but as much as I wanted to give myself over to the sensation, I was even more curious what he'd discovered about Jack Bly while I was scanning the lab. I slipped my hand inside his overcoat and brushed the bulge of his sidearm. "What were you and Agent Buzzcut talking about?" I asked.

"Not much."

"C'mon. You two were all over each other."

"He's not my type."

I knew that—it was the only reason I could tease. "I dunno, he's got those pale eyes you like so much."

Jacob's tongue trailed wet heat down the sinew of my neck. Against the wetness, he whispered, "Colored contacts."

What the heck? I'm pretty well-versed in manly behavior, at least as much as it pertains to the police force. I couldn't imagine anyone at the Fifth Precinct wearing contacts unless it improved their aim. And *colored* contacts? They'd just as soon slap on a tutu and a tiara. Federal agents weren't that much fancier than local law enforcement, so what was Bly's deal? Obviously the guy was some sort of FPMP tool, although Dreyfuss would know I presumed as much, and maybe he wanted that presumption to distract me from Bly's real…hell, I had no idea. And Jacob's hot breath playing over my throat was making it less and less likely I'd come up with a plausible theory anytime soon. My natural inclination would be to stop the presses and hash out what Bly might be hiding, but that conversation was too detailed to have right there in our own foyer where the FPMP could potentially hear it. If we cranked up a loud, nasty porno, we could whisper speculations to each other below the cover of all the fake grunting and groaning. I knew just the disc, a plotless wonder of a fuckfest set in some poor schlep's basement. The actors don't trade dialog for long, thankfully, since their delivery is painful to watch. Hell, the sex is painful to watch, too. They slam each other hard enough to bruise. I found my pants fitting funny just thinking about it.

The back of Jacob's hand brushed up against my burgeoning hard-on, and we both sucked air. That hiss of breath reminded me of the porno, which made my breathing even more labored. That, in turn, made Jacob's groping take on a real urgency. It had been a while since we'd had a chance to really go at it. Too long. I made one last attempt to come up with some encoded way of comparing notes on Bly, but I kept getting sidetracked by the gentle rake of Jacob's teeth below my right ear.

Maybe if we started banging each other, whoever monitored our channel would tune out. Unlikely, given that if I were the one on the receiving end, I'd turn up the volume and call my co-workers into the room, too. But my judgment was compromised by the pressure of Jacob's hands roving up and down my sides.

We shoved at each other's clothes. I reveled in the feeling of us clawing at the overcoats and suits and holsters in the way—too urgent to bother undressing or even go upstairs. We used to keep a super slippery lube perfect for shower sex in the downstairs bathroom, but that was before we had a roommate. Now it'd be weird. Plus, even an adjournment to the first-floor bathroom could kill the sudden, precarious moment.

I worked open Jacob's belt buckle and butted my groin against his hip. He grunted. A few shoves and he was exposed, that fat slab of stiffening cock hanging out from his open fly, the rest of him disheveled and flushed. I mouthed the word *yeah*. Dirty talk was never my forte, and I was even more tongue-tied with the thought of the FPMP listening in. Fine. We'd communicate via body language. When he took a step back and shoved me to my knees, I dragged at his slacks, twin fistfuls of fabric, to keep my kneecaps from cracking against the tile. I kept my hands where they were, balled in Italian wool, while Jacob grabbed me by the head and plugged my mouth with his cock. Yeah, it was rough. And yeah, it was perfect. I felt my own hard-on straining down my pant leg, cool at the tip where a wet spot would be spreading over the lining of my pocket. I focused on that, my own aching hardness and the strain in my jaw, the invasion of that salty hunk of flesh fucking my face, in and out, in and out, pubes rasping my lips as Jacob's fists tightened in my hair.

"We should go upstairs," he huffed.

I noted he made no actual attempt to stop pummeling my mouth and head for the staircase. I made a sound like, "Ngh," and ground my upper lip into the base of his cock. It made no sense to interrupt the proceedings now, not with us riding a sweet wave of momentum. I walked my hands up the front of his slacks, one handful at a time, until I had him by his ass, a firm globe in each hand. I squeezed, hard, and he started really wailing on me.

"Close," he grunted. I'd figured as much by the way his thighs trembled. "You wanna swallow?"

I gave a shadow of a nod, which he felt through his death-grip on my hair. Without warning, a weird notion popped into my head: if it were Bly kneeling there instead of me, Jacob wouldn't have any hair to pull.

Immediately, my gut insisted that Agent Bly was definitely not gay. Not even curious. Although I can be oblivious to the fact that someone's into me (specifically) until their tongue is in my mouth, I'm good enough at guessing someone's overall inclination. Plenty of men my age shaved their heads these days, not just gay guys. It didn't mean a thing. Unless you added colored contacts into the equation. And the way I'd felt like Bly was watching me more closely than he needed to. And the loadedness of the question, "How do you like being a PsyCop?" Which could have just meant he was a Psych groupie…though it didn't explain the colored contacts.

Firmly resolving to put Bly out of my mind, I focused on the prod of Jacob's cockhead at the back of my throat instead, and gave it that extra bit of suction to hasten the experience toward the big finale. Jacob released a stuttery breath and bit back a moan. Pretty soon he needed to tear a hand from my hair and slam his palm against the wall behind me to keep himself upright. With one hand on the wall and the other cupping the back of my head, he dragged me onto his dick for the final few thrusts. When he let loose, he was so far down I couldn't quite taste it. But I could feel the thrumming in his shaft as he shot.

He pulled out, then let go of my head to plant his other hand on the wall, mashing his brow into his forearm while he shuddered all over and sucked air like I suck white light. I let go of his ass, sagged back against the wall and gave myself a few quick strokes through my pants. The wet spot was huge, but thanks to my mental image of Agent Bly with his hinky eyes and his tanned scalp, my stiffness had unstiffened.

Jacob dropped a hand to my cheek and cupped my face with the touch of a butterfly wing. "I thought you were into it."

First the sleeping pill incident, now this. I tried to be less obvious about chafing my dick to attention as vigorously as I was. "I am. It's good."

He pulled me to my feet, then kissed me…on the *forehead*. "I'll go make dinner."

"Don't you dare, Mister." I snagged him by the sleeve and pulled him back. "I'm not done."

I could tell by the way he snugged up against me that while he'd been offering me an easy out, he was glad I hadn't accepted it. He nudged his thigh against mine. I shifted myself to rub off on his bulging quad, took his face in both hands, and kissed him hard. Our quickening breath danced between our wet mouths, and reclaiming the mood was no hardship. Just focus on Jacob, I told myself. His lips. His tongue. The solid press of his body, the insistence of his hands. Pretty soon Bly was a distant concern, a negligible curiosity that would definitely keep while I tended to more urgent matters. I grabbed Jacob's hand and covered my crotch with it. My body responded to his touch, same as it always does. I might not be a teenager anymore, but the plumbing works just fine…when I was able to clear my mind and keep my focus on the matter at hand, anyway.

My eyes had drifted shut, and I decided that keeping them open—keeping my attention on Jacob—would be my best bet. Not that I could see much more than a blur while he was kissing me. But it was a nice blur. The way he'd started jerking me off through my pants was pretty sweet, too. My breath caught, and he sighed encouragement into my mouth and started pawing at the front of my pants.

As he pulled back to undo the fly, he shifted position. Right behind him, the front door filled my field of vision. I was bombarded by images of it flying open, and me standing there with my dick out and a dumb look on my face. First I pictured Lisa framed in the doorway. Then Lisa and

Crash. Then Lisa and Dreyfuss. And Crash. And Carolyn. And bringing up the rear? Agent fucking Bly. All looking at me wide-eyed with horror.

I clapped my hand over Jacob's just as he unbuttoned my waistband. "What?" he asked.

I indicated the door behind him with my eyes. Ever pragmatic, he reached back and slipped on the security chain. "There." He turned back to me, sized me up, then dropped his voice. "Now lace your fingers, put your hands behind your head, and don't move a muscle unless I say so."

Oh-ho. Now *that* tone of voice got my attention. I did as I was told. My overcoat bunched around my neck and my holster rode up my side. A yank from Jacob hobbled my knees with my own slacks. A draft from the mail slot played across my exposed groin—*don't think about the door*—but then his hot mouth was on me, his eager, greedy mouth, and I consoled myself with the idea that all anyone would really see, were some passerby to peer through the mail slot, was the back of Jacob's head.

I had a top-view. Some scalp showed through the short-clipped hair. Not as much as a certain Agent…I was *not* going to think about that guy. Focus on Jacob. His broad shoulders. His heated breathing. His molten wet mouth. His fingers clamped around the base of my dick, jacking me hard while he sucked. I walked my feet out just a bit—I hadn't been granted permission to move, after all—and I locked my knees so I didn't need to think about anything but the blowjob. The sweet, sweet blowjob. Jacob's rhythm picked up, and he started kneading my bare ass cheek with his free hand, the one that wasn't steadily jacking me toward my peak, just the right speed, not too fast, not too slow, just right, and his mouth was just right too, so wet, so good, and pretty soon I'd be spiraling toward that….

A car engine revved outside. Headlights shone through a gap in the mail slot. I caught my breath, loud. Jacob stilled and listened. Across the street, a storm door slammed.

False alarm. Just a neighbor. Unfortunately, the moment of panic had pushed me most of the way back to the starting gate. Jacob stood, still jacking my spit-wet dick. He ran his hand down my upper arm where it was still parked behind my head, petting me from protruding elbow to shoulder. With a smoldering look, he purred, "I *will* make you forget about whatever's bothering you."

"It's just…"

He fit his mouth to my ear and said, "A good, hard fuck is what you need." A thrill surged down to my groin so forcefully that I wondered if he felt my agreement in my dick. Or maybe it was the way my breath hitched that tipped him off. He stopped jacking me off and spun me by the upraised elbow. "Upstairs. Now."

I broke position in order to catch my pants and keep them from sending me tumbling back down the steps. Jacob let the minor infraction slide, but as soon as I crossed the bedroom threshold, he was right behind me. In a smoky voice, he said, "Strip."

Although he was stripping down too, his movements were slow, deliberate, almost lazy. By contrast, my hands were flitty and ineffective, struggling at buckles and buttons that had managed to turn into a dozen small puzzles since the last time I'd touched them. I yanked off my holster as I stomped out of my shoes and pants, forced my shirt over my head without bothering to undo all the buttons, and then it was just me, and just Jacob, skin on skin. We kissed, wet and a bit salty, and the heat of Jacob's body engulfed me. I couldn't be sure if it was all physical heat, or if something in his subtle bodies spoke to something in mine, and they were already mingling and merging in anticipation of what we were about to do in the physical.

It seemed awfully ambitious of him, promising to fuck me after I'd just sucked him off, but when my hand drifted down between us, I found him raring to go. Again. He smiled proudly against my mouth—and I hummed my agreement. We stroked each other, kissing, basking in the anticipation. And then Jacob caught me by the wrist, spun me, and forced me facedown onto the bed.

If he ever forced me for real, it would be a one way ticket to Freakout Land. But I trusted him in a way I'd never trusted anyone before. When he shoved my hands up over my head and knocked my thighs apart with his knee, I was utterly certain that he'd stop the second I asked. With that certainty, I was able to really let everything go. Everything. Whatever the hell I'd been mulling over—so what? I'd never admit in a million years that the thought of being someone's fucktoy was a major turn-on, since that's not at all the way I saw myself. But the stiff prong nudging up and down my ass crack told me that Jacob could see me like that, and the thought of him taking me, spreading me, using me…that idea blotted out everything else but the feel of his body against mine. His strong fingers pressed into my wrists, one-handed now as he rummaged through the nightstand. His thighs spread my knees and I struggled back against the pressure, pushing against him, relishing the sensation of being unable to clamp my legs shut even if I'd wanted to.

And then, slickness.

He swiped lube over my ass, jamming a thumb inside, and I gave a strangled moan into the comforter. My dick was trapped beneath me at a weird angle, but I didn't protest. We were too deep in the fantasy. I rocked from side to side to right myself, fake-struggling, and Jacob shoved my wrists into the mattress and spread my legs even wider.

A blunt nudge at my ass. All my awareness rushed down to my privates. Jacob took it slow, drawing it out. He folded himself over me, chest hair tickling against shoulder blades, and murmured in my ear, "Now…who're you thinking about?"

"You," I said into the mattress.

"Me. Just me." His cock prodded me again—was he going to make me beg for it? The thought filled me with dread, though it was spiked with a sick little twist of anticipation. He situated himself on his elbow and reached between us with his greased hand, but instead of diddling me, he grabbed hold of himself, and he lined us up. He didn't push in. Instead, he started stroking my crack with his greased cockhead. I recognized the move. He'd tease at my hole 'til I squirmed, then sink that fat meat in once I was ready to scream. A giddy rush of blood shot down to my groin at the mere thought. We'd been together long enough that even the reruns in my brain got me hard. I closed my eyes and focused on the blunt feel of his tip probing, prodding, but not quite sinking in.

I murmured, "Yeah," and he echoed it, and I realized I'd begun rocking against him, promising him how good it'd feel once he actually did take the plunge. My throat was raspy and my jaw hurt, and pretty soon my ass was gonna sting. That thought sent another jolt straight to my balls.

"Now what're you thinking?" he asked.

"How good it's gonna feel."

"That's right." A blunt prod—again, not hard enough to penetrate. But a taste of what was to come. "And that's all you need to know. Me. Buried in you."

He rocked against me, cock poised, pressing, pressing, and then… the thrust. I actually cried out into the mattress when he shoved in. He lost hold of my wrists, but I kept my arms up over my head and grasped the blankets instead. I reveled in the stretch while he grappled with my hips, trailing lube across the crest of my pelvis, angling me so that he'd butt up against my sweet spot with every deliberate thrust. He shoved in deep. "There?"

"Down a little…fuck, there. There."

He'd come only a few minutes before, so he'd be able to go for a good long while. Since I was rubbing off against the blankets, I could aim for the long, slow burn, too. His bunching abs skimmed the curve of my low back. His pecs brushed my shoulder blades. All down my back and thighs his fur tickled my bare skin, at least until we'd been at it long enough to work up a good sweat that slicked his body hair down. He shifted his angle, still pummeling my sweet spot, but now driving my hips into the mattress even harder. The friction against my dick intensified, and suddenly all the stroking and sucking and fucking was just about to pay off. I clenched around him as I hurtled toward my orgasm, with thoughts of nothing now but the tightness in my nuts and his fat cock pounding me. He felt me start the climb. His breathing changed, stuttered, and his whole body tensed. I hadn't realized how steady, how precise his movements had been, until that control started to give. The chink in the armor always does it for me. I love that small moment when he breaks, when he lets loose long enough to give over to the release, even if it's just for a second. I tried to slip a hand beneath me to finish myself at the same time, but he knocked my hand aside to do the reacharound himself, fucking me, jacking me, gasping my name wetly into my hair.

The moment stretched, a long slow peak that was less like a crashing wave and more like the flood tide coming in. We both made some noises that didn't sound like they'd come from human throats. And we both came, hard.

The build had been slow, and now the ebb was just as slow, flowing seamlessly into sleep.

CHAPTER 11

I DREAMED.

I was in a vast white room. Two rows of black-suited agents stood at attention facing one another to form a long aisle. They were all the same guy. Agent Bly, maybe, but more generic, like someone had made a crappy mold of him and pushed out a few dozen almost-Blys. At the far end of the row, a single figure galumph-walked into place at the head of the line, the position of power. He faced me with his whole body and said, "Your car sucks. Heh-heh."

The generic agent closest to me leaned in and said, "Are you gonna let him talk to you like that?" I realized it was Jacob. "He's not half the Psych you are."

How could I answer? Poor Einstein had come through Camp Hell, same as me. Then, once he was through being tortured by the orderlies, poked and prodded and drugged by the mad scientists, Stefan and I were eager to pile on more abuse. I owed him now. Respect. Or at the very least, patience.

I was about to tell Jacob I had my reasons when the shooting started.

The two rows of black-suited agents drew their weapons, all in synch. One row turned to face the gunfire, and the other row stepped up to interweave with them and form a single unbroken line of men in black leveling their semi-automatics. All except one, Jacob, who broke rank to get between me and the gunfire.

I grabbed him by the shoulders and said, "Get down!" Confidence is one thing, but let's be realistic. He's not really a man of steel.

Bam-bam-bam...I couldn't see the shooter in the field of white, but

I curled up tight to present the smallest possible target. The shooting stopped, and then an alarm went off, followed by a woman's voice. Probably one of those automated computer voices that count down the seconds to self-destruct. Except I could swear it just said my name. And that it had a hint of a Spanish accent.

Lisa? At the FPMP?

I shuddered awake to the phone ringing in Jacob's office. The answering machine beeped.

"Okay, I'm gonna go sit in my car now. I hate to keep pestering you guys, but one of you needs to get up and let me in."

"Oh fuck," I groaned. Jacob's head snapped up from my pillow, not exactly awake, but startled, ready to dive for his sidearm if need be. "It's okay," I told him, "go back to sleep. I locked Lisa out with the safety chain, that's all." He said something unintelligible and rolled so that all the covers wrapped around him, leaving about a foot of comforter for me.

There was a hooded sweatshirt hanging off the doorknob, but aside from that, the only handy clothes were from the suit I'd stripped out of earlier. I pulled on my dress slacks without underwear, jammed on my shoes with no socks, topped off the look with the old gray sweatshirt and ran downstairs by the light of a few strategically placed nightlights.

I was halfway down the front walk when the cold hit me—fucking hell. A light dusting of snow had settled, and it kicked up onto my bare ankles as I jogged toward Lisa's Volkswagen. I planted my palms on the frame of the passenger door, and the window powered down. "You didn't need to come running out here, Vic. You could've just called and told me the chain was off."

Well…maybe I would have, if I hadn't been in the midst of a creepy FPMP dream that incorporated her message. As more waking parts of my brain lit up, it occurred to me that she hadn't sounded particularly alarmed on the answering machine. Of course not, the sight of our cars must have told her we were home, and a few simple sí-nos that we'd nodded off. Though it was below freezing, her car was right there to keep her from getting frostbite while one of us struggled toward wakefulness.

A simple mistake. No reason to panic. Embarrassed that I'd just wigged out over a phone call, I dropped my gaze to her passenger seat.

A giant bouquet took up the whole surface. While I couldn't name any of the flowers, I was guessing it was pricy. Not a cheap carnation in the bunch. As I tried to come up with something amusing to say about it, something to break the pause in conversation that was growing awkward, I realized there were more flowers on the floor. And more in the back seat.

"You're dating a florist?"

She gave me a look.

"Why are you leaving the flowers in your car? They're all frozen. Bring them in the house so you can, I dunno, stare at 'em or something."

She clicked the lock open and said, "Grab that one, it's still fresh."

I hauled it off the seat while she slung her purse over her shoulder and collected a doggie bag from the back seat. I caught a whiff of spice as the bag shifted. The food smelled better than the flowers, which smelled like a funeral home. I wondered how smart I'd been in telling her to bring them inside, after all.

A couple of vases had managed to make their way into the cannery after Jacob's retirement party. I'd been shifting them farther and farther out of sight every couple weeks with hopes of sneaking them into the trash by Christmas. I pulled the biggest vase out of the cupboard, cracked a big chunk out of it on the kitchen faucet, then pitched it into the trash with a surprising amount of regret. I filled the second-largest vase halfway with water and set it on the countertop uneventfully. Lisa tried to jam in the bouquet all at once, but it was too big. I grabbed a random handful of stems and pulled about a quarter of the flowers and fronds out of the batch, and said, "Try that." A card fell out. Without being too obvious, I had a look at it while she hoisted the rest of the bouquet into the vase. It landed face up, which was good. I could be smooth about reading it. However, it was in Spanish, which was bad. It read *Para la rosa más hermosa* in quirky, back-slanted cursive.

Once she stuffed all the flowers in the overflowing vase, she said, "I don't think they'll fit inside the tent with me."

As floral arrangements went, it was very large. I wondered if she'd bothered telling her mystery man that she wasn't really a hearts-and-flowers type of girl. That she was an ex-cop who'd gone over to the New Age side when she couldn't hide her abilities anymore, that she was more interested in goofball comedies than sweeping romances, and that she preferred french fries to caviar. But other than her unfortunate liaison with a slimy Casanova of a shaman at PsyTrain, she'd been single the whole time I'd known her. She probably exclaimed over the flowers like they were the best damn thing in the world, so as not to rock the boat. I'd been single plenty of years myself—in her situation, it's what I would have done. "We can put them on the coffee table," I suggested.

"Then we won't be able to see the TV."

True. I shifted a cutting board out of the way and hauled the vase over to a part of the kitchen counter that could be seen from the main room—though if there wasn't a roof in the way, you'd be able to see the damn thing from orbit. "There. Whaddaya think?"

After a pause, she said, "Victor…." in a tone that conveyed she was about to say something I didn't want to hear. Something about leaving.

"I'm really sorry." I focused at the flowers and not on her, so as not to spook the conversation. "Locking you out was just a dumb…it was totally a mistake. It won't happen again."

"I know. It's fine. I'm not mad."

"Okay, good. Because we love having you here—it was just a dumb mistake and you totally shouldn't read anything into it."

"I'm not."

"Good."

I risked a sidelong glance at her, sensing that whatever we were trying to talk about was nowhere near resolved. Now she was staring fixedly at the vase. I decided to shift tactics. "So does flower guy have a name?"

She did look at me then, up and down, taking my measure. Then she said, "It's after midnight, and you get up early for work. We'll talk about it tomorrow."

Why did a simple first name require a lengthy discussion? "I'm not gonna jinx it."

"We'll have dinner tomorrow, okay? You and me. We'll talk. And you can ask me anything you want to ask." She gave me a quick hug, retreated to her tent and zipped up the flap behind her.

If I didn't know better, I'd wonder if some of our gay had rubbed off on her and she hadn't quite figured out how to introduce her new girlfriend. Because uncharted gender territory was the only reason I could dredge up for her not letting me in on her secret valentine. That didn't make any sense, though. Of anyone, I would be the first person she would confide in (other than the lucky lady) if she started pitching for my team…right?

The card I'd spotted didn't offer much by way of clues. I went back and looked at it again. It was in Spanish, but I already knew her paramour was Hispanic. It was in cursive, which you don't usually get nowadays from the under-thirty crowd. I'm pushing forty and I print everything in block lettering myself. Maybe she was seeing an older guy (or gal). But I couldn't really infer it from the card. For all I knew, it had been written by the florist.

She wanted to tell me about her new thing in her own time and her own way. Fine. But maybe she'd be willing to tide me over with a quick sí-no to help me determine whether Dr. Chance was still lurking around the FPMP, or whether I'd be shit outta luck in getting "set up" with a good supply of drugs. But then her silhouette assumed the phone position and murmured something in Spanish, and I realized my question should probably wait until morning. Especially given that I'd become vividly aware that my pants felt like three kinds of wrong—freezing and wet on the hem, stiff at the pocket and slimy in the seat. Since I was already downstairs, I treated myself to a quick blast in the shower before I headed back up in a towel to wrest some blankets and bedspace back from Jacob and fall into a deep, thankfully dreamless sleep.

The sex must've done me good. I slept straight through to the alarm—something I rarely do. When I dragged my bleary ass downstairs, Lisa was gone.

"Where the hell would she be at six-thirty in the morning?" I complained. I was talking loudly to make sure my bitching could be heard over the hum of my electric razor. Then I saw I'd somehow missed a strip of hair on my jaw, even after three fucking passes.

Jacob knotted his tie. "Yoga."

"This early? If I didn't have a day job, I'd go for the later yoga. The one that takes place after sunrise. After rush hour, for that matter."

"I gather she likes the teacher."

CHAPTER 12

LIKES, AS IN *LIKES*? HM. I could see Lisa going for a yoga instructor. But would a yogi have the financial wherewithal to shower her with all those massive floral testaments of their devotion? And would she really need to be so secretive about seeing this person? Given all the esoteric stuff I've been exposed to, I'd hardly scoff at a little yoga. I tried to imagine the yoga instructor. He'd be limber, naturally. If he was a hippie-type, he might have a beard. Not a manicured beard like Jacob, either, but one of those natural beards that go all the way down the neck. Heck, his face might even be mostly concealed by a nest of hair. If he had a saving grace, it would be the eyes. They'd be sparkly eyes, a lighter color. Blue, or maybe green.

Or gray. Pale gray, the type of eyes you really don't see on anybody… unless they're wearing special contact lenses. "What's with Bly's colored contacts?"

Thankfully, Jacob didn't suggest anything dumb, like maybe the guy had always wanted gray eyes. "Don't know."

"Maybe I could get Dreyfuss to put us all together, and you could have another look at—"

"Vic, wait. I can't look at Bly. Now that you've pointed me at Laura Kim, I feel like I'm right on the verge of something. Yesterday I spent the day in archives. According to the paperwork, Laura claimed she was sick the morning Burke was shot. She left the FPMP before noon. I'm tracking down video surveillance from her apartment building now. It's slow going, but I found some footage that might tell me if she went straight home or not."

It seemed like a shame to waste a bunch of time trying to determine something the sí-no could tell us in five seconds. Yeah, it was being flaky about whether Laura was the shooter, but maybe we could get it to verify her location and save Jacob a lot of tedious work. I figured I'd send Lisa a vague text that she could answer at her leisure once she'd rolled up her yoga mat and put on her shoes. I was halfway to my phone when our ridiculously loud doorbell nearly blew out my eardrums. I checked the clock. Still early—twenty to seven.

I doubted that anyone who'd show up on my doorstep at twenty to seven was someone I'd be eager to see.

My sidearm was upstairs, so I palmed a kitchen knife before I answered. Because Jehovah's Witnesses and Avon Ladies don't just pop over at twenty to seven—and installing a peephole was one of those household chores that Jacob hadn't yet gotten around to (and I didn't dare attempt for fear of destroying the door.) I crept up, knife in hand, and considered kneeling down and peering out through the mail slot. That would just give me a view of someone's knees, though. Then I saw the security chain, the one that had been the cause of my screwed up FPMP dream last night, and I slipped it on before I answered.

I opened the door, then did a double-take. The early morning visitor framed by the two-inch gap was Sergeant Warwick. I slammed the door and yanked the chain off, then re-opened it. Though not all the way.

"Uh…hi." Was I supposed to invite him in?

"Let's take a walk," he said.

While I'm pretty sure any government surveillance around the cannery is confined to the building's perimeter—and therefore, his visit would already be duly noted—I decided whatever he wanted to say to me would probably be less awkward without the presence of the male stripper jigsaw puzzle and the tent in the living room.

Warwick's gaze flickered over my shoulder, and I felt Jacob's presence at my back as a subtle creak in the floor, or maybe a shift in the air pressure. Warwick greeted him curtly with, "Detective."

"Sergeant." Jacob didn't bother mentioning it was "Agent" now. But he did slip the kitchen knife out of my hand and tuck it behind the bag of sidewalk salt without Warwick being any the wiser. "Would you like some coffee?"

Warwick scowled. He wasn't accustomed to politeness—he was more in the habit of being direct. Which, I realized, I didn't actually mind. "We were just going for a walk," I said. Jacob had the grace to act as if it was a perfectly normal thing for me to do, despite it being painfully early and unpleasantly cold.

I stepped into some shoes, threw on a coat and joined Warwick on the front stoop. Ted Warwick is a solid tank of a guy, with a neck as big around as his head. I've seen photos of him in his military days. His short thinning hair had been darkish blond once, but had gone tarnished platinum with age. At the best of times, he was ruddy. Now, in the cold, he was practically fluorescent.

He walked. Fast. I struggled to keep up without taking a header and landing on the frozen garbage in the gutter. Once we'd gone three unrelenting blocks, he said, "Your absence…is it voluntary?"

My first impulse was to defend my choice to report to the FPMP offices rather than the Fifth Precinct, at least until I realized what he was actually asking. The Sarge—worried, about me? I hardly knew what to make of it. "Yeah, it's…yeah."

He paused and gave me a sharp look, a look that had been honed over the decades to cut straight through bullshit. "You're sure you're not in over your head."

I shrugged. I probably was—but at least my eyes were open.

"If you needed to take a last-minute trip…I know a guy who can sell you a used car and hold the title, keep it hard to track…."

"I don't need a—it's fine, it's nothing weird." Relatively speaking. "It's no worse than anything else I do."

We turned a corner and stopped talking while we passed a frazzled-looking woman strapping a wailing toddler into a car seat. Once we were clear, Warwick said, "A few years ago, a PsyCop from the Twentieth was moonlighting where you're working now: Detective John Wembly, an empath." He let out a sigh, and the wind carried its white tendrils away. "He disappeared."

"From his job?"

"From everywhere."

The image of the repeater who'd swallowed a bullet in the conference room flashed through my mind's eye. Could an empathic cop be neutralized by locking him in a room with his sidearm and a bunch of suicidal head-cases? Talk about an elaborate way to take someone out. Not that I thought it was implausible, mind you. I've seen too much weird shit to discount the possibility. Just that it seemed like a hell of a lot of effort.

"I think it's in their best interest to keep me around," I said. "Who else can monitor their ghosts?"

"And if one of the higher-ups had to choose between keeping you around and making sure no one else had the benefit of your expertise? Don't get cocky. Everyone's expendable, Bayne, even you."

If I was expendable, I'd *be dead by now.* I didn't say it. Hell, I was shocked I'd even thought it. Shocked and angry. I was tempted to tell him to fuck off for calling me expendable, but what came out was, "At least the things I do there matter."

His reply was a level glare.

I did my best to glare back without tripping over a crack in the sidewalk. "How many of my collars get acquitted?"

His eyes widened—he hadn't seen that one coming. But then he took stock and said, "Too many."

We both looked away and focused on our brisk, pointless walking. After another block we'd already passed twice, he said, "Defense attorneys are starting to realize they can play the Psych angle and hang a jury, at least if they're lucky enough to land a judge who doesn't ride the fuck out of 'em in the courtroom."

"Oh my God."

"Look at it this way…a public defender ain't gonna use that tactic. The criminal's gotta hire high-priced defense to get off like that. These scumbags mortgage their houses, their families' houses, sell everything they own and then some to pay for some slick lawyer to work it. They'll be paying the rest of their lives."

Maybe so. But not like they should. Not like the guys in orange jumpsuits.

"If you need that car," Warwick said, "call and ask me about your 'mileage receipts.' I'll leave the guy's number in the planter in front of the diner on Kedzie by the end of the day."

Part of me thought all the cloak-and-dagger was an elaborate hoax, because this was the boss who'd been glaring and barking at me for the past dozen years. Ted Warwick bitched about my penmanship and my Auracel use. He didn't dream up elaborate schemes to procure getaway vehicles.

"And if I were you, I'd start investing in prepaid credit cards, gift cards, any kind of untraceable plastic. Christmas is coming—it's a good time to stock up without anyone noticing. And make sure you pay for them with cash."

Why hadn't I ever thought of that? "All right. Yeah."

We were nearing my street, and he slowed as if to determine whether we'd need to go around the block again. "And what about Zigler?" he said.

"What about him?"

"Do I really need to spell it out?"

Apparently he did. I shrugged.

"Is he laying low to buy you time off," he asked, "or do I need to go check on him too?"

"He's out of town for a funeral." At least, I presumed he was—but maybe Dreyfuss had told him to say that to steer me toward the FPMP. Who the hell knew anymore? "Check with Betty. I'm sure he gave her a call."

Warwick grunted, not exactly in agreement, but not disagreeing, either. I turned down my block, thinking he'd follow. He didn't. He kept right on walking…to wherever it was he'd actually parked.

Now my nose was running from the cold. I should have just invited

Warwick in and spared myself the exposure. According to Lisa, the cannery's free from surveillance devices. In addition, Jacob's gym pals sweep it regularly for electronics, although they've never found anything. And Crash does a sage smudge and protection ritual every new moon.

We also run the blender when we talk about anything important. It's especially loud if you fill it a quarter of the way with water and add some ice.

I gave Jacob the skinny on my talk with Warwick and the mysterious Detective Wembly. "One day he was doing a side-job for Dreyfuss," I said, "and the next…gone. I'm guessing he got himself shot. There are five gunshot victims in that building, five that I've seen. Probably more if Richie's continual exorcisms are rubbing them out."

"So you think I should drop the Laura Kim angle and start looking into this Wembly?"

"I don't know what to think." Wembly wouldn't have anything to do with Jacob's case—the timeframe was all wrong. "You've got your hands full. I should be the one looking for Wembly." That seemed a lot safer, too. I'd hate to have someone check on Jacob's work and find him digging up dirt that had nothing to do with Burke's shooting. Jacob's physical investigations could be traced, whereas I could always stand around looking dumb if I didn't want anyone else to know what I was doing.

"Okay, I'll see what I find on the video surveillance and establish a timeline. What about you?"

"Jennifer Chance has got Dreyfuss seriously freaked out. She's supposed to be number one on my hit-list." Maybe it was for the best if I focused on finding Chance and kept as many repeaters as possible intact. I might need them if I wanted to see for myself how Wembly met his end. I had a feeling he was the suicide in the boardroom—but maybe he wasn't. Maybe he was Triple-Shot. Or Throat Bullet. Or some other poor sap in a suit getting mowed down over and over in a dark corner they'd neglected to show me. Without a photograph of Wembly, there was only one way I'd know if his repeater was still moonlighting at the FPMP.

"Yoga must be over by now," I said, "don't you think?"

I pulled out my phone, but Jacob touched me on the wrist before I could hit my memory-dial. "Vic…not a good idea."

"You don't even know what I'm trying to do."

"You're going to ask Lisa a sí-no about that PsyCop, which violates the FPMP privacy policy, on a cell phone that anyone can pick up with a cheap antenna."

Okay. He had me there. I put the phone back in my pocket and turned my mind to rehearsing dinner conversation for later, when I'd have Lisa to myself. Could I get away with asking the murder-related sí-nos I'd been building up before we started talking about her love life, just in case the conversation turned out to be more difficult than I was anticipating? It was probably something dumb she was being so cagey about. Some total non-thing. It just seemed like a big deal to her because she was caught up in the thick of it…which I really didn't want to imagine, given that she's the closest thing to a sister I'd had since foster care.

The blender changed pitch as the ice cubes were pulverized into a thin slush. I rested my finger on the off-button, but before I pressed it, I whispered, "No matter what I do, I feel like I'm playing right into Dreyfuss' hands."

Jacob shook his head. "We should have known there'd be nothing straightforward about this exorcism you owe him."

I'd never expected anything at the FPMP to be what it seemed. Dreyfuss wanted to string me along? Fine. All the more skeletons I'd dig out of his closet. Plus…all the more "payment" for me.

CHAPTER 13

WHEN I REPORTED TO THE Operations Coordinator's desk, she seemed surprised to see me. "You came in! I wasn't sure…I mean, when you didn't show up…"

My general level of anxiety usually lands me everywhere five minutes early, but thanks to Warwick's unscheduled visit, both Jacob and I were half an hour late. "Yeah. We ran into a little snag at home."

She leaned in, dropped her voice, and said, "I'm really glad you're here."

Jacob had been about to stride on back to the archives, but he slowed to catch the rest of our exchange. I can't say I blamed him. Given that I could place Laura at the scene of Roger Burke's unsanctioned execution, she should've been a hell of a lot more leery of me. "You are?"

"Agent Duff is *exterminating* this floor today." She gave me a meaningful look. "He does it every Thursday, but now with you here for backup, there's a chance of it actually sticking."

Great. Just what I needed. Richie mucking around in my sandbox. "Where is *Agent* Duff, anyway?"

"Agent Dreyfuss' office. They usually spend a good two hours there."

"Do you think I could…?"

"I'm buzzing him now." A pause. "Detective Bayne just reported. Yes. Okay." She hit a button and said, "Agent Marks can walk you there."

As Jacob and I were clicked through the airlocks, I did my best to convey, "Great, now they're going to rub out any chance of me figuring out what happened to Wembly," with a widening of my eyes. Jacob acknowledged this micro-expression with a brief eye-widening in return.

The door to Dreyfuss' office was open, and Richie's voice carried down the hall. "…thinking about taking it back. They should make these things easier to use. One minute it's working, and the next minute the screen is black with the words 'no disc' flashing in the corner. All I wanted was to see what was on ESPN2."

Jacob left me to Dreyfuss' tender mercies and let himself into a locked office just down the hall. The Regional Director himself glanced up at me from behind his desk. "Well, look who decided to join us for another day of fun and games."

"What did you expect?" I said. "I wasn't finished."

I cut my eyes to Richie to indicate my displeasure with this whole exorcism I hadn't been invited to. Dreyfuss returned the shadow of a smile. And then I realized that I didn't *want* to talk to him via micro-expression. That channel should be reserved for Jacob and me, damn it.

"It's Thursday," Dreyfuss said placidly. "And on Thursdays, this is what we do. Richie is a stickler for his schedule…and we wouldn't want to upset the talent."

"If you ever worked here for real," Richie said, "you can't be late more than once a week or your paycheck gets docked." As he educated me about the FPMP's policies, his helper, the world's most stoic black man, was rolling out a printed floor mat. It was almost like a game of Twister, except instead of various colored circles where you'd plant your hands and feet according to the whim of a small plastic spinner, there were circles indicating where candles should go at the cardinal points, as well as crosses and doves and writing in what looked like Hebrew.

Probably not quite as popular at parties.

Dreyfuss said, "Agent Bly tells me you paid a visit to the lab. I'm surprised, given your track record with exam rooms and medical personnel."

I tried to think of a smart reply to that when I was distracted. Under his scrappy hooded sweatshirt, I noticed, he was wearing gloves. Thin white cotton gloves.

"Find anything of interest down there?" he asked. I shook my head. He watched me for an extra couple of seconds, narrowing his eyes like he was waiting for me to have second thoughts and feed him an interesting tidbit

I'd been withholding. I dropped his gaze and focused on the white gloves.

"Maybe you should spend a little more time among the test tubes. Dr. K's psychic enhancements aren't strictly pharmaceutical in nature. He has some interesting toys."

"What toys?" Richie asked.

"All the latest and greatest Psychic paraphernalia you've come to know and expect, Richard. Your prayer mat. Your Vatican holy water. Your beeswax candles from Assisi. Our research department collects it all, from the stoutest Bible-thumping, Jesus-loving Christian icons to the airy-fairiest woo-woo New Age trappings. You need gear? Dr. K can set you up. Meanwhile, Detective Bayne is so poorly supported by his agency he's gotta score his own salt down at the corner minimart."

Richie snort-laughed, then wiped something unfortunate that had sprayed out of his nose onto his cuff. Then he said, "No wonder your ability runs hot and cold."

Given the level to which I obfuscate my talent, that remark shouldn't have pissed me off. Yet somehow, it did.

"If you're lucky enough to get a job interview," Richie told me, "they make you take a polygraph test. Just make sure you don't lie while you're doing it. 'Cos somehow, they figure it out."

"Good to know." Maybe I'd pass the polygraph and maybe I wouldn't. The day I put in my job application at the FPMP, they'd be driving snowplows in hell.

Richie and his assistant—Carl, his name was, judging by the *Carl, do this* and *Carl, do that*—set up their exorcism with the precision I might use to tidy up the hallway where Jacob was constantly dropping his dirty socks. I sat in one of Dreyfuss' office chairs and tried to figure out where to look. Should I burn the images of the repeaters into my mind's eye? It was unlikely I could dig up an official snapshot of Wembly the PsyCop on the Internet for a match, but maybe, through my cop-connections, I could score a casual photo of him. I was leery of staring at the repeaters for too long, though, for fear of broadcasting that I had an actual visual on them…and that I could medium circles around "Agent Duff" with his Vatican holy water and his irritating laugh.

I could watch Richie, but it seemed to me he spoke louder when my eyes were on him. He got a little strut in his awkward walk, and he made Carl hand him things that he could have reached perfectly well himself.

And of course, not five feet away from me was Constantine Dreyfuss. He would have loved to engage me in conversation…which, of course, meant he was the last guy on the planet I wanted to talk to. "So," he said. "cold enough for you out there?"

I wasn't sure if he was attempting ironic weather-related small talk or if he was asking about ghosts. I grunted.

"It's okay to sit back in your chair," he told me. I hadn't realized I'd been perching on the edge. "Enjoy the show. I'll pay you for your time today, Detective. Never fear."

Maybe it was for the best he was having Richie take a stab at the repeaters instead of me. That way I could refer back to them once I dug up that photo of Wembly. Still, it wasn't in my nature to sit on my hands and wait. I allowed myself a glance at Dreyfuss to see if I could tell what he was really up to, and my gaze fell on those cotton gloves again. Some new psychic tool I should be aware of? Or maybe a blatant attempt to get me to leave fingerprints on something without contaminating the evidence.

"Go ahead," he said. "Ask."

"What?"

"You want to know what's up with the gloves."

I shrugged.

He tilted back in his big leather executive chair and crossed his ankles on the corner of his desk. "It's an attempt to break a comforting lifelong habit. My fingernails are nasty, so I'm told."

Was he bullshitting me? I narrowed my eyes.

"You think you feel gay when you're playing Brokeback Mountain with Agent Marks? Try getting a manicure." He sighed. "Then chew through the freaking thing two hours later."

The sharp pungency of frankincense prickled my sinuses. My eyes watered. Richie announced to the room, "We're gonna start now."

"By all means," Dreyfuss replied.

Carl had placed red velvet kneelers at the east and west points of the diagram. He and Richie settled in, rosaries wrapped around their hands, and Richie began to pray. "Our Father who art in heaven, hello be thy name...."

Hello?

I felt Dreyfuss' eyes on me and couldn't resist looking back at him. He was smirking.

If I didn't know better, I'd think Dreyfuss hired an actor, a character actor with a gift for channeling an utter moron, and planted him here so I'd be broadsided by a work ethic I didn't even realize I harbored. *Hello be thy name?* How could Einstein possibly manage to exorcise a repeater when he couldn't even recite the Lord's Prayer?

Then again, he hadn't exorcised these particular repeaters yet, despite the weekly attempt. I swiveled my seat to watch, horrified, as Richie ran through the prayer without an iota of understanding, reducing it to a bunch of meaningless, disjointed words and sounds. He then moved on to a Hail Mary, creating bizarre, run-together word groupings. "Holy Mary, mother-of-God, pray-for-us-sinners, now and at the hour-of-our-death, amen."

Throat Bullet went down in a spray of spectral blood.

"What I wouldn't give for the Victor Bayne ticket to this event," Dreyfuss murmured. "You're right on the fifty-yard line."

"And today's exorcees," I whispered. "Who are they?"

"Dunno. I was living in Tampa at the time."

So he claimed. "If you were to guess...."

"I just so happened to put together a few likely candidates." He hit some keys on his keyboard, and his triptych monitors lit up with a grid of photos. Some mug shots, some candids, some work I.D.s. "Maybe you have a 'sense' of who it is we're actually talking about here."

Did he actually want the repeaters identified for some mysterious purpose of his own, or had my entire conversation with Sergeant Warwick been recorded and analyzed, and he knew who I was really gunning for?

I scanned the photo lineup. There were a couple dozen in all, most of them thirty-something white guys, with a couple of Hispanics or Arabs sprinkled in. One black-suited guy looked familiar—not from the repeater show, though. Maybe from yesterday's lunch, or the underground parking lot. Which would mean Dreyfuss had seeded the lineup with fake hits to see if I was lying. I dunno if he thought I'd pick wrong because I couldn't really see the repeaters, or because he thought I wanted to misdirect him on purpose.

When you think about it, including that one guy I half-recognized was pretty clever of him. For all I knew, the majority of the guys in those mugshots were still living and breathing and driving around in their FPMP Lexuses. Which meant that unless I wanted to come off as a fraud, I'd need to point out the real guys. And he knew I knew it.

"If I did happen to have an opinion," I said, "why should I share it with you?"

"Because I think it's high time we put this idea that I'm the next Hitler behind us."

"Hitler, no. J. Edgar Hoover, maybe."

"I've got reports on each of these guys." He placed a large sealed envelope on his desk, then pinned it down with his gloved hand before I could grab it. "I believe you'll find anything bloody that went down here is old news. Hijinks from before I took this job five years ago. I'm willing to bet a pair of Bears tickets on it."

"Just a pair?"

"Hell, a whole skybox and a blowjob from the quarterback. If you've got the cajones to be honest here, I know it's a bet I won't lose. Because I might push your buttons, and I might piss you off. But I've never lied to you. Not once."

Apparently our sparring had fallen out of the whisper range. Richie began praying louder to indicate he was not amused that we were talking through his exorcism. "*...and blessed is the fruit-of-the-loom Jesus....*"

Unbelievable. Was my head going to explode from the dumb? I thought it just might. "Okay," I whispered, "so what if the repeaters aren't yours?

That only proves you don't kill people in your office."

"Aha!" he hissed. "They're only repeaters then. A skipping record. Psychic residue."

Fuck. I hadn't meant to let that slip. Fuck, fuck, fuck.

"That's why you can't just ask them who they are," he added.

"I never said that."

As he gloated with a big, smug smile over scoring the secret, I threw caution to the wind and snatched the envelope out from under his fingers. Maybe he could have even held onto it, if it weren't for those gloves. But I yanked that paperwork right out from under him and sprinted out into the hall as I tore it open. He was quick—but I had a head start. By the time he caught up to me, I'd fanned out the dossiers to ensure I wasn't being baited with an envelope full of blank paper.

I wasn't. Some were clean computer printouts. Some were speckly photocopied documents. One was a purple-inked mimeograph. But at a quick glance, they all looked like the real deal to me.

Dreyfuss ripped off his cotton gloves and flung them down on top of the torn manila envelope I'd dropped. He didn't try grabbing the papers away from me, though. Instead, he planted his hands on his hips and gave me a narrow-eyed look that challenged me to find out exactly who the repeaters were.

Hopefully, I could do more than that. Hopefully I could find out what had become of Detective Wembly.

It was easier to go through the stack out there in the hallway. Richie's mangled prayers were less distracting, and the sting of incense was less pronounced. I looked at each photo carefully, noting age, hair, facial features. I also glanced at the writeups. One guy was in the Russian mob. Another was CIA. Someone else was with the phone company. No Wembly.

It all looked real to me—but that's what forgers do, create documents that look real, and I had no doubt Dreyfuss had access to a competent forger. And, of course, there was the guy I'd seen at lunch, though when I got to his mugshot, it claimed he was a Turkish ambassador's bodyguard.

I handed his sheet to Dreyfuss and said, "Nice try."

Dreyfuss scanned the paper. "You lost me, pal."

"Stacking the deck with FPMP employees isn't exactly the best way to earn my trust."

Dreyfuss looked at the sheet again. "Ha! The missing Turk is the spitting image of Russ from this angle. Wait 'til I show him!" His reaction was incredibly spontaneous, and it seemed totally sincere. A good act, but that only meant Dreyfuss was a good actor. He folded the paper, slipped it into his pocket, and said, "Forget about him, then, is anyone else a hit?"

I stuck my head through the doorway.

"…full-of-grace, the-Lord is with-thee…" Richie bellowed. Triple-Shot was looking fainter than usual.

I pulled my head back out before the Fruit of the Loom cycled around. He must have been praying a rosary, which meant I had fifty opportunities to stop myself from slapping him upside the head.

"What did you see?" Dreyfuss whispered.

A big dumbass who, by all accounts, should not be able to exorcise a dead fly. "Do you want the repeaters obscured for a week, or do you want me to I.D. them? You can't have it both ways."

"So his ritual actually does something?"

I shrugged. "It's like painting over a water stain on the ceiling. These guys are vivid enough that eventually they leach back through. But yeah. In the short term, it works."

"Whaddaya know? Victor Bayne actually told me something worthwhile without putting me through the wringer first. I'm beginning to think you might be sweet on me."

"Must be the manicure."

He strode back into the office and put a halt to the exorcism. Carl stood up, knees cracking, and went about snuffing the candles. Richie didn't know what to make of the interruption, though. "I'm only on my twenty-second Hail Mary. If I take a break now, I'll have to start from the beginning."

"That's fine."

"But...I wasn't done."

"We pay you for your time and expertise, Richard. You're not doing piecework in a factory. If you need to start again later, what difference does it make?"

Richie didn't seem particularly mollified, but Dreyfuss' tone was edgier than usual. As I waited to see if Richie really was stupid enough to keep arguing with the guy who'd just scored him a skybox to go with his Lexus, Dreyfuss' phone buzzed. He reached across the desk and hit a button. "Go ahead."

Laura's voice said, "Washington on the line."

Dreyfuss didn't look very excited. In fact, he seemed annoyed. "Okay, gang, I gotta take this. Time for a coffee break." He shooed me out into the hall with Richie and Carl.

"Oh well," Richie said. "I don't drink coffee, but the cocoa is real good."

We settled in the lounge with the cushy leather furniture and the walls decked out in framed magazine covers. Carl went into a tiny kitchenette off to the side and set about making the coffee without being asked. I'm not sure if it was because he knew Richie enjoyed being waited on, or if it was better not to let the hot water fall into the wrong hands.

"That thing Agent Dreyfuss said about you and Agent Marks..." Richie said. "Was he just trying to be funny, or is it true?"

"Which thing?"

"Brokeback Mountain. Are you good friends, or are you ho-mo-sexuals?"

I hadn't realized Einstein could listen and pray at the same time. "Both. We live together."

Richie scowled as if he was thinking very hard. Finally, he said, "There are plenty of ladies you could have sex with, y'know."

"I'll keep that in mind."

"Really. The bars and restaurants are full of them."

I took another good look at him and beheld him in all his bald, stoop-shouldered glory...and I wondered if wing night at the Blue Room might be code for something spicier than Buffalo wings. And then I wished I could rinse off my brain.

"Now that you have a choice," he said, "you could find a lady to have sex with instead."

I'd been about to go help Carl with the coffee (whether he needed my help or not) but the thin, brittle remains of my patience went *snap*. I pushed back into my seat like I was hunkering down for trench warfare, and said, "I don't know what kind of whacked out religious Tea Party propaganda you've been listening to, but it's bullshit. Being gay is not a choice. I've been queer ever since I can remember and I never stopped to deliberate over which gender would float my boat."

"Uh, I don't know too much about tea or boats. I just figured that in Heliotrope Station, you had to go along with Stefan because he was the strongest empath. Now that he's not messing around in your mind, you can do whatever you want."

I couldn't have been more stunned if Richie had picked up a coffee urn and broken it over my head.

"He was mean," Richie added.

The fragrant coffee went down like mud. My first impulse was to insist that there'd been no need for Stefan to give me a nudge. Back then, I was twenty-two, attitudinal and horny. He was a goth boy in eyeliner with a naughty smile that went straight to my guts. We'd been a match made in purgatory. And that was without taking our psychic abilities into consideration.

Mean? Yeah, he was mean. That was probably what I liked about him. Because when you're nothing more than an overgrown teenager, "mean" is imitating the way people swing around to face you when they talk; it's mimicking the last insanely stupid thing they said, then recreating their annoying laugh. It's implying their rooms are haunted, or making them burst into tears for no good reason.

You could chalk up our bullying to a lot of things—my guess is that we were overcompensating for being a couple of gay punks, psychic misfits to boot, by acting unbearably obnoxious. But at some point you grow up and become a functioning member of society. When I saw Stefan's practice, the way he was helping people cope with their old demons, I figured him for a fully fledged grownup.

And then I found out his metamorphosis was all on the surface. Underneath, he was still the guy who'd made Movie Mike shit himself in the cafeteria.

"How big is your TV?" Richie asked.

I stared at him longer than a normal person would have, though I don't know if the rhythms of normal conversation made an impact on him or not. I saw him now, homely and middle-aged, but I imagined him then, a doughy little wimp. Not like I'd see spirit activity, not in a sixth-sensory way. But in my imagination I saw what he used to be, and I saw what he'd become. The whole thing was discouraging.

"Mine's a seventy-incher," he went on, "high-definition. It gots the internet on it…well, that's what the box says. I can't figure out how to turn on the internet part. The remote's really stupid."

And even after all these years, it was tempting to say, "Oh, I'm sure it's the remote that's stupid." But I resisted.

"It gots 3-D too, but I need to hook up the blue-ray for that."

I was considering suggesting he just flip the TV onto a pair of sawhorses and use it for a dining room table when Dreyfuss joined us. "Sorry for the interruption," he said glibly. "Let's get back to smoking some ghost."

CHAPTER 14

RICHIE WAS EASY ENOUGH TO read—at least until he pulled out a big zinger from the past—but Dreyfuss was about as transparent as a film canister. Still, it seemed to me that after his private phone call, his good cheer had become a bit more forced, and his eyes were sharp enough to leave wounds.

Richie finished his hot chocolate and said, "Are you sure you really want an exorcism?" He'd adopted the tone of a mom asking her incontinent kid if he really didn't need to go potty before embarking on a car ride. "Because it's pretty dumb to stop halfway through."

Dreyfuss appraised him, and then he turned to me. "What do you think, Detective? Have you seen all you need to see?"

Damn it, he knew I hadn't. "Maybe I could do another sweep of your office first. Before the ritual. Establish a baseline."

"You're the guest." Dreyfuss pulled a wad of bubble wrap out of his pocket, handed it to Richie and said, "Take care of that for me, would ya?" and motioned me to precede him while Richie hunkered down in a lounge chair and got to work. A series of pops ensued that followed us down the hall, though the sound stopped abruptly once the stout door behind us whispered shut.

I never thought I'd be relieved to be alone with Dreyfuss.

The prayer mat was right where Carl had left it, and the charcoal puck was still smoking gently. The presence of the religious paraphernalia itself hadn't faded the repeaters, but the partial rosary had caused Triple-Shot to go flickery. I watched him take his three bullets, jerking as each one hit. His face was a twisted mass of fear and shock. I wasn't sure I'd be able to match him to a stoic photograph.

I turned to Throat Bullet instead, and took a good, long look at his face, suspecting that I already had a match. Then I stared at a few more random places in the room so as not to broadcast what I'd actually been looking at. Dreyfuss was at his desk, gloveless, gnawing a cuticle as he watched me search. I gestured, and he handed over the dossiers. I flipped through and found my match.

"By the way," I said, "you owe me yesterday's pill."

Dreyfuss pulled out his pillbox, dug out a red, and set it on the desk in front of me.

I swallowed the massive amount of saliva that had suddenly gushed out of my glands, and decided identifying a few repeaters might see me all the way through the weekend if I bartered for each individual ghost. Since I was already pushing my luck, I said, "I'll I.D. your first victim for three Seconals."

He plucked out three more pills and lined them up beside the first one. I quelled the urge to smack myself in the forehead. Obviously I should have asked for more, but I couldn't exactly backpedal now. I sucked at negotiation.

According to the paperwork, Throat Bullet worked for the Chicago Tribune. His missing persons report had been filed eight years ago. The photo was an obvious match, and the identity and dates would be easy enough for me to verify, so I presumed it was real. I pulled the page and handed it to Dreyfuss. He glanced at the paper and bit off the corner of his fingernail. "I would've thought this guy was off sunning himself in the Caribbean. He took a lot of dirty money to keep stories quiet."

The guy by the bathroom was even easier to I.D. thanks to his dramatic hairline. Russian mob. Supposedly. That put me up to seven pills. It also left the most disturbing repeater unidentified.

Triple-Shot took his three bullets and went down. I considered my sheaf of photos. It was possible the repeater wasn't even in the stack. Still, I scrutinized each one. I could eliminate two thirds of them easily, but there were five possibilities I wasn't so sure of. Grim white guys in suits tend to look a lot alike. I wanted to put a name to this face, and not only for the Seconal. The PsyCop program had been running in Chicago for just over a dozen years—I should know, since I was one of its charter members. When had Detective Wembly turned up missing—last year, or last FPMP directorship? I wasn't sure. Sarge had been vague. Maybe I should have set Jacob on researching Wembly and not Laura Kim. At least we knew what Laura Kim looked like and where she was.

I straightened up, not realizing I'd been hunched, while my back cracked like a chorus of castanets. I stole a look around the room as I stretched. Dreyfuss was watching me, all that snappy wiseass energy of his now quiet, calm and focused. The only thing moving was his hand as he picked at a ragged cuticle while his eyes remained on me. Sometimes my people-instincts are spot on, and sometimes they're shit. I wasn't sure which of those variables I was currently experiencing…just that I thought maybe, *maybe*, I finally knew him well enough to get a read off him. "Tell me something," I said.

"If I can."

"The guy in the boardroom who shot himself in the head…."

Supposedly the only thing I knew about the boardroom was the presence of a now-eradicated cold spot. His eyes widened. I'd never supplied such a precise level of visual detail to anyone outside my most trusted inner circle.

"…was it the missing PsyCop, Wembly?"

His face froze. Only for a nanosecond. And then he said, "Definitely not."

Maybe that was true, or maybe every word out of his mouth was a lie. I might not know if the suicide repeater was Wembly, but one thing was for sure: I'd seen that pause. I knew Dreyfuss had plenty to hide.

Was he lying? Having Carolyn Brinkman in my life has taught me there are plenty of ways to lie. Not every falsehood is a bold-faced whopper. There are lies of omission. There are subtle misdirections. If Con Dreyfuss says he's never lied to me, I'm inclined to think that might be the case.

Technically.

So if the missing PsyCop wasn't the boardroom suicide, then…I cut my eyes to Triple-Shot.

"That's not Detective Wembly either," Dreyfuss said.

"I wasn't looking at anything."

"And I'm the Queen of England." He turned to his keyboard and dismissed the photo lineup on his monitors. "If the third ghost isn't in my stack of likely candidates, then maybe he's someone I don't know about yet. We can do a composite—I've got the software—and pull some more suspects."

"It's not that. He might even be one of these guys on the shortlist."

"Maybe a trained sketch artist could help you figure out—"

"I know how to I.D. features, that's not the issue. It's that people tend to look a lot alike when they're screaming."

That shut him up. He tore off the hunk of cuticle he'd been picking. The nail bed on his ring finger started bleeding. Profusely. He gave a disgusted grunt and blotted it on the hem of his hooded sweatshirt.

"Plus he's all flickery now from the Hail Marys."

Dreyfuss leaned forward in his chair. "So you can actually see the effects of Agent Duff's rituals take hold?"

I shrugged.

"And, in theory, you could exorcise this guy for good…once you were satisfied you knew who he was, and that I didn't kill him."

I was tired of hedging. Plus, it seemed pointless. "Yes."

"Well, then." Dreyfuss sucked a bead of blood off his finger. "What about the reverse? Could you bring the spirit back and get a better look?"

My knee-jerk reaction was to insist I couldn't. But as I opened my mouth to deny it, I began to wonder. Maybe Dreyfuss was on to something, and maybe I actually should be looking at my ability that way. Making the ghosts sharper wasn't something I ever set out to do—or, more accurately, it wasn't something I was aware of attempting. But every time I scoured a crime scene for psychic evidence, every time I chased a flicker I saw in the corner of my eye, wasn't I hoping to find some clear and obvious piece of evidence that would help us make our pointless arrest?

"Maybe," I said finally.

He was watching me, hard. He knew he'd piqued my interest. "Never tried, have you?"

I shook my head.

"I've always thought it was a crying shame you were stuck ticketing jaywalkers with those bozos on the force. You know I'd love to put you on the fast track for personal growth and development."

Excitement surged through me as he reached into his pocket, and I figured I hadn't blown my chance at those last three Seconals after all. But it wasn't his magic pillbox he pulled out this time. It was a keyring. He opened his lowest desk drawer, took out a slim black folder and placed it on his desk, careful not to bleed on it. "All the Psych trainers in the world can tell you to clear your mind and breathe and chant and ring the Tibetan prayer bowls…but it's all a bunch of theory. None of them can really guide you from a place of experience."

He'd lost my attention with the folder. People don't keep their pills in a folder. Unless there was a prescription in there…but he'd already told me a Seconal prescription was out of the question.

"After all," he said, "who's gonna tell Michelangelo how to paint a ceiling?" He was happy to supply his own answer. "Not the guys down at the Home Depot. That's for sure."

Unless it was a prescription for some kind of psyactive that might allow me to talk to Triple-Shot. After the mickey I'd let him slip me in Santa Barbara, I didn't want anything to do with Dreyfuss' experimental drugs. Unless they were benzos.

"But there is one person who can provide Victor Bayne with the benefit of her experience." He opened the folder, but the sheet of paper inside wasn't a prescription at all. It was a piece of notebook paper, slightly yellowed. My heart sank at the sight of it—because while he'd been trying to arouse my curiosity as to what it might be, I really had sold myself on the idea of a new prescription. He was watching my face fall—and I didn't care. All that setup, for a stupid note?

And then he said, "Marie Saint Savon."

"It's in French." I tried to sound cocky, but my voice was shaking. 'Cos once I registered what he was showing me, scoring pills was the last thing on my mind.

"I took a few semesters in high school," Dreyfuss said, "but I was too busy watching Conchita Suarez in the front row twirling her long black hair to remember much more than the basics. They wouldn't let the Cuban kids take Spanish just to raise their GPAs. Lucky for me."

"So you don't know what this list says?"

"I didn't say that. There's such a thing as a translator, y'know."

I read a line. I was so excited I kept going back on myself, reading and re-reading, trying to make sense.

Resentir un frisson. Okay. For all I knew, the *Frisson* was an overpriced luxury sedan. I looked to Dreyfuss for an explanation. He read the line out loud, and while I wouldn't know a good accent from a bad one, he sounded pretty damn French to me. "It means to feel a sudden drop in temperature," he explained, "along with a big case of the willies. A cold spot."

He read the next couple of lines. "*Le voir mourir*—seeing a death…not a spirit, but the death itself. You call 'em repeaters. *Parler a l'ame*—chatting with spirits."

Holy hell. Marie Saint Savon had left behind a laundry list of medium abilities. In order of difficulty, no less. I read the final line out loud. "*Craquer les morts.* What the hell is that supposed to be? Dead crackers?"

"Now *that* would be an interesting snack to serve at a football game." Dreyfuss gazed down at the yellowed page. "*Craquer* is more about forcing them to do what you want. You know, like when you're questioning a suspect and they finally crack. Breaking them."

Breaking the dead? Maybe that wasn't so farfetched. Look what I'd done to Jacob's biggest vase.

"You know what I don't see on this list?" Dreyfuss asked.

"Do I even want to know?"

"Astral projecting. Fully awake. Standing up."

"I don't actually have that ability," I said quickly. "It was the drugs. I was pumped full of crazy-strong psyactives and I was running on pure adrenaline—"

"Relax." His shrewd eyes were right on me, unflinching, and he spoke in a voice so calm and low it was hardly more than a whisper. "Your secret's safe with me. After all, you're holding onto my nearest and dearest confidence yourself. So it behooves me to keep certain matters between us."

"As a rule, I don't project," I insisted. "It's never happened to me anywhere but PsyTrain."

"Never mind the specifics. What I'm trying to say, if you'd put a lid on your panic attack, is that you've uncovered some new abilities above and beyond Marie Saint Savon's chart, and that with certain augmentations, you can achieve them. If you can do the difficult stuff, the unheard-of stuff…then the skills on this page should all be do-able. Put your mind to it, maybe you can compel spirits."

"It doesn't work that way."

"So you say—but I doubt you've ever tried. You want to know who that third repeater is?" He knew damn well I did. "Force his spirit to tell you."

I considered asking Dreyfuss to leave so I could concentrate, but I knew that scenario would give him an advantage. If he was in another room, he could do whatever he wanted unbeknownst to me, while my every move would be visible to his psychic eye. So I let him stick around. I pretended it didn't bother me, either.

My white light level was pretty high, though most of the juju was currently pumped into my protective shell. Keeping up with the armor was second nature. Once I'd visualized it in place, I hardly gave a thought to maintaining it. Using the white light to affect other beings was more problematic for me, because I had to let the energy flow through me and then into something else. Jacob was better at letting go than I was. He could steal the light and blanket the room with it…but since he can't actually see what's going on, having him assist would be like blindfolding him, handing him my sidearm, describing a target and expecting him to hit it by squeezing out a spray of bullets. I'm guessing it worked with the Fire Ghost because he could hardly miss her. Plus she was so eager to get out of there, she met us halfway.

I approached the repeater, a fortyish Caucasian guy in a dark suit. A bullet to the thigh jerked him back, then another to his opposite hip flung him the other way. The final bullet in his shoulder spun him around. Shoulder wounds aren't normally fatal, so it must have been an arterial hit. Probably so, judging by the spray of blood. Maybe, since his death was imminent, that third bullet knocked his spirit loose before his physical body actually expired. Thinking along those routes made me anxious about predestination and free will, though, so I told myself the actual moment of death wasn't in question. It was the identity of the repeater… and whether I could figure that out.

He was flickery from Einstein's ritual. Was it possible to un-exorcise him? Maybe white light didn't run on a one-way street. If not, I could theoretically throw an exorcism into reverse. If Richie was able to affect the repeater with those ridiculous botched prayers, it seemed to me I should be able strengthen the ghost signal. Not with prayer—I'm not completely sold on the idea of a guy with a big white beard in the sky—but with energy.

I watched the critical moment unfold. Thigh. Hip. Shoulder. Blood spray. My intent was usually to break up the energy and send it off to its proper place. Not a physical location, but a plane that overlaps it. I'm not sure the name mattered—astral, ethereal, the metaphysical scholars try to label these planes of reality, but they never seem to agree with one another, so it was vague in my mind. *Go wherever it is that you belong. Not here.* That's the gist of my usual command.

What would that look like in opposite-land? I did my best to ignore Dreyfuss, ignore the repeater, and focus on the question. The opposite of "go away"?

Come back.

I felt a shift in my understanding, a realization that calling something back should, in theory, work. I wouldn't need to make a big show of it, either. While I do use my physical voice to talk to sentient ghosts, I'd long ago stopped speaking with repeaters. They never reacted as if they were hearing me, and I could salt them perfectly well without saying anything aloud.

To be honest, I could salt them perfectly well without salt, too. But I hated the way my hand felt after I reached into my pocket and pulled out my psychic fairy dust. My own salt was currently in my overcoat, which was in the lounge. I was in no mood to try to explain to Richie what I was doing by going out there to retrieve it, so I supposed my salt packets would have to stay where they were. Given the choice of letting the FPMP supply me with salt or using my own non-physical stock, I opted to tap my own mojo and suffer the clammy-hand later. I'm sure I didn't actually need to reach into my pocket either, but I'd never bothered to break the habit. It was good camouflage to keep the people around me thinking that I needed to employ some sort of physical prop in order to perform.

I planted my feet, centered myself, and dipped my left hand into my pocket. I felt the telltale tingle immediately. Not surprising. My white light was in overdrive. I fixed myself on the repeater…and floundered. It wasn't just that I told them to scram, I realized. There was a whole feeling attached to it. A feeling of untangling a knot, and of scrubbing a stubborn stain off the bathroom sink. A feeling of cleanness. Of rightness. Of release.

How the hell was I supposed to feel that in reverse?

"Filthy captivity" wasn't exactly the vibe I was aiming for, I knew that much. Solidity, maybe? Substance? I sucked a big gulp of white light and imagined the repeater growing more opaque. Controlled.

Lucid.

The fairy dust was ready now, more than ready. My hand prickled unpleasantly, as if tiny shocks of static were playing over my fingertips. I wasn't strong enough to leak ectoplasm on my own, not without the help of a big fat psyactive. So while there wouldn't be any jelly involved, I would end up with a creepy, numb hand to show for my efforts. I was eager to get to that stage of the game, because at least then, I knew the "ick" would begin the process of wearing off.

I pinched. A granular sensation played between my fingertips, crackling with energy. With my internal faucet pouring white light into me, and the idea of solidity fixed firmly in my mind, I pulled out my fairy dust. I thought, *come back,* and I salted the repeater.

My vision flashed white.

It was a little bit like the sparkles you see when you press on your closed eyelids, except it had nothing to do with my optic nerve and everything to do with my sixth sense. I'd just focused a load of white light, maybe more than my wiring was designed to handle, and the conduit needed a second to cool off.

Maybe it wasn't even an entire second. More like a moment, a breath. Even so, I was logy with relief when the dazzle wore off and I got my physical sight back. I glanced at Dreyfuss first. He sat behind his big desk, eyes boring through me while he picked at his cuticles without knowing he was doing it. Good, that was good. I could deal with him watching me, especially since I didn't have any other choice.

The repeater, unfortunately, hadn't reacted to my attempt quite like I'd expected.

He'd frozen.

It was something straight out of a sci fi flick, where the camera pans around some exaggerated action while the actor stops in an impossible pose. This freeze-frame was the shoulder hit, the critical hit. His body was torqued, with his legs, hips and right arm flung forward, and his left arm, shoulder and head snapped back. The spectral bloodspray was a galaxy of tiny frozen globules fixed in the air around the point of exit. One of his shoes was half off.

"I don't think he's gonna talk," I admitted.

"Because he won't," Dreyfuss asked, "or because he can't?"

"He can't."

"Because…?"

"He just can't. That's not how it works."

Dreyfuss leaned forward, but he kept the big desk between him and me. And the repeater. "What's the complication? Maybe we can MacGyver a fix."

That spot between an unsolvable problem and an earnest problem-solver is one I always try to avoid. "There's no workaround, okay? He's a repeater. Repeaters don't talk."

If Dreyfuss was surprised I admitted spirits talk to me (in actual *words*) he didn't show it. "So repeaters are shells."

"Not even that," I said. "They're more like a snippet of film."

"Energy."

Everything's energy, or so the theorists tell us. But thinking about the way everything's made of atoms—or the empty space between them—makes me start to wonder if everything was really nothing, and as thoughts went, it wasn't a very appealing notion.

"Energy from the moment of death?" he asked. I nodded. "But spirits are different." I didn't confirm or deny that, but it seemed he didn't need me to. "Okay, so what if you don't focus on the repeater. What if you focus on the person instead, and you invite them back for a little chat?"

"How is the repeater not the person?"

"It's totally different…isn't that what you just told me? A repeater is a moment, an imprint of a moment of violence. But a person's mind, their spirit, the essential them-ness—that's the part you'd need to tap if you want to talk to this guy and get an I.D."

"I can't focus on the person if I've got no idea who he is."

"You've been going at this for a long time and you're starting to get fatigued. I understand. But we're right on the verge of something here. Don't you feel it?"

All I felt was weariness and frustration…until he pulled out his pillbox. As I debated whether I'd be pushing my luck by asking for five pills for this final I.D., he said, "Maybe you don't think you're able to call this guy back, but a dozen reds says you can."

CHAPTER 15

AND SO I TRIED. I sucked white light, and I tried to picture Triple-Shot speaking to me, and I imagined that my white light was calling to him. I tried and I tried, 'til my mouth was dry, my head throbbed and my pits were damp. Finally, when I was so woozy I needed to sit down, I lowered myself into a chair and said, "It doesn't work that way."

"Are you sure?" Dreyfuss said tentatively. My head snapped up as I registered his tone. It was unlike him to be anything other than one hundred percent certain. "Maybe you just need a little help."

He rolled his chair over to the credenza behind him, turned a key in its lock, and slid open a panel. Inside was the tube of an old-fashioned TV.

It wasn't like the massive tube TV from the bed and breakfast in Missouri, and it wasn't like the old console in my basement. But there was no doubt in my mind it was a GhosTV.

He caught my eye. "What do you say?"

"Gimme a minute." I swabbed my forehead with the sleeve of my jacket, and though I hated to ask for anything, I said, "Can I get a water?"

Dreyfuss rolled over to another panel and unlocked it. There was a small fridge inside. *He locks his fridge*...and here I thought *I* was paranoid. Still seated, he pulled out two waters and tossed them both to me, one after the other, in an easy underhand. "One for each of us. You pick."

It was a relief that I didn't need to be circumspect about how little I trusted him. I tossed one of the waters back. He caught it neatly, cracked the seal, and drank. I did the same. My temples were pounding. A Valium would help some. An Oxy would be better yet. No doubt Dreyfuss could score them if I asked, and no doubt he would pop one right along with me to put me at ease. But I didn't—because I was clearly the worst negotiator on the planet, and asking for a painkiller would probably undercut my Seconal. Besides, I'd rather hold on to the headache, as a reminder to stop being so sloppy around him and keep a few of my secrets for myself.

No matter how badly I wanted those pills, I could tell by the twisting of my guts and the painful tightness in my neck muscles that there'd only be one more "try" in me that day. "Okay." I might as well get it over with. "Turn that thing on."

He powered up the tube. I did my best to breathe, and center myself, and relax. GhosTVs bring on headaches for me, and since I was already in the midst of one, I'd need to pace myself. No telling if a headache is only an angry firing of the nerves or an important vein fixing to pop.

"It's set to the parameters we got from Jeffrey Alan Scott," Dreyfuss said, hushed and reverent, as if he was announcing a golf match. "Let me know if you need 'em tweaked."

I waved him off and he shut up. One more try…and I didn't have energy to spare for a chat while I was attempting it.

As I adjusted to whatever it is the ramped up TV signal does to my brain, the repeater grew solid—rock solid, like I could mistake him for physical, if not for his mid-air spinaround. Given the posture, he seemed more like a waxworks figure than a ghost. Or a frozen moment of violence. Or whatever he actually was.

The level of detail was freakish. I could see the jacquard pattern of his tie fabric, count the blood globules. I eased around him. Not a nail-biter, this one. Hairy forearms, though. I could count the hairs. Hell, it felt as if I could pluck one, if I'd wanted to…but I didn't try. Touching it might shatter the illusion before I'd seen what I needed to see.

I focused on his face. So much detail that it transcended my discomfort at rubbernecking this guy's final moment—but enough detail to I.D. him? Maybe not while he was screaming like that. I looked at him, hard, and gave the relevant details that would narrow the search. Hair:

medium brown. Eyes: medium brown. Skin: medium-toned Caucasian. Birthmarks: none. For such a spectacle of a repeater, he was nearly impossible to fucking describe.

I tried sending the paranormal film loop forward or back a few frames, to the point where his face looked more like his everyday face, more like something I could match with a mug shot. Nothing. Whatever I'd done with the fairy dust had cemented him in place, good.

I sucked some more white light and gave him a focused nudge. Nothing.

I imagined his selfness, his soul, coursing back through the cosmos to inhabit the gruesome shell, to tell me something, anything of use. Nothing.

My head was pounding now. I had Dreyfuss tweak the knobs, increment by increment. Together, we found a setting that felt so sharp-edged sparkling hyperclear that I wondered if maybe I needed to go get my eyes examined. If the first settings represented what I'd come to accept as "clear," maybe middle aged farsightedness was finally taking hold. The repeater was so acutely vivid now I could practically count his skin cells. And there was still nothing I could use.

His eyes were wide and shocked. His face was contorted. His mouth gaped in a scream…but now, I could count his fillings.

Maybe I should ask for dental records. I thought it facetiously, but actually, it wasn't a bad idea. We should probably act on it right away. The repeater might fade with time. Or he might be stuck here for good. There was no way of knowing. I needed to go lie down, but I might only have this one chance.

"Our top five," I said to Dreyfuss, with my eyes fixed on the frozen repeater's molar, "can you get me their dental records?"

"I'll give it a shot."

My head was about ready to detonate. I turned toward my chair to take a load off, and caught myself doing a double-take at Dreyfuss. Something hinky was going on, but it wasn't the freaky eyeball phenomenon I'd witnessed at PsyTrain. While the multiple glowing eyeball look wasn't pretty, I'd seen it before. It wouldn't have startled me. This was different. The air around him was occupied, but not by repeaters.

I sat down, slouched in my chair and pinched my temples, then stole a look from under my palm. It was barely there, whatever it was, difficult to make out, but definitely centered on Dreyfuss. Smoke? No, it didn't move quite like smoke.

He picked up his phone and there was definite movement in the non-physical, as if his motion had disturbed whatever it was. As if it was reacting to him. "Laura," he said, "prioritize this. I need you to dig up some dental records, I'll send you the list—and don't wait until you have them all, bring them to me as quick as you turn them up. Thanks."

He hung up, and the non-physical stirred again. It was as if an alternate plane occupied the same physical space as Dreyfuss, and in that plane, there was stuff. Cloudy stuff. Floating stuff. Stuff he couldn't feel, although it seemed to sense him. It wasn't a mist and it wasn't a vapor, though. More like…I squinted. What the hell did it look like? For someone who was supposedly a visual thinker, I sure had a hard time figuring out what I was seeing. The stuff around Dreyfuss looked less like clouds, and more like…jellyfish.

My body reacted before I did, probably because my brain was busy trying to convince me that I wasn't really seeing what I saw. I flinched, and tried to turn the motion into a kind of cough to cover my twitchiness.

Dreyfuss glanced up. Small glowing tracers followed his eyes, though that was normal, for him. "Are you okay?"

Don't look, I begged myself. But I couldn't tear my eyes away. The psychic jellyfish didn't just happen to occupy the same physical space as Dreyfuss. They were tethered to him by long, thin strands of noncorporeal goop.

"Bayne?"

"Headache," I lied. My headache was now a dull sheet of pain that I hardly felt, because my entire awareness had been hijacked. All I could think was, *What the fuck are those jellyfish things?*

"Do you want something for it? I've got aspirins with a pinch of codeine that'll knock it right out." He reached into his pocket, and all the jellyfish shifted. In fact, every time he moved his hands, he created a noticeable disturbance in the jellyfish field. The goopy tethers, I saw, were connected specifically to his hands.

My first thought was that maybe the Con Dreyfuss in front of me wasn't really him at all. Maybe he was a poor husk who'd once been Con Dreyfuss, a snotty skatepunk who'd ollied through the wrong place at the wrong time, and the evil jellyfish overlords had taken over his body, puppeteering him into position all these years to take over the FPMP.

I watched him pull out his deep, deep pillbox and place it on his desk while the jellyfish trailed behind the motion. It didn't look like the jellyfish entities were pulling the strings. They were actually kind of languid, like he'd wandered through a field of them and gotten himself tangled up. Now they were just being dragged along for the ride.

He flipped open a compartment, pulled out four pills and rattled them like dice. The transparent jellyfish quivered on the ends of their tethers. He set two pills in front of me, popped the other two, and washed them down with a slug of water. "Chalky."

Keeping my headache no longer seemed important. Numbly, I did the same.

He said, "You really don't look so hot. I've got an M.D. on staff, maybe I should have her sit in."

"It's fine," I said automatically.

As he leaned back in his chair to consider how not-fine I actually was, I spied motion in the jellyfish field. Vibration coursed down one of the strands as the floating body where it originated gave a gentle undulation. Dreyfuss brought his hand to his mouth and clipped off the edge of his cuticle between his teeth, and the undulation stopped.

I turned away and gulped water.

"If you're gonna hurl, aim for the wastebasket."

I'd seen one of those jellyfish things before, or something like them, at the hospital the Fire Ghost was haunting. The image popped into my mind like it was yesterday: a dark, cloudy thing trailing behind the gurney of a homeless woman with an impossibly high blood alcohol level. Had it been strung to her with a goopy tether? Hard to say, I'd only gotten a glimpse. Fuck, oh fuck. I cradled my head in my hands. I'd tried to follow up, but couldn't get anyone to give me her name. Then I let it drop.

I didn't know it was this bad. I didn't know.

No, that's not true. I knew, I'd seen the thing, and I dismissed it. There was too much other stuff going on, and I let it slip away. I cradled my head in my hands.

A button clicked, and Dreyfuss said, "Laura? Get Dr. Santiago up to my office, ASAP."

"No," I said, forcing myself to sit up and look normal, whatever that might be. "It's fine. I'm fine. It's passing."

"Doc's cool, a smart lady, you'll like her."

"It's fine."

Dreyfuss cancelled the doctor, sat back in his big leather chair, and watched me watching him. He patted his hair, and the jellyfish field swayed. "Bedhead? Lint? What's so fascinating up there?"

What the hell was I supposed to tell him—that apparently he had fingernail demons floating around over his head? Connected to him? Feeding off him? Okay, demons might be too strong a word. Gremlins, imps…. No matter how I tried to frame it, no way did it sound even remotely reasonable. "I need to try something," I said finally. "Don't move."

His eyebrows rose expectantly, but he stayed put as I stood and approached him.

"Okay," I said, "close your eyes."

"Is this a trust exercise? Like falling backward and expecting you to catch me?"

Actually, I just didn't want him to see me sprinkling my invisible fairy dust. "What's there to trust?"

"You're armed. I'm not."

I ejected the magazine and handed the Glock to him. He placed the unloaded gun on his desk with a shake of his head, like the move was a bit melodramatic for his taste, then shrugged and closed his eyes.

When I dipped into my left pocket, I found my supply of fairy dust was three, four times what it had been before. Sucking white light in front of a powered up GhosTV must've been the reason for the extra mojo. I grabbed a good handful, and I flung it at the jellyfish. I didn't tell them to scram, not out loud, but I must not have needed to. There was a disruption in the field, all those transparent bodies rippling and roiling. Dreyfuss winced and flexed his fingers. I scooped out another big handful of fairy dust and flung it. *Beat it*, I thought. *There's more where that came from. I can keep this up all day.*

As I reached for a third handful, one of the fingernail demons detached itself and undulated away, rising up and disappearing through the ceiling tiles.

All day long. I flung another handful, and two more detached and fled. Every time I reached into my pocket, the level of dust was higher. Once the first few took off, the remaining jellyfish lost their nerve. One by one they pulled loose and floated up through the ceiling. *And don't come back,* I thought, *'cos I'd be more than happy to dust you again.*

I was staring at the ceiling, waiting to see if the fingernail demons were gonna try and sneak back for more, when I realized the pulse was pounding in my ears so loudly, I was surprised Dreyfuss couldn't hear it from where he sat. I ramped my focus down a few notches and did my best to breathe, I fell back a few steps, then told Dreyfuss, "Okay."

He opened his eyes and looked at me. "Was there a ghost on my head?"

"Not…exactly."

He pulled off his scrunchie, shook out his corkscrew curls and groaned as he raked his hands through his hair.

"There are non-physical things that aren't quite ghosts," I said, hoping to make him feel better. Though as I said it, I realized it was probably no great comfort. "It was nothing *dead*."

"I have a medium who costs me a cool two million a year, and it takes a fucking public servant to see…you got rid of it, didn't you? Tell me it's gone."

As much as I dislike Dreyfuss, I couldn't help but feel for the guy. "Yeah.

You're good now."

"That's just peachy. Look, I don't mean to sound like an ingrate, but some days it just doesn't pay to get out of bed." I knew the feeling. "I'm not lying when I say I'd love to have you on my team. Name your price."

"Let's not get ahead of ourselves. I know you don't like burning your favors, but Jacob needs to get into the Metropolitan Correctional Center. You've got to make that call yourself."

"And here I thought you'd ask for more drugs." He raked his hair back into a sloppy mess of a ponytail, pulled out his pillbox again and popped a Valium. My throat gave a little pulse like it wouldn't mind swallowing one too. Before I could hint that it was rude of him not to share, his phone buzzed. He pushed a speakerphone button, and Laura's voice said, "I located some dental records."

"Bring them in," Dreyfuss told her. Then he said to me, "If this was police work, you'd be waiting on a subpoena right now, and you know it."

Since I was fully aware of that fact, I didn't bother replying.

Laura came in and set a few sheets of paper on Dreyfuss' desk. If she was alarmed to see an unloaded 9-millimeter sitting on it, she didn't show it. "I have Dr. Santiago standing by," she told him. "Are you okay? Your hair's kind of—"

"It's not me. It's Detective Bayne."

Laura looked me over critically, and I said, "I don't need a doctor. It's just eyestrain." Or was it psychic overload? Or Seconal backlash? Either way, I didn't want to get into it. "It's practically gone."

She glanced at the window and said, "I'm sure this glare isn't helping any."

I'd been so engrossed in the repeaters and the fingernail demons I hadn't noticed any glare, but now that she mentioned it, the light was pretty intense. The roofs of the buildings in the train yard were covered in snow. Those roofs were sooty white, the November sky was murky white, and the light bouncing off them and pouring through the floor-to-ceiling window was making us all squint.

Laura marched up to the window. Somehow she managed to avoid stepping through any of the repeaters on the way. She veered around Richie's prayer mat, too. With a yank, she whisked the curtains shut. The room went dim, and afterimages shaped like the window drifted across my field of vision. I heard her re-cross the room as her high heels made gentle thumps against the berber, though when my pupils adjusted and my vision faded in, I was surprised to find her still standing beside the window where the curtain had been. Until I realized it wasn't Laura I was looking at.

It was Jennifer Chance.

CHAPTER 16

DR. CHANCE IS THE SAME stature as Laura Kim, five and a half feet tall, fit, somewhat angular. Like Laura, the ghost wore a plain dark outfit, but her blonde hair was a quick giveaway. That, and the bullet hole in her forehead. Chance's ghost leaned back against the wall beside the window with its arms crossed, scowling, watching Con Dreyfuss intently through narrowed eyes. How long had she been lurking around behind that curtain? All morning? All year? What had she seen—and what had she heard? And more importantly, what secrets of mine did I inadvertently spill to Dreyfuss that morning, and by extension, to her?

Sentient ghosts don't terrify me. They're not exactly at the top of my list for "Things I Want to See Today," but they don't leave me soiling myself and crouching in the corner, either. I'd be lying, though, if I said the ghost of Jennifer Chance didn't creep me out, especially now, knowing that in all this time it had never moved on…and that it still had its eye on Dreyfuss.

Make no mistake, Chance had been creepy in life, too. Whenever I hear a female character's voice on TV go a little singsong, I get a flash of her coming toward me with a syringe. On bad days, the visual is accompanied by the tactile memory of her brushing my hair off my forehead while she gazed into my eyes.

I looked up at the ceiling so she didn't know I'd spotted her. Dreyfuss looked up too, as if he needed to guard against head ghosts descending on him.

"You really should have Dr. Santiago take your blood pressure, at least," Laura told me. "Just to be safe."

"I'm fine."

"Laura's prone to migraines," Dreyfuss said. "They lay her out for days if she doesn't nip 'em in the bud."

"It's not a migraine," I said. "It's almost gone."

Laura looked me over as if she didn't quite believe me, but she knew enough to pick her battles. She said, "If you don't need anything else, I'll get back to the dental records."

"Thanks," Dreyfuss said absently, scanning the ceiling for threats he couldn't see, while Jennifer Chance peeled away from the wall and strode after Laura.

Although I thought I was being smooth, when Chance passed by, a chill stole over me—and a major case of the heebie-jeebies. I flinched, visibly. She stopped in her tracks and looked me in the eye. Emotions played over her face, one after another: shock, anger, and finally, excitement. "It works?" A flicker, and then there she was right there, looming over my seat, Laura Kim forgotten, eyes wide with wonder and a hint of mania. Way too close. "This particular tuner setting works?"

I was not having this conversation in front of Dreyfuss. I squirmed away from Chance, gathered my sidearm and bullets from the desk and said, "I gotta use the john."

Dreyfuss looked at me a bit strangely, but he couldn't exactly forbid me to go to the bathroom. I ducked in, then closed and locked the door behind me while Jennifer Chance floated right through it. Then I turned on the taps in the sink and the shower to provide a bit of white noise, contorting myself to avoid brushing up against her. While I'd been loath to present my back to Laura Kim in the parking garage, my instincts with Chance's ghost were the opposite. I found myself protecting my solar plexus like a shoplifter guarding a five-finger discount stuffed down his shirt.

"You see me now," Chance said. "I know you do. I've been lying low all day and suddenly you have a visual. It must be the tuner."

"Back up." I snapped the ammo cartridge into place, which apparently only intimidates people in movies. Normally I would've used a "drop your weapon" tone, but instead I whispered since I wanted the conversation to stay between her and me. Hopefully the water splashing would be enough to confuse surveillance devices, at least without advanced filtering. I holstered the useless weapon. My headache was so blinding by now, I was dying to perch on the closed toilet seat, or maybe lie down on the floor to keep physical damage to a minimum in the event I keeled over. Since that would make me a stationary target, though, I stayed on my feet, angling away from her constant, solicitous touching. Still, it was only a single bathroom and there weren't exactly a lot of places to go. When she grabbed me by the arm, I felt the tips of her fingers sink in. And in. And in. I jerked my arm away and sucked a huge gulp of white light, then threw it around her to keep her to herself. "I said, back the fuck up."

"Calm down, Detective. I'm only checking your pulse."

"Touch me again I'll salt your ass where you stand. Get it?"

"Actually, I don't…but I presume it's nothing good." She raised her hands in exasperated surrender. "Your breathing is rapid, there's a mottled pallor to your cheeks, and you're perspiring. It's in your best interest to let me—"

"No."

"At the very least, make a cool compress and put it on your forehead." She made a big show of keeping her hands up, ironically, as if it was entirely unreasonable for me to distrust her. "There's a washcloth right there."

The contrarian in me wanted to tell her to shove the washcloth up her ass, but I was eager for something, anything, to dull the knife edge of my head pain. My "cool compress" was a wet wad of thick white terrycloth that I swabbed across my brow while I kept my eye on Chance. It was difficult to restrain myself from checking out the mirror, since the guy I'd glimpsed looking back at me was hollow-cheeked and waxy. Visual confirmation was unnecessary, though. I knew I felt like shit. What mattered was keeping my eye on the ghost.

This particular ghost looked pretty much like she did in life. The thing was, when I'd known her, she'd been posing as my general practitioner, with breezy hippie-chick clothes and a practical, nurturing bedside manner. The real Jennifer Chance was purely mercenary, and with my GhosTV-enhanced perception, she looked as solid as Dreyfuss or Laura. Her shoulders bunched together and her collarbones stood out, even though there weren't any physical collarbones there to cast her chest in stark relief. The eyes that had faked compassion so credibly now seemed clinical and hard. Looking at those eyes made me feel so uncomfortable I actually fixed on the bullet hole instead. It shifted and shimmered under my gaze. When a single drop of crimson blood drooled out, I finally looked away…though only a bit to the side, still keeping her in my sights while I asked, "Why are you still here?"

"Isn't it obvious?" I expected to hear *Because some FPMP goon shot me down in cold blood*, but instead she said, "Dreyfuss has my tuners."

The tuners? Holy hell, she was *babysitting* the GhosTVs. "Gadgets you made…and yet you seem surprised that they actually work."

She said, "We hardly got anywhere with them before the police ruined everything with their kidnapping charges—I wanted to *ask* you to test the tuners with us, but Burke said you'd never go along with it, not ever. He said no amount of money could get you to willingly take a psyactive, and given the way you were tripling your Auracel dose, I believed him. I trusted him." She sighed. "I trusted him, and he was nowhere near as invested in the project as I was. In the end, all he cared about was bargaining his way out of prison."

"No big surprise."

"With your talent and my invention…. I wish I'd known about the barbiturate habit. I could've sourced them for you—all the Seconal you'd ever want—but I let Burke talk me into doing things *his* way, and look where it got me. I'm dead. You're performing like a dancing bear for a handful of pills. And the vultures here are circling my research, trying to reconstruct it and take all the credit."

She wasn't even pretending to be coy about listening in on my dealings with Dreyfuss…but what about the flower shop? Was that really a sacred space, or had she been lurking among the potted ferns? Since that field trip was the only time I'd discussed owning a GhosTV with anyone from the FPMP, maybe I could determine whether the charms and protections actually worked, or if she could go anywhere she damn well pleased. Including my home. "So Dreyfuss has all of your…tuners?"

"Not all." I braced myself to see if she'd allude to the florist talk, and instead she said, "They shipped one off to PsyTrain…it must've been a few months ago. Between the lab here and whoever they're working with at PsyTrain, they'll probably get their Nobel nominations within the year—for *my* invention."

"That's what this is all about…the Nobel Prize?"

She rolled her eyes. "They don't give out posthumous Nobels." Well, duh. *Everybody* knows that. "The best I could hope for at this point is the National Medal of Science. That, and keeping the vultures from claiming my work as their own."

Given that she was dead, I didn't really see how winning some kind of medal would make any difference one way or the other. It wasn't as if she'd get the satisfaction of flaunting it in front of her rivals. Still, if the obsession keeping her here was not about her murderer but instead the GhosTV, maybe she could be reasoned with rather than exorcised. If she could be reasoned with, maybe she'd be willing to bargain. It would be a crying shame to let all her FPMP surveillance go to waste. "I'm looking for some information," I said. "What would it cost me to find out how a missing PsyCop named Wembly disappeared?"

Cocking her head, she gave me a look of pity and moved to pat me on the arm. It was a glimmer of the old Dr. Chance—the fabricated Dr. Chance. I backed away before she could touch me, and her sympathetic gaze turned frosty. "There's one tuner that Burke didn't manage to turn over to the authorities—the prototype. Get your hands on it before Dreyfuss does. Release it to the scientific community with my name on the research. And demonstrate that the technology works."

It seemed like a hell of a lot of legwork to go through. Maybe, once upon a time, I would have entertained the possibility. But since I'd probably be able to come by the Wembly information with a few sí-nos, it hardly seemed worth it. Unfortunately, she picked up on my unwillingness before I was able to lead her on with a few promises I had no intention of keeping.

"That's the price—but obviously you'd never be willing to pay it. Because Dreyfuss has you convinced that the minute the public knows who you are and what you can do, you're as good as dead."

"I didn't say that." Although it struck me as chillingly possible.

"You don't need to. It's written all over your face." She reached for my wrist—I pulled back. I sent a blast of psychic light into the white balloon around her, too. She scowled. "You're a coward," she said, "just like Burke. Since I can't dash off a prescription, you have no intention of helping me."

"That is entirely not…" She whirled around and sailed through the far wall. I was alone. "…true."

That last blast of psychic juice had cost me, physically. In addition to the blinding headache, I was nauseated now, lightheaded and exhausted. I swabbed my face again and turned off the taps. The mirror was steamed up, so I switched on the vent, then sat on the closed toilet seat and pressed my face into my hands. She was making me out to be some kind of selfish creep—and if I was so damn selfish, would I go around trudging through murder scenes in my futile attempts to bring the killers to justice? Would I subject myself to mangled repeaters and salt them for the sake of closure if I only cared about myself? Who in their right mind would shout out, "Look, world, I'm a big ol' medium who can prove to you this GhosTV's got reception," if their only reward would be a bullet to the face and an unmarked grave…right next to Detective Wembly.

While I don't know exactly how Con Dreyfuss' remote viewer talent works, I was pretty sure that between his Psych skills, his surveillance equipment, and his uncanny knack for picking up on everything I didn't want him to know, I'd emerge from the bathroom to him sending Jennifer Chance his regards. But instead he said, "Did you hurl?"

"I'm fine."

He was mousing through a bunch of web pages on his triple monitors, mostly text, though a scientific diagram flashed by on the left-hand monitor and a closeup of a bright red capsule on the right. I stepped around the Russian repeater and sat myself down across from Dreyfuss so he couldn't see how unsteady I was on my feet. He said, "So is it just the downers with you, or do you need uppers to peel yourself out of bed?"

"Why, are you running a two-for-one special?" The pain in my head spiked, then hung there, impaled. I glanced at Triple-Shot. He was as still and solid as a department store mannequin.

"If you don't need to double-dip now, one of these days you will, and it's a nasty cycle. Barbiturates are archaic and crazy-addictive, and the upper-downer cocktail is nothing to mess with. I'm not throwing stones, here. Just sayin'—pharmaceuticals have evolved."

"You're running low on reds. Is that it?"

Dreyfuss gave a long, exasperated sigh. His eyeballs left a short string of tracers behind. "You think you're the only one who has trouble sleeping? Hardly. But if the ultimate goal is survival, this is not the most promising route you could take. Dr. Santiago could help you wean yourself off the reds with something more twenty-first century—and then transition from those into something cleaner. Herbs. Acupressure. Biofeedback. It'd be totally off the record. No one needs to know but you, me and Santiago. If you find yourself feeling sentimental for that Seconal buzz—you can always console yourself with a few Jägerbombs."

"Drinking ramps up the ghosts. And I tried hypnosis. It seemed like it was working, too. Unfortunately, *someone* bribed my no-good therapist ex into reporting back with all my personal details." To compound irony with irony, the dead doctor in the bathroom just claimed she would've given me all the Seconal I could want, while the pothead was trying to make me go holistic. I almost laughed, until even worse pain lanced through the existing pain in my skull. "Look, forget about the sleep aids for now. Could I get a couple more of those codeine aspirin?"

Before he could whip out the magical pillbox, Dreyfuss' phone buzzed. Laura's voice said, "Dr. Santiago is here."

I said, "I told you not to—"

"I didn't. Laura did." He gave an unconvincing apologetic shrug, then said into the intercom, "Send her in."

Like I needed a doctor to tell me I'm taking too many pills as it is. The muscles running up the back of my neck were as tight as piano wires, but when I went to massage them, I nearly jumped out of my chair. It felt like someone had just draped a frozen gel pack across my skin. I touched my fingertips to my cheek. Cold. Not like frostbite—my fingers weren't red and they didn't sting or burn. But pressed against a normal-temperature part of my body, they felt like they should've been frozen solid. The worse part? My palm was ever so slightly damp. And not with sweat. Numb, too. Mostly in my left hand, my salting hand. But I felt a little tingle in my right hand as well. Great. An FPMP doctor was on her way, and I was leaking ectoplasm.

There was a jaunty knock. Dreyfuss buzzed open his door and a busty Latina in a clingy wrap dress and four-inch heels breezed in. Her thick black hair hung past her shoulders in loose curls, her lipstick was fire engine red, and she didn't look a day over thirty. She also had a third eye in the middle of her forehead, which I told myself I probably shouldn't stare at, though it was easier said than done. "*Hola*, Constantine."

"*Hola*, Doc." He indicated me with a sweep of his hand. "This is—"

"Victor Bayne," she said, before he could finish. "Agent Bly's new PsyCop friend." Her Spanish accent was thick and lilting, almost as if she was playing it up for effect. She looked me over with a sultry, knowing smile. Meanwhile, I found myself wondering if I'd managed to pass out and wake up in one of those weird Mexican telenovela soap operas where the male characters are a bunch of average schmoes and the women are scantily clad and smoking hot, and everyone acted like extra facial features were totally normal.

Dr. Santiago gazed into my eyes with all three of hers. Assessing my pupils, or reading my mind? I started singing *Row, Row, Row Your Boat* to myself just in case. "Laura says you have a pretty bad headache. When did it start?"

"Today?" I wiped my hand on my slacks to chafe some warmth back into it and rub off the goo, hoping she'd just figure it was sweaty. "Maybe an hour ago."

"Ever had one like it before?"

"I…guess." I was hesitant to pour out my soul to Santiago. If she was employed by the FPMP, aside from her psychic talent, she was probably no slouch in the doctoring department, either. Maybe Dreyfuss already knew everything there was to know about me, but I wasn't eager to run through my medical history in front of him, even though, ironically, he'd be a lot more likely to patch me up with a handful of pills. For sure I couldn't let on that I was leaking ecto too, if I didn't want to end up staring at Dr. K's gaptoothed grin from inside a Plexiglas box.

Merrily, merrily, merrily, merrily...

"Any idea what triggers it?"

"It's kind of like eyestrain. Like staring at the TV too...long." As I said it, I realized there was an inanimate object I could blame that would get me out of revealing too much personal information. I didn't care to admit the pain was caused by fumbling around with the talent I spent most of my time trying to ignore. "GhosTVs are hell on my head. That's all."

Dr. Santiago looked puzzled, and Dreyfuss let out a laugh. "He's talking about the psychic tuner."

"You're running it right now?" Santiago exclaimed. "Then start by turning it off."

"But the—" I gestured toward Triple-Shot, worried that my chance to identify the missing PsyCop was about to dwindle to a pinpoint in the center of the tube once the signal was cut.

"They've been here for ages," Dreyfuss said. "They won't disappear when we pull the plug."

"Wait," I said.

Dreyfuss stopped with his hand poised above the dial.

"Before you touch anything, I want to jot down those readings." Because if I started with these crystal-clear settings, maybe I could experiment at home. Figure out how to prep myself for the next time I was called upon to do some heavy-duty ghostbusting. Figure out how to get a repeater to talk, so that the next time I faced the remnants in the FPMP building, I could determine whether Dreyfuss had anything to do with Wembly's disappearance or not. I approached the credenza, pulled out my notepad, and thanks to the numbness that had now spread over both my hands, dropped my pen. Fine. I was about to get down on one knee to look at the dials more closely anyway. I picked up the pen, fumbled it, and dropped it again. Then I dropped the pad. And the pen. Again.

"Allow me." Dreyfuss grabbed the pad and pen out of my numb hands before I could drop them yet again, jotted down the settings and switched off the TV.

My head pain ebbed slightly.

"You should leave the building," Santiago recommended, "walk around a little. Have lunch. Anything it takes to get out of the tube's range. Whatever it does, whatever signal it produces, we have nothing to measure it with. So we don't know how long it really takes to shut off completely."

The signal decayed as soon as the power was cut, but I didn't go into it, not when I might be able to use the leverage of that knowledge later. Besides, I had other concerns. Dreyfuss had finished noting the last reading and was handing the pad back to me. Since I wouldn't put it past him to "accidentally" record the wrong readings if it suited his mysterious purposes, I double checked the note to make sure they were correct. And then I got a good look at his handwriting....

A quirky back-slanted cursive.

I'd figured the way he greeted Santiago with *hola* was a chummy affectation. I'd figured wrong. I pictured the card that had fallen out of Lisa's bouquet. *Para la rosa más hermosa.*

"So…" I was shocked at how calm my voice sounded. "Which is your better language—French, or Spanish?"

"Definitely Spanish," Dreyfuss said. "My first wife was from Monterrey… and it behooved me to know what she was telling the family back home about her insufferable spouse."

Sonofabitch. No wonder Lisa was being so cagey about her new love interest. It was no yoga instructor, no fireman, no torrid lesbian affair. All this time, my best friend had been playing grab-ass with the Regional Director of the FPMP.

…life is but a dream.

CHAPTER 17

LISA. AND DREYFUSS. TOGETHER. LISA, *my* friend, making phone calls to Constantine Dreyfuss in *my* house, speaking in a language I didn't fucking understand. Here I thought eavesdropping on me through Stefan was a low blow.

Worse still, I couldn't so much as think about it. Not there. Not yet. Because Dr. Third Eye was able to creep inside my mind, so my every thought might as well be public record.

Row, row, row your boat....

I stood, head swimming, and jammed the GhosTV settings into my pocket before any telltale ectoplasm could leak onto the paper. Dreyfuss was watching me. Santiago was, too. I ran through some multiplication tables—*nine, eighteen, twenty-seven, thirty-six*—and my God, did Jacob know? Did he know what was going on and choose not to tell me? He must know. How could he not? He worked with Dreyfuss and he lived with Lisa, and he was the smart one.

A is for Apple. J is for Jacks. Cinnamon toasty Apple Jacks...

No wonder Jacob wasn't as close to Lisa as I was. I'd thought he felt vulnerable around the sí-no, but if he knew about her thing with Dreyfuss, no wonder he'd been keeping her at arm's length.

"I need to talk to Jacob," I said, while in my mind, I focused on the peephole that needed installing and the water bill we couldn't forget to pay.

Dreyfuss buzzed Laura and asked her, "Can you locate Agent Marks for us?"

"He's in the archives."

Researching Laura, I realized.

And I'd just swung the attention of her surveillance directly at him. Dreyfuss looked to me. "How interruptible do you need him to be?"

As I realized I'd managed to make a target out of Jacob, my brain scrambled frantically for the camouflage of a jingle, a saying, a rhyme, anything to blot out the realization before Dr. Santiago could pluck it out of my head. I couldn't think of a damn thing. "Uh…I don't really…what I mean is…." White light. White fucking light. I sucked it down so hard and threw such a fat wall of it around myself that my ears started to ring. "Never mind. It's not important. I'll ask him later."

Despite my best efforts not to, I pictured the archives I'd toured with Agent Bly: banks of computers, microfilm, even filing cabinets. Then I pictured video of those archives now playing on Laura Kim's computer, just as Jacob was nosing through her records. Whether Jacob had known about Dreyfuss and Lisa suddenly made no difference at all to me. Disagreements came and went. Those, we'd work out. But if anything happened to Jacob's career—hell, maybe his life—because I'd leaked a thought I should have kept private, I'd never forgive myself.

"Maybe we should break for lunch," Dreyfuss said. "Unless you'll just yak it back up."

"Right, lunch." Keeping myself from thinking incriminating things was damn near impossible, and I couldn't afford to slip. I had to get out of the telepath's range. "Not here, though. I think Dr. Santiago's right. I should put some distance between me and the TV."

"I'm not cutting you loose so you can wander around out there alone," Dreyfuss said. "You're looking pretty tweaked-out to me. I'll have Laura page Agent Marks so he can join you."

"Wait." A rough plan began to take shape, but I didn't want to give it too much thought, not in front of Santiago. The gist of it was this: it didn't make sense to pull Jacob out of archives…and maybe I could buy him more time by distracting the surveillance instead. "Actually, I was planning to invite Laura."

To say Laura Kim looked at me funny when I invited her to lunch was an understatement. With the GhosTV turned off, I couldn't tell on sight if any of the suits wandering past were capable of reading my mind, so I sheathed myself in a white light wetsuit just in case. That meant one part of my attention was on shielding myself, so the portion of my brain responsible for talking was underpowered, and none too slick.

"I figure it's gotta get boring, staring at these four walls all day." It didn't seem like a pickup line. I hoped. I dropped eye contact and noticed a folded Tribune with an ad for a hot dog joint called Jim's Original on top. "We could try that place," I suggested, and then I felt like an idiot. I'd just asked The Fixer, who wore diamond earrings and tailored suits, to go out for a *hot dog?*

Her face lit up, and she grabbed her purse.

Aside from my time behind Camp Hell's razor wire, I'm a lifelong Chicago North Sider. As such, I get all turned around south of Roosevelt. I think it's because the main diagonal artery cuts through the grid in the wrong direction down there. Plus, with my head throbbing and my brain occupied by white light allocation and random-thought generation, chances were I'd end up in Lake Michigan if I attempted to get anywhere myself. Luckily, Laura Kim was absolutely delighted to be my driver. Turns out Jim's Original was located in her old stomping ground on Maxwell Street, the neighborhood where her detached car door was nearly lost to an overeager bargain hunter.

Maybe my lunch companion was miked, maybe not, and I was going with the supposition that anything that was said between us would get right back to Dreyfuss. Still, she hadn't sprouted a third eye in the lambent glow of the GhosTV. At least my thoughts would be my own—and believe me, the wheels were turning. While Jacob was placing her at Burke's shooting, maybe I could figure out whose orders she'd been carrying out, if anybody's. Given the fact that the FPMP was one big speed-dating pool, for all I knew, the motives in play had been entirely personal. I'd been pondering how, exactly, to bring up Burke when Laura slowed down and began trolling for a place to park…or double-park as the case may be. Jim's was a bright yellow building fronted by sliding windows where people ponied up to order, then wandered off eating their sloppy hot dogs and Polishes as they walked, or drove. There was nowhere to sit and nowhere to park, but the stream of diners seemed unconcerned that they weren't offered these basic amenities with lunch. Maybe they were grateful enough that for a measly $3.50 they'd get fries with their sandwich.

"Are you sure the nitrates won't make your headache worse?" Laura said.

"It's fine." I wasn't even fibbing. "I feel a lot better now."

"I kept a headache journal for over a year. Lots of people can't handle any kind of processed meat. Lucky for me, hot dogs weren't my trigger." And I knew my ebbing head-splitter was due to psychic strain, dubious drugs and a GhosTV, though I didn't volunteer it.

Laura eased her Lexus beside a thuggish SUV with a naked lady silhouette decal on the window. "I'll order, so we can put it on the company card," she said, "but you should probably stay with the car so we don't get ticketed. The Polish with grilled onions is amazing."

"Sounds good. I'll take two."

I pressed my still-cold fingers against the heating vent and watched her approach Jim's. There were three lines going, all of them doing brisk business. But the line closest to the car, I realized, had a dead panhandler wandering through it. And by through, I mean literally *through*. His semi-transparent body wove in and out of the people waiting in line as if he was getting his jollies from touching their insides. Laura strode past him, planting herself in the line farthest from him, and I recalled how eager she was for me to exorcise Dreyfuss' repeaters. Maybe for good reason.

The GhosTV hadn't revealed any gruesome psychic features on her, but mediums are hard to spot. Our subtle bodies ride loose in our skins, and for me to really shake free to the point where the multiple limb syndrome is visible to my inner eye, I either need to be psyactive- or TV-enhanced. In a lower-calibre medium, I imagine the multi-body effect would be phenomenally subtle.

A few minutes later, the smell of awesomeness filled the car. "I saw some parking spots down the block, if you don't mind us eating in here."

She laughed nervously. "I mean, it's so much better when it's still hot."

"Your fancy Lexus isn't a no-food zone?"

"A car's not important, it's just a thing. A material possession. Besides, I can always have it detailed."

She pulled into an empty space while I spread a plastic bag over my lap and divvied up the Polishes. The personal motivation theory for offing Burke, the lovers' quarrel or steamy vendetta, was seeming less and less plausible. It was possible they'd crossed paths at the FPMP. But from what little I knew of her, and from what little I'd seen of the real Roger Burke, I couldn't imagine them together for longer than the duration of a single incompatible conversation. She was a philosopher—Burke was a sociopath. All my questions about their relationship evaporated, and what I said instead was, "Are you psychic?"

She looked at me, shocked, then started to laugh. Still a nervous laugh, but more robust, like she actually thought I was being funny on purpose.

"You've been tested," I said, "right?"

"Extensively. Me and everyone else at the office. But, no. My Psych scores are totally average."

Psychic evaluation is straightforward for most talents. Can you call a sequence of cards because you see it in your head? You're clairvoyant. Are your readings coming from the person administering the test rather than the test itself? More likely, you're a telepath or empath. Can you peg what will happen in the future? Precog. You probably can't move things with your mind, given that I've only ever met one guy who could do that…but if you could, you'd be telekinetic. Mediums, though, are slippery to test.

To measure someone's sensitivity, why not run them through a gauntlet of awful repeaters and see how many they swerved to avoid? I'd seen Laura veer around four ghosts in the past two hours. Totally average people don't do that. In general, people might avoid a haunted locale. But once they were up close and personal, they'd stand there blissfully unaware while non-corporeal panhandlers manhandled their guts. And even if a bunch of ghost energy was available for testing purposes, the only person who could grade the exam would be someone who could actually see what was going on—another medium. A really strong one.

"Who administered the mediumship part of your test," I said. "Richie?"

"Well, yeah, who else? And I'd been meaning to tell you, as soon as I got the chance, I think it's really sweet how you are with him."

I needed to turn that statement around in my head a few times. People don't generally call me sweet. Plus, I had no idea how I was with him. "What do you mean?"

"The bodyguards would rather be assigned to anyone but him. They have some kind of betting pool running as to who's going to get stuck on Richie duty. They all throw a few bucks in and…well, I'm not sure how they win, they would never do it in front of me."

"Why not?"

"I'd rip 'em a new one. Then I'd guilt them into donating to the Manatee Rehabilitation Fund. There's no need for them to be so cruel." Funny, I'd expected Laura Kim to spook me with her ice-cold assassin grace and to floor me with the extent of her callousness. I was floored, all right, but for entirely different reasons. Jacob was right, this coldblooded killer was more of a bleeding heart. "Yes, this is a high-stress job, and it's hard to listen to Richie being so obnoxious. But all the agents have been briefed on Fetal Alcohol Syndrome, and they know his personality issues are classic."

Uh oh. "I don't know anything about Fetal Alcohol Syndrome," I admitted, hoping I could right my worldview, which was suddenly alarmingly askew.

"Oh. I thought you…uh, I mean, since you were friends at Heliotrope Station."

Where we all just thought he was stupid. Not that he had an actual condition. "Maybe the staff knew. But the inmates didn't have much to do with the staff."

She glanced at me sharply over my use of the word *inmates*, though she didn't choose to open that particular can of psychic worms, and steered the conversation back to Richie. "If the mother's alcohol consumption isn't known or documented, the syndrome can be diagnosed based on facial features, they're that distinctive. You wouldn't know it so much to look at him now, he looks like a regular guy, but there's a baby picture in his file. In that photo he looks like a textbook example. The bow of his upper lip is so flat it's practically missing. Plus, his eyes are really small. He has no peripheral vision—which is good, in a way. It's the reason Agent Dreyfuss uses to explain to him why he wasn't issued a sidearm."

Two Polishes with fries sat like a greasy rock in my gut as I pictured Stefan and me swinging around to face each other and laugh our mocking, "Heh-heh."

Laura brought me back from my Camp Hell ruminations with the question, "Why are you asking about my tests, anyway? I'm not a medium. I can't be."

"Yeah…back when the testers pegged me there wasn't a word for it other than *schizophrenic*."

"But you don't get it. I can't even deal with cartoon ghosts and rubber masks—I'm that scared of dying. If I ever saw a spirit, I'd totally lose it. Death is just so…so…."

"Messy?"

She laughed once, nervously, at my attempt to lighten the mood. "So final."

Now the way her level of anxiety spiked around me made a lot more sense.

"I guess I don't see it that way," I said. "What gets me is the unfairness of people dying because of someone else's jealousy or maliciousness or greed. But once we're dead…I guess it's some comfort to know it's not just a black pit of nothingness in store for us. That when we're done here, we start on another leg of the journey."

She dabbed the corner of her eye with a greasy napkin while I pretended to be very interested in brushing poppy seeds off my overcoat. "Wow, is it really that late?" she said brusquely. "We should probably head back. I don't like to be away from my post when Washington's been calling."

"Is that code for…the President?"

"No, no. The executive branch doesn't want anything to do with Psych.

It's Con's boss, the National Assistant Director. Our attorneys have been advising a clairvoyant in Iowa—poor thing lost her investment banking job to jealousy and internal politics—and Washington wants us to pull out. Con's been stalling it. One of his precogs told him he could get this woman a good severance package if he dawdled long enough."

It was bad enough I needed to shift my view on Richie's mental capabilities. I was not willing to re-evaluate my thoughts on Dreyfuss now, too. Especially since I knew the precog in his pocket was probably the same one who camped in my living room.

The trip back up Halsted was outrageously short, though it was long enough for Laura to convince me to "adopt" a manatee. Well, why the hell not? It only cost twenty-five bucks, plus it got me out of participating in a 5k walkathon. Once we were parked, I dug out the cash while she crammed the evidence of our lunch into a plastic bag: the waxed paper, the mustard packets, the greasy napkins and hot pepper stems. As I handed over the manatee money, a pair of very non-agent-looking people got out of a Lexus parked near the lab door and let themselves in with a magnetic key card. "Have you been through the lab?" she asked.

"Label-makers Gone Wild."

"A few years ago I had an assignment down there. I was helping them crunch a huge pile of data, a room full of forms, all of it on paper, nothing digitized or searchable. It was nice and quiet, no ringing phone, no interruptions. But even so...." She gave a shiver. "I was glad when it was over. It's creepy down there."

I'd been spooked too, though my own issues were caused by my history with Camp Hell. Although if Laura Kim said a particular location creeped her out, I was inclined to wonder why.

I was also inclined to wonder why I'd ever taken her to be a murderer. Sure, she'd been in front of the federal prison that day, but so had hundreds of other people. In our recent conversations, she'd mentioned working offsite on occasion, and also that her job involved a fair amount of analysis. If Con Dreyfuss wanted a set of physical eyes and ears downtown the day that Roger was released, it made plenty of sense to send someone as savvy and observant as Laura. So what if Roger Burke implicated her—what did that actually prove? Burke had drugged a good two dozen coffees and handed them to me with a smile. How far-fetched would it be for him to point me in the wrong direction, either to cover his own ass, or to glean a final moment of sick satisfaction by pitting me against someone I might actually like?

As we walked toward the elevator, I realized I'd learned plenty about Laura during our lunch, but nothing I could use. Proving that she wasn't the shooter could at least be a step in discovering who the killer actually was, and maybe now that she and I had broken bread together, she'd be willing to hint at her real reason for being downtown that afternoon. Doing my best to sound as casual as if we were still talking about manatees, I said, "D'you remember the day Roger Burke was released?"

"Do I ever." Laura paused in front of the elevators, but didn't hit the button. She leaned toward me and said, "I had such a bad migraine, I would've checked myself into the emergency room if I thought it would do me any good. I left work early and took so many meds I was out of it for days."

Although shooting someone in the head might easily be stressful enough to trigger a reaction in the body, this didn't strike me as the type of response the shooter would give me. I tried to sound sympathetic. "And it was probably a mess to get home, all the chaos, all the traffic."

"No, not really. I just caught a cab."

"It was a mob scene down there. My partner needed to lay on the flashers and siren to get out of the jam."

"Oh sure, down by the Correctional Center. But I'm talking about the Near North Side before lunchtime. As far as I can remember, traffic was pretty light. If I'd been caught in that mess down in the Loop, I dunno what I would've done."

We rode up to the fifth floor while I tried to determine if she was really saying what I thought she was saying. "Then you weren't downtown," I clarified.

"Nope, I missed all the commotion." The elevator doors opened. She went back to her desk and tossed our fast food remnants in her trash. "I'm glad you suggested lunch, Detective. My stomach won't thank me later, but for now I'm one happy camper. As to your donation, I'll make it anonymously to protect your privacy, and send your adoption certificate home with Agent Marks."

I stood, nodding stupidly, and wondered how to say, *But we talked to each other that day, as surely as we're talking right now.*

Given some of the mind-bending stuff I've seen—fingernail demons and shapeshifting succubi—and given the fact that the sí-no wouldn't peg her as the shooter, how could I be one hundred percent sure that the woman I'd spoken to in the bus shelter that fateful day was really Laura Kim?

CHAPTER 18

SO I'D GOTTEN OUR MAIN suspect alone, but now I was more confused than ever. Nothing was adding up. Laura, the potential assassin, got choked up when she thought too hard about the plight of plankton and krill. Meanwhile, Con Dreyfuss, my personal nemesis, was filibustering Washington over a single lost job.

Although…the fact that Dreyfuss and Washington didn't see eye to eye could be significant. What if Washington was calling some shots that Dreyfuss didn't authorize? Maybe it was Washington that told Laura to take out Roger Burke. And Jennifer Chance, too.

Sure. Right after Laura talked everybody into adopting a manatee.

I'd been girding myself for another head-splitting visit with Dreyfuss and his repeaters, so I was relieved when Laura gathered Richie, Carl and me in the lounge and said, "A meeting came up. Agent Dreyfuss can't join you this afternoon, so he'd like you to sweep the perimeter for the rest of the day." She then said to me specifically, "That's outside, under viaducts and along the highway. The wind off the river is brutal. If you need gloves or a hat—"

"It's fine." I am so not a hat person. "I'm used to working outdoors."

We all donned our overcoats, then stood there looking at each other. I waited for the FPMP agents to get going. Carl looked to Richie to lead the way when Richie said, "Well, go ahead."

"Which kit should we bring?" Carl asked. It was the first time I'd ever heard him speak.

"Pick one," Richie snapped. If Carl cared about the attitude, he didn't show it. I'm guessing he'd been thoroughly briefed about the Fetal Alcohol

Syndrome. I'm also guessing he received adequate compensation in return for his patience. He chose a spiffy briefcase, then looked again to Richie. Richie gestured toward the elevators and said, "Get going, then—why do I always have to do everything?"

Carl turned and led the way without so much as a raised eyebrow.

I hadn't realized that being interrupted mid-rosary would leave Richie in such a snit. I'd need to bone up on his condition myself, although reading about it would no doubt leave me wracked with guilt over the way I used to treat him. In an effort to be nice without coming off as condescending, I asked, "Big plans for Sunday?"

He looked me over coolly, and said, "Nothing special."

Cripes, I knew the game wasn't quite as thrilling if the Bears weren't playing, but I'd figured it might cheer him up to talk about the Falcons and the Patriots. Guess not.

It was cold outside, not a crisp winter subzero freeze that made everything fresh and new, but a damp late autumn cold driven home by a persistent wind. Still, the dank stretches under the viaducts probably smelled better now than they would in the summer, just judging by the occasional whiff of pee I detected despite the chill breeze.

Although you'd think anyone in their right mind would want to get the perimeter sweep over with and get back inside for a nice hot beverage, Richie poked along, prodding Carl to take the lead. Finally he said, "Explain to Detective Bayne what you're doing. I'll monitor."

That request did earn a brief look of surprise, but Carl took the directive with his typical stoicism. We walked their usual route. Between the train tracks, the El, the highway and the warehouses, it was not exactly pedestrian friendly. But with the proximity of the Salvation Army, Carl told me, it did attract a fair amount of homeless people who were happy to tuck themselves away in a nice deserted spot to try and get out of the cold. Occasionally, one of them would expire. And the FPMP wasn't keen on anyone they couldn't see lurking around their offices.

"If Agent Duff thinks it's necessary in any spot," Carl said, "we do a blessing."

Richie trudged along beside me. Not his normal free-wheeling galumph, either. He hunched against the cold with his hands shoved deep in his pockets and his shoulders up around his ears. "Do you normally find much that needs blessing?" I asked.

"Are you testing me now?" Richie said. "What do *you* think?"

I thought it was way past someone's naptime, but I refrained from saying so.

The end of the day couldn't come soon enough. Between dour Carl and crabby Richie, I found myself wishing Dreyfuss would put in an appearance. At least he could hold up his end of a conversation. His Washington meeting kept him busy for the rest of the afternoon, though, and I ended up heading back home without checking in on Triple-Shot to see if he'd moved or faded, or if he was even still there at all. While I'd gotten to know Laura a lot better, what I'd discovered about her left me stumped. Still, the day hadn't been a total bust. I'd figured out how Con Dreyfuss spent his evenings. And who he'd been spending them with.

Jacob wasn't home yet when I pulled up behind Lisa's car in front of the cannery, and that was fine by me. Although I had absolutely no idea what I was going to say, I'd still rather talk to Lisa alone. I'd had a bit of time to simmer down, and my initial shock at realizing the identity of the mystery man had worn off. I'd also had time to consider the fact that she'd been working up her courage to tell me all this time, and had planned on spilling the beans tonight. Still. What the hell had she been thinking?

I didn't exactly mean to slam the front door, but thanks to an extra nudge from the wind, it sounded as if I did. So much for the subtle approach. Maybe that was for the best. After my meat grinder of a day, the only thing I wanted to do was get all my difficult conversations over with and enjoy one of my precious red pills in peace. I was debating how dickish I'd sound if I opened with, *Okay, so I know about Dreyfuss*, when I swung into the living room and found Lisa slumped at the dining room table, head in hands, poring over a pile of paper. She looked up at me, red-eyed. She'd been crying.

"Are you okay?" I crossed the room in a few steps, then stopped short, not knowing if I was supposed to hug her or pat her shoulder or what, baffled as to what I should do with my hands. "What happened?"

At my inept show of concern, the waterworks started. While Lisa cried, I jammed my hands in my overcoat pockets, ignoring the grittiness in my left pocket that might be spilled salt or might be a sifting of fairy dust I'd managed to summon without meaning to. Lisa swiped brutally at her eyes with a soggy wad of tissue, then blew her nose, took a centering breath, and said, "I gotta tell you something."

"Okay." I pulled a chair around and sat so I was facing her with my knees brushing her thigh. Luckily, her fiddling with the wet tissue excused me from needing to decide if holding her hands was expected of me or not. "It's, y'know..." I decided not to blurt out what I already knew. If I was lucky, maybe Dreyfuss would break it off with her once he realized I was so desperate for reds, he didn't need to use Lisa to get to me. "Whatever it is. It's fine."

"The guy I've been seeing..." she chewed on the end of the sentence for a while, then finally said, "it's Constantine."

And there it was. "I suspected."

It sounded gentler than *I know*. Still, she was surprised. "He didn't tell you. You didn't see us together." She didn't bother hiding the fact that her mental process had become one giant sí-no. "Anyway, it doesn't matter, it's not important. He says his office is haunted for sure—and not the repeaters. Something was *on* him. What the hell was it?"

"Well..." shit, where to begin? "Sometimes, when a GhosTV is playing, I see things in the astral or wherever. Not ghosts." I could tell that if the word *jellyfish* left my mouth, she'd freak. "Energy, maybe. I don't think it's dead. I don't think it was ever a person."

"He had an astral thing on his head?"

"It wasn't..." I held up my hands and flapped them in the air above me. "Not *directly* on his head." I figured I'd better not mention the goopy tethers, either. "In the general vicinity."

Lisa frowned and thought, though I couldn't imagine what she might be asking the sí-no now.

"Dreyfuss was the one who jumped to the conclusion there was a ghost on his head." Not that I could blame him, considering he had three nasty repeaters around his desk and a sentient ghost lurking behind the curtain, and the medium on his payroll thought the Hail Mary involved boxer-briefs. "I tried to tell him, but…" I shrugged.

Lisa's eyes tracked back and forth as she processed my explanation while I looked down at a tear-stained scrawl on a torn sheet of notebook paper.

Entity—yes. Ghost—no. Invisible—yes. Alive—? Sentient—? Evil—?

Ask the sí-no if it was a fingernail demon. Yeah, right. "It seemed to react when he bit his nails."

She stared at her inconclusive notes, then said, "Oh."

"Maybe it was like…a habit?"

"Oh my God."

I put Lisa's notes in a pile, tamped the paper edges into alignment, then began nudging the loose puzzle pieces underneath into an even row. "I got rid of it."

She nodded.

"Come on," I said, "you should be glad. Since his cuticles gross you out."

She was quiet a long time, staring at the puzzle pieces I was arranging. Finally she said, "He didn't tell you about us?"

"Not exactly. His handwriting did."

"I thought you'd be mad." She considered the statement, then corrected herself. "I *knew* you'd be mad."

I had been. But seeing what a wreck Lisa was over the fingernail demons…well, who the hell am I to judge? "Tell me you gave Dreyfuss a going-over with the sí-no and he's not just interested in your psychic ability, that he's interested in you."

"He is," she whispered.

Dreyfuss was no Mexican firefighter, that's for sure, but… "I guess I can see how he might come off as charming. If you like the wiseass type."

"I wasn't in the market, you know. I figured I was done with men, at least until I sorted out what happened at PsyTrain." But since the two of them had met in Santa Barbara, she explained, he would occasionally consult with her on matters of FPMP intelligence. This was news, but like so much in my life, it didn't exactly surprise me. After all, Lisa never seemed to be hurting for cash, so she'd obviously been working somewhere.

Dreyfuss, being paranoid, would only talk to her in person. He figured it was best to make their meetings look like dates to keep Lisa from attracting any anti-Psych attention. On their third fake date, in a dilapidated movie theatre with sticky floors, Lisa realized Dreyfuss was gazing at her with something more than businesslike interest when the lights came up. She was inclined to brush off the idea that the Regional Director of the FPMP was harboring romantic notions, but she couldn't resist checking in with the sí-no…which confirmed that Con Dreyfuss had indeed taken a shine to her.

I wanted Lisa to be happy, I truly did. If Dreyfuss could survive the sí-no's scrutiny, more power to him. Still, I needed to be clear. "It's really none of my business who you date," I said, "but please…don't discuss me with him, okay? You might trust him, but that doesn't mean I do."

She shook her head sadly. "This isn't about you."

"Sure. And the idea that I claimed he had a ghost on his head randomly popped into your mind."

"But he was really freaked out and…all right. I get it. No talking about Vic." She picked up a piece of grayish jigsaw and snapped it into the background just as Jacob's key turned in the deadbolt. "I hope Jacob takes the news about me and Con as well as you did…but he won't."

I felt bad for her. It must be rough to enter into a conversation knowing it was gonna tank. But I also felt elated for me. Not only had Jacob been in the dark about the Dreyfuss affair, which meant he wasn't hiding anything from me—but I'd also figured it out first. I'd have to do my best not to look smug.

"Maybe you should tell him," Lisa murmured.

In the cannery, sometimes sounds bounce off the floorboards or brick in ways you don't expect, usually sounds you'd been hoping to keep to yourself. This particular utterance was one of those sounds. "Tell me what?" Jacob called from the vestibule.

He found me sitting in my overcoat beside Lisa, who was puffy-eyed and red. Gravely, he repeated, "Tell me what?"

"I'm involved with Con Dreyfuss." Stunned silence. "Dating him," Lisa added, just in case he'd taken her "involvement" in some platonic way.

Jacob's response was low—but thanks to the cannery, it carried. "What are you thinking?"

Clearly the wheels were turning. Lisa was looking hard at the table, and she wasn't working on the puzzle. I scrambled for something to cut the tension and came up empty-handed. Finally Lisa said, "You know what? There's nothing I can say that won't make it worse."

"I maneuver around that guy all day long, he's listening to my phone calls and recording my movements, and now I find out that in the only place I thought I was safe from his psychic *whatever*—my house, my own house—"

"Jacob," I said. "Take a breath."

"I'm not spying on you." Lisa's voice shook.

Jacob said, "Out of every other guy on the planet…you pick Con Dreyfuss?"

"What difference does it make? I would never spy on you. How could you think I—oh. Right. Might as well come right out and say it. Because at PsyTrain I was with Bert. Is that it? I made one bad choice, and now everybody thinks I'm the weak link."

Jacob said, "What I think is that Dreyfuss is manipulative, and you were vulnerable."

Uh oh. Bad choice of words on Jacob's part. Lisa brought out the big ammo. "I'm vulnerable? Who brought home a demon-thing that exploded in his bed? Not me."

"Okay," I interjected. Life was so much easier when we skirted all the ugly topics. "What's done is done. Lisa's personal life is her personal life. Jacob, you work with the guy. At first I was worried about that, but so far it's fine. If Lisa says she's not discussing us with Dreyfuss, I believe her."

Whatever I'd said, it must've been the right thing. The mood lifted tangibly. Lisa took a deep, cleansing breath, then let it out. Jacob's shoulders relaxed. "I'll start dinner," he said, and headed toward the kitchen.

"Good," I said, "we're all good." What a relief. If I was worried about Lisa moving out before, I was twice as leery now, considering where she would end up going if she left anytime in the near future. True, she wouldn't be able to spy on me if she were living with the enemy. But that still meant I'd lose her. The first few weeks of a new boyfriend were always the heady days. Hormones were raging and everyone was on their best behavior. As soon as the initial fervor died down, no doubt Dreyfuss' cockiness would wear thin, and their relationship would shift from the torrid and clandestine affair it currently was to that awkward thing they'd both just as soon forget. Best not to be stuck living in the guy's apartment when that happened.

I glanced over at her to reassure myself that we were all good, and light glinted off the tiny decorative key she'd taken to wearing around her neck. If at any point I spotted a matching lock somewhere on Dreyfuss, I wouldn't be able to stop myself from hurling. "As long as you don't rush into anything."

"Rush into what?"

"Just...anything."

She frowned. "Like what?"

Uh oh. "Take it slow. That's all I'm saying."

"You moved in with Jacob like a week after you hooked up. So it's okay for you, but not me?"

"Look, that's not what I...you don't need to move."

"I'm not talking about moving anywhere. But I don't need to 'take it slow' either. Con says he loves me."

A startling crash made us both jump. Jacob muttered something, then squatted down to begin picking up broken shards of ceramic. My heart was pounding...and I told myself it was just the dropped plate I was reacting to. With Lisa watching me very closely, I kept my face cop-blank.

She didn't need to read my expression to know how I felt about her announcement, though. Not when she had the sí-no. She squared her shoulders, looked me in the eye, and told me, "And I love him too."

Although sound carries unbelievably well in the cannery, at that moment, you could've heard a pin drop. I grasped for some remark that would make it all better—a well-timed quip like the folks on sitcoms always seem to make. A wry comment to smooth everything out and return everything to the status quo, so anyone who'd missed an episode wouldn't feel lost when they tuned in next week. Unfortunately, our lives kept getting messier, and no one-liner, no matter how witty, would sweep that mess under the carpet.

Jacob flung half a broken plate into the trash. It hit with a thunk that made me flinch. "I'm gonna grab some takeout," he announced.

"Wait." Lisa stood. "Stay. I'm going out. This is your place, you shouldn't have to leave. You two want to talk. And I have things I need to do."

I said we should all just calm down and order some pizzas, but that suggestion was about as effective as it'd been the last time I'd floated it. Lisa grabbed her purse and her coat, and was out the door in less than a minute. Jacob didn't come out from behind the kitchen bouquet until she was gone. Although he was still wearing his distinctly-unhappy face, having the space to talk to me in private took some of the edge off him. "You never even got a chance to take off your coat," he said, offering me a hand up from the dining room table. I took it, since it seemed preferable to heaving myself back onto my feet of my own volition. But then I saw his expression shift when he touched my hand. "It's freezing."

I sighed.

He didn't let go, and I didn't make any effort to hide it. Not from him.

He took my frigid hand in both of his, tenderly, and cupped it to his face. The five o'clock shadow on his warm cheek felt rough and familiar. He held my hand there, saying nothing. I stayed quiet too. Maybe I didn't know exactly what we were communicating, and maybe I couldn't quite name this mood, but I knew that the last thing I wanted to do was kill it.

Holding my hand still, he turned his face so his lips grazed my palm, and he blew. His hot breath tickled my palm, but despite the fact that it sent shivers down my spine, I didn't pull away. My fingertips nestled in his goatee. He blew again…or maybe it was the ghost of a kiss. For the first time that day, I allowed the thick barrier of white light I'd been lugging around to drop.

"It's not warming up." His lips caressed my palm as he spoke, and his goatee tickled.

At least it wasn't leaking.

Since I'd spent my day sweating through my shirt, which left me feeling generally clammy and rank, I attempted to warm up with a shower. Jacob followed me into the bathroom, though he sensed that I wanted the whole spray to myself and waited while I hosed off. It wasn't unheard of for us to talk around the sound of running water, either. Though we needed to speak loudly enough to be heard through the frosted glass, it provided some illusion of camouflage.

"I'm not mad at Lisa," Jacob said. Could've fooled me. "It's just that she's so damn young, and I don't want her to make the same mistakes I did. I think back about how I was at that age. Thought I knew everything."

"And you've changed how, exactly?"

He lobbed a bar of soap over the shower door. It bounced off my shoulder. "You couldn't tell me a damn thing. I knew better. Even when I started sleeping with my Criminal Psych professor."

"Undergrad?"

"Grad."

That was marginally less creepy. I've seen pictures of Jacob in grad school. Once he'd shaved off his eighties mustache, he had a smooth baby face that was all smoldering eyes and lush lips. Biggish hair, too, but that was par for the course. I can't say I blamed the naughty professor for wanting to hit that. "So how old was he?"

"He said he was thirty-eight—but I'm guessing he lied."

"I can't imagine what the two of you had to talk about when you weren't bonking. And don't tell me Criminal Justice."

"That's exactly it. We didn't actually have much in common. At the time, though, I didn't see it."

Okay, that was encouraging. What could Lisa possibly have in common with Dreyfuss? Presumably, sex—which I really didn't want to imagine. And his whole fetish for ethnic chicks…ditto. And their similar careers. And the fact that they were both off-the-chart Psychs who no one in their right mind could handle dating for long….

Best not dwell on it, since all I could really do was let things run their course. Any attempt to nudge them apart would only make them cling together more stubbornly. I rinsed, turned off the taps, and opened the shower door. Jacob was waiting there with a towel. It would've been more efficient to dry myself, but it felt a lot better when he did it. I pressed my forehead against his shoulder while he ran the towel up and down my back, with more groping than drying. I said, "I guess I should be grateful you never ended up sharing a suburban bungalow with Teacher."

"Turns out, he was married."

Luckily, I was positioned so he didn't see me biting back a laugh. Jacob is utterly sure about everything he does, and nine times out of ten, he's right. But the look on his face when he isn't? Priceless. "I hope you at least aced the class."

"A-*minus*," Jacob grumbled.

I bit the inside of my cheek to wipe the smile off my face.

Good thing, since he was scrutinizing me. "You look a lot better now than you did when I got home." He took my hand and pressed it to his cheek. His face still felt warm against it, but the temperature difference was nowhere near what it had been before. "How do you feel?"

"I'll live. I just need to go easy on the white light."

CHAPTER 19

THE HARDWARE STORE ISN'T EXACTLY my first choice for a scintillating night out. But after my shower I was feeling about as normal as I ever do, and when Jacob said he had a quick errand to run, I opted to go along. We presume both our vehicles are monitored. On the way there, I filled him in on my day—the GhosTV, the repeaters and their dossiers, the white cotton gloves, Richie's Fetal Alcohol Syndrome and even his bratty mood swing. Then Jacob parked at the far end of the lot, and as we walked toward the building at a glacial pace with the wind whistling around us, I whispered all the things I'd kept to myself. Between the fingernail demons and Santiago's third eye, I'm sure Jacob was dying to react. He kept his cool, though. Even when I detailed my conversation with the elusive Dr. Chance.

Once we cleared the automatic doors, Jacob touched my arm with two fingertips to signal me to keep quiet. Surveillance cameras overlooked the doors. I'd always figured them for anti-theft devices. Now, though, it was simply easiest to assume every retail camera in the city led back to the FPMP.

As hardware stores go, it wasn't a very big shop, just a mom-and-pop strip mall operation that had been bought by a national chain some years back. It probably wouldn't last much longer in the face of the mega home centers so big they needed their own zip codes, but it was putting up a good fight. Silver garland was strung through the store and Christmas carols were playing, although the only people planning for December at this point were retail stores and obsessive gift-givers. At least the main display that greeted us still featured Thanksgiving gear: turkey fryers, roasting pans, pilgrim window decals, and of course, snow blowers. I paused and considered how much useful noise a snow blower could potentially generate, and filed that information away for future reference. Sure, I'd probably cut off my own foot if I cranked it up. But Jacob came of age in Wisconsin. He'd know how to work it.

It was a blustery weekday night. There weren't many other customers, just a young Hispanic couple searching for the correct light bulb and a guy in navy work clothes browsing the plumbing section. The only things in the store that interested me were the distinctly non-hardware items. I wondered if the stained acoustical ceiling tiles had ever been white, or how many people actually bought beef jerky from a communal jar on the counter. Jacob paused in front of a section labeled "Door Accessories." It never occurred to me doors might need to accessorize. Among the thresholds and mail slots and replacement screens, Jacob found what he was looking for hanging from a small cardboard tag: a peephole. But instead of heading up to the register with it, he stopped at the key cutting station and rang the service bell.

Since I'm apparently so hyperaware of the location of my keys, I don't own a spare set, though I supposed it couldn't hurt to have one made. However, Jacob didn't pull out his keyring. He fished a loose key out of his pocket instead, which he handed to the pimply-faced Asian kid who'd come to wait on us. "Ten copies," Jacob said.

The kid paled, and stammered, "Ten? I dunno if we have enough blanks."

"Whatever you have, then."

Although the blanks were sorted by brand, number and shape, the clerk felt his way through the spinner as if he needed to touch each key to reassure himself he wouldn't end up cutting a handful of scrap metal. While we watched, he matched the key, compared it to two more blanks, then settled on his first pick. "I have eight."

"That's fine."

"It'll take a while. You can go shop. I'll come find you when they're done."

"We're in no hurry," Jacob replied mildly, but the kid was so flustered that he ended up juggling the blanks in his attempt to keep from dropping them. Jacob wasn't being particularly demanding, but that combo of self-assurance and intense eye contact (the demeanor that made me think naked thoughts) occasionally had the opposite effect, which left people intimidated and cowed. I could see it in their furled shoulders, their darting eye movements, their nervous laughs. Speaking of which…

"I think all my questions are making Laura nervous."

Jacob gave me the "quiet" signal again. The kid plugged a blank into the machine and turned on the power. The grinding squeal that came out of the machine was impressively loud. Jacob motioned for me to continue. I told him about the way she'd been totally cool and deadpan about claiming she was never at the scene of Burke's shooting, while inconsequential parts of the conversation evoked an uncomfortable laugh. "Thing is, I just can't see her pulling the trigger. I spent a good half hour with her at lunch, too. I figured it couldn't hurt to keep her busy while you were digging through her records."

I didn't realize how ham-handedly I'd been fishing for a compliment until Jacob looked more chagrined than impressed. "Actually, I spent the whole day trying to track down Detective Wembly."

"Oh." I'd been hoping my cloak-and-dagger routine would yield better results. I'm guessing his secret agent moves didn't turn up anything we could use, either. Otherwise he would have mentioned it by now. "What did you find?"

"Nothing." He gathered his thoughts to the whine of the key machine. "A whole lot of nothing, though. A suspicious amount of nothing. It's as if he never existed. No record of him at the Twentieth—but I remember the name. I can't put it to a face, but it's an unusual name, and I've definitely heard it before. I'll bet we've both met him at some PsyCop function, or at least seen him. If Warwick says Detective Wembly worked at the FPMP, I tend to believe him. Plus there were a lot of redacted records right around three, four years ago. And the weird thing? The subject wasn't blacked out…but the investigator was."

We pondered our best bet at finding a photo of Wembly to jog our memories, figuring one of us must know someone who knew someone at the Twentieth—someone who hadn't cleared the memory card on their digital camera in a while.

"And what about Laura?" Was it insensitive of me to bring up the possibility of paranormal creepy-crawlies so soon after we were reminded of the unfortunate fate of Jacob's duvet? "As sick as it might seem, I'd rather hear that whatever I talked to downtown, whatever Burke saw, it wasn't really Laura at all."

We clammed up as we strolled past the surveillance cameras on our way back to the parking lot. As Jacob sprinkled the freshly cut keys into the steel trash can just outside the doorway with a surprisingly loud metal-on-metal clatter, he said through the noise, "I guess I'll need to prove it *wasn't* Laura Kim."

Buying the peephole was one thing. Installing it was something else entirely, because installation involved tools. Tools involved the basement. Looming shadows. The smell of old concrete and new rubber flooring. A GhosTV lurking under the stairs. I stopped short of the tool collection and stared at the blank screen. There was a vague plan taking shape, but for that plan to work, I'd need to figure out a better storage plan for the TV. If the GhosTV spooked me, I wondered how Lisa felt about it. She'd actually been stuck in an astral nightmare for days—and this dusty console was a vivid reminder. Me, I'd just seen some stretched heads. Which was pretty bad, too.

I couldn't leave the GhosTV sitting in the alleyway for any ol' passerby to scoop up. It was too valuable to destroy. And giving it back to Dreyfuss would be an admission of my fear. Plus, while I hoped the time would never come, I might need the damn thing someday.

Jacob veered around me and headed for his tool chest, unaware of my conundrum. He opened a red metal drawer full of tool-things, then handed me the hang tag. "What size drill bit?"

I held our soon-to-be peephole up to the light—the print was minuscule—and read the directions three times to ensure I was telling him the right thing. "Half inch."

He began plundering the drawer.

I focused on the finished part of the basement, the home gym. It didn't see use every day, but I gathered it served its purpose. He never came upstairs looking twitchy from being underground. I said, "I was thinking…we could put in another bathroom down here, right? And extend the drop ceiling, make up a couple of finished rooms…." I wrapped my arms across my stomach and shivered.

"You mean, a bedroom?"

I nodded. "Something nice. Like a little apartment."

Hesitantly, I moved deeper into the murk of the basement's unfinished half. There were no vermin currently in residence, at least not of the rodent variety. Jacob had located and grouted holes fastidiously, and we hadn't snapped a trap in months. The spiders could be startling…but that's what white walls were for. To discourage anything creepy from sneaking up. It was hard to imagine fresh white drywall. Difficult to picture ceiling tiles and laminate flooring. Right now, my senses were too busy screaming "basement" to properly visualize a private guest suite, a place Lisa might consider staying in the long-term.

"Grab that tape measure," Jacob said.

As I'm not what you'd call "handy," I needed to ask myself, "Does he mean that thing?" until I came upon the square metal item that registered as a tape measure. That's probably how working the sí-no felt. Not as natural as knowing something immediately, but finding information accessible after a small lag and a moment's consideration. I grabbed the tape measure and followed him to the stairs. He paused at the foot. "You're talking about a real bedroom for Lisa. Even though she's with…him?"

"I give their couplehood another few weeks. A month, tops."

"You sound pretty sure."

"I just spent the week working with the guy," I said. "It was like being sandblasted with sarcasm."

Jacob stared down at the hang tag, turning it in his hands. I waited while he gathered his thoughts. Once he did, he said, "I can't believe I didn't see it."

"You were too wrapped up in Burke's shooting."

"It seems so obvious, in retrospect. There were shopping bags from a jeweler in his trash, but I figured he'd bought another new watch. And I thought the florist was another one of his surveillance partners."

"It probably is. That, and a safe zone where he doesn't have to worry about dead spies." Usually, I'd add a remark about it being simpler to abstain from killing people if you didn't want the deceased to listen in… but I found I was no longer certain where Dreyfuss' actions ended and the ghosts began. Especially not if Lisa was willing to trust him. Sure, she was probably blind to his faults now, in the throes of her infatuation. But at the beginning, before they fell for each other, back when he was just the FPMP guy with a smart remark for every occasion? She must have run him past the sí-no then. Or maybe that's just what I wanted to believe.

I wasn't entirely sure of Jacob's commitment to keeping Lisa in the cannery until he drilled the hole through our front door. When I suggested we put it at her eye-level rather than ours, he agreed without a moment's hesitation. Then I had to pretend I wasn't feeling choked up and mushy by turning away and reading the minute print on the hang tag again.

Ten o'clock rolled around, then eleven, and still no Lisa. Finally, against my protests, Jacob texted her to see what time she thought she'd get home. She replied within a few minutes, which was good. But her reply was, "Late…don't wait up. Cya." We both overanalyzed it, of course. Jacob said he thought it sounded friendly. I said nothing—because the Lisa-height peephole was probably too little, too late, and I felt my best friend slipping away into the clutches of Con Dreyfuss.

It looked like she'd come home during the night, since the shoes she'd been wearing were now beside the door, and there were a few long hairs in the bathroom sink. But by the time we were up and around, she was already gone. I even waited 'til the last possible moment to leave, more than fifteen minutes after Jacob, and still, no Lisa. Finally I gave up and headed to the FPMP myself.

I nearly missed the garage ramp. Again. Hard to say if Dreyfuss would admit there was some kind of psychic camouflage on it, or if my brain simply had a few fried synapses in the spot that should recognize the building. After circling the block I'd so recently walked on foot, though, I made it to the elevator bank with no time to spare.

"Hold the elevator!"

I squelched the impulse to "accidentally" nudge the close-button. Not only was I on time by the skin of my teeth, but now, embarking on my fourth day at the FPMP, my patience for Richie was paper thin. I'd done some research on Fetal Alcohol Syndrome while I was waiting up for Lisa, though, which made me feel guilty for getting so frustrated with him. I stuck out my foot and bounced the doors open.

He jogged in from the parking garage and said, "Thanks." It was a far cry from the enthusiastic handshake he usually greeted me with—then again, his hands were occupied with a cardboard tray that held four tall drinks. He saw me eyeballing them and said, "There's a new smoothie cart down on Hubbard."

Business couldn't be very brisk, given that it was November, a particularly dank November. And we were basically in the middle of nowhere—bordered by warehouses and storage facilities, highway ramps and a rail yard.

"By the gym," he said.

I tried to imagine who'd travel to a neighborhood like this to work out. "Oh."

"I got one for you."

"Oh." In light of the unexpected gesture, I felt like even more of an ass for dreading his inevitable monologue about football statistics and the unsuitability of my car. He held up the tray and nodded toward the tall cups, and I took one. "Thanks."

"Chocolate malt," he said.

I nodded and wondered if I was supposed to give him a few bucks for it. But then I decided that buying a bunch of smoothies for his coworkers might be akin to inviting strangers off the street to come join him in his skybox. A way for him to feel generous. Or maybe to buy people's friendship and approval.

On the fifth floor, he marched up to Laura's desk and said, "I got you a smoothie."

She looked surprised, but she took it and thanked him.

"Aren't you going to drink it?"

"I just brushed my teeth." She set it on her desk. "I'll try it in a while."

"It's chocolate malt." He squinted at the smoothie on Laura's desk. I felt condensation bead the outside of plastic cup I was currently holding. Keeping his eyes on Laura, Richie found the straw of the closest smoothie with his mouth and took a long sip. "It's really good."

"Great," Laura said. "Thanks. You know I love chocolate." Richie stared at her a moment longer, and she added, "I can't wait to drink it. Later."

As he realized she wasn't about to suck it down on the spot to appease him, his mood curdled. He made a sniffing sound, turned, and stalked off toward his office.

Who knew he'd still be in a snit about yesterday's exorcism getting interrupted? "That was weird," I said.

"I probably shouldn't drink it anyway. Certain kinds of fruit enzymes trigger my headaches. Even if this is mostly chocolate and yogurt, there's no guarantee the blender was clean to start with."

"He seemed awfully eager for you to drink it." Maybe he'd hocked a loogie in there. I peeled open my lid and peered in. Now that I'd thought of the phlegm ball, there'd be no drinking of mine, either. I took both smoothies and dumped them down the lounge drain, then reported back to Laura. "Can you let Dreyfuss know I'm ready to sweep his office again?"

"Not today." she leaned forward and dropped her voice. As if that would make any difference. "The Metropolitan Correctional Center finally agreed to let a team re-process Roger Burke's cell, and also the location of his shooting. We've been trying to get a team in there for months. It could be the big break in Agent Marks' case." Well, the office repeaters weren't going anywhere, I supposed. "Any physical evidence would be long gone. But psychic evidence…maybe you'll get lucky."

My gut wanted to like Laura, so I figured I should give her a chance put some kind of spin on her story—to let me know she'd been privy to information that absolutely necessitated Burke's elimination. Or imply that she'd been coerced. "If I did happen to get lucky…any idea what I might find?"

"You'll figure out whoever did this. We'll all feel a lot safer once we know."

I held her gaze even though I was practically squirming with the desire to drop it, and tried to will her to come clean. She looked from eye to eye, reading me, hopefully struggling with the urge to tell me whatever it was she'd been holding back, so I stayed strong, and I forced myself to wait. Finally, she said, "If anyone can figure this out, it's you."

What was that supposed to mean?

CHAPTER 20

WE CONVENED IN A SMALL meeting room: me, Dreyfuss, Richie, Jacob and Bly. I kept my eyes peeled for Dr. Chance, but she didn't put in an appearance. Not that I knew of, anyway.

Bly's shaved head gleamed under the recessed lighting. Richie had dressed marginally better than usual in charcoal and black, and he'd even buttoned his shirt correctly and tucked it in all the way around. Jacob was his usual cool, composed self. Dreyfuss looked a bit worse for wear: bleary-eyed and subdued. I did my best not to picture why he'd been up so late with Lisa.

At least I didn't need to endure any of his smarting off. With tasks to assign, he was all business. "Here's the deal," he said. "We've got two mediums on the team, a Stiff and an empath."

Wait, who's the…? I looked Agent Bly. He was watching me blandly. I tamped down my surprise as best I could—since, apparently, he could feel it.

"No exorcisms today, no matter how tempting it might be. Treat anything you find, physical or otherwise, as evidence. Leave it intact." While Dreyfuss outlined a schedule and ran through the areas where we'd been granted special access, I wrestled with the knowledge that Agent Bly could pluck the state of my emotions right out of my head, and no amount of times tables or nursery rhymes would make a damn bit of difference. Worse yet, it was possible my mental gymnastics around Dr. Santiago had all been for nothing. Maybe she was an empath too, and all I'd managed to do was generate a big wave of anxiety in her presence.

As we headed toward the car, Dreyfuss hung back with Bly for a whispered conversation. Cripes, he couldn't even be bothered to be subtle about telling Bly to spy on me? Dreyfuss retreated to his office and Bly caught up with the group. "What?" he asked me.

I gave a sullen shrug.

Jacob glanced back over his shoulder but kept his mouth shut. At least he couldn't be read by Bly. In fact, knowing Jacob like I did, I probably understood him better. I took some comfort in that.

"You've got your orders," I told Bly. "I get it. Nothing personal."

He didn't look particularly concerned. "Not everything's about you, Detective."

Maybe not. But it was a lot safer to assume it was.

I stared at the back of Bly's shaved head as he drove us downtown, predictably, in a humongous black Lexus SUV. I expected Richie to point out a dozen automotive features I didn't care about. He was still out of sorts, though, and he spent the ride to the prison staring out the window. Jacob and Bly discussed possible angles of approach. I kept my mouth shut and tried to map the location of the bald spot that caused Bly to embrace the clippers…but I couldn't find one. The stubble on the back of his head was full coverage.

Back in the day, the only guys with full heads of hair who would opt to shave it off were skinheads. The shaved head was probably still some kind of fashion statement now, though in my mind, it didn't exactly go with the dark suit. I could see Bly buzzing himself bald as an intimidation tactic. Or maybe hair interfered with his emotional radar.

I would expect to be quietly melting down over the idea of heading to a federal prison without so much as a gram of Auracel in my system, but it was actually comforting to be accompanied by three other Psychs, even if Richie was inept, and even if Bly was only there to get a read off me and report back to Dreyfuss.

Empaths are pretty common. It's estimated that a percentage of the population with high social aptitude is actually empathic to some degree.

In giving us our assignments, Dreyfuss hadn't specified any levels—but if he had, I'm guessing Bly's rank would've been impressively high.

For the most part, empaths don't spook me. At least…they didn't. Not until Richie reminded me that a strong enough empath can actually project an emotion—and that it was possible Stefan had been doing just that. Back then, I hadn't known enough to protect myself, either. Now I knew. So I was hoarding white light like it was going out of style, all the way downtown.

Usually, when Zigler and I walked through a scene, it was a pretty low-key affair. We'd find our grid. I'd give him any impressions I formed. We'd leave. He'd type up our findings and due process would ensure whatever we found exonerated the perp. But as we pulled up to the MCC and I got a load of the setup, I realized our investigation at the prison was a much bigger deal.

What I initially thought was a construction barrier actually turned out to be a set of corrugated metal walls put up to shield us from the rest of the world while we combed the very spot Roger Burke went down. It would have taken a lot of pull to have a safety box built on a morning's notice. Then again, it took a lot of pull to commandeer a skybox on Thanksgiving.

The thing was, if anyone had consulted with me, I could've saved them a lot of work by mentioning there'd be nothing in that particular location to find. I'd seen Roger Burke's spirit whisked away before his corpse started to cool. I'm not sure if I believe in hell. But if it does exist, I think that's where he is right now, stoking the big furnaces and sharpening the pitchforks.

Jacob spoke to the guard in charge—military, very intimidating, though not intimidating to him. I watched the way they looked at Jacob, too. His air of entitlement, his calm ease, his whole attitude—coupled with the way he actually looked and listened to everyone he came in contact with—earned him the instant respect of every manly man who crossed his path. I stood up straighter in hopes of being categorized with Jacob and Bly, rather than Richie…who'd undoubtedly be asking some stone-faced soldier what kind of car he drove and offering an unsolicited critique. But when I risked a sidelong glance Richie's way, he was just watching and waiting. What a relief.

The guard escorted us in. It felt strange in the cube. Maybe a bit claustrophobic. A fresh tape outline had been placed where Burke had fallen, and an evidence marker showed where the slug had lodged in the side of the building after it exited Burke's skull. Like the rat-holes in our basement, the granite was now patched. I'd expected the enclosure to be open to the sky, but no, of course not. Not with all the El tracks and high-rises around it affording a perfect place for a sniper to set up shop. "What type of gear do you need?" Jacob asked.

"Obviously I can't work without my incense and whatnot," Richie said.

"But that's exorcism gear," Jacob said. "Dreyfuss said to treat it as a crime scene and leave paranormal evidence intact."

"Well if you know everything," Richie snarled, "then why'd you bother asking?"

Jacob must've been briefed on the Fetal Alcohol Syndrome. Still, I imagine it cost him to keep a straight face. He motioned to a pair of guards, who wheeled over something heavy covered with a tarpaulin. Something trailing a very long extension cord. The hair on my forearms prickled even as the object was revealed.

The GhosTV guts from Dr. K's lab had been mounted in a plexi box like a specimen in a museum. Richie's eyes went wide, then he looked away quickly as if he hadn't noticed. He must know what it was. As the organization's top medium, he'd probably sat through some sort of experiment in the lab…although I'd wager he was pretty bummed when he realized it didn't get ESPN.

"Maybe you should do the honors," Jacob told me. It made sense, since I was the only one getting a useful boost out of it, but I couldn't help but notice Richie staring at me disconcertingly as I approached. I did my best to chalk it up to his vision issues, checked the settings, found the power switch and turned it on.

A moment later, a red network of veins popped up in Jacob's forehead. I was especially curious what Richie would look like, since my enhanced vision didn't seem to work in the mirror, and I wasn't sure what I looked like when my subtle bodies were on display. He crossed his arms and looked at me. His arms left tracers behind. Not too scary—I could handle that. Then Agent Bly turned to face us, and he looked like the Visible Man.

At least now I could match the visual to the talent. My brain interpreted empathy as thin skin. Literally.

Bly looked shocked, in a way that only someone with no eyelids can look. Shocked, and eerily eager. The tip of his nose was gone, and the absence of lips made it look as if he was grimacing. Under the influence of a GhosTV, I'd seen other thin-skins before. But despite the missing nose, Bly looked more like himself than the others had. Must've been the shaved head. The muscles in his forehead came down at an angle from either side where they attached to the top of the skull, forming a V in the middle that echoed his stubble hairline.

That meant Dr. Santiago was likely a telepath, so my times tables and earworms had probably been effective in shielding my true thoughts. And also that she probably thought I was either really clever, or batshit crazy. Now if only I could get Bly out of the way so I didn't have to dwell on moderating my emotions. "It'll be better to have the mediums walk the grid alone," I said. "Less interference in the subtle bodies."

If Bly detected my bullshit-generating emotion in play, he didn't let on. He and Jacob stepped outside the corrugated metal box, leaving me alone with good ol' Einstein in the very spot I'd seen Roger Burke die.

Richie put his hand on my forearm. With all the articles I'd read fresh in my mind I now knew he was dealing with compromised motor skills, so I figured he was steadying himself. But we weren't exactly walking, or doing anything else that should make him unsteady. Just standing there. He said, "Thanks. The other agents can be a pain in the ass."

I was tempted to point out that Jacob was *my* pain in the ass, but it wasn't worth getting into. Not when Richie didn't really understand half of what was said to him, and laughed along to cover for it. Especially when it might lead to some conversation where he'd imply I was secretly straight all these years and I just didn't know it. I shrugged off his hand

and said, "Okay, how do you want to do this?"

He visually scanned the enclosure in a long, slow sweep and said, "Are you getting any impressions?"

I sighed. "No."

"We'll adjust the settings."

"The settings are fine." I walked a grid just to be sure. Once I'd found nothing there, I sucked in a bunch of white light and focused hard on the vague tape outline of Burke's body. Nothing there, either. I even tried mentally calling to him, since I was full of light and GhosTV signals. I wasn't entirely sure what I expected to discover even if I did get to speak to him. It wasn't as if I'd ever had success in trapping him in a lie. I wasn't up for the mental sparring, but if I was lucky, maybe I could see if he had any insight as to why Laura Kim, of all people, would want him dead. Or maybe I could figure out why he'd want to frame her. Burke never showed up, though, so I was spared the effort of teasing out his truth from his lies.

With nothing happening on the spirit front I shifted my focus to the physical, though I'd been trying so hard, it took a moment to reorient myself. I was adjusting my internal faucet when Richie grabbed me by the arm again and said, "What are you doing right now?"

Since when was he Mr. Feely? I peeled out of his grasp. "Normal centering stuff. You know, like The Nun taught us. White light. Why—do I look any different to you?"

He squinted at me and shrugged.

Once I thought about it, I realized his learning style might be more kinesthetic than visual, since one of his many issues was compromised vision. But since I didn't want him grabbing me again, I decided not to mention it.

"You're not sensing any activity?" he asked. "Not even with the tuner activated?"

"There's really nothing here to sense."

"We need to calibrate the settings." What did he think it was, a car engine? I must've been looking at him funny, because he added defensively, "That's what Dr. K would do. Hee-hee."

Since I wanted to figure out what happened to Roger Burke as much as anybody, I hunkered down in front of the set and nudged the dials one way, then the other, using the tracers my hand generated as a guide.

"That's how you gauge the signal?" He was right on top of me. "Why?"

I sidled over to put a little space between us. "I get a little, uh, visual disturbance when…" now he'd probably think I was mocking his eyesight problem. "Just a small…it's not important. The settings are fine. But there's really nothing to see here. This particular ship has sailed."

He half-turned and gazed down at the tape outline. "That's a shame."

It was. But maybe it was for the best that I wasn't dealing with Burke himself. Even if I managed to call him back, he'd probably manage to muddy the waters worse than they already were. Criminals are notorious gossips, though. Secrets are one of their main forms of currency. Hopefully we'd find someone inside who knew why a hit was carried out on Roger Burke, and who might have ordered it.

Sure, I'd been inside the Metropolitan Correctional Center before. Seeing the visiting areas is one thing. Having access to the cell block is another. I was allowed to keep my sidearm, as were Jacob and Agent Bly. After reading up on Richie's condition, I was doubly thankful that he'd never been issued a service weapon.

I'd found the metal box outside claustrophobic. The six by ten cells, by comparison, were suffocating. Two people lived in this closet of a room, day in, day out? The stainless steel toilet was right there in the open, which made me clench all over at the thought of taking a dump where a cellmate could see and smell it. Worse, the sink was built into the side of the toilet, and a drinking fountain was fixed in the sink.

I'm no germophobe. In fact, rimming my boyfriend is my idea of a good time. Still, I suspected I'd expire from dehydration before I drank water that shot up from the back of a toilet.

If shitting was bad, sleeping in the cell would be no treat, either. The bunk beds were fixed to the wall, a pair of narrow metal shelves that screamed out "morgue." You couldn't even call the mattress they held a futon. It was more like a flimsy pad. A pair of drawers was suspended from the lower bunk, a small desk-like shelf jutted from the wall, and a backless concrete column of a "chair" rose from the floor before it.

Among all these details—the close quarters, the profound and dehumanizing sparseness, the toilet drinking fountain—what struck me the most was the window. I'm no architecture buff, but I do know the MCC caused a big stir in the seventies when it was constructed. The building itself is a big pointy triangle, and the windows are vicious slits. From the outside, the rows of vertical window recesses make the building face look like a cuneiform tablet, but from inside the cell, the single window dominated the room. It was a bizarre postmodern slot, taller than me, maybe seven feet tall…and only five inches wide. How many inmates lay tucked into their morgue shelves on their hard, thin pads, staring at that awful slot, wishing they could extrude themselves out through it, into freedom?

Then again, how many scumbags who bludgeon their girlfriend to death with a dog dish get to skip the penitentiary simply because some of their evidence was gathered by a PsyCop?

Maybe life wasn't always fair…but for the inmates of the MCC, their living conditions were some kind of payback. I reminded myself of that as I steeled myself to step through that reinforced door. "I'll go first," I said, thinking I should get it over with before I changed my mind. I wouldn't have minded Jacob being in there with me, but if I suggested pairing off, chances were I'd end up with Bly. He didn't look like he'd been flayed anymore, so the GhosTV must be out of range. But he was still a big, square guy, and the potential of him following me into that cell had "Camp Hell flashback" written all over it. "It's pretty tight," I said very, very calmly. "You guys stay out in the hall while—"

"We can fit," Richie said, and shoved me into the cell.

I spun around on him, flinching, and snapped, "What the hell is your problem?"

"Hee-hee. What's wrong…scared?"

Calm down, I told myself. *He's mentally handicapped.* Or differently abled. Or whatever. "You don't just go shoving people into a prison cell." With some effort, I lowered my voice. "Especially after what we've been through at Camp Hell."

"What do you mean?" he asked, the picture of innocence.

I sucked white light and quelled the urge to whap him upside the head. Despite his crazy-making presence, I should be able to perform. I must have managed to absorb some coping skills during my time on the force, after all, some way to compartmentalize the anxiety until it was safe enough to unwind. Jacob was poised in the doorway, ready to drag Agent Oblivious out of the cell if I gave the word, but I indicated with a small shake of my head that it was okay. I was okay. Being in Roger Burke's cell was a rare opportunity. I wasn't going to squander it by letting Richie throw me off my game. Closing my eyes, I took a deep, centering breath.

It smelled like feet. I wasted no time in exhaling.

"Haven't you ever been in a jail cell before?" Richie said. "You're supposed to be a cop."

I let the cop part of the statement slide, since he was obviously trying to get back at me for interrupting yesterday's exorcism, and instead said, "Jail, lockup…that's different from prison. Prison is long-term. Decades. Life." I snapped on a latex glove and ran my finger along the edge of the bed. It was round, blunted down to prevent anyone from getting hurt. Still, no doubt a sufficiently motivated cellmate could use it to cave in a skull. I guess there wasn't any good way to make a prison cell inmate-safe without removing every last thing in it and making every room single-occupancy. And then some inmate rights group would complain about the solitary confinement and sensory deprivation constituting cruel and unusual punishment.

"Kind of makes you think about the 'guest suites' back at the FPMP," I said.

"What do you mean?"

"They're miles apart in terms of accommodations. But maybe that only means it would take longer to lose it in a nicer cell."

Richie clutched my forearm and said, "What difference does it make if someone's sitting in a cell or a mansion? We're only as free as we can be in our own heads."

An unpleasant sensation twinged up my arm, like hitting on a shred of tin foil with my molars, and I pulled away roughly enough to let him know I didn't appreciate all the manhandling. "Quit touching me, okay? I need to concentrate."

CHAPTER 21

ASIDE FROM THE STRIKING AROMA of old socks, Roger Burke's cell was clean. Maybe that was for the best. If there'd been a repeater in residence, it wouldn't have supplied me with any useful information. And if there'd been a sentient ghost lingering around, I would have exposed the extent of my ability to Richie and Bly by talking to it. Seeing Jacob's eyes, the longing look he cast on the door of the cell, wrenched my heart. If we couldn't get to the bottom of Burke's final mind-game, he'd be stuck squandering all his FPMP time trying to solve a puzzle with key pieces that were long since lost.

Agent Bly said, "We should see if the staff would let us join them for lunch." When he piped up with that suggestion, I realized he hadn't said much. Maybe it was Jacob's investigation, but Bly had been an FPMP agent longer than him. Richie actually had seniority…but obviously, his opinion didn't carry much weight unless it had to do with cold spots or football.

Some phone calls were made and lunch was confirmed. While the MCC guards didn't have any say as to where we were allowed to go, there was nothing written in stone about them needing to go over and above to accommodate us, and certainly nothing forcing them to have a deep heart-to-heart chat with us over our lousy sandwiches and vending machine chips. Sure, they'd all done their jobs. Burke had made it out through the facility's front doors alive. But my experience with the people in these types of professions is that they give the facts and leave it at that, for fear of bringing down some kind of recrimination on their own heads. So it floored me when the guard and the nurse we broke bread with were downright friendly.

Don't get me wrong—I know exactly how charming Jacob can be when he sets his mind to it. But before the sandwiches were even unwrapped, these guys opened up to him like long lost brothers. The guard said, "I dread getting an ex-cop on my cellblock. Fucking dread it." He was a middle-aged Latino guy with "don't fuck with me" written all over him. "But Burke could handle himself, and there was something about him… the other inmates took to him a lot better than I thought they would. He spent as much time as he could in the library, trying to figure out how to get off. He probably told a few of the other ones he'd help them get off, too."

I'd wager he didn't mean "get off" in the porno sense, given that Burke would rather cut off his own dick than let another guy handle it.

I took a bite of my sandwich, an institutional approximation of a BLT that tasted like the plastic wrap. The bread was spongy, the lettuce was soggy, the tomato was crunchy, and the bacon—if that's even what it was—had the consistency of beef jerky. The meatlike-substance was so bad that even Richie the carnivore peeled open his spongy bread and picked it off. Then he tried a bite of the veggie mush-and-mayo sandwich and opted to not eat it at all. Jacob was probably crying inside while he ate, but he didn't show it. The prison staff seemed accustomed to the cuisine. "However Burke finally worked it for himself," the guard said, "however he got his sentence overturned, looks like it didn't pan out too good for him after all."

The nurse was a younger guy, tough, black, and just as big and imposing as the guard. "Even if he stayed," the nurse said, "there's no guarantee he would've been safe. Couple months later, flu ripped through the inmates. Took out a half dozen guys in his cellblock. Makes you wonder about the hand of God. Maybe when your time is up, nothing you can do to get out of it."

I was well aware of the mortality rate of the latest flu outbreak. We'd had our share of cases in the Fifth Precinct's residents…though the cause of death was plain enough that they didn't need me to confirm it. I said, "It must've been brutal to contain it here."

"You got that right," the nurse agreed. "Keep everything as clean as you can, don't matter. Whatever's catching, it spreads."

"The inmates who passed…any of them friendly with Burke?" I asked.

The guard ran through his mental roster of recently deceased inmates. "Could've been. Like I said, he got along a lot better than you'd expect."

"And did the flu patients die here, or were they transported elsewhere?"

"Flu or no flu," the nurse said, "these are dangerous felons. They treat them here, in the infirmary."

I looked up and met Jacob's eyes, and he rewarded me with the grim shadow of a smile.

Certain types of places just seem like they'd be haunted: cemeteries, abandoned houses, disturbed Indian burial grounds…places people avoid, and places people die. Since plenty of convicts probably have an axe or two to grind, enough unfinished business to cause them to stick around, I figured the Correctional Center's infirmary would be swarming with spirit activity.

So, of course, it was clean.

Jacob and Bly took one of the doctors aside, a greasy looking guy who seemed eager to be distracted from his job. There were a few patients in hospital beds. I wasn't sure if they were as out-of-it as they looked, or if they were faking because they had no desire to help the Law. Richie moved slowly up and down the center of the room, scrutinizing each patient in turn. I had no idea why he was insisting on making eye contact. I personally didn't want to interact with any surly, diseased convicts. But I suppose I should've been happy that at least Richie wasn't subjecting us all to his exuberant galumph-walk.

A second doctor sat at a desk toward the back of the room, arms crossed, scowling down at a pile of reports as he read. His demeanor struck me as more serious than the other doctor's, since he was less eager to drop what he was doing, I suppose. Maybe he would have heard something about Roger Burke's final plans. And maybe he'd be willing to tell me about them. Not here—I imagine there'd be a possibility of recriminations for him here. But I could get his number and have Jacob call him later.

"Doctor, I'm Detective Bayne. We're investigating the homicide of former inmate Roger Burke."

To say I startled the guy was an understatement. He nearly fell out of his chair.

I scanned for a name tag, but he wasn't wearing one. Caucasian male, average height and slightly overweight. Age, approximately fifty. Gray hair, a sparse beard, and thick glasses. And he was staring at me like I'd just crept up behind him while he was reading and yelled "Boo!"

Hoping to let the whole startle-thing slide, I acted like I didn't notice the spooked look he was giving me, and said, "Were you acquainted with Burke?"

"What *are* you?" he said.

I got a better look at him and saw his elbow was intersecting the plastic arm of the office chair. The nearest inmate was peering at me through slitted eyelids, probably wondering why I was introducing myself to thin air. I had a potential witness—a really solid ghost—but I also had a bunch of people around me I couldn't simply shoo out of the room. One guy was in traction. Another one was on dialysis. I couldn't exactly give the ghost my business card and have him meet me after work. Could I?

I dug out my paper PsyCop license and placed it on the desk. The doctor didn't try to pick it up, but he bent over it and read. "I've heard of Psychs, but you can see me? Actually see me? And hear me too?" I looked him in the eye and nodded. "I always thought this psychic business was a bunch of malarkey. I see I was entirely wrong. You'd think I would be used to it by now, too." He gave a grumpy huff, crossed his arms and shook his head.

There was a desktop computer and laser printer on the desk. I pulled a pen out of my pocket and a sheet of plain paper from the printer, and began to write.

"Patient records are privileged information," the greasy doctor called from across the room, not seeming particularly alarmed that I was monkeying around on his desk.

"Just making a few notes," I called back.

"That guy's an idiot," the ghost doctor said. "He's given up, you know? Lost his practice and now he's here, and he can't give two shits about the job."

You worked here? I wrote.

"Eight years. Eight long, ugly years."

Did you know Roger Burke?

He stared at the question for a moment, stroking his beard in thought. "The ex-cop. Ex-fed. So that's why the big guns are here."

I'd hardly call myself a "big gun" but luckily I was able to keep my side of the conversation to a minimum.

"I didn't know him," the ghost said. "But I'd heard of him."

Any idea who'd want him dead?

He leaned back in his chair, though his chair didn't move, and folded his hands behind his head in a show of excessive casualness. "They say he kidnapped a cop. Does the cop have an alibi?"

My first impulse was to roll my eyes and assure him I could be fairly certain I knew where that cop was…and then I realized that I was damn lucky I didn't have the FBI breathing down my neck. Lucky…or enjoying the protection of the FPMP. Eager to find something, anything of use, I wrote, *Did any of Burke's pals die in the flu outbreak?*

"Could be. There were a dozen casualties. Me included."

Can I talk to them?

"Can you?" he echoed. "I don't know. They're gone. I moved them along, the ones that were troubled, confused. Hard to explain why I bother, it's just something I feel the need to do. So they're not here."

Talking to spirits who'd moved along would be like trying to call the ghosts back to the repeaters. It seemed possible, but only in theory. I felt like I had access to a telephone, but dialing random numbers was getting me nowhere fast. *Where are they?*

"Wherever it is we go when we finish our earthly business. Heaven?

Reincarnation? The Elysian Fields? Wherever we go, that's where they are. Whether you can call them back from beyond the veil, I have no idea. I'm a man of science, not superstition. It never occurred to me that the afterlife was anything more than a morality tale to keep people from slaughtering each other." He glanced at the guy in traction. The patient was covered in prison ink, including three tattooed teardrops at the corner of his eye—one for every life he'd taken. The dead doctor sighed. "Not a very effective morality tale, either."

While part of me found it encouraging that some dead folks stuck around to keep the spirit population in check, I was disappointed that they seldom told me anything helpful. Maybe Miss Mattie would know how to contact the dead-and-gone. I'd avoided asking her since she'd probably say something cryptic about believing in myself and suggesting I pray, but I supposed I shouldn't presume that's what her answer would be.

Since this dead guy's vocabulary seemed a lot closer to mine (or maybe it's just we were both clearly pessimists) and since he was willing to discuss the matter with me, I tried to puzzle through another question that would help me figure out how to broaden my reach. I was about to write, *Can you hear my thoughts?* when a hand clapped down on the back of the office chair, and now I was the one to nearly jump out of my skin.

Richie.

"We gotta go," he gasped. He was covered in a sheen of sweat. "I need to eat something. I'm going into hypoglycemic shock."

The dead doctor must've been good and startled, too. Now he was gone.

The greasy-looking doctor actually concurred with Richie's diagnosis. I figured Richie had just read the word *hypoglycemic* on someone's chart and repeated it because he wanted to be the center of attention. Luckily, there were glucose tablets at hand. But with the FPMP's house medium cranky, shaky and sweating, the Metropolitan Correctional Center outing Dreyfuss had called in his favors to arrange was over.

On the force, I work weekends as often as not. But today, Friday afternoon meant release from my bondage, and thanks to the FPMP, I could finally appreciate the sentiment behind TGIF.

Lisa was out—I did my best not to visualize with whom—and after wolfing down an early dinner, Jacob and I had become one with the couch. I slouched, sprawling back into the pillows, with his head cradled in my lap. While we hashed over the day, I twirled his short dark hair between my fingers, absently forming small liberty spikes that unraveled as soon as I let go. I looked forward to this one-on-one time all week. I felt like I could relax my shoulders and breathe all the way in. His features softened from not needing to hold his cop-face in place. In the spaces where our words trailed off, the silence was soothing. We had a lot to talk about, though. Even without running the blender. The infirmary convicts must've been on some pretty good opiates; Jacob said he'd found them surprisingly chatty. They told him Roger Burke was always up to something. He was maneuvering to get me to recant my testimony—and if that hadn't paid off, he was hoping to barter some very special technology for his release—the remaining GhosTVs.

Compared to the convicts, the dead doctor hadn't told me anything useful. Still, I recounted the conversation for Jacob the best I could. He listened in that way he does whenever I talk ghost, so focused I can practically hear the gears turning. "We know Burke contacted you about your testimony," Jacob said. "But what about the GhosTVs?"

"I'm under the impression that Dreyfuss scooped them up. Maybe someone was trying to stop him from grabbing them…but who would want to keep the GhosTVs under wraps?" I asked. Anti-Psych groups? The government? I can't imagine how I'd ended up with a console of my very own growing cobwebs in my basement if anyone knew the half of what they could do. The only group that understood the GhosTV's potential was the very organization investigating Burke's shooting. Ironic? Maybe not. It was entirely possible the right hand didn't know that the left was covered in gunshot residue. "We thought it was a good idea for one of us to keep tabs on the FPMP," I said, not getting into the fact that we'd disagreed which one of us was the best guy for the job. "But what if we were wrong? What if we should stay as far away from them as possible? Because people disappear there. Jennifer Chance. Detective Wembly. All those repeaters on the fifth floor. Someone's taking people out—maybe not Dreyfuss, I've got to hope Lisa eliminated Dreyfuss before she shacked up with him—but someone."

Jacob didn't disagree. He thought for a while, then said, "Lisa couldn't eliminate Laura Kim."

"But she didn't say Laura did it, either." The thought of collaring Laura made me sick. I genuinely liked her, and my gut was telling me she acted nothing at all like a killer.

There were all kinds of Psychs on staff, though. What if Laura Kim hadn't voluntarily pulled that trigger? What if a powerful Psych had forced her hand? My fingers stilled mid-twirl. "Jacob…."

"Mm?"

"We need to take a better look at Agent Bly."

CHAPTER 22

I SLEPT LIKE CRAP WITH visions of that morgue-like bunk bed shelf and the toilet fountain dancing in my head. I'd thought murderer-ghosts would be the thing to trigger my anxiety, and instead it had been the sight of the cells that spooked me. I'd waited too long to take a Seconal. If I took one now, I'd sleep my Saturday away. I indulged in a Valium instead. It made my limbs feel heavy, but left my thoughts returning to the sight of the prison cell. I gave up trying to get back to sleep pitifully early. Even so, Lisa had come and gone before I could catch her and question her about Agent Bly. Jacob didn't need to tell me I'd be an idiot to utter his name over any phone, or to even say it outside of one of our safe spaces, without alerting the whole FPMP to the fact that we were on to Bly.

"It's six fucking thirty," I snapped. "Does she have *yoga* on Saturdays?"

Jacob was still in the land of grog. "Actually," he said into his pillow, "I think she does."

There was no guarantee she'd be coming home afterward, either. Armed with a map printed off the Internet, I made my way to Lisa's gym. Since there was only one door, I planned to snag her on the way out and figure out what the hell Agent Bly's game was…and whether he'd managed to force or coerce Laura Kim into killing someone.

I sat in my car sipping my big coffee, watching the windshield gradually fog over. It started around the edges, creeping toward the center, but I had my eyes on the prize. After the email-theft incident, Lisa had opted against joining Jacob's gym, which was full of beefy gay guys who look pretty much like Jacob. In contrast, hers seemed more like a mom-gym, the type of place where even I wouldn't feel too intimidated. The clientele

I saw going in and out was mostly female, and a big poster in the window advertised free child care. The few guys who did show up seemed like they probably had booster seats in the backs of their minivans. I'd spied Lisa's VW in the lot, though the parking places on either side of it were taken. That was fine, as long as I had a good view of the door. There was a yoga session scheduled—I'd checked when I printed off the map—and just as my clock showed 7:33, a stream of mostly women emerged from the front door. They had pastel yoga mats slung over their shoulders and water bottles clutched in their hands. Their body language was easy, as if they all knew each other, holding open doors, chatting amiably, waving goodbye.

Lisa's not one for neon colored workout clothes. She dresses like a cop—navy, black, white, gray, denim and khaki. I recognized her navy jacket right away…and then the crowd shifted, and I recognized a certain atrocious knit hat. And the guy shameless enough to wear it.

Con Dreyfuss strode beside Lisa with a day-glow yellow yoga mat clamped in his armpit and an acid green water bottle with a loop-top swinging from the pinkie of the same hand. He needed to keep his other arm free, obviously, to prevent Lisa from escaping. That's what I told myself. Even though she appeared to be trying to cradle her head on his shoulder as they walked with their arms around each other, swerving like drunks. And even though they were both smiling so brightly they practically lit up the dingy parking lot.

I slid down lower in my seat and squinted, relieved that there hadn't been a spot free near Lisa's Beetle after all. No way she'd miss me if she walked right by my car. I was two rows over, though, and she had no reason to look. She was too wrapped up in Dreyfuss anyway. They paused by her car to disentangle from one another, and he took a moment to tuck a strand of hair behind her ear while he gazed into her eyes and said something that was undoubtedly charming. I'd seen him look that way before, dopy with longing, when his astral body went to sit vigil by a medicated Faun Windsong's bedside, so seeing this side of him didn't shock me now. Like before, he didn't know I'd borne witness to it, so I could hardly tell myself he'd trumped up a show of devotion simply for my benefit.

They climbed into her car. I sighed, and my window grew foggier still. Through the mist, I could tell by the way they bent their heads together, there was spit being swapped between Dreyfuss and my best friend. I watched their silhouettes with a sick fascination, but luckily for me, they kept their makeout session brief. They pulled out of the parking lot and were on their way. I started my engine so my blowers could get to work on clearing my windshield, and I wondered how I might manage to pluck Lisa from Dreyfuss' grasp. Not forever. Even I'm not selfish enough to throw a wrench in the works when she was so obviously happy. But long enough for her to help me figure out how Bly had managed to force Laura to do his dirty work. Even if things like fire ghosts and fingernail demons flew out of left field to shred my carefully constructed scenarios, I had to start somewhere. As a working theory, Agent Bly forcing Laura Kim's hand made more sense than anything else I could think of.

I wasn't super-familiar with the gym's neighborhood, and I discovered a "no left turn" intersection exactly where I'd planned on getting back home by turning left. I toyed briefly with the idea of turning anyway, since all I'd need to do was flash my badge if I got stopped. But the thought of seeing the look on a traffic cop's face as he stared at me and thought, "Really? You?" wasn't exactly appealing. I kept going straight, and then found a snowed-in park at the next point I wanted to turn, and pretty soon I realized I wasn't far from Bob Zigler's house.

Maybe I couldn't question the sí-no about Bly's secret motives, not until Lisa came up for air and detached from Dreyfuss, but Zig would be the perfect person to ask about the missing PsyCop, Detective Wembly. I pulled up and checked out the house. No Impala—he must've still been out of town. I couldn't exactly call him or send him an email without the whole FPMP knowing about it. There was a mail slot in his front door, though. I could leave a note.

Need any info you can get on Detective Wembly, missing Empath from 20th Precinct. Photo especially. -Vic

If I could get a look at this Wembly guy, I could say whether or not he was the boardroom suicide, or even some other repeater I just hadn't had the pleasure of stumbling across quite yet. If his picture didn't ring any bells, maybe any other information Zig could dig up on him would give me an idea of what to be wary of. After all, I had to make sure I'd never be known as "That *other* PsyCop who mysteriously vanished."

As I opened the storm door to slide the note through the mail slot, it occurred to me that the walk was freshly shoveled. Maybe Zig had left his kids behind—they were teenagers, old enough to fend for themselves. They didn't strike me as the type of kids to destroy the house with a wild party the second their parents left them unattended, either. I rang the doorbell, figuring I should give them the note in person and let them know it was important their dad got it.

Since I was expecting one of the kids, I did a little double-take when Nancy Zigler answered. They were back from their trip after all. I was surprised Zig hadn't checked in with me when he got in, but maybe he got in too late to call and figured he'd see me Monday morning. "I haven't seen you in ages," Nancy said, all smiles. "I didn't realize you were coming over—the house is a mess."

I highly doubted that. The Ziglers' house looked like something out of a home decorating magazine. She called her husband downstairs while she held open the door for me—okay, there was a basket of laundry on the coffee table being folded while the TV played a gardening channel, but other than that, I didn't spot anything out of place. She seemed to be in such a good mood, it was too bad I needed to bring up the subject of the funeral. Unfortunately, funerals are one of those things you can't sweep under the carpet. "I'm sorry to hear about your friend."

"Which friend?"

Great. I probably shouldn't have said anything. "The…funeral."

Her smile turned puzzled.

I heard footfalls on the stairs. Zig turned the corner of the landing and hurried down to join us. "Vic," he said. Just my name. Sensing something was up, I waited. He gave me an inscrutable look, and then said, "We need to talk."

While I wasn't surprised, Nancy seemed genuinely perplexed. Zig's grim tone was pretty clear, though. "I'll leave you to it," she said, heading upstairs.

Zigler ran his hand over his face. It was early and he hadn't shaved yet. His whiskers glinted silvery gray. He looked tired—physically and mentally tired. "There was no funeral," he said.

"Okay."

"I just needed some time."

Even though he was still standing awkwardly in the middle of the vestibule, I wandered into the living room and slumped into a wing chair. He followed, perching on the edge of a recliner, distinctly uncomfortable. "So why sneak around?" I asked. "You could have told me."

"It wasn't planned…you know you need to submit the requests five days out."

"Shit, Zig, what the hell do I care? The timing made sense. We were wrapping up the bloodmobile anyway—although I wish you'd stuck around long enough to write up the narrative. I suck at that."

He gave an unpleasant sniff of a laugh and shook his head. "Doesn't matter anyway."

"What do you mean?" I suspected I knew.

"He'll get off. They all get off. So what difference does it make?"

So. He'd heard about the dog dish guy too. He subscribed to the same journals as I did. And Zig was thorough; he actually read them. It's not that I was glad Zigler was despondent over the creep's acquittal. But I was relieved that he hadn't been doing an unauthorized side job all week. The image of him exchanging information with some sinister figure in a shadowy alley popped into my head. He had a good idea of the extent of my abilities. I'd hate to think he'd sell me out…but what if he would? What if he was feeling worn down and fed up, and the right person came along with the right offer?

"Nancy doesn't know about the time off," he said. "I guess I'll need to tell her now. I've been parking down by the river, and staring at the water, and thinking."

"Aren't you still talking to…" a shrink? "You know. A professional."

He shrugged. I'm not sure if that was supposed to mean he'd stopped therapy, or that he was still going but it wasn't doing him any good.

It was just about a year ago, I realized, that we'd blundered into the world's most hideous basement scene together, a room full of animated corpses on gurneys flapping around like dying fish. All the elements of my worst fears were there: basements, medical equipment, confinement and ghosts. Yet, somehow, the scene hit Zig twice as hard. He wasn't inured to the horror like I was. Maybe, had he seen the ghosts moving the bodies, the trapped spirits clumsily tethered to their former shells, it might have been slightly less terrifying.

Or maybe not.

In the past year, Zig seemed to have aged at least five. His salt-and-pepper mustache was mostly gray now. His sagging skin had a gray undertone, too. Here he was, dealing with supernatural stuff that scared him shitless. Now, on top of it, the collars he made were going free thanks to some slick lawyers and the average NP's distrust of Psychs. He looked ragged and depleted. He looked miserable.

I was about to suggest he apply for a transfer—but then I wondered if that was even possible. PsyCops don't have anywhere lateral to move. The only way out for them was retirement. That wasn't a one-way ticket on the disappearance express, was it? Jacob retired, and now he was in his glory as a federal agent. As far as I knew, Maurice was fine. Earlier in the week, he'd emailed me some photos of him and his wife surrounded by a buffet full of shrimp on a Caribbean cruise. "Maybe it's time to look at retiring," I said, as neutrally as I could.

"No way I could swing it, no way. Not until Robbie's through with undergrad."

"How long is that?"

"He's a high school junior now. Six more years…assuming he gets his

Bachelor's in four. Which he'd better."

Shit. With Zig aging in dog years, six years from now he'd be a mummy. He'd almost quit last winter and I talked him out of it—I'm guessing that was before he got his first college-level tuition bill for his oldest kid. I was about to suggest he go ahead and take a medical leave to get himself together, if that was what he needed...but then I thought better of it. Maybe he was smart to keep the chinks in his armor from showing. For all I knew, it was some vulnerability of Wembly's that got him disappeared.

"Look, I'm sorry I blew your story with Nancy. But from now on, you can tell me what's really going on, y'know? Who am I to judge?"

He nodded, staring at his knees. "I just need to wrap my head around some things. That's all."

"I get it, Zig. I really do." I stood up and handed him the note I'd been holding all this time. "But if you can spare the mental energy while you're soul-searching, it would help us both out if you dug up a little something on a missing PsyCop."

Waiting for Lisa to come home was driving me nuts, and my edginess was driving Jacob nuts, so he holed up in his office while I cleaned the rest of the cannery very loudly. Every now and then I'd pause in my stomping and banging to consider texting something that might lure Lisa back home, but then I'd remind myself who she was with. Any coaxing on my part would be a big red flag inviting Dreyfuss to turn his psychic attention our way. So I mopped the floors. And I slammed the kitchen cabinets. And I bided my time.

I was beginning to think Lisa might not come home at all when finally she rolled in around eleven, carrying one of those styrofoam clamshell doggie bags. I'd sat down fast in front of my puzzle, hoping to appear as if I'd been too riveted by the topless men in bowlers to go to bed. But just as surely as I'd figured out which thing on the hardware shelf was a tape measure, she took one look at me and knew I'd been waiting up for her. Thanks, sí-no.

"Why are you mad?" she said.

"I'm not." She'd know I sure as hell was, and yet I denied it on principle. "I just wanted to…" I sighed and knuckled my dry eyes. "Lisa, I really need your help."

She put away her leftovers, then came and sat down beside me. "It's hard, you know? I can tell you don't approve."

"Forget it—you don't need my approval. I'm not your father." We both sat with that statement for a while. Lisa's dad was a beat cop who'd died in the line of service when she was a teenager. No wonder she was a magnet for older guys.

"But you are my friend," she said.

I stared at her hand on the table. She was wearing nail polish, iridescent purple, and she's not a nail polish girl. It was a slick professional job, too—no doubt she and Dreyfuss had hit the nail salon together, since they were joined at the hip. "If he ever turned you against me—"

"Why would he? Victor, he likes you." She watched me until I met her eye, then said, "Yeah, you get on his nerves, but he likes you anyway."

It pained me to think it, but maybe on some level, Agent Smartass and I were too much alike. Maybe I could trust him…if only he weren't so cagey about Detective Wembly. "Can you answer me a sí-no?"

"What is it?"

"There's a missing PsyCop named Wembly." I almost asked if Dreyfuss had him erased…and then I reminded myself that I was talking about her boyfriend. Also, that I should probably establish a baseline first. "Is he dead?"

Her expression went somber. "No." We sat there together beside the stupid puzzle and watched one another, and finally she said, "He's okay."

"Did Dreyfuss tell you to say that?" I blurted out. Her eyebrows shot up. I realized I'd just crossed a line, and I tried to backpedal. "He almost had me strip-searched, you know. You can't blame me for wondering."

She stood abruptly. "It's late. We're both tired. I'm going to bed."

"This guy Wembly is gone, Lisa. A PsyCop who disappeared. Dreyfuss knows what happened to him, right? Maybe you won't answer me, but

I'll bet the sí-no planted the answer in your head anyway. Just saying, if Dreyfuss had something to do with it, you'd be better off knowing. Don't go into this with blinders on. If Dreyfuss is disappearing PsyCops, you need to know."

It was a desperate attempt—but I figured it was the only shot I had. She'd be up at the crack of dawn doing Pilates or Zumba with the guy, and he'd brainwash her into telling me whatever it was he wanted me to hear. But instead of swinging around and proclaiming yes or no, she shook her head sadly and said, "I'm not getting between you two. If the PsyCop is okay, then drop it."

CHAPTER 23

NOW THAT JACOB'S WEEKENDS ACTUALLY fall on the weekend, he could potentially begin sleeping in. He never does, though. With only one lifespan of waking time and infinite bad guys to outsmart, he'd feel too guilty for indulging in an excessive amount of sleep as often as two days a week. I'm not one for lingering in bed either, though my reason is less purpose-driven than Jacob's. Even when I've been slumbering in the tender arms of Seconal, it's my natural edginess that peels my eyelids open, usually before Jacob wakes up. Which was why I was surprised to find his side of the bed empty and cool.

Sometimes he gets ambitious and makes a big breakfast, but unfortunately, I didn't smell anything cooking. I sat up, fuzzy, thinking about Dreyfussasking me if I needed uppers to pry my eyes open. Anxiety handled the wakeup call…but lately it was taking more than a few of those caffeine shots to lift the fog. Now *there* was a vicious cycle I had no intention of riding. No, all I needed to do was cut back, divvy up the capsules into halves like I had before, and be really firm with myself about limiting my dose. Just think how long they'd last if I was really consistent. My dealer might even be able to score more before I ran out.

I staggered into the hallway to go mainline said caffeine when I heard the clack of a keyboard coming from Jacob's office. I took a detour, and found him working away at his desk. Strangely enough, though, not at his computer. His monitor was pushed back and his keyboard shoved aside while he typed on a crappy laptop.

"Dare I ask?" I said.

He docked his MP3 player, fired up some 80's college-rock, and motioned for me to come close. When I was in range, he dragged me down onto his lap. The office chair groaned in complaint, but hopefully it would hold us for a few minutes if we didn't start doing anything too rambunctious. He locked his arms around my middle, then whispered against the nape of my neck, "Laura Kim's apartment building runs surveillance on the lobby. The files are a common format—same types of files you'd download from a porn site and watch on any computer."

That would explain the lobby footage playing on the laptop's low-resolution screen in front of us. I recognized the date in the corner, that fateful day last February. The time signature beside it ticked by at double speed. He'd borrowed the files, rather than sifting through them in the FPMP archives. It seemed like a smart move, though I suspected if he got caught taking home the extra credit, there'd be hell to pay. That's why he was using an untraceable computer. I grabbed a plain plastic bag off the mountain of unread periodicals on the desk and fished out the receipt from a 24-hour pawn shop. One used laptop, paid in cash, purchased two hours ago. Guess I wasn't the only one having trouble sleeping.

A figure blurred by, and Jacob reached around me and hit a key. The footage reversed. He watched again at half speed. It was a man carrying groceries. He hit another key, and the footage sped to double time. The time signature hit 14:00:00. "You've been watching since she got home?" I whispered.

His affirmative nod nudged the back of my head. "Eleven thirty. Consistent with her testimony."

I settled back against his chest and watched the footage with a sick sort of fascination. Nothing moved but the time stamp in the corner, yet I was totally engrossed. Jacob's fingertips toyed at the lower edge of my sternum, but the weight of his focus remained on the screen. A few minutes later, another blur passed, which turned out to be the mail carrier, first coming, then going. And then a blue-haired old lady. And a black guy. And then…Jacob's breath caught.

Five hours after Laura Kim went home for the day to crawl into bed and nurse her debilitating migraine, there she was, heading back out again.

After carefully picking through the footage, we determined Laura was not at her apartment at the time of Burke's shooting. Jacob would need to figure out where she'd been heading. We spent the morning brainstorming angles for him to pursue. Luckily she'd left her car at work. Cab receipts might tell Jacob where she went, if the cab companies still had them at this point, and were willing to divulge them without a subpoena. But he'd need to make that request from the FPMP, not the cannery, if he wanted a chance at getting his hands on the goods.

We'd done all we could from home, but of course it killed Jacob that he couldn't do more. While he worked out his frustration at the gym, I headed to Wicker Park to pick up Crash for our monthly sage smudging. I wasn't sure how well the smudging ritual blocked Dreyfuss' prying eyes, but especially now, it seemed like we should keep up our defenses. Plus it was a good reason to slip Crash a hundred bucks.

Instead of double-parking and calling him to come downstairs like I usually do when I pick him up, I found a spot and regular-parked. It was doubtful Miss Mattie would know what had happened to Detective Wembly, since she kept her focus directed on Crash. She did understand how the world of spirit worked, though. While she might frame everything in terms of God's love, maybe she could help me understand if it was possible to coax back a repeater's spirit and question it.

And if I could master that trick, maybe I could drag Roger Burke out of hell…and maybe I could force him to give me some straight answers, too. I was so focused on my mission, I nearly collided with an older woman in the vestibule as she exited the boarded-up palm reader shop. "'Scuse me," I mumbled, and flattened myself against the mailbox bank so she could pass me.

Instead, she paused and looked me up and down. She was pushing seventy, with long gray hair and deep creases in her skin. She looked like a quintessential Brothers Grimm witch, at least from the neck up. But her Blackhawks jersey and stylishly distressed designer jeans ruined the Hansel and Gretel illusion. "Can I bum a cigarette?" she said, raspy-voiced.

"Sorry. I don't smoke." I pointed to the palm reader's door "Are you the, uh…?"

"Lydia."

"Vic." She nodded, but didn't offer to shake hands. I suggested, "Maybe Crash can spare one."

"He quit…a few months ago."

While I tried to tell myself I hadn't noticed he'd quit because his shop is always full of traces of lingering incense and burnt sage, I felt profoundly oblivious anyway. In an effort to appear more observant, I inclined my head toward the plywood. "Did they ever catch the guys who did the break-in?"

"Are you kidding? Those cops are a bunch of useless jerks. All they care about is giving out parking tickets." She considered me while I did my best to look un-cop-like, and then she said, "I normally charge seventy dollars for a reading. But for ten bucks, I'll pull a card for you."

And normally I would take a pass, but with the break-in and the lack of insurance, I felt bad for her. One card suited me just fine. Lydia would get her nicotine fix, and I'd only be delayed for a few minutes.

She ducked back inside without inviting me in, but I did catch a glimpse. Broken glass glittered along the baseboards, and a hole was punched through the drywall opposite the door, right in the center of a jumble of distorted blackletter gang initials. Robbery had a motive I could understand. But knocking a hole in the old lady's wall and then tagging it was adding insult to injury.

She came back out with a tarot deck and began shuffling the second she had both hands free. The cards were manufactured with rounded corners, but even so, those rounded edges were further blunted by age and use, and the backs of the cards were matte, the coating worn off by thousands of shuffles. She handled them with the confidence of a blackjack dealer. "Don't touch the deck," she said. "Just point." She fanned the cards.

I pointed randomly. She nudged the fan with her thumb and a card poked out. "That one? Are you sure?"

Since I hadn't been pointing to any one card in particular—and since I was much more concerned about seeing if Miss Mattie was around—I told her it was, hoping to speed the process along and give Lydia her ten bucks.

"The Page of Pentacles." She flashed the card at me. It was the traditional Rider-Waite deck, showing a young guy in tunic, hose and a big red hat. He held up a pentagram-etched disc the size of a dinner plate. "You're good with money. Mature about money. Pages can be flighty, but not this one, he's serious."

She noticed I'm serious? That was like noticing winter was cold. Plus the money thing—given that I didn't balk about paying her for a quick reading, it was a logical enough assumption that I wasn't hurting for cash. Still, I supposed she had to tell me something for my ten bucks, so I nodded and played along.

"Page of Pentacles takes care of himself. He's industrious and frugal."

I kept nodding, thinking her "reading" could apply to anyone.

"A hard worker. Sometimes moody. A magnetic personality."

Really? People never say that about me—the magnetic part, I mean. Once they know I'm a medium, most everyone avoids me like the plague. I must have frowned, and no doubt Lydia was experienced at reading expressions and body language. She leaned forward and peered at me. "No, this isn't you. Your eyes are too light…and you're too grim for a page, even the Page of Pentacles. Knight of Swords? No, you're too pale. Knight of Cups, that's your card. So who's this? Someone younger. Dark hair, dark eyes. Dark and serious. Could possibly be female. Do you know anyone like that?"

Cripes, that was so vague it could be anybody. Maybe Laura Kim, maybe Lisa…but seeing as how I was only subjecting myself to the reading as a vehicle for delivering a pity ten-spot and I had no intention of talking about my actual life, I just shrugged.

"If you don't…you will. Someone dark will come into your life very soon, maybe today. Not dark as in evil. Just dark-skinned."

I dug out my wallet and said, "I'll keep my eye out." Thankfully, the appearance of the money drew the reading to a rapid close. As Lydia snatched the ten bucks out of my hand, my phone rang. She took off in search of cigarettes before the phone even cleared my pocket.

It was Crash. "I hope you don't expect me to take a bus in this weather."

"Actually, I'm—"

At the top of the stairs, his front door opened…but it wasn't Crash who emerged, I could see that much even from where I stood one story down. The guy wasn't quite as tall, and he had a shaved head. Plus…he was African American. Page of Pentacles. You had to give Lydia her props. She might not be psychic, but she was observant enough to pay attention to who was going in and out of her building.

"I'm right downstairs," I said into the phone, and backed out of the vestibule. I had no desire to mingle with one of Crash's tricks. It wasn't jealousy, exactly. More like awkwardness.

"Okay," he said. "I'll be right down." I pocketed my phone and followed Crash's overnight guest with my eyes as he strode out the door and past the boarded-up window. He was so striking I couldn't stop myself from gawking. His skin was dark and his lips had a pouty curve to them. I wished I could see his eyes, but he was wearing mirrored wraparound shades. Although I had no evidence to support the idea, I suspected he had great eyes, too. He'd brushed past without taking any notice of me. He was at that age…the one at which guys *my* age are pretty much invisible. Twenty-five, tops.

And now, with the daylight hitting him, I could see his head wasn't shorn quite as close as Bly's. He had about a quarter-inch of hair, and it was dyed a purply plum black. His pencil jeans were overdyed too, pink on black, and tight enough I was surprised he could even bend his knees to walk. His cropped biker jacket came down to his waist, barely, showing off the jeans. I tried to not notice how good his ass looked as he walked away. I failed wretchedly.

At the top of the stairs, the door to Sticks and Stones jingled open again, and Crash pounded down the stairs. Since I didn't want to look like a pathetic letch, I did my best to pretend I hadn't been ogling his one-night stand. He didn't ask, thankfully, just herded me toward my car with his shoulder. "Let's go—Jacob wants me to be extra thorough. Says he's worried you're all bringing home FPMP energy. I'm not sure if that's even possible…but why take chances?" We'd need to be back in Wicker Park in time for him to open shop at eleven, too, so visiting with Miss Mattie was out. I hopped back in my car. Crash fell into the passenger seat and launched into a spiel about the way his candle wholesaler was gouging him on shipping, I was glad enough to simply listen, and nod, and avoid thinking about the Page of Pentacles.

I was positive I was in the clear when Crash's side of the conversation took an abrupt turn from candles and headed straight into something personal. "I don't know how you can stomach the whole relationship thing."

What? "Uh…."

"Because it's not like anyone ever does what you expect them to do."

"That's true."

He shoved a piece of gum into his mouth and cracked it loudly. I worried for his tongue stud. Or maybe his molars. "Like this guy Red, who waltzes back into town expecting to pick right up where we left off." Red—like my favorite drug? Figures a hot black guy who rocked purple hair and pink jeans could also carry off the name Red. I felt about a century old. "Like I've just been sitting here for past couple of years, waiting around for him to come to his senses. What the fuck, man. What the fuck."

I was so unsure of what I was expected to say to that, I didn't so much as grunt for fear of putting the wrong inflection on the sound. Encountering a friend's one-night stand makes for moderate awkwardness. Ex-boyfriend issues surpassed that level entirely. I stared straight ahead and wished the route to the cannery could magically be half a mile shorter so I could get out of the car and avoid lodging my foot in my mouth.

"You don't just leave when things get tough," he said. "And then come strutting back. And go around acting like everything's fine and dandy."

"…no."

"I made good money, you know, back when I was a stylist. And then I fell for him—the boss' pet—and everything went to shit." He huffed and shook his head, and stared out the window. "He could've been a man about it." He said it so quietly, I wished the radio's volume had been a smidge higher so I hadn't heard him. It felt too personal, too raw for the likes of me. "He could've made a choice—the owner, or me. So what does he do? Says 'fuck the whole thing' and takes off. Completely fucking ditches it. Everything. And runs."

"If you're not in a good space to do the ritual, we should probably reschedule."

"It's fine—it's a perfect time for me to fortify the defenses, while I'm all riled up."

I wasn't sure I believed him, but I knew better than to question any pronouncement of his on psychic matters, even on a good day. Contradicting him now would leave me singed and gutted for sure.

"Anger's a powerful emotion," he said. "Might as well channel it."

As long as he didn't aim it at me. I was just an innocent bystander in this whole thing. We turned onto my street—nearly there—and I thought I was about to get away clean when he said, "I mean, I'm boyfriend material. I'm the type of guy you'd consider settling down with. Right?"

Holy crap. Was that a rhetorical "you"?

Before I came right out and asked him to clarify, he added, "I'm not bad to look at. I can hold up my end of a conversation. I'm actually fairly easygoing on most subjects—and open to negotiation on most others. As for the deal breakers…well, I'd never diddle around with someone to begin with if they weren't a decent human at heart."

"Of course not," I said, hoping it was what he was wanting to hear.

His hand landed on my knee. I did my best not to visibly flinch. "It's the gray areas that get you. Bad things done by good people, because they're confused. Or because they want everyone else to 'like' them." He removed his hand to make the air quotes, and I relaxed, marginally. "Or because, when it's all said and done, they're cowards."

You've gotta love how the guy who just claimed he was easygoing was actually the most opinionated person I've ever met. I did not point that out. I pulled up to the cannery, thinking I was in the home stretch, and he said, "Supposedly he realizes he made a huge mistake. Supposedly all this time he's been agonizing over what he did."

I gave an "I dunno" shrug that hopefully looked sympathetic rather than condescending.

"But if I was his soulmate—as he claims—then how could he bail to begin with?"

"If you think he's jerking you around…maybe you should check with Lisa."

Although I suspected he was just venting and not looking for any actual guidance, he considered my suggestion for a long moment. Long enough for me to wonder if we were done talking and it was okay for me to get out of the car, or if I'd come off as being an asshole for breaking off the conversation right there. Figuring I didn't want to compound the problem by bailing on him too, I stayed put. Finally, he said, "It is tempting. Maybe I'd skip to the unvarnished truth for a different kind of relationship. A casual friend, a business associate. But in matters of the heart…it seems like I'd be missing out on the good stuff if I don't let things take their natural course. Could be that the whole point of tangling with someone is to see how it all unfolds."

I wasn't so sure about that, given that Lisa was floating around on Cloud Nine with a guy nobody in their right mind would trust, but I wasn't about to argue with him. I'd hoped to get him settled in his house-blessing mode and go hide at the diner with a cup of coffee and a magazine when I saw he was walking not toward the cannery, but toward me. Hopefully he didn't want a hug. I don't make a habit of hugging people unless I'm gonna put out. Thankfully, instead of grabbing me, he bumped his hip against mine and left the full-body contact un-hugged. "You're a good listener. Thanks."

Luckily, it seemed a reply wasn't required. While I did consider thanking him for thanking me, in the end I decided to keep my mouth shut. There's no sense tempting fate.

CHAPTER 24

IRONICALLY, THE STINK OF BURNT sage was pervasive in the cannery on "cleansing" day…and a few days after, too. We kept our suits in garment bags and ran the bathroom vent so we didn't smell like we'd just walked through a burning field for the rest of the week. But still, a crispy aroma clung to us.

A fan was propped in the front door, blowing out, and Jacob had a pot of garlicky sauce simmering on the stove. I sat at the dining room table. I'd pieced together three sets of bulging quads and placed a nipple in its proper spot when Lisa came home. I almost asked if she'd been avoiding me, but only an idiot would start a conversation like that. I decided to channel my "good listener" mode and let her talk first. She sat down at the puzzle, sorted some darker grays from some lighter grays, then said, "Are you reporting back to the Fifth Precinct tomorrow, or…?"

"Didn't we agree you weren't going to talk about me with Dreyfuss?" I snapped.

"We did. And I told him I didn't know." We both glared at the puzzle. "I can't be like Carolyn and always say, 'I'm not talking about that.' It doesn't feel right to me, and besides, it makes it seem like I've got something to hide."

True.

"I just wondered if you were going back to the FPMP." When I shuddered at the sound of the acronym, she gave me an analytical look and said, "You know the way you feel about Con? Guess what—I feel the same about Sergeant Warwick." I must've looked pretty stunned, because she gave a bitter laugh. "He stuck me in a holding cell for fourteen hours for working on your case while I was suspended."

I thought of the toilet fountain and swayed in my seat.

"Jennifer Chance is still there," Lisa said. "And she's a threat. No, that's a huge understatement. If you don't get rid of her, she is going to do something bad."

Convenient how Lisa claimed not to be precognitive until she needed to make a point. "I saw Chance once, for maybe five minutes, and then she ditched me. I went through that place from top to bottom and I can't find her." I have one skill—and I was feeling defensive about it failing. "Explain to me how she's a threat if the only one who can see her is me. Because Richie—hopefully I don't destroy my karma by saying this because he can't help it—is a complete moron, worse than useless. If he happens to feel her cold spot, all he needs to do is put on another sweater. If no one can see her but me, she's no security threat."

"Yes, you're the only one who can see her."

Ah. If I played my cards right and didn't ask a question that shut Lisa down, I could take an unexpected crack at the sí-no.

"So I've been thinking about Laura Kim…."

"Victor, I just told Jacob I wasn't gonna—"

"One little thing—is she a medium?"

Lisa looked surprised. And then even more surprised, when she said, "Yes." The answer sank in, and then she added, "She hasn't been hiding it—she doesn't even know."

"There's a guy in the lab staring at plants. Telekinetic?"

"Yes."

"And what about Jack Bly?"

"I don't know him."

"I'll bet that doesn't matter. He's a psych, an empath. Is he strong?"

"Yes."

"Strong enough to do more than sense an emotion? Strong enough to project one?"

Lisa looked concerned. "Yes."

I'd figured as much judging by how flayed and ghoulish he'd looked in the glow of the GhosTV...but it didn't hurt to have my suspicions confirmed. I was relieved there was no empath in the room to pick up on what a struggle it was for me to keep my questions flowing without implicating her precious Dreyfuss in any way. I wanted to ask if Dreyfuss had charged Bly with manipulating me so I would feel comfortable enough to keep coming back to the FPMP, but instead I took Dreyfuss out of the question and said, "Has Bly been tinkering with my head?"

"No."

"What about Jacob—he can't mess with Jacob, can he?"

"No, Jacob is stronger. Even if this Bly person wanted to, he couldn't."

Really? Then why was he always staring at me? I trusted Bly even less than I trusted Dreyfuss. Maybe Dreyfuss could spy on me without the aid of electronics. But Bly could actually make me—I gasped. "Did Agent Bly manipulate Laura into assassinating Roger Burke?"

"No." Lisa's eyes were huge. "Thank God, no. You think an empath could actually do something like that?" She paused, and presumably answered her own question. "That's scary."

No kidding. In some sense, I'd wanted to be right—because at least then I'd know what happened and who was involved. But for now, we were all still in the dark.

At the end of the night, Jacob was squinty-eyed and stiff—and not in a good way—by the time he finally crawled into bed. I gave him a second to see if he was going to roll onto me and try something. When he didn't, I slipped my knee across his thigh, fit myself against his side and settled my head on his shoulder. I felt him sigh and relax. "I bought a disposable phone, drove to the middle of a forest preserve, walked two miles from the car and called the cab company. They won't give me anything without a subpoena."

I nudged his leg into a more comfortable spot and pressed against him harder. "Try again tomorrow from work. You'll probably get a different supervisor, plus you'll look a lot more impressive on their caller ID."

Even though it had turned out to be a bust, I told him about my bum theory of Agent Bly using Laura Kim as a shooter. He was quiet for so long, I listened for the sound of his breathing changing in case he'd drifted off on me, but finally he said, "If the sí-no won't pinpoint Bly, maybe it wasn't him…but the FPMP is full of high-level Psychs." He sat up and shed his exhaustion like a sweater in a sauna while I quietly wondered if I would've been better off waiting 'til morning to talk shop. "If a strong enough empath can plant an emotion, maybe a strong enough telepath can plant an idea and make someone else think it's theirs."

He headed downstairs glowing like a kid on Christmas morning and coaxed Lisa into unzipping the tent flap. Personally, I wouldn't have woken her up for a sí-no, but Jacob had been picking at this case for months without solving it, and now he'd scented blood. No way was he about to let it rest until morning. I leaned on the railing and looked down at the two of them while he did his best to seem both charming and apologetic. Maybe he pulled off the charming part, then again, I'm pretty biased. "You still think Laura Kim didn't shoot Roger Burke?" he asked eagerly.

Lisa shot a peeved look up to the loft, as if I were the one down there asking sí-nos at midnight. She said, "I'm not looking at Laura. How can I get that through to you?"

Jacob plowed ahead as if he didn't notice her annoyance. "But did the bullet that killed him come from Laura's weapon?"

Lisa went quiet. I held my breath. It felt like the whole cannery held its breath. When my lungs started to ache, she said, "Yes."

My mind was racing, but before I could sort out any implications, Jacob asked, "Did one of the other Psychs force her hand?"

Although Lisa's voice was quiet, in the still of the cannery, it carried loud and clear. "No."

"Was she the one who fired it?"

"Do you know what you're asking me to do?" Lisa asked plaintively. "Con trusts Laura with everything. With his life. You're asking me to tell you she's responsible, she's involved—that maybe she even did it—and it's not fair to put me in that position if the sí-no isn't clear. It's just not fair."

"Maybe Dreyfuss should be more concerned about her," Jacob said. "Maybe he needs you to look out for him."

"Laura is not a danger to Con, or to me. Period. And if the sí-no isn't saying whether she fired the damn gun, then you need to either figure out some other approach or let it rest. You know that if ballistics matches the bullet to her weapon, it's all over for her. How do you think I'll look if you take Laura down, and it turns out she was somehow in the wrong place at the wrong time—and then Con finds out you acted on a sí-no? I'm willing to try to get him to drop the investigation and move you into something else so it's not your problem anymore—because, face it, do you really care who took out Burke after everything he did? Laura could lose her job. She could go to prison. So I'm not pointing the finger at her—I'm not willing to take responsibility for any of this."

She zipped up the tent with three quick jerks as if she really wished there was a door to slam.

Jacob was too keyed up to drift off, I could tell, so I treated him to a quick hummer in hopes of helping his sleep mechanism kick in. Even so, once I was done getting my hair pulled and my tonsils prodded, I was the one who was drifting off when he broke the silence with, "I was hoping you'd be done at the FPMP by now."

Despite the fact that I was half asleep, or maybe because of it, I caught a faint note of wistfulness in Jacob's delivery. It wasn't exactly a lie—he really was hoping the exorcism would be short and sweet, and I'd get it over with and roll on with my life. But part of him would be sorry to see me go. He felt conflicted, and that made two of us. I couldn't see myself getting involved with a bunch of eavesdroppers who shot people in their offices. Except psychic police work was an exercise in futility, and the stuff that Laura Kim claimed they did at the FPMP had merit. But how did the missing PsyCop fit in? I shuffled the problem to the back of my mind. No sense in trying to make any big, sweeping decisions since I didn't need to, not yet. Tomorrow's assignment was clear. I still owed Dreyfuss his damn exorcism.

CHAPTER 25

WHEN I REPORTED TO LAURA KIM the next morning to see how I'd be deployed, I hoped to linger for some chitchat. I wasn't about to tell her she was a medium—she seemed just as happy to be in the dark on that matter, and I can't say I blamed her. My main concern was figuring out how she was involved in Burke's shooting. The more time I spent with her, the more likely it was I might find some small inconsistency that would unravel the whole assassination scenario in a way the sí-no would definitively confirm. To say I found her fascinating would be an understatement. Today she wore a black suit with a burgundy shirt and matching lipstick, and while she wasn't beauty-queen pretty, her features looked striking and exotic to my Caucasian eyes. Definitely too hot to have tied the knot with Dreyfuss.

He'd mentioned multiple ex-wives before—I didn't recall exactly how many—but as I watched Laura taking a call while she pulled up some database on her computer, I imagined the two of them walking down the aisle. And then I began to dread him presenting my best friend with something more permanent than a diamond tennis bracelet.

"If you're feeling that bad," Laura was saying, "I should send Dr. Santiago to your place and have her check you out." A pause. "Be honest with me… did you watch the game at a bar? Were you drinking?" Another pause. Laura sighed. "Make sure you drink plenty of water. You're probably dehydrated."

It almost sounded as if she'd been talking to a teenage kid, but I doubted the FPMP's staff physician would be deployed in the case of a tailgate gone too far. When she ended the call, I said, "Richie?"

She nodded. "A few years ago, he developed a bad habit of 'extending' his weekends. Agent Dreyfuss put a policy in place stating he wouldn't get sick pay without a doctor's note if the absence occurred after a day off. So when he calls in on a Monday, I know it's serious. It's too bad. He's predisposed to drinking, and he doesn't have the impulse-control to say 'when.' Add that to his low blood sugar incident at the prison on Friday…." She trailed off and sighed. "It's just too bad."

"Maybe you should reconsider sending Dr. Santiago on a house call."

"He started losing his temper when I even suggested it."

The smartass in me wanted to suggest they send empathic Agent Bly over to smooth his ruffled feathers. But even though the sí-no cleared Bly, I didn't want to invite any more interaction with him than was necessary. "If Richie's out today, who'll be the other half of my buddy…system?"

The elevator doors whooshed open and three guys in black suits stepped off. I didn't think there was much cause for concern, given that everyone at the FPMP was a suit, until I noticed Laura's eyebrows hitch up. Two of them strode past her desk, keycards in hand, without acknowledging her. She stood up and asked, "What is this?"

Suit #3 flashed a pass of some sort and said, "We're collecting some equipment from Agent Dreyfuss' office. Then we'll be out of your hair." Mild words. They were totally at odds with the bully-boy body language, which said, *stand aside, peon*.

Laura was quick, though her movements were controlled, not panicked. She buzzed Dreyfuss and said, "Three Agents from Washington on their way in. Their access cards overrode the locks. I couldn't stop them."

Through the intercom, there was a sigh. "Understood. See if Santiago and Bly can…well, hello, gentlemen." Dreyfuss cut the connection.

The elevator dinged again, and this time it was Dr. K who staggered out. His bushy hair was wild, his glasses were crooked, and his paunchy cheeks were so flushed I thought he'd keel over in a fit of apoplexy. "Dey barged into the lab…" his Russian accent had gone thick. "Dey took the tuner."

Laura nodded, fingers flying over her keyboard. Uneventful exterior shots of the FPMP from each angle filled the quadrants of her monitor.

More typing, and four angles of the underground garage took the place of the exteriors. Men in black stood at the ready beside a black armored van…and it didn't look like anything out of the Lexus catalog. She dispatched Bly and Santiago immediately. "Find out what's going on," was all she told them. Although for someone with as much psychic firepower at her disposal as Laura had, she didn't seem very hopeful she'd get to the bottom of things. I could imagine why. What good were high-caliber psychs against a bunch of goons in black who were just following orders? The muscle probably didn't know much more than what they were supposed to grab and how much damage they were allowed to inflict.

A couple of the parking garage shots showed nothing but parked cars. Laura dismissed those, keeping two goon shots onscreen. She then pulled up live camera from Dreyfuss' office, two angles. Dreyfuss stood to one side with a sheet of paper in his hand, shaking his head in disappointment as the goons swept the office with a handheld meter. At the touch of a keystroke, we had audio. "We'll need you to unlock your desk, sir."

"Sorry," Dreyfuss said. "Not until I've read this form."

"You haven't…looked at it."

"And I'm a very slow reader. Sometimes I wonder if I'm dyslexic."

As Dreyfuss stalled the team in his office, Santiago and Bly approached the team in the garage. Bly blended right in with the other grim guys in suits. He didn't engage them in any way—he simply stood by while Santiago sashayed up in high heels, blood red lipstick, and a slinky floral print dress. None of the goons ogled her, but they all stiffened as if it cost them something to resist giving in to a catcall and a leer. We didn't have audio on her, but it wasn't necessary. Her huge gestures were stage-worthy, and her line of questioning wouldn't be any more complicated than, "Oh my God, what are you people doing?" Because that question was just a cover for what was really going on. Her mind, probing theirs.

One of the invading agents did finally break down and look her way—and I saw Bly, off to the side, unnoticed, was looking right at the agent who'd cracked.

Bly found the chinks in the opposition's armor, and Santiago dove in for recon. They handled themselves like old dance partners. Just like Jacob and me. The footage was too grainy, too small, to really make out the looks on the goons' faces. But it seemed to me the goon under Bly's sway had an actual expression on his ugly mug, rather than the disconnected blank stare they usually wore—the Big League equivalent of my cop-face.

Dr. K clapped a hand on my shoulder, swaying. "Do you know how much work they will ruin? Why now? Why so sudden? If I had a chance to wrap things up…" he turned away, shaking his head in disgust.

I'm not sure what it was that got to me. Was it watching Bly and Santiago tag-team the intruder? Or hearing Dr. K lament that the work he'd been doing would all be for naught? Or was it just that I'd grown accustomed to the FPMP, and I didn't appreciate a bunch of outsiders walking in and acting like they owned the place…in which case, I could assume I was suffering from Stockholm Syndrome. Maybe I actually was, since I found myself rooting for Con Dreyfuss.

"They took my computers, my reports, my phone, even my notebook," Dr. K moaned. I suspected his backups were toast, too. And for what? I'd seen the lab in action—and I'd taken part in enough experiments exactly like the ones he was running to know he wasn't doing anything that should merit this level of interference. Where the hell were these assholes when I was kept awake forty-eight hours at a stretch, when I was poked and zapped and squirted up with psyactives that scorched through my veins like battery acid? Nowhere. And now some bored telekinetic stares at a plant while a GhosTV is playing in the background, and the whole damn cavalry charges in…at whose bequest? Washington's?

"I take it Dreyfuss' boss is none too happy about his stalling tactics for the banker in Iowa," I commented.

Laura responded with a humorless laugh and turned up the volume in Dreyfuss' office. "There's really nothing interesting in there," he told the goon who was fitting a power drill to the manual lock on his credenza. Another suit plucked the CPU out from under his desk. "And there's nothing on my hard drive that's not sitting right there on the mainframe for everyone's reading pleasure. But go ahead, take it. It was time for an upgrade anyway. Those components are such a pain in the ass to recycle."

The whine of the drill blotted out the sound, but only for a few seconds until the credenza was open. Dreyfuss was saying, "Help yourself to some yogurt if you're hungry."

Maybe there was nothing more exciting behind door #1 than a refrigerator. Soon enough, though, with the help of their industrial drill, they exposed the GhosTV.

It wasn't that they were deliberately rough—but clearly, they had nothing invested in preserving the unique technology, either. Whereas the TV in the lab could be hauled off in one piece, Dreyfuss' TV had been fitted specifically to the credenza, and as the goons pulled it free, a bunch of electronics spilled out behind it like entrails. I could give two shits about the GhosTV—I'd been fucking kidnapped to test the damn thing. So when the federal repo men started cutting wires, why did I feel each and every snip echoing in the pit of my gut? "Should we stop them?" I said.

"Don't," Laura said. "They'll be authorized to use whatever force necessary." She turned her attention to her phone, pressed some buttons, and said into her headset, "This is Laura Kim…no, in fact I prefer not to hold. We have an unacceptable situation in Chicago and I need to— Damn it."

"Well, I'm done here," Dr. K said. "I might as well go get a drink."

Laura's phone lit up. "Stop him," she told me. "He's wrapped his car around a telephone pole before. This time he might not walk away." She turned away to field the calls, leaving me to deal with Dr. K.

Currently, the scientist was jabbing the elevator call button repeatedly, hard enough to break the thing. "Whoa, whoa," I said. "Maybe Con's got a copy of your data somewhere. I'm sure you've got schematics. You could build your own."

"Believe me, I would have…we'd be testing them all over the country by now if I knew what it was about the old tubes that made them work. It wouldn't just be a government project, either. Once business saw the potential, money would pour into development. Every company would want their own remote viewer, and anyone with enough money would be able to make their own."

"I don't follow you."

"That's what it does. Not like a television set—you can't turn it on and see what was happening somewhere else. But sometimes, when the tester is in an alpha state, he can see things. Report back on them. Do you understand how important this is? Ever since the Cold War the military has been trying to develop remote viewers."

I'd seen remote viewing in action, and I'd seen the GhosTV doing its thing. Dr. K was talking about apples and oranges, although I could see where the end result would seem the same.

Dr. K shook his head. "Once the tuner technology is refined, it could make anyone clairvoyant."

"If everyone is potentially psychic, the anti-Psychs don't have anyone to harass," I said. The GhosTV didn't actually "make" people psychic. Mostly, it loosened up their subtle bodies and allowed them to go astral. The majority of them didn't remember their trips. Even so, it would be a game changer. If Dr. K managed to take the GhosTV to the next level, eventually he could make the FPMP obsolete.

As my head reeled with the implication of the research, the Washington goons filed out of the lounge. One was hauling the GhosTV guts toward the elevator. Another had Dreyfuss' CPU. Dr. K and I backed away, giving them plenty of room. "You may want to hold off on that," Laura called after them. "I'm on the phone with your boss right now." But they ignored her—*just doin' my job, ma'am*—and once the elevator doors shut behind them, they were gone.

CHAPTER 26

DREYFUSS STROLLED OUT BEHIND THE goons looking thoughtful and unhurried. Dr. K charged up to him, gesticulating wildly and begging him to do something, but the drama didn't sink in. He was tuned in to his own thoughts—and he was staring directly at me. He patted Dr. K on the shoulder, calming him, then turned back to me and said, "Detective? Let's go for a walk."

I'd expected another excursion to the flower shop, but once we were outside, he led me toward a gap in the concrete wall beneath the viaduct instead. It occurred to me that it might lead to some kind of escape pod, or maybe a panic room. It then occurred to me, as I squeezed through the rough concrete, that there could be someone waiting on the other side of the gap to put a bullet in my brain. If there were, that person couldn't be very big. Jacob wouldn't have been able to slide in greased and naked. I could barely cram through myself.

There was no hit man on the other side of the gap—but no fancy secret emergency equipment either. Just railroad ties and rusted freight cars. Dreyfuss had led me into a small lot formed by an exit ramp abutment, a peeling outbuilding and an unfrequented corner of the rail yard. He squinted up at the gray morning sun peeking between the distant North Loop skyscrapers with his phone pressed to his ear. "*Hola*," he told whoever was on the other end, then, "Y'know that place I hoped we'd never meet? I need you there."

When he tucked his phone back into his pocket, his sweatshirt rode up and flashed the edge of a holster. I've never known Con Dreyfuss to carry. Ever. The idea that he found it necessary to bring a firearm with him made me wonder if I should have thought twice about following him in.

"What's going on?" I hated how my voice shook.

His stony expression didn't change. He turned away wordlessly and began to walk. I stood there for a moment and considered squeezing back through the concrete gap, finding my sorry car and heading home, but what then? Jacob was still inside the FPMP. Anything I failed to do could have ramifications for him—ugly ramifications. And so I turned up my collar against the bone-chilling wind that whistled relentlessly through the rail yard, and I followed.

Not only was Dreyfuss freer to move around in his sneakers and sweats, but he was a hell of a lot more nimble than me. We rounded a corner and came upon a tumble of cinderblock, timber and rusted drums. He scaled it like a mountain goat while I picked up a few dozen scratches and splinters clambering along behind him.

The wall of rubble was a pretty good sound baffle. I hauled myself over the top. Dreyfuss was farther ahead. When I called for him to slow down and my voice was swallowed by the ambient noise, I realized the crank and rattle of the train yard was deceptively loud. I tore my slacks on a protruding nail hurrying to catch up with him, and barely caught myself from sprawling when I tripped on a loose board. He didn't even break stride. Somehow, I followed.

He'd led me to a maze of old outbuildings. The wind changed, moaning through the corridors created by the corrugated walls of industrial sheds and the sides of rusting freight cars. I smelled oil and dirt and winter-cold steel, but underlying it all—and growing stronger the farther in we delved—was the elusive scorched-air scent of electricity. The air above our heads was criss-crossed with cables, some as fat around as my thigh, supported by knobbly old wooden posts that were still shaped like tree trunks, roughly skinned, now petrified black with pollution and age. The cable hung in great tangles and spools off the posts, strung around the rail yard haphazardly, as if a giant baby had crawled up and looped it from one pole to another like a big ball of string. Somewhere beyond the metal and cable labyrinth, a bell began to clang, cutting through the murk of noise in its sharp percussiveness. A train was coming, but I didn't hear it. I felt it through the soles of my shoes, and I smelled it as a spike of burnt electricity in the air. Dreyfuss hugged the edge of the maze, creeping toward a building now, a low brick building that looked like old Chicago, like the occasional cobblestone street that peeked through when tree roots or weather heaved the blacktop open. Like the cannery when I realized it had not always been my home, and I pondered the origin of the strange machines lurking in the unfinished half of the basement.

Somewhere beyond the maze, the rumbling slowed. A long metallic squeal joined the chorus of noise, and a stunningly loud hiss crackled over the top of it all. Dreyfuss ducked around a corner and I rushed after him. It was a shallow dead end. I backpedaled quickly to keep from flattening him against the far wall. But it wasn't a wall, I saw, when he moved aside a rotting plank covered in dead weedy vines. It was a door, an ancient door of hewn timbers weeping with rust where the corroding nails held them together. The verdigris covered lock above the doorknob was much newer than the door itself, but that wasn't saying much. Fortunately, it was new enough for Dreyfuss' handy dandy bump key to work on it. He pulled the magical piece of metal out of his pocket, wriggled it in, and gave it a whack. The door probably creaked as it opened, though the sound was lost amid the rail yard din. Beyond was darkness.

He pulled a pocket flashlight and slipped inside. I followed.

The ceiling of the small room was so low I couldn't stand up straight, and the whole thing reeked of age. It wasn't entirely sheltered from the elements. Broad cracks in the walls let gray daylight knife in, and gaps in the plank flooring allowed the dust sifting from the decaying mortar to settle into whatever emptiness lay beneath. Except for strings and coils of electrical cable that looked none too safe to touch, the room was empty. I expected Dreyfuss to unearth another door and lead me to a place where everything would suddenly make sense. Instead, he planted his feet in the center of the room, and he waited.

"What's going on?" I asked again—and the words were swallowed by a thick electrical hum that felt more like a stiffness in my eardrums than an actual sound.

Dreyfuss peered at me coolly. I think he heard, but he didn't answer.

My forearms prickled. Beneath my sleeves, my arm hairs were valiantly attempting to stand at attention. So was the hair on the back of my neck. I swallowed. My spit tasted like nickels. I could only imagine what the electromagnetic field was doing to any eavesdropping devices we hadn't known we were carrying. While it was a relief to know any unwanted communications signals would be scrambled, I wasn't so sure what it meant for my own molecules. I'd always thought the people who claimed they contracted mysterious diseases from living around high tension wires were just looking for someone to pay their medical bills. I'd been wrong—the electricity was definitely affecting us. Even worse, if it was screwing with the physical, I could hardly imagine what it was doing to our subtle bodies.

When Dreyfuss finally spoke, he said, "Might as well make yourself useful and see to it that no dead people are listening." He dug something tiny out of his pocket and threw it at me. I felt it ping off my overcoat, and although I couldn't hear it hit the floor over the drone of the electrical hum, I suspected it sounded like a Seconal capsule. "Your payment."

He wasn't wrong—nothing would freak me out more than to swing my flashlight beam around and find Dr. Chance had been lurking in the shadows all along. But I could do without the judgment.

I walked the perimeter of the shack, feeling for cold spots, looking for movement, but as far as I could tell, the place was clean. I wasn't sure if the electricity could affect my ability, though, so I salted the area just to be safe, stretching my tiny pocket-sized supply to cover the length of all four walls. I topped it off with a few spritzes of my re-purposed breath spray, pumping until nothing but air came out, and then I flooded it with white light. It was the best I could do. Hopefully it would be enough.

My white light was symbolic, though. It didn't do a thing for my physical sight. Between the darkness and the distracting hum, I hadn't even noticed that there was a second door in the far wall. I first saw it as a slice of light, which filled me with a surge of panic, at least until I realized that the light was entirely mundane daylight, and all I'd need to worry about was the silhouette that now filled the doorway. I blinked away tears while my eyes adjusted. Despite the fact that the hair on this silhouette floated up in a dark nimbus as it came into contact with the overflowing electricity, over the past few months I'd grown plenty familiar with this particular silhouette from outside the blue nylon tent wall.

Lisa.

A chain dangled from her hand. The antique key she'd been wearing around her neck protruded from the lock of the Depression-era door. Beyond her, a Grand Avenue bus wheezed by as if everything was same-old, same-old, but I was viewing it now from the other side of the looking glass. Here Jacob and I thought we'd been so clever with our key cutting and ice grinding. The lengths Lisa and Dreyfuss went through to talk privately made Jacob and me look like a couple of kids playing secret agent.

Lisa closed the door behind her and we were plunged into near darkness again. An afterimage in the shape of the doorway danced in front of my eyes until they adjusted to lack of light, and when they did, I found them kissing. Lisa and Dreyfuss. Right there in front of me. Not in a lovey-dovey way, either. Desperate. Like the world was gonna end.

They tore their lips from one another, but Lisa kept a two-handed hold on his face. "What happened?" She called over the droning hum.

"I'm completely fucked. They know what I can do and I'm as good as dead."

"No they don't. Tell me what happened."

"Washington's coming down hard. They dismantled our biggest project. Next thing they'll haul off is me."

"No…no. I promise. No."

He closed his eyes and took a deep breath. "Is today my day to die?"

"*No, llegarás a mañana.* Just you wait and see."

"Who brought Washington down on my head?" Dreyfuss pulled away from her and pointed directly at my face. "Was it him?"

Me? He thought I'd been the one to bring Washington in? Not on purpose. Inadvertently, though? I hoped not. I hadn't even realized

Dreyfuss wasn't the only one spying on me—but I'd been careful not to leak anything. I was always careful. So I couldn't possibly be the one who'd triggered the GhosTV raid. My mouth worked, though I couldn't think of anything intelligent enough to say that would merit screaming it over the electrical hum. Lisa replied with something a lot longer than a simple yes or no. I didn't hear what it was. Neither did Dreyfuss. He cupped his palm around his ear and shouted, "What?"

She shook her head sadly, then steeled herself and yelled, "I can't tell you anything about Vic."

"You've got to be kidding me," I hollered. I was fairly sure I'd done nothing wrong, and obviously she could make an exception to the sí-no if it were to exonerate me. I grabbed her by the shoulder and shook her, and blue static sparkles danced around her wool coat. "Tell him! I didn't do anything." Or, at least, I didn't mean to.

Lisa glanced from me to Dreyfuss and back again. Her brow was furrowed. It should have looked hilarious with her hair floating all around her, but it didn't, not one bit. I wished I was privy to whatever she was asking herself—but I supposed I'd need to be a telepath to hear it. Lucky me. I just saw dead people.

Would she really hold back something that would clear my name all for the sake of proving a point, or was she protecting me? Whether I did something or not, I didn't want Lisa to take the fall for my mistakes. I repeated, "Tell him."

She stared at me hard, her dark eyes boring into me for a long moment, then she turned to Dreyfuss and said, "No. It wasn't him."

Dreyfuss shouted, "Someone told upper management about the GhosTVs. And exactly where they were kept."

"Oh, come on," I yelled, "plenty of people know that."

Dreyfuss smiled grimly. "Actually, no. Only a handful of people knew about the set in my office."

And I was one of them. Fantastic. In my defense, I had absolutely no idea it was that big a deal. He'd given a set to me, after all…though he'd also given me a warning that I'd better not go blabbing about it. So what if I knew he locked the TV's credenza. He locked his goddamn refrigerator, too.

Lisa tried to haul Dreyfuss toward the door. "They got what they came for," she said. "They're gone now—they're not listening. We don't need to do this."

Dreyfuss and I were too busy having our own standoff to worry about something as mundane as the electrical field scrambling our guts. We both stayed put and tried to stare each other down. "Other people knew besides me," I insisted. Richie and Carl must have seen it at some point—I knew absolutely nothing about Carl, but it's always best to watch out for the quiet ones. Maybe Bly, too. And then there was Dr. Santiago, who could've had some kind of rivalry going on with Dr. K I didn't know about, a rivalry where she'd benefit by sabotaging his work…although even as I thought up that scenario, I knew I was grasping at straws. All those people must have seen it at some point. All those people, plus Dreyfuss, and me…and Laura.

My gut wanted to trust Laura Kim, but my gut's proven itself to be spectacularly wrong on numerous occasions. The thought of suggesting Laura was the culprit made me sick. Especially when I couldn't temper the accusation with an apologetic tone of voice. No, I'd need to scream it out in all its ugly glory, and I realized I wasn't willing to. Not without definitive proof. Still, I felt the need to deflect the blame from myself, because even though Lisa had just conveyed the sí-no's blessing on me, Dreyfuss looked like he wasn't buying my innocence. Lisa dropped his arm, stepped away from him, and paused at the door. She looked to me, pleading with her eyes for me to leave the humming, crackling room with her. But I had a point to make. "I'm not the only one who knows about it," I insisted. "The thing didn't install itself in your credenza."

"No, Dr. K put it in. So he sabotaged his own project?"

"All I'm saying is that what happened this morning could've been in the works long before I set foot in this place."

"No," Lisa chimed in. So much for that argument. She looked a bit stunned, like she hadn't been expecting the sí-no to spill out at that very moment. But now that it had, her internal stream of questioning was running through her mind. "It happened while you were here, Vic. This week. You know the person who's responsible. A woman. It's a woman."

I felt the blood drain out of my face.

"Not Laura Kim," Lisa called out. I could see it in her eyes—she was as relieved as I was that the sí-no was finally taking a firm stance on Laura.

"Then it's Santiago," I said. "I never trusted her."

"Not Santiago," Lisa snapped, pressing her shoulder impatiently into the door.

"There is no other woman there," I said. "Unless you're talking about someone I saw in passing, in the lunchroom or the hall."

"No, you know her. You spoke to her. Where…? In the dining room? No. In Con's office."

I ran back the tape in my mind and tried to figure out what she meant. Thoughts of the exorcism and the botched rosary brought back memories of repeaters and jellyfish. I supposed it was possible the jellyfish were female, and I did chat with them, even if it was just to tell them to hit the road. Maybe they were something more than habit-demons. Maybe they were some kind of spying device. But if they were capable of carrying information back to Dreyfuss' superiors, who the heck would receive it in Washington? Even if they had a Psych hopped up on psyactives interpreting the message, all the jellyfish could do was undulate. They weren't sentient enough to carry on a conversation. Not like….

I closed my eyes and swayed on my feet. Not like Dr. Chance. It fit, it all fit. A female I knew. In Dreyfuss' office. Pissed off at Dr. K and positive he was poised to snatch a Nobel for her GhosTV. "Is it Chance?" I asked weakly. Her name was swallowed up in our noise shield. I needed to come clean, even though it meant admitting that I'd been holding back the majority of what I knew. If the dead doctor had managed to figure out a way to exact her revenge, I'd need all the help I could get. I braced myself and shouted, "It's Dr. Chance."

Dreyfuss went ashen. Lisa closed her eyes, took a steadying breath, clutched Dreyfuss' hand and said, "I'm not saying one more word until both of you come outside."

CHAPTER 27

GRAND AVENUE WAS DEAD IN the gap between morning rush hour and lunch. Although the wind was bitter and sleet pelted our faces, it was an enormous relief to escape the electrical hum of the dank, low-ceilinged utility hut and to slide back into the real world, although that reality felt a bit flimsy now that I'd integrated so many new and scary concepts in such a short span of time.

My ears were still ringing from the hum, and I worked my jaw hoping to make my eardrums flex and shake off the residual drone. We could speak freely now since the sí-no assured us no one was listening in, and while it was a relief to stop shouting over the noise, it was no relief at all to hear that Dr. Chance was indeed the one who'd told Washington about the GhosTVs.

"One thing I asked of you," Dreyfuss muttered at me. "One damn thing. To take care of Chance."

"There wasn't any time. I was feeling her out, then she got in a snit and took off. I haven't seen her since—and I did try."

"I've seen you try, Bayne. You try to do the things you deign to do, like pinning those lousy repeaters on me. You try 'til you puke. But how hard did you really try to find Chance? Don't answer. I'm sure by now you've rationalized that you're the good guy, and you're convinced you really did give it your all."

Lisa took Dreyfuss by the elbow and murmured, "You didn't eat anything today." He shook his head in disgust. "Baby, you need to eat or you'll make yourself sick. You need your head in the game right now."

The smoothie cart Richie'd discovered was less than a block away, and

Lisa had her eye on it. The old guy manning the cart was swaddled in winter clothes with his breath streaming away from him in a cloud. Not exactly the best enticement to try a slushy cold drink. Even so, it was quick, portable and available, so the three of us trooped up to the cart. As we watched Dreyfuss' strawberry mango swirl churning through the blender, I tried to come up with a way to explain myself, to assert that I'd done what I thought was right at the time. Except I couldn't, because now it was obvious I should have been less concerned with identifying the repeaters and more worried about tracking down Chance. Lisa ordered a chocolate banana smoothie for herself, then asked if I was getting one. Although I knew it was completely illogical, and although we'd be able to see the guy making them, I declined. I couldn't get past the notion of Richie hocking loogies into the drinks. He'd been out of sorts lately too, crabby and quick to take offense, and now he was home sulking.

Wasn't he?

"Is Richie hungover for real this morning?" I asked Lisa.

"No."

"So he's pissed off that I interrupted his rosary."

"No."

"Does he want to get back at me for Camp Hell?"

"No…why do you ask?"

"Because I was a raging asshole to him—yeah, I know, you're shocked."

"No. He doesn't see it way. No."

What an unexpected relief. I still felt guilty as sin, but I deserved to carry that burden. What mattered was that I hadn't messed him up any worse than the hand of Fate already had. "So he's okay."

Lisa cocked her head and furrowed her brow. "No." She sí-noed in silence for a moment, then said, "I don't really know what that means."

I'd had a sneaking suspicion something was up. "I'll give him a quick call and see what's what." I pulled out my cell phone and asked Dreyfuss, "Do you have his number?" My little screen didn't light up when I flipped the phone open. Figuring it was turned off, I hit the on-button.

Nothing. Dead.

Dreyfuss poked his smartphone's on-button a few times, then stuck the unresponsive thing back in his pocket with a sigh. "Can the day get any worse? Don't answer that, *querida*, it's rhetorical. Let's just hope Laura can fix it."

"As if my morning wasn't stellar enough," Dreyfuss said, "now I killed my phone." He tossed the dead smartphone onto Laura's desk. It hit with a clatter.

I placed mine carefully beside it. "Mine too." Lisa didn't need to join in. She'd left her phone in her car—presumably because the sí-no told her to.

Laura glanced at the phones. "I hate to ask what you were doing," she said, "but I suppose I need to know."

"High tension wires might or might not have been involved," Dreyfuss allowed.

"Then cross your fingers." The Fixer pulled a fresh battery out of her desk, swapped it into Dreyfuss' phone, and lo and behold, the little touchscreen lit up.

He took the phone from her. "It was just a drained battery? How is that possible?"

"I have no idea—but the same thing happened to me the last time I got an MRI. Apparently my purse was too close to the machine." She slipped open the back of my phone and peered at the battery. While my phone is nowhere near as old as my car, it's still a cheap model. I'm as hard on cell phones as I am on blazers, and since I end up in the phone store a couple times a year having my data transferred out of a crushed hunk of plastic, I don't invest in anything fancy. "I don't have a battery for this," she said, "but I do have a charger."

Dreyfuss, meanwhile, was scrolling through his messages. "How many times did you call me, Laura? I've gotta try and figure out our next step here, pronto, and I hate to think what else could've gone to shit while I was out of range."

"It's Agent Duff. He's being really weird…and really persistent. He's insisting that I leave work and go to his house, but he won't tell me why."

"He probably wants you to show him how to program his new remote," I said, hoping it was something as simple as that. But Lisa shook her head, no.

Behind us, the elevator whooshed open, and out tromped Carl, Richie's unflappable assistant, looking a lot more animated than I'd ever seen him. He took in the agitated cluster of folks around Laura's desk and zeroed in on Con. "Agent Dreyfuss, I really hate to interrupt you—"

"It is a phenomenally bad time."

"—but Agent Duff is losing it."

"I do not have the resources to wipe Duff's ass for him at this particular moment. Not now. Not today."

With the aplomb of someone who knew when to pick his battles, Carl dug in his heels and said, "He tried to talk me into getting Laura over to his place. By force."

That revelation did give us all pause, despite the GhosTV-raid fallout. "Did he mention why?" Dreyfuss asked calmly.

"No. But he offered me ten thousand dollars to do it."

Dreyfuss considered that information, then turned to Lisa. "I have a feeling it's all connected," she said.

Feeling. Right. Like the way I "sense" things in mixed company when the ghosts are telling me exactly where their bodies are buried.

"What about those repo men who paid us a visit today?" Dreyfuss asked Lisa. "You think he might have invited them to Chicago?"

"I…don't know."

Maybe Lisa wasn't willing to confirm or deny anything, but Dreyfuss decided he'd found his leak. "After all I've done for him, this is how that cretin repays me? Son of a bitch."

If there's one thing I've come to expect from Constantine Dreyfuss, it was his ability to bounce back from anything with a smile, a wink, and smartmouthed quip. I'd never seen him seriously angry outside the astral—and now he was spouting off things he'd normally keep to himself. Watching him teetering on the brink prompted me to fling my psychic faucets open wide and bring my protective white light thundering on down.

Now that Carl had his boss' attention, he added, "I think Agent Duff came in over the weekend, too. Someone went through my desk—and no one else has the keys but him and me."

"I'll check his keycard," Laura said. I expected Lisa to use the sí-no to save some time, but Lisa kept her mouth shut. Either she didn't want to broadcast the extent of her clairvoyance, or the sí-no was being flaky again. "He was here Saturday," Laura verified, "from 10:12 to 10:41. Do you want me to pull the surveillance? It'll take a few minutes."

"Do it," Dreyfuss said.

Surveillance had become a major pain in my ass. But when I wasn't the subject of the mechanical eye's gaze, I had to admit it was pretty convenient to have a record of exactly what had gone down. Once Laura pulled up the files, we watched as Richie entered the office he shared with Carl, and proceeded to systematically go through one desk, then the other.

"What's he looking for?" Laura wondered aloud.

And whatever it was, why wouldn't he know whose desk it was in—his, or his assistant's? Then again, it was Richie we were dealing with. Unless there was a football stat attached, he didn't sweat the details.

Onscreen, Richie flattened a booklet on one of the desks, then peeled a sticky note from a cube and jotted something on it.

"Is that the internal phone directory?" Dreyfuss asked.

"Looks like it," Lisa said. Which I took to mean that it definitely was.

"From my desk," Carl said. "That's *my* desk."

I made a mental note to never touch anything of Carl's without asking him first.

Richie pulled a tissue from a dispenser on the desk, knocking the box askew, and blew his nose. "That was the first thing I noticed was moved. Then he went and put the notepad back in the lower drawer—oh mercy, his germy hands were all over my desk. Every single drawer and knob."

"Pull his phone records," Dreyfuss told Laura. "Cell and landline."

"Already on it. But even if he was the one who called in Washington—what is it he wants with me?"

Dreyfuss turned to me. His hair was corkscrewing free from his scrunchie, the creases on either side of his mouth were deep, and his flecky hazel eyes looked like they'd been on the seeing end of too damn much. "You know him better than anyone here. I want you to go check this out. You never agreed to do any fieldwork for me, and I can't order you—but I'm asking you."

Did he honestly think I was enough of a prick to say no? "Yeah, I'll… okay. Yeah."

"Not without backup. Laura, get Bly, Santiago and Marks up here. That should be enough firepower to find out what his deal is."

Laura hit a button. "Agent Marks' phone is going straight to voicemail." She turned from the phone to the keyboard and typed a flurry of commands that pulled up a map on a quadrant of her monitor. A few keystrokes, and a moving red dot appeared in the schematics. "He's in the building."

Her casual tracking of Jacob gave me a chill. I no longer needed to wonder whether or not I was being tracked, but how. Would my dot still show up, should the FPMP care to search for me, or had the electromagnetic field disrupted whatever was transmitting my signal?

"Actually," Laura said, "it looks like he's already on his way."

Jacob stepped into the fifth floor lobby and leveled a look of calm assessment at everyone in the room. My adrenal system was already on threat level orange from watching my partner show up on a tracking system. As if that wasn't enough, there was something else, something in his demeanor that twanged my warning signals. His shoulders were squared, his stride was purposeful and his eyes were intense. Yeah, his bearing's normally assertive, but there was a brusque stiffness to it now that felt intimidating. I trusted him with all our semi-serious power plays in the bedroom, and his current body language had me a bit spooked, so I could hardly imagine how formidable he must look to everyone else.

Jacob cut through the crowd, heading straight for Laura. As he reached her desk, he pulled a plastic evidence bag from his overcoat—a bag that contained a gun. Wordlessly, he set the weapon down in the middle of Laura's desk, and he looked at her.

She stared back at him, uncomprehending. We all did.

The moment stretched, silent, awkward, unbearably long, until finally Dreyfuss said, "Okay, I give up. What's this about?"

"A team just pulled this Sig from a marina downstream from the Metropolitan Correctional Center. Once ballistics runs their tests, they'll confirm it fired the bullet that killed Roger Burke."

If that was Jacob's murder weapon, you'd think he would seem happier to have it in his possession. A hell of a lot happier. He was anything but happy, though. And he was staring into Laura's eyes with excruciating intensity as he explained about the weapon. She stared right back, too, but not in a defiant sort of way. More like she couldn't imagine why Jacob was telling *her* about the Sig Sauer in the plastic bag.

Jacob dropped his voice low and said to Laura, "It's registered to you."

Laura laughed, a single awkward sound that was almost a sob, because it was painfully obvious Jacob was not kidding around, and said, "That's not my gun." Jacob said nothing—no one said anything—and Laura insisted, "My main weapon is right here," she checked her desk drawer to be sure, "and no one can get to my backup but me."

"I wasn't randomly dragging the river, Laura. I located it with GPS tracking. *Your* GPS tracking."

"There's got to be some mistake," Laura went on with a frantic edge to her normally-unflappable voice. "I store my backup in a safe deposit box, and I haven't opened it since Christmas."

While Laura turned to her keyboard to call up more records, Jacob said, "Surveillance footage shows you visiting a safe deposit box approximately forty-five minutes before the shooting."

Laura's hands started trembling so hard her typing went sloppy. A sprinkle of random dots lit up the map, and she smacked the keyboard in frustration. "How could I have gone to the bank? I was flat on my back with the worst migraine of my life!"

"Okay, kids," Dreyfuss said, "everybody simmer down. Let's not jump to any hasty conclusions." He reached across the desk and picked up the evidence bag by a single corner. The gun dangled heavily from his two-fingered grasp. "Laura, route the phones to the switchboard and meet me in my office with Dr. Santiago."

Laura's eyes widened and she went the color of chalk. "You're going to *interrogate* me with a telepath?"

"We need to figure out how your gun got involved. That's all."

Although the words were delivered in a calm and reasonable way, I didn't really buy them. I'm not sure any of us did.

CHAPTER 28

BLY'S CAR CHARGER DIDN'T LOOK like it would fit, but I jabbed the plug at the hole a few times just to be sure. No good. I pocketed my drained phone.

In front of me, the Agent himself adjusted his rearview. I caught a glimpse of his pale gray contacts and looked away. Frankly, I wished he'd stayed behind at the FPMP for Laura's dissection. Not for Laura's sake…it was bad enough she was getting brain-raped by Dr. Santiago. For my own sake. Selfish, I know. I would have preferred to work alone with Jacob. So what if Bly knew the way? That's what GPS is for. I just didn't like being in a car with someone who could read my emotions, since emotions were impossible to camouflage with times tables and mindless songs.

I vowed to try and keep a lid on my feelings anyway, though it was distracting, to say the least. I'd always thought being a Stiff was a lot more handy than we all realized—and this was a prime example. At least one of us could withhold his inner life from Bly. Hopefully mine was messy enough that he could chalk it up to my perpetual state of nauseated anxiety.

Jacob sat in the passenger seat beside our unwanted empathic partner, sketching out a Richard Duff timeline in his notepad. "How did Agent Duff seem to you at the prison?" Jacob asked.

Bly shrugged. "It's a prison. He was stressed out—just like everyone else."

So much for empathic insight.

"Look," Jacob said, "my ex-partner is a telepath. If I were going into this situation with her, she'd be getting some kind of useful read off him.

You could try doing the same."

I'm sure Bly didn't appreciate Jacob challenging him—and I was glad I wasn't the one who'd had to do it. Bly grit his teeth and drove in silence until we pulled onto a side street and he nosed into a parking spot. As he cut the engine, he said, "If you ask him what he wanted with Laura, he'll come up with some kind of lie. You need to make suggestions. Maybe they were planning something together. Maybe he was going to blackmail her. Heck, maybe he thought he could hold her for ransom. Ask anything you can think of, and I'll touch my chin if I get a hit."

It was nothing at all like the way Carolyn worked, but if anyone could handle the shift in operating procedure, it was Jacob.

I wasn't sure what I expected Richie's house to look like, but when we took in the two-story brownstone, all I could think was that it looked perfectly normal. The property was well-maintained, from what I could tell beneath the old snow, anyway. His mailbox sported a Bears logo. His brown Lexus was parked in the driveway.

All his shades were drawn.

I mentioned the shades, and both Jacob and Bly unconsciously shifted their holsters. We got out of the car and approached the front stoop. Maybe Dreyfuss had never issued Richie a service weapon, but that wouldn't necessarily mean he didn't own a gun. It might behoove us to try and sidestep Richie as soon as we could, since he didn't have much peripheral vision at his disposal thanks to the Fetal Alcohol Syndrome.

At least I wasn't front and center. Bly had been to Richie's place before—playing pinochle, no less—so he volunteered to take point. I was happy to let him.

Bly rang the bell. We waited. Richie yelled from somewhere inside, "Bring it around the back!" And then, quiet.

Bly rang again. Pounding footsteps. Galumph-walk? Maybe a very angry galumph-walk.

"I said, bring it around the—" the door pulled open, only as far as the security chain. "Agent Bly? I thought you were someone else—the FedEx delivery guy, he's useless." The door closed and the chain rattled while he called through the wood, "Is Laura with you?"

"She couldn't make it. They need her at the office."

"I ask for one simple thing…" the door whipped open and Jacob and I both sidled away, since for all we knew, he'd been readying a semiautomatic. But it looked like it really was only the door chain that had been engaging him and he was empty-handed. He turned to look at Jacob in a sort of swooping motion that was all head and shoulders, and then at me. His face lit up and he said, "Detective Bayne!"

He didn't offer to shake this time. For which I was relieved.

"Can we come in?" Bly said.

Richie pivoted to set his sights on Bly, then me, then Jacob, then me again, taking his sweet time in formulating his answer. Finally, he said, "Sure…but it's kind of messy. I'm right in the middle of a repair."

The brownstone had a tiny foyer, just big enough to hang up a coat, which led into a combo living/dining room. The carpet was beige, the walls were papered in boring neutrals, and furniture…well, hard to say about the furniture. Every square inch of surface was covered with bits of electronics.

"My television is defective," Richie explained.

"It was probably under warranty," Bly said.

"Anyway…can I get you something to drink? Tea? Coffee?"

Jacob and Bly both declined, but I said, "Coffee's fine." I figured the longer we stayed, the more congenial we managed to act, the more likely it was that Jacob could slip some questions in about Laura Kim and we'd figure out exactly what had sent Richie off the deep end, and why he was overcome by the urgent need to see her.

First things first—I needed to make sure Richie didn't hock a loogie in my cup.

I followed him into the kitchen. It was done in chrome and granite—expensive, and again, monochromatic and dull. The kitchen table was dominated by a laptop and a printer, both new, judging by the matching boxes stacked by the garbage can beside the back door. The overflowing garbage can…which had a trio of cereal boxes poking out from the top, processed sugary stuff that would make even a five-year-old cringe.

He must've known I was on loogie-patrol. He was extra solicitous when he ushered me over to the shiny new coffee pot, even attempting to slip an arm around me…which I avoided. Because, ick. It was Richie. And he was acting phenomenally creepy.

Calling in sick, taking apart his new TV, acting like a freak…. Everything must tie together, but how? My best guess would be that Richie was bipolar—maybe the FPMP already knew that, or maybe the condition had gone undetected due to the Fetal Alcohol Syndrome—and he was roaring through a manic phase right now. That's what all the "projects" and the shopping spree suggested to me, anyway. I've known plenty of bipolars and I've seen them cycle, though. Richie's body language was awfully calm for someone in manic phase.

Aside from the normal stuff, like canisters and paper towels, the countertop was cluttered with a bunch of tools I couldn't name—meters and wires and electrical looking things. The cabinet-mounted work light was on, shining down on the gear. Richie shuffled through it like he was playing three-card Monty. He turned back to me with a prescription bottle in his hand. "Want a Xanax?"

Wait, what? "No. Thanks."

"Are you sure? They make you feel really good."

Surprisingly enough, I wasn't even tempted to take one and save it for later. "Coffee's fine. Really."

"I thought you liked pills."

"Best not. I'm…on the clock."

With a "suit yourself" shrug, he turned back to the cabinet beside the sink and said, "You're the tall one. Can you get the coffee down for me?"

Classical music was playing in the background, I realized, and his tone was eerily coquettish. I did my best to block out the idea of him doing Brokeback Mountain research over the weekend and deciding he might be ho-mo-sexual, but the mental image flooded my mind's eye anyway. "Stop being weird," I told him as the old Hardcore Vic defensively reared his head. "You can reach it perfectly well from there."

His smile faltered, then went broader than before. But it didn't reach his eyes. He set the coffee on the countertop, swooped around to face me, and said, "You'd better make it yourself. So it's just the way you like it."

Since I preferred my coffee loogie-free, I thought that was a pretty good idea. While he filled the pot with water, I found the filters and dumped a random amount of coffee into the basket. I also sucked down a bunch of white light, enough to make my ears ring and my hands go chilly. While intellectually I knew his mental issues couldn't migrate over to me, I still felt better with a sturdy psychic barrier between us.

I was trying to seat the basket when I heard Jacob bark, "Drop it!" I flinched so hard I sent the coffee airborne, and dry grounds rained down on me like hail. A splash of water hit me from the side, and the carafe fell to the floor and shattered. I whirled around to find Bly in the doorway with his weapon drawn and Jacob flipping Richie face down onto the kitchen table.

"Don't move," Bly bellowed at me. At *me*. Dumbass.

"Just what the fuck do you think I was doing?" I snapped back.

"Vic, stay still," Jacob shouted—and his tone, I realized, wasn't bossy at all. It was frightened.

"To your right," Bly said. "Live wire. Don't move."

Oh.

The length of electrical cord lay on the floor where Richie had dropped it—no crackling, no sparks, nothing to indicate it was a potential hazard. But the far end of it, I saw, was clearly plugged in. The business end where an appliance would normally be attached was bare, three coppery wires with about half an inch of rubber shielding stripped away. And there I was, soaking wet, standing in a puddle maybe a foot away from the exposed tips.

Bly grabbed a pot holder off the stove and pulled the plug, then yanked the cord away from me just to be safe. "Okay. You're good."

Jacob, meanwhile, was attempting to subdue Richie without breaking those flabby little arms. "Settle down," Jacob said, "just settle down, and no one will get hurt."

Bly glanced at Richie—he focused—and Richie stilled, then gradually relaxed.

Maybe Einstein did just try to electrocute me…but it spooked me the way that single empathic glance had laid him out as effectively as a bottle of Xanax. I re-doubled my white light in case Bly decided maybe I needed to be forcibly calmed, too.

With my right side soaking wet, I was now hyperaware of the disassembled electronics all around me. Doing my best to keep myself to myself, I eased up to the table and looked down at Richie. He was so relaxed that his subtle bodies had been jarred loose. The border of his head was out of register. He looked slightly doubled all around, as if his outline had been mis-printed.

"What were you thinking?" I asked him.

"It was a joke," he said, "only a joke. Like a joybuzzer. Hee-hee."

Bly shook his head in disagreement, though being face-down, Richie couldn't see it.

"Come on," Richie said as Jacob fixed his hands behind him with a vinyl wrist restraint. "Can't you take a joke?"

The moment Jacob let go of his hands, Richie's astral body rippled. Whatever Bly had done with his power-empathy, it left Richie struggling to contain himself. His fingertips slid out beyond his physical fingers without Jacob's grasp to hold the bodies all together. I needed to de-escalate the situation, but what could I say? "Let's all calm down," I started with…and then I saw that the fingertips protruding from Richie's stubby fingers were too tapered, the nails were too neat to be his—hell, his laugh didn't even sound right—and I realized the subtle body inside Richie wasn't Richie at all.

The disassembled TVs and classical music suddenly made a hell of a lot more sense. The person so desperate to see Laura Kim wasn't Richie—it was Jennifer Chance. My head reeled as I worked back to the last time Richie had been his blithe, Bears-loving self. Chance must have been riding around in Richie's defective body for days, suffering from his crappy eating habits and his tunnel vision. She must be jonesing for a better ride. As an untrained medium, Laura Kim had no experience keeping tabs on her subtle bodies. Her physical shell would be a much better fit than Richie's, too. But if Laura wasn't available, I realized with a shudder, Chance was willing to settle for me.

Bly did a double-take at me as the revelation rocked my world—but he wasn't a telepath. He'd get the gist, but not the particulars. Even the strongest empath in the world wouldn't pick up on the specifics of what I knew, only the fact that I'd just had a big "a-ha" moment. In this case, a way to transmit the details would have been phenomenally useful. It's hard to convey "we need to keep Chance from sliding into me while I salt her" with a meaningful glance. I had to settle for flapping my hands in a "keep him still" gesture, and I focused on my part of the operation: the exorcism.

I cranked my internal faucet to maximum, flooding myself with white light, and grabbed for my salt…although before I even touched my empty pocket, I remembered I'd used it all earlier that morning. Fine. I needed salt, but luckily I was standing in a kitchen. No problem. I began pawing through the cabinets. Apparently the real Richie isn't much of a cook. While Jacob keeps crocks of granular sea salt with his herbs and spices, the closest thing I spotted in Richie's kitchen was a shaker of butter-flavored popcorn salt. Although I've been known to work with some dubious equipment, I didn't want to risk letting Chance float free because synthetic butter flavoring was tainting my supplies.

I dug some more, not that I expected to find a big jar of myrrh hiding behind the barbecue spice blend and the marshmallow-studded hot cocoa mix. I searched for sage, cinnamon, basil—all the common pantry stuff that had good vibrations for esoteric work—but anything basic or straightforward was nowhere to be found.

I jammed my hand in my pocket and tried to summon ethereal salt, but with my heart racing a mile a minute, I wasn't able to shift the white light out of protection mode into a more creative capacity. The attempt made pain lance through my head, a sickening pain that warned I'd better watch myself. Maybe sidewalk salt would do the trick. It might not be exactly the same as table salt, but it was a hell of a lot less adulterated than anything in Richie's cabinets. "Everyone stay put," I said, looking from Jacob to Bly in hopes that they could keep the situation intact long enough for me to prep the world's most impromptu exorcism.

I darted back toward the front door and found a half-empty sack of something called Safety Step...which didn't seem very promising. I scanned the packaging. Magnesium? Uh oh, that didn't sound right. I thrust my hand into the bag, while back in the kitchen, Chance said, "At least untie my hands," through Richie's mouth. "I'm half your size—what kind of threat could I possibly pose to the two of you?"

"It's for your protection as well as ours," Jacob said, while I scooped out a handful of Safety Step and aimed a big stream of white light into it.

No reaction—nothing. Nada. Zip.

I dumped the Safety Step on the floor and wiped the last few pellets off my damp palm. It left a swath of grayish white across the front of my black wool overcoat. Richie probably owned real exorcism gear somewhere—and I'd probably be able to utilize it, even if it was hyper-Catholic—but unless it had a big neon sign on it that read *Ghost-be-Gone*, there was no way I'd find it before Chance got wise to me and ditched Einstein's body. I slipped back into the kitchen and headed for the popcorn salt.

"Let go, Marks, you're dislocating my shoulder," Chance whined through Richie. "I'm telling Dreyfuss you idiots treated me like a common criminal."

I'm not sure if she actually felt Richie's pain, or if she was angling to free a physical set of hands. Her ghost arms were more or less aligned with Richie's, so either she was anchored in Richie, or she was forcibly keeping herself inside to keep his personality from reasserting itself. My best guess was that she could leave whenever she wanted.

"I think it would be okay to un-cuff him," I said, doing my best to tell Jacob with my eyes to follow my lead. I needed Chance to stay in Richie, at least for the moment, and I worried that she'd give up the physical body if the physicality was too painful. "Like he said, it was just a joke. Our practical jokes go way back—we were always pulling pranks on each other. No harm done."

Jacob reached for a pair of tin snips on the countertop…and Bly knocked them away. "I'm bringing him in."

"Wait, hold on—" I said, but Bly steamrolled me.

"For everyone's protection." He hauled Richie's body up by the arm and forced it toward the doorway. With no way to fit through it three-abreast, Jacob let go.

It was like double-vision, but only for a split-second. As soon as Richie's body was pulled from Jacob's grasp, Jennifer Chance tumbled out, translucent, rumpled and disoriented. She shuddered and rolled her shoulders like she'd just woken from an unsatisfying nap with a crick in her neck, and then whirled around and looked directly at me. Commotion—Richie's body went down like a sack of bricks when Chance ejected—but I couldn't worry about that while Chance was loose. The look in her spectral eyes set off all my warning bells, the look of someone with nothing left to lose. I snatched across the countertop for the popcorn salt, but I grabbed short. It tipped over the side and bounced off the floor, and a scattering of electronics rained down on top of it. Desperate, I drew down a gulp of white light and steeled myself as she set her shoulders and barreled toward me—and then the only thing I knew was the concussion of a spectral being slamming into my chest.

On impact, I sucked the white light into my protective membrane. My peripheral vision sparkled and my knees went weak, from the force of the impact, or the sudden flow of psychic energy, or both. I knew I was still me, though, and only me. And the more she battered her spirit against my white light condom, the more sure my barrier grew. It was like the first time I'd parallel-parked without hitting the curb. It didn't guarantee that every future parking job would be perfect—but it did leave me with a pretty good idea of the way it should feel when I got it right.

Chance was impossible to keep a visual on. She'd cranked up her spectral transparency somehow, and I saw her as an overlay to the melodrama that was going on in the kitchen doorway, Richie sprawled on the floor with Bly clearing his airway. Jacob was in the act of pulling out his phone when Chance's assault slammed me into the fridge. Jacob abandoned Richie and made toward me.

He only wanted to help—I knew it in my gut—but I didn't want to risk Jacob's idea of "help" translating into him stealing my white light and leaving my solar plexus open to a hostile invasion.

"Stop," I yelled, at him, at Chance, and I made a grab for a ghostly arm. If I could get hold of her, I hoped, maybe it would keep her at arm's length so she couldn't sneak in. My hand passed through her arm like a fork through aspic. Jacob paused, then kept coming, "I need the light," I snapped, and I grabbed for Chance again. This time, though, I made a small tweak to my protective sheath, shifting the membrane from outside my ethereal body to just beneath it. I grabbed again—and this time I caught something.

Jacob, meanwhile, had taken me literally. He flicked on a work lamp that was clamped to the edge of the kitchen table, and swung the force of the hundred-watt bulb directly in my face. My breath whooshed out in a great gasp of surprise, frozen, visible, illuminated by the glare of the high-wattage bulb. Although the room was warm, my breath escaped me as a big blooming cloud of frost.

It shouldn't have mattered—it was only a light, for crying out loud, only my breath—but the moment my concentration slipped, Jennifer Chance went gelatinous again. She snapped out of my grasp and disappeared with a sticky, wet "pop."

"Jesus Christ," Bly hissed. He and Jacob were both staring at me with the whites of their eyes showing all around.

"It's fine," I said, "take care of Richie." The last of the frost snaked out of my breath, ebbing as quickly as it had come once the supernatural source was gone. Now I felt shaky and feverish. A bead of sweat snaked down my forehead, hit the permanent furrow between my eyebrows, and made for my left eye. I brushed it away…and left a trail of frigid slime across the bridge of my nose. I looked down at my numb hand. It was covered in a chunky bluish coat of ectoplasm that hung so thick it pattered to the floor around my shoes. I held my goopy hand away from myself, and I shuddered.

There'd been no contingency plan for possession—no shorthand or procedure in place. I'd formulated an ad hoc plan, though, to grab hold of Chance and salt her with popcorn salt before she could slide into anybody else. Too bad I couldn't explain it in three words or less while we were all getting knocked around the kitchen. Although I'd done my best in a lousy situation, I wouldn't go so far as to say I was satisfied with our performance. Jacob backed me up, although since he couldn't read my mind, he'd ultimately done more harm than good.

I shook cold goop off my hand—it splattered the linoleum—and I gave Bly the nastiest look I could muster. Him, I was pissed at. Because that jagoff actually could read my mind, and he'd set the whole shitstorm in motion by second-guessing me anyway.

CHAPTER 29

THE GOOD NEWS WAS THAT Richie would be okay. When his crusty eyelids fluttered open and he got his bearings, it tugged at my heartstrings. Looking back, I could kick myself for not noticing he'd suddenly quadrupled his vocabulary and acquired a new gait. When someone's acting weird, my first thought has never been that they might be possessed… although now, I suppose I'd always consider it a possibility, especially if the weird person was a medium.

Although the destruction of the 70-inch flatscreen would be a major shock to Richie's system when he finally pieced together where all the tiny electronics in his living room had come from, mercifully he had no memory of the weekend. I wasn't surprised. When the Criss Cross Killer took me for a joyride, he'd blotted out my consciousness too.

The bad news was that Richie said we should call Dr. Santiago right away, and that we should tell her he had "one of those blackouts"…again.

The even worse news was that now we didn't know where Jennifer Chance was hiding.

The worst news of all was that right now Laura Kim was frazzled and vulnerable—and it wouldn't surprise me a bit to learn the events of the day had triggered a headache. Bad timing. A convenient migraine would allow Chance to slip into Laura, then quietly hunker down inside her and wait out our investigation.

Since Richie was asking for Dr. Santiago, we unanimously decided that getting him back to the FPMP made a lot more sense than calling an ambulance. At least at the FPMP they'd take us seriously when we explained he hadn't been hungover when he called in sick that morning—he'd been possessed. Who better to monitor against re-infection than Dr. Santiago, who was familiar enough with Richie to spot a pattern of un-Richie-like thoughts now that she'd know to keep an eye out for them. Hopefully they could pull Laura Kim down off the torture rack since we now had good reason to doubt she got up off her sickbed and blew a hole in Roger Burke herself. I couldn't begin to guess why Dr. Chance would want to plug her old partner, but I'm sure we could tease out her motivation now that we knew where to look.

Richie didn't need all three of us to run him back to headquarters. I decided to take a detour and pick up some protection for Laura. If we were lucky, Laura's interrogation would actually work in her favor. Hopefully Chance would prefer an unfettered spirit body to a borrowed physical body that was being questioned by a remote viewer and a telepath. I knew of a charm that could keep her spirit out, so I cabbed it to Sticks and Stones in search of the protective shaman necklace that had once been the pride and joy of Faun Windsong.

"D'you have a phone charger in here?" I asked the cabbie, a squat Eastern European guy in sore need of a shave and a stick of deodorant.

He glared at me in the rearview and pretended he didn't speak English.

It would have been helpful to call ahead and have Crash meet me on the street with the necklace, but it would only take me a few minutes to run up and grab it. Plus, I wanted to have a quick chat with Miss Mattie. Hopefully she could give me some pointers on exorcising a sentient ghost who had no desire to move on.

Since the cabbie drove like a cabbie—which is to say, like a maniac—we made great time. Until we got to North Avenue, that is. And then traffic ground to a halt. "What's the problem?" I said, but we were still playing the no-English game. I glanced at his license. "Sonofa...look, Bogdan, could I use your phone?"

He glared.

Fine. I pulled out my badge and clinked it against the plexi barrier between the front and back seat. "Give me your phone. Now."

Bogdan understood that.

My thumb went for memory-dial three, the store, but of course that wouldn't be any good. I called information instead and had them patch me through to the Sticks and Stones landline. It was busy. I tried again. And again. Busy. Traffic crept forward a few feet. Somewhere up ahead, sirens whooped, the long drone of emergency vehicles punctuated by the directional noise blat that would tell the rest of the drivers where the hell the sirens were coming from.

"Shit." I slumped against the door and pressed my head to the window... and then I realized the window was greasy. I sat up again, tried Sticks and Stones a few more times, and I waited.

Traffic went nowhere.

It was half a mile between North and Division—less, now that we'd rolled forward another block—so I decided my best bet was to hoof it. I threw Bogdan's phone at him along with a twenty. Not that I expected much, I told him to wait for me in front of the boarded-up palm reader's if traffic ever moved again, and I took off for the store.

I've never found it helpful to jump to conclusions, at least when I wasn't in a position to do anything about them. So I did my best to stay in denial until I was close enough to see what was going on with my own eyes. The fire trucks, the EMTs, they could've been there for anyone. The buildings in that part of Wicker Park were stacked up against each other like firewood—bad analogy—and it could have been any building on that block dripping with the sooty aftermath of a blaze.

Only as I neared, I saw it wasn't just any building. It was Crash's building.

I broke into a run.

"Move—police—move!" I didn't bother with the badge. I used my body and my no-nonsense police bark to elbow through the crowd. When I got to the front and found some uniforms keeping the bustling throng at bay, I whipped out my badge to get myself in there and find out who was in charge.

The fire was called in just before nine, three hours prior, and firefighters spent well over an hour extinguishing the blaze and keeping it from spreading. No word yet as to how it started. It was out now, and crews were sifting through the sodden wreckage to figure out if anyone had been trapped inside, and to make sure nothing was still smoldering. "Casualties?" I was surprised at how calm and businesslike I sounded.

No, I was told. None yet.

Even though I knew enough to stop pestering the firefighters and let them do their jobs, I was beside myself with fear. Second floor, second fucking floor. And a store full of flammables—books, paper, cardboard, charcoal—not to mention accelerants like oil, aerosols and saltpeter. I took a deep breath in a morbid attempt to try and catch a whiff of sandalwood on the aftermath of the fire, but all that remained was the rank stink of muddy soot.

Without thinking, I pulled out my phone and hit memory-dial two, Crash's cell. I hit it four or five times before it registered that my phone was still dead. Neighbors—someone would know him. I started working the crowd, badge out, questioning the rubberneckers as to whether they'd seen him. No, said the ones who knew who I was talking about. Haven't seen him. Not today.

Right. Because at nine, the time when the fire had started, he wouldn't be standing around loitering on the sidewalk. He'd be rolling out of bed to nuke himself a bowl of generic oatmeal, down some coffee, and get ready to open his store. If he was even awake yet. Jesus Christ.

As I searched through the milling onlookers, desperately seeking a telltale glimpse of bottle blond, I spotted three separate news crews entrenching themselves at various locations that had a clear line of sight to the aftermath. Automatically, I stooped and did my best to blend in. The FPMP indoctrination had done its job. Not only was I now paranoid about being tracked by Dreyfuss, his Psychs, and even his ghosts, but I was more worried about being spotted by someone who had a bone to pick with Psychs in general, and who'd love nothing more than a nice tall target to aim for.

A ripple of urgency went through the emergency response personnel as firefighters called in EMTs. The camera crews tried to push in while the cops pushed back. The wait for the EMTs was excruciating, though it couldn't have been more than a few minutes between the time they ducked into the building and the appearance of their gurney nudging out through the broken remains of the doorway. Even though I saw plenty over the heads of the rest of the crowd, I craned my neck to get a glimpse of who was on that gurney. The only thing I saw was a sheet-covered body.

My world tilted. I pressed into the guy beside me, who shoved back with his shoulder and rocked me upright, and with my feet under me, I burst into action. "Police—stop right there—police—I need to see—"

There was too much crowd between me and the ambulance, though, and it rolled away before I could bully anyone into lifting up that sheet. I was left standing there inside the barricade in a pocket of quiet like the eye of a storm. I had to call Jacob. He must be at the FPMP by now. He'd have all those resources at his disposal, all those contacts. He'd figure out what's what. I planted my hands on my hips, glaring at the milling crowd beyond the barricade that filled in the ambulance's wake just as if it had never been there, and I scanned for a rubbernecker who was a likely candidate for commandeering a cell phone. Every time I feinted toward someone with their hand to their ear, the crowd swallowed them up.

Maybe a uniform would give me a crack at his radio. Wicker Park would be the Fourteenth Precinct…did I know anyone from the Fourteenth? As I searched in vain for a familiar face, a woman's voice piped up close by. It took me a moment, over the murmuring drone of the crowd and emergency vehicles, to realize it was the only voice inside the barricade that was currently shouting.

"It was an accident—you make sure you put that in your report. Do you hear me, you useless pig? I said, do you hear me?"

I whirled around and found Crash's downstairs neighbor giving a nearby police officer a piece of her mind, while the cop ignored her and helped another ambulance maneuver into position without running over any bystanders. I took two bounding steps toward her before I realized that everyone else was damp, charred and sooty, while Lydia was clean and dry. Her long, wavy gray hair was loose, her sweatshirt had a glittery

Tibetan OM symbol on the front, and her skinny jeans belonged on a woman at least thirty years younger. Hard to say what her shoes looked like, as they were kind of transparent. Her feet too, for that matter.

"Lydia," I called—and she spun around to look at me. I was flooded with relief, though I couldn't say why. Crash's neighbor was dead, after all—I should be dismayed. But in all my profound selfishness, the only thing I cared about was that I'd finally found someone who could tell me where Crash was. I pulled out my drained phone and held it to my ear, hoping that I'd look like a perfectly normal guy having a phone conversation, and I called out to her again. "Lydia, c'mere."

She squinted at me for a sec, then said, "Well, if it isn't the Knight of Cups." She approached. The closer she got, the more ethereal she looked to my mind's eye. Solid, but luminous. "Just my luck—the only one out here willing to give me the time of day, and he doesn't smoke."

The last thing her lungs needed was a smoke. "Have you seen Crash?" I asked her.

"Nope. Not lately."

"The fire—"

"It was not arson. I bought some paint thinner, I'd been cleaning that damn graffiti off my walls. I must've spilled some on my clothes. I must've fallen asleep with a cigarette lit."

"Sure." My heart sank. Maybe she'd be willing to try and find Crash for me, but first I'd need to tell her she was dead. Once she realized she'd said what she needed to say (to someone who was able to hear it) she might very well move on and leave me hanging. Still…it didn't feel right to keep talking around the charred elephant in the room. "Lydia, here's the thing. You didn't survive the fire."

She stared at me for a moment, as if to decrypt a sick joke I might be attempting to make at her expense, and then she looked back at the fire-blackened wood panel that had been covering the vandalized remains of her front window. "Oh." She looked at her hands, then looked at the charred building again. "Oh."

"I'm not really talking on the phone. I can see you because I'm a medium."

"Oh." Lydia considered her hands again, front and back. "Right. Yeah." When she looked up again, she gazed directly into my eyes. While I couldn't name the color of her irises, and while I couldn't begin to guess why a ghost would be wearing clumpy mascara, there was a gravity there, a wisdom, that calmed my racing heart. I shivered and took a deep breath, though carefully now, since my shallow, rapid panic-breathing had left me oxygen deprived and woozy. She said, "I guess that's why I'm not burnt."

"It probably would've been pretty painful if you hadn't...."

"No kidding. They say burns are the worst." She looked back at her hands, then snapped her fingers a few times. "It's not like lucid dreaming, is it?"

"I wouldn't know."

"Well, I can't make a pack of smokes appear."

"Listen, I'm worried sick about Crash. Could you...?" I left it open-ended, hoping she might come up with a bright idea.

"I'm sure he's fine," she said dismissively, waving her fingers like an illusionist, and scowling when the goods she'd been trying to materialize didn't appear.

"How about Miss Mattie," I suggested, "do you know Miss Mattie? Have you seen a big African American woman in a scarf?"

She ignored the question. "If my mind created these clothes I'm wearing—or if they're some non-physical equivalent of my actual clothes—then where are my damn cigarettes?"

Maybe she was blocking them...after all, if it hadn't been for her cigarette mishap, she'd be alive to smoke another day. "Forget about your cigarettes. Do you know Crash is fine, or are you just guessing?"

"If you're asking whether I'm plugged into the cosmos, then no. At least...not yet. I do feel different, though." She maneuvered her hands like a she was trying to create a ball of energy, though if she was successful, I couldn't see the results.

"Maybe if you try to focus on him," I said. "See if you pick up any—" on the street behind me a horn blared, loud and insistent. I turned to see what the problem was, and found a cab wedged up against the curb, with Bogdan hanging out the window, gesturing to me.

"Hot damn!" Lydia crowed. I spun around to find she'd summoned a spirit tarot deck while my back was turned. She fanned the cards and presented them to me with glee. "How about I draw a card for you, Mr. Medium? Go ahead, pick something—this one's on the house."

I was torn. On one hand, Lydia should be able to sift through the wreckage and figure out if Crash was still in there. Unfortunately, she was newly dead and didn't quite have her bearings. Plus, I wasn't entirely convinced she'd be willing to help me out even if she did. And then there was Bogdan, laying on his horn. Maybe I was better off calling Jacob, letting him interface with the emergency workers through FPMP channels. Hell, for all I knew Crash had FPMP tracking on him, and within minutes, a red dot on a computer monitor would let us know he was sitting in a coffee shop somewhere watching his building smolder.

I'd jogged a couple of steps toward Bogdan when Lydia called out, "Hey, Knight of Cups!" I turned with the intention of tossing back a quick apology for ditching her, but I saw she was holding up a card: The Tower. It was only a drawing, not a particularly sophisticated rendering at that, but the sight of the flaming tower with people leaping out the windows gave me a chill nonetheless.

When she had my attention, she said, "Flawed structures can't stand… see the lightning bolt striking the tower? That's knowledge, a new knowledge that rocks your world. Something you believe to be true is revealed as false."

Images of Jennifer Chance's spirit tumbling out of Richie's body flashed past my mind's eye. "That's already happened."

"Sorry, kiddo. I'm looking at your future."

Bogdan's horn bleated. I shifted my weight, staring at the awful card, torn between the urge to stay with Lydia and the urge to call for help.

Lydia must've seen something in my expression that she took pity on. She tamped her deck into a neat pile and said, "Crash has been staying with that fancy black kid—he rolls in just before eleven, in time to open the shop with maybe two minutes to spare. He'll be fine. Actually, *fine* might be an overstatement. If he was on schedule, he got a good eyeful this morning, what with the fire trucks and the crowds. But he wasn't home when the tower fell."

CHAPTER 30

FUNNY, HOW THE INSIDE OF that rank taxicab felt comforting and familiar now, compared to the chaos outside Crash's building. I sagged with relief against the taxi's greasy window and cradled Bogdan's phone against my cheek. Jacob told me he'd found a message from Crash on his cell when he checked his messages on his way back to HQ, so he'd known about the fire. Unfortunately, there'd been no way for him to fill me in before I found out the hard way. If Crash wasn't caught in that blaze, though, that was all that mattered. I was confident he would handle the logistics of the fire the same way he'd handled that irate customer, which freed up my mind to figure out what to do about Jennifer Chance.

We'd need to formulate a plan in a secure space—on this, Jacob and I could both agree—and we weren't talking about dodging surveillance electronics this time, either. I briefly considered the flower shop, but I realized that the florist wouldn't necessarily have the things I might need for an exorcism. Let's face it, the next time I met up with Chance, I'd need to be armed with something a hell of a lot more effective than butter-flavored popcorn salt.

"I'm bringing in the heavy artillery." I didn't want to come right out and say *GhosTV*. Not that I thought Bogdan cared one way or the other, but for all we knew, Chance's ghost was breathing right down Jacob's neck with her spectral ear pressed against the side of his phone. "The very large and bulky heavy artillery—the one that almost crushed my hand in San Diego."

Jacob said, "I'll come get it…if that's what you think is best."

I actually had no idea whatsoever. All I knew was that we had to do something.

There was evidence that Lisa had left the cannery in a hurry that morning. Mail was scattered over the vestibule floor. A full cup of cold coffee sat beside the jigsaw puzzle. Lights were on. The TV was on too, playing a soap opera that none of us watched, at least as far as I know. I took a few steps toward the TV, then backtracked to where we stored Crash's house blessing supplies in the kitchen…until I realized we'd moved it to the downstairs closet, or was it Jacob's office? I'd performed a lumbering line dance, taking two steps in each direction and wasting half a minute, and I was no closer to exorcising Jennifer Chance than I'd been when I walked through the front door.

Get it together.

I paused, took a deep breath, and checked in with myself. White light? I hadn't thought about it in hours. The faucet was on its normal flow, a kind of medium-low, the minimum amount it took to keep a basic barrier between my subtle bodies and the rest of the world. I cranked it up to fortify my defenses, and I considered which tools I had at my disposal. Yes, I did feel a vibration in the sage and incense Crash used on ritual day, however I personally had good results with perfumey off-the-rack Florida Water. Plain old table salt did me just fine, too. Even the iodized stuff.

Now was not the time to start experimenting, but memories of the way the potassium Safety Step lay dead in my hand led me to second-guess myself. Maybe I was limiting myself by using table salt. Maybe if I activated some of that chunky grayish sea salt, my exorcism would pack a bigger punch. I broke for the kitchen and grabbed the fancy stuff in the round glass crock with the cork top—it even came with its own precious little wooden spoon, tied to the neck of the crock with a length of jute. The spoon clattered to the floor and slipped under the kitchen cabinet base when I ripped the top off and flung white light at the chunky crystals. The mineral lit up to my inner eye like a bonfire. Finally—something that worked. I crammed it in my pocket. There were so many other spices in there—normal spices, not the weird processed stuff like Richie had. Bay leaves, pepper, thyme…my Camp Hell lessons tugged at my memory, and I started wondering if I should have made more of an effort to try out different herbs, if I'd been selling myself short all this time…if I was a miserable failure of a human being and I fucking deserved to have Jennifer Chance wearing me like Halloween costume, driving my car, handling my gun, sleeping in my bed, touching my man….

Panic would *not* help any of us. Deep breaths. Deep, even breaths.

A key rattled in the front door, and Jacob called my name. "Vic?"

"In here." Jacob was home. He'd read all that tedious, cryptic exorcism material, and he probably remembered it all, too. He'd know what to do. Relief flooded me, and I turned toward the front hall.

Agent Bly stood awkwardly in the doorway. My panic returned full force—*body swap*—until I realized that Jacob was right behind him. In his own body. I turned away and did my best to look like I was searching for something very important on the coffee table and my hands were not shaking. Deep, cleansing breaths. Reality was not coming apart at the seams. It wasn't. Everyone was themselves. Mostly. Unless they were a medium. In which case, they might not be.

"I came to help with the heavy lifting," Bly explained.

I grunted. His sympathy annoyed me. No doubt he'd felt my panic spike like a slap in the face, but he merely stepped aside to let Jacob past, and then cocked his head and considered the big blue tent. I tried to pretend he wasn't even there, since the worst thing I could reveal was the fact that I didn't really know what I was doing, which he must have already known.

I focused on Jacob. Just him. "Here's what I've got. I juice myself up—salt, chemical psyactives and the GhosTV—I pump myself up with everything I got. Then I send that freak packing to the other side."

Jacob nodded. And that was that.

Until Bly chimed in with, "How are you going to keep her contained? She might slip into you and do some serious damage before the rest of us figured it out. How do the rest of us help while you're dealing with her spirit? And how are you going to find her to begin with?"

While I was dying to tell Bly to shut up and mind his own business, he did have a point. Several of them.

"You know," Jacob said, "the protection necklace might be gone…but the shaman who made it could help us."

"He's in Chicago?"

"Florida, last I knew."

"There's no time—"

"Vic." Jacob stopped me with a pointed look. "We don't need him here. Your talent runs ten times hotter than his, but face it, he's studied longer and he knows what he's doing. Talk to him first, before you rush in. That's all I ask."

It galled me to go crawling to someone I hated for advice, but Jacob was right, Bert Chekotah was the only authority on exorcisms we knew.

Jacob made all the arrangements, then set me up in his office. It was disconcerting, the green light on the webcam and the little box in the corner of the screen with the three of us in it, me scowling, haggard and pale, looking like I'd just been through the wringer. I scowled harder. I would have preferred a simple phone call, less fuss and muss, but given that no one seems to have a common vocabulary for dealing with Psych stuff, I couldn't deny that a video chat would be our best bet at understanding each other.

Jacob and Bly were both looking grim and frazzled, too. They stood to either side of my chair like a pair of beefy, crop-haired bookends, except Jacob had soulful brown eyes, while Bly had those pale colored contacts that made his irises look hinky. It was all I could do not to stare at them. I watched the contact bar instead. A phone icon lit up green and the computer made ringing sounds. Jacob reached over my shoulder and clicked the icon…and then Bert Chekotah filled the screen.

I did a double-take, because the shaman I remembered was always harried from keeping too many plates spinning in his professional life, and too many women from finding out about each other in his personal life. But the guy settling back in his chair adjusting his headset mike looked about five years younger. His tan was deep and his hair was longer, windswept and carelessly flattering. Instead of the rumpled linen suit in which I always pictured him, he had on a faded T-shirt and a beaded turquoise necklace. He looked like a surfer now, or maybe beach bum stoner, or an artist who made sculptures out of driftwood and sold them to tourists. He looked handsome, too, the type of good looks you can't really ignore, not if you're being honest. I'd seen the mewling, spoiled brat inside him, and even so, it was just as hard to keep my eyes off his sculpted cheekbones as it was to not stare into Bly's creepy contact lenses.

"One thing you need to understand about an exorcism," Chekotah told us, "is that there are spirits, and there are ghosts. My people believe that everything in the world is imbued with spirit. Not just human beings and animals, and not just living things, like plants, but everything. Lakes. Mountains. Rocks." He held up a sports drink in a plastic bottle. "Even this. I think that what my people refer to as 'spirit' would be called subtle bodies in other cultures."

Made sense to me. Mediums' spirits rattled around looser inside them than everyone else's, too. Maybe our spirit eyes were askew from our physical eyes, and our spirit ears were pitched slightly different. Whatever the misalignment, it allowed us to sense things in that other plane of existence, be it repeaters, or ghosts, or even spectral jellyfish.

"Spirits aren't all beneficial," Chekotah said. "Some are tricksters, and it can go beyond harmless mischief. Some enjoy causing pain and suffering. They can't be exorcised since they're not really dead, but they can be bargained with, or even appeased. One person's aggressor might be someone else's protector."

"So a pissed-off dead woman who's hijacking other people's bodies," I said. "Spirit, or ghost?"

"The angry remnant of a human being…that's a ghost." Chekotah looked grim. "Traditionally, my people kept none of the belongings of the dead—they put the body out for the elements, along with all of its belongings. They left it in the swamp and didn't look back. Nowadays, though, think about how materialistic modern culture is. No one's going to get rid of their dead relative's stuff. It might be valuable, so they'll want to keep it for themselves, or maybe sell it on eBay. Every last item they hold on to leaves a tiny pinhole that pierces the veil between death, and life. Enough small items—or something with a big enough emotional charge—will weaken that veil enough for ghosts to cling to this world and avoid crossing over. A ghost cares about one thing, and one thing only: luring the people who were once its friends and family into the land of the dead, so it doesn't have to suffer alone."

That explanation gave me an idea on how to find Chance's hiding place, though I wasn't convinced that all ghosts cared about was death. After all, I had it straight from the source that Jennifer Chance's big concern was who got credit for her GhosTVs. Not that she wouldn't get a kick out of inflicting a ton of collateral damage too. "Spirit, ghost, whatever she's called, how do I get rid of her? Salt? Or something else?"

Chekotah considered my question in this new thoughtful, unhurried manner he'd adopted, then said, "In the beliefs of my people, even a mineral has a spirit. If salt is what focuses your energy, then use salt. The energy comes through you, and you harness that energy with ritual. But ritual is a personal thing. You need to do what resonates with you."

"I'm not asking you how to focus my ability. I need to know what it is you do to the ghosts once they're in range that makes them cross over. Do you visualize a door and give 'em a shove through it? Or hit their spirit body with a blast of energy that makes it evaporate? Or…what?"

Chekotah looked startled in his video. So did Jacob and Bly, in the small box down by the corner. I wasn't accustomed to letting people know I literally saw these things, and I didn't trust either Chekotah or Bly with my secrets. I didn't have the luxury of being cagey, though. I needed to stop Chance from inhabiting anyone else.

"I'm in trance for that part of the ceremony," Chekotah said.

"You must remember something. The Criss Cross Killer, sticking to Jacob. What were you thinking when you scraped him off?"

Chekotah closed his eyes, took a deep breath, and whispered to himself as he rocked back and forth. I shifted impatiently in my seat. Jacob and Bly looked grim. But before I could say, *You know what, forget it, I'll just wing it like I always do,* Chekotah spoke. "Hugo Cooper had his feet firmly in this world, but his connection to Jacob felt weak, like a spider's web. All I had to do was brush it away. He was filled with anger, but it wasn't enough to keep him here, not without the connection."

Like the silver cords that connected astral travelers to their bodies. And the goopy tethers that anchored the jellyfish to Dreyfuss' fingernails. Something was connecting Chance to this world, something only I could see. "So I find the tie, and I cut the connection. Got it. Thanks."

"And then you guide them to the veil. The door you were talking about might work for this, if you see it as a door. But they won't go willingly. You need to escort them to it."

"By visualizing them going through?"

"No, with your spirit. Guide them to the edge of the veil, and then the pull will take over."

Oh, hell. "Lemme get this straight," I said. "You project out of your body, grab the ghost, shove it up against the veil, and trust your silver cord to keep you from getting sucked into Deadland too."

He thought about it for a moment, then nodded. "Basically."

I had a hard time believing that someone as selfish as Chekotah would put his own subtle bodies on the line. Maybe the pull of Deadland was strong for actual dead people, but it must not be too intense for someone with a living physical body to call home. Not if that weenie was willing to brave it. Then again, maybe he was stronger than I'd been giving him credit for. It's not as if mediumship rankings meant anything…not that they'd ranked themselves at PsyTrain anyway. But he had managed to put up those sturdy astral barriers around his room, so maybe he did know what he was doing after all.

"Do you need some chant to help you shift your vibration?" he asked. "I could send you some MP3s."

Chant wouldn't do squat for me. Those painful experimental psyactives would work perfectly fine. "No. Thanks."

"Let me know if there's any other way I can be of help."

While I couldn't stand that guy for what he'd done to Lisa, my current situation with Chance was pretty dire. Any ally was a welcome ally. Even Bert Chekotah. I thanked him one more time and then moused around, searching for the button that would end the chat session, while he reached up and took off his headset. And then I saw it.

A wedding band.

Jacob put his hand over mine, guided the cursor to the signoff point, and clicked my finger into the button. Chekotah's image was gone now, but the image of the wedding band was firmly branded into my brain. That creep had *married* someone just a few months after the astral debacle? Not only was I enraged for Lisa, and for every other decent woman at PsyTrain, but for his current wife, too. Because if he hadn't cheated on her yet, I'd lay bets that he'd be sleeping around by New Year's.

"I'm gonna hit the bathroom," Bly said, fleeing the room before anyone could tell him where it was. Apparently my bitterness was so pronounced I could use it to deflect empaths.

I glared at the icon Bert Chekotah had chosen for himself, some Native American stylized feather. The way he hid behind his "I'm so spiritual" crap turned my stomach. "I'm sure he'll make an *awesome* husband… and it had better not be Faun Windsong who married him. Because she should know better."

"No, she's still in Santa Barbara. I don't think we've met the lucky girl."

"Good. But whoever it is, he doesn't deserve her."

"Yeah, I know, I give it less than a year."

I was sorely tempted to seize on my indignation and call the guy back before I cooled off. Once I had some time to think about it, I'd probably decide it wasn't worth getting a few digs in, and Chekotah would still be going around oblivious to what an ass he was. Jacob, standing behind me, settled his hands on my shoulders and dug his thumbs into the muscle on either side of my spine. I hadn't even realized I'd been gathering tension there. Sometimes it's hard to differentiate between pulling down white light and painful clenching. I rolled my neck a few times and sighed. "Of everyone at the FPMP with a big SUV, you had to bring an empath into our house?"

"So that's what's really eating you."

"If he could see into all your nooks and crannies, I'll bet it would be eating you too." I spun the office chair to face him. "It pisses me off. If it weren't for him strong-arming Richie when I specifically told him not to, Chance would still be in there. We'd know where she was, and we wouldn't need to go on a ghost hunt right now."

Jacob planted his hands on the armrests, leaned in, and spoke whisper-soft. "I had my eye on him."

"I thought he wasn't your type."

"I'm serious. Yeah, he's shifty, and I had my reservations before, but I've made my peace with them. If Bly hadn't read Chance's intentions and stepped in, she might've managed to zap you out of your own body so she could take over. You're armed. How would you feel if she used your weapon—your hand—to take the rest of us out?"

I tried to swivel away, but Jacob's hold on the chair didn't budge. The small struggle, though, made me suddenly aware of the way he was straddling my outstretched legs and leaning over my body like he owned it. When we roleplayed at being bossy, it was all an act for me. For him, though? He really was that butch. In fact, he was probably holding back so he didn't dislocate my shoulders when he forced my hands over my head and pushed my wrists into the mattress. That was fine in bed—he'd had plenty of practice over the years at being just forceful enough without taking things too far. In terms of Psych, though, he was flying blind.

"Here's the thing about working as a team," I said. "I need to be sure everyone's got my back."

"We do."

Maybe. But that didn't mean they knew what they were doing. "Bly thought I was oblivious that something was seriously wrong with Richie and he pushed too hard." And Jacob swung a light in my eyes…but the last thing I wanted to do was undermine that enviable self-confidence of his. "You and I need to get on the same page with our Psych talk."

"Okay."

The words I used to describe my subjective experience of Psych were painfully dumb, but it wouldn't do us any good to reinvent the vocabulary at this stage of the game. "There's energy all around us. Once, when we were all hopped up, you said it felt like vibration. For me, it looks like white light." Jacob nodded. This wasn't news to him. But I don't think he really understood its importance. "You handle this energy, whether you know it or not—Chance couldn't slip out of Richie until you let go of his arm. If my subtle bodies are rattling around loose inside my shell, I'll bet yours are fused in so tight it'd take a psychic earthquake to dislodge them. It wouldn't surprise me if you were actually better at handling the light than I am…but the problem is, you can't see what you're doing. I can."

"Then you're in charge." Jacob pressed his forehead into mine, and though Bly was lurking around the cannery somewhere, I felt some of the knots inside me untangle as I focused on Jacob's nearness, the immensity of his presence. It was big, like everything about him is big. Yet somehow, that huge presence didn't drown out my essential me-ness, but rather, amplified it.

He glanced at my lips as if considering whether or not we could afford to squander a precious moment for a kiss, and I leaned forward and made that decision for both of us. His lips parted. Our teeth grazed together. I swept my tongue in, bold, and his breath caught. Mine too, sharing this inhalation between us, dwelling for one shining moment in our trust, fortifying ourselves with the single, fleeting kiss, shoring me up before we embarked on an exorcism in which I absolutely could not allow myself to fail.

I relaxed into the familiarity of his mouth…and then I felt it. The gentle tug. Startled, I pulled back. "Did you feel that?"

The moment was ripe for a wisecrack, but Jacob must have sensed I was dead serious. "I'm not sure. I mean…" he broke eye contact and glanced away, somewhere in the vicinity of my ear. "It's always intense."

"I'm not talking about—"

"I know. Neither am I. Not entirely."

I squirmed my hands up between us, grabbed him by the face, and squared up his eyes with mine. "Listen. I've been gorging on white light all day. I've seen Jennifer Chance puppeteering Richie's body and I'm spooked as hell. That can't be me on the end of her strings, get it? That can't ever be me."

"I get it."

"So you can't grab my light. Heat of the moment, things get crazy… you've gotta keep your head on straight."

"Wait a minute. You're saying that when I kissed you, I—?" We stared at each other for a long moment, and when I didn't back down, he said, "Can I try it again, just to see if I can feel it? If it's safe, I mean, if you don't think I'll siphon out all the—"

Since I still had him by the face, it was up to me to pull him into the kiss. I doubted he'd steal the whole shebang. Last time he did that it was a different situation entirely, with sky-high adrenaline and a very disturbed ghost in the room. Besides, even if he did nab some juice, it couldn't hurt to rev him up before we charged into battle. I'd have time to replenish on the way back to FPMP headquarters. His mouth was hot and wet against mine, but his tongue was shy. Now he was really holding back. I could feel a tremor in the arms of the chair where he gripped them so tightly his hands shook. I moved slowly. We didn't have the time to be leisurely, but I wanted to forge the connection right. My tongue skimmed the edges of his teeth, but no telltale tug followed. Even when I tuned in to the great glut of light I'd been hoarding, it was all still there, roiling around inside whichever subtle body contained it.

I tongued him deeper, encouraging him to try and take it from me, but I could tell that light wasn't budging. Whatever he'd been doing before when I felt that tug, it wasn't happening now. Anxious to get going, I gave a little push…and then the floodgates parted.

My world went as bright as a sunrise over a fresh snowfall, but without the accompanying squint-inducing pain of overtaxed pupils struggling to adjust. I felt the light rushing into him through this connection in the physical, this kiss. It could have been any kind of touch, though, from a pinch to a caress. I don't think that detail really mattered. What escalated the luminous flow was our intent.

I ended the kiss gently. The transfer had been substantial, but I still had a sizable stockpile remaining. Jacob's eyes fluttered open. His cheeks were flushed. "You felt it," I said. I didn't need to ask. His awed expression said it all. "So that's the mojo at the heart of it all. If you grab it from me, you might as well tie me up before I shoot anybody, and then fly that asshole Chekotah out here to evict Jennifer Chance. If I can see the white light, it's likely she sees it too, and she'll slip in the second she spots an opening.

Jacob's eyebrows twisted up earnestly. "Wait a minute, who says this has to be a liability? If I can drain your white light, shouldn't I be able to top it off too?"

I typically cede to Jacob's greater intelligence, experience, and overall competence on all matters. Psych, however, was my thing, the only arena in which I had an advantage. I didn't want to burst his bubble, but given the stakes in this game, I couldn't afford to coddle him for the sake of—

He crushed his mouth to mine and jammed his tongue in, hard. His hand slid into my overcoat and grazed my holster while his fingertips dug into my ribs. His breath came in ragged huffs—and my physical body was starting to think this exchange was more about getting its rocks off than gathering light.

And then I felt it, like pins and needles, like a whack on the funny bone or a deep huff of aerosol propellant, an edgy, squirmy, frighteningly exuberant sensation that morphed from tactile to visual as it passed from Jacob's body into mine…from his spirit into mine. Sparkling, buoyant light. The same stuff as mine, but with a slightly effervescent cast imparted by the act of forcing itself through both our filters. My breath caught, and my groin throbbed. My physical body wanted to do something completely different than ghost hunting with this heady potency coursing through my veins.

Power is power, and I knew better than to squander it in my pants. I pulled away with a wet gasp before Jacob could ram all his light down my throat. If Bly was listening in, it probably sounded like we were banging each other. And if he was eavesdropping with his psychic empathy…well, it probably felt pretty much the same. Jacob's lips slid to my ear. He was breathing hard. "You felt that," he gasped urgently, like he'd just discovered my G-spot. "I know you felt it."

I felt it, all right.

Big time.

CHAPTER 31

ONCE JACOB AND I CONFIRMED that yes, the light flowed both ways, and once we adjusted our manhandled clothing and half-hard dicks, we headed downstairs to find Bly sitting on the big leather couch, leafing through the latest issue of Inner Eye. I'd rolled up the magazine and squeezed it in a sweaty fist so many times it read more like a scroll. The empath looked totally innocent, like he hadn't been catching massive waves of gay emanating from the upstairs office. Other people's lust must get old after a while. Or maybe he'd simply learned how to tune that type of stuff out.

We all headed down to the basement. I might not be entirely sold on Bly's presence in my home, but I was glad enough to take advantage of the extra pair of hands and strong back. I tested the set first to make sure it was working. Red and veiny? *Check.* Completely flayed? *Check.* Tracer fingers? *Check.* Then we unplugged the behemoth, eased it into its padded clamshell case, and set to hauling it up the stairs. I'd assisted with the encasement, but there wasn't room for all three of us in the stairwell. I darted up ahead and slid furniture and throw rugs out of the way to prevent anyone from tripping and getting crushed by the last remaining GhosTV.

I toed three pairs of shoes out of the way—why do women need so many shoes?—and scooted a wastebasket up against the wall as Bly backed out of the stairwell, carefully maneuvering his side of the massive crate. Scouting ahead, I discovered the typical scattering of mail on the vestibule floor. I gathered it up and was about to toss it on the blowjob bench when I saw that one of the envelopes didn't have a stamp or a return address on it. Only my name, in Bob Zigler's precise handwriting.

"Front door," Jacob called out, breathless. I crammed Zig's letter into my coat pocket and yanked open the front door just in time for the guys' momentum to carry both them and the TV crate through it. As Bly backed over the threshold, a vision of Washington goons flooding in to relieve us of the technology came to mind. Or worse, gunning us down in the process. I was relieved that at least Bly would be the first one to take a bullet…and then I felt guilty for thinking it. I was also relieved that he wasn't a telepath, and the worst thing he'd read off me was a confusing jumble of anxiety. Which was probably pretty typical of my headspace anyway.

Bly's gargantuan SUV did come in handy after all. The back row not only folded, but also split down the middle and swung to either side. Meanwhile the middle row had the capacity to fold down individually, just in case even more cargo room was required. We could've fit a keg in there alongside the GhosTV, as well as a new 70-inch flatscreen for Richie. The dashboard was pretty impressive too—satellite radio, MP3 dock, onboard navigation—though the main thing I cared about was that it could charge my phone, since I'd gone through the trouble of remembering my car charger.

Maybe Bly was part of my new Spook Squad, but I still didn't want to sit next to him where he could stare at me in his peripheral vision. I climbed in back, figuring I'd leave that honor for Jacob, since Bly could stare at Jacob all he wanted without reading a thing.

I opened my faucet to the infinite supply of white light and started loading up for the big showdown with my ex-doctor, and as I did, the image of the lightning-struck tower floated up through my consciousness. *Something you believe to be true is revealed as false.* I'd thought Dreyfuss was the worst guy in the world Lisa could have hooked up with, but one look at Chekotah was enough to convince me that I'd been wrong. I saw Dreysuss' face when he looked at Lisa—the guy was hopelessly besotted. If I could find room in my heart to relax my suspicions on Chekotah and Bly enough to accept their help with this exorcism, I could probably find a way to go a little easier on Dreyfuss for dating my best friend. Behind my back. And doing *yoga* and *manicures* together, for crying out loud.

We were still a couple minutes away from FPMP headquarters by the time I remembered the note from Zigler burning a hole in my pocket. If I learned something ugly about Detective Wembly at this stage of the mission, it might throw me off my game. Investigators with redacted names are unlikely to turn up sipping mai tais on a Maui beach…and if I found out Dreyfuss (or Bly, or both of them) had been the ones responsible for disappearing the missing PsyCop, it might undermine this cautious truce.

I fiddled with the envelope for a while, then folded it in half and slid it toward my pocket…and then I considered the fact that it wasn't very full. I flexed it a few times. One sheet of paper inside, tops. Zig would hardly be able to show definitive proof of what had become of poor Wembly in a single sheet. It was probably nothing more than a quick note, a phone number, a lead. Or maybe a reassurance that Wembly'd simply left the force and moved to Poughkeepsie. I folded the envelope. Unfolded it. Sighed. And slid my thumb under the seal. Because whether or not there was something upsetting inside, the not-knowing would create a gap in my focus where my white light could leak out. Now was not the time for me to be leaky.

There was indeed a single sheet inside. It wasn't a note, though. It was a photo printed on plain paper off a computer—a small picture, like you'd snap with a cell phone, but despite its small size, I felt a jolt of recognition. I knew the room, and I knew the people in it. Maurice and I had been in that room countless times, doing our boring duty as PsyCops to sit through tedious PowerPoint presentations on statistics and bone dry protocol lectures. Front and center, three PsyCops posed awkwardly with their thumbs in the air as if to say, "Yeah, this really is as lame as it looks." Carolyn Brinkman on the left. Valdez, the South Side precog, in the middle. And on the right, The Guy With the Hair—that's what Maurice and I always called him. He was a tall, paunchy ex-narc with this thick, full head of dark hair like you wouldn't believe, and it was always sticking up like he'd slept on it wrong. Apparently The Guy With the Hair was

John Wembly, according to the words *Brinkman, Valdez, Wembly* jotted below the picture. It stood to reason I knew him, or at least knew *of* him, but in light of his disappearance, connecting a face with the name just made me sad.

Until I got a better look at the photo and realized that Detective Wembly, minus the paunch, the pallor, the brown eyes, and the big, crazy head of hair…was sitting directly in front of me. His eyes flickered up and met mine in the rearview, and I looked away fast. No doubt he felt my emotions peaking yet again. It must be exhausting for an empath to be around me—although this time, I'd hauled out a set of feelings that didn't really see much use: surprise, wonderment, relief. Maybe even cautious optimism. Whoever had transformed John Wembly into Jack Bly had done such a good job of it, neither Jacob nor I realized we'd met the guy dozens of times before. Heck, he'd come right out and asked me how I liked being a PsyCop. Without the picture, though, I might have never made the connection.

Something you believe to be true is revealed as false. It had sounded so ominous at the time (and the illustration of the lightning-struck tower contributed to the overall sense of dread) but I was stoked to learn Detective Wembly was alive and kicking. His reward for helping the FPMP in some clandestine investigation hadn't been a pair of concrete shoes after all, but rather a shiny new badge, an SUV that cost as much as a small bungalow, and one hell of a makeover. Not only that, but I'd been badgering Con Dreyfuss about Wembly's whereabouts all week. Hell, I'd gone so far as to imply Dreyfuss was responsible for having him knocked off. It must have been pretty tempting to point me at Agent Bly and say, "There's your missing PsyCop, dickwad." But Dreyfuss had resisted the urge to set the record straight, even though it left him looking like a murderer.

My optimism even shed a bit of its cautiousness as I realized I was privileged to have some solid Psychs in my corner. Yeah, Jennifer Chance still creeped me out. But I could take her. Especially with all the backup I had at my disposal.

I had Jacob unplug my phone and hand it back to me, hoping to keep myself from blurting out "I know who you are!" by scanning through my messages before we rolled into the FPMP underground lot. A quick glance showed nearly forty missed calls—busy morning—but mostly they were hang-ups, with only a few messages.

First, Bob Zigler. "I dropped something off for you. Hope it's what you're looking for."

It sure as hell was. Although for a guy who'd just uncovered something the FPMP had tried really hard to bury, he sounded pretty down in the dumps.

Second message, Crash. His voice was shaking. "So, your phone keeps going to voicemail. Anyway. There was a fire. The store is gone." A long pause. A clamor of raised voices in the background. Breathing. Although I knew he hadn't been hurt, my heart still hammered when I heard him tell me the news himself. "I'm okay. I'm…yeah, I'm okay. I wasn't home." A sigh, and another long pause, where I thought he'd probably hang up and start attending to the endless snarl of red tape he'd need to unravel to start getting his stuff in order. But then he added, "You know, it's funny. I thought I'd just made a great big change in my life, since I decided, *What the hell? Might as well go for it.* With Red, I mean. Absence doesn't really make the heart grow fonder, but the thought of him pining away for me while he was off in San Francisco made me feel a lot better. Petty, huh?" He gave a wry laugh.

While Crash's empathy wasn't as sensitive or accurate as Bly's, I'd bet he had a good sense of how much regret this poor Red guy actually felt. You might be able to lie to an empath with what you say or don't say, but lately I'd gained firsthand experience on how challenging it is to shift the way you feel.

"Just goes to show, my idea of change is jack squat compared to what the universe had in store." He sighed again. "I'll bet it went up like a fucking bonfire. The incense, the resin, the books, the herbs, the charcoal. Shit. I hope Lydia's okay."

Lydia. Existentially speaking, she was fine. But my heart sank to hear the concern in his voice. I scrolled through more missed calls to see if he had any more news for me, but the rest of Crash's calls were all hangups. I would have phoned him back there and then, except for the identity of the caller who'd left the third message: Stefan. Briefly, I considered deleting the message from my Judas ex unheard and going on with my life, but I couldn't bring myself to thumb past without hearing what he had to say.

"So, are everyone's calls going straight to voicemail, or just mine?" His voice.... I've never met anyone with a voice like Stefan's—deep and rich, like you could sink right in to it, drown...and die with a smile on your face. He should've been working in Hollywood, or at least radio. And even though if I ran into him on the street I'd be happy to jab him with a sharp stick, the sound of his voice still left me breathing funny and swallowing dry. "Listen, I get that there's a lot of bad blood between us, and I know you don't understand why I did what I did, but set all that aside for now. Since you're some big-shot detective, I need you to help me find someone from Camp Hell."

The fact that he'd called me "some big-shot detective" in a dismissive way shouldn't have tripped my trigger. Of course, it did. Our triggers ran deep.

"I suppose you'll want to know why, so you might as well hear it from me. I joined a twelve-step program. It's just as hokey you'd think, too. All that B.S. about a higher power, and helplessness, and surrender. 'I'm Steven, and I'm an addict.' 'Hi, Steven.'" It jarred me to hear him call himself by the new name the FPMP had assigned to him, even though it was only marginally different than the name I'd imprinted on. "The success rate is nowhere near what they claim, either, but I had to try something. This past summer I got stopped by a traffic cop for making a lane-change without a signal—who the heck gets stopped for that?—and I realized there was a roach in my ash tray. What if that cop had searched my car? I could have lost my practice over something as ridiculous as a lane change."

Says the guy who smokes weed in his office, covers it up with air freshener, and thinks no one notices. I decided that maybe someone jonesing that hard for a hit really might benefit from Narcotics Anonymous. Then I wondered if there were supernatural jellyfish on goopy tethers hooked into his lungs. I rolled down my window and sucked in a few cleansing breaths before I hurled a stomachful of sour coffee onto Bly's plush leather seating.

"I'm on step nine, making my amends. I'm generating a lot of resistance to doing this, y'know? So it makes me think there must be some growth waiting for me on the far side of the process."

Could I forgive him for what he'd done to me—going behind my back, telling all my secrets, pumping me for information that he turned right over to the highest bidder? Could I even handle hearing the apology? I had no idea.

"Maybe no one's ever going to convince me that the little dweeb didn't deserve at least some of what he got, but I feel like I need to apologize to Movie Mike…if I can manage to find him."

Fucking hell, that asshole Mike? What about me?

"But you know who was doing unexpectedly well?" Stefan asked. "Richie Duff—good old Einstein. We were brutal to him, weren't we? Especially that imitation of his pathetic laugh you were always doing…I get goosebumps just thinking of it. He was a lot more gracious about my apology than I would have been, although maybe he's blocked a lot of it out. Haven't we all? He seemed pretty eager to chat about Camp Hell, but he couldn't remember anybody's name."

I could take that at face value, since Richie actually was doing unexpectedly well, or I could presume Stefan had recently been duped into providing Jennifer Chance with a long roster of Psychs. Given that he didn't make a snide remark about being invited to see the Bears play on Thanksgiving, it was more than likely Stefan Russell been making his amends to a ghost.

CHAPTER 32

STEFAN GAVE ME MOVIE MIKE'S actual name and ran through which channels he'd already searched, then said, "Maybe you've got better resources at your disposal than I do," and hung up without telling me he was sorry. I would have called him back and demanded my apology if it weren't for the fact that I was busy reeling over the idea of him chatting it up with Jennifer Chance. That, plus the fact that we'd arrived at FPMP headquarters, where I needed to leave my personal life on hold.

Dreyfuss was waiting for us beneath a cheesy sign that read, *Wow her with two dozen red roses!* His arms were crossed, clenched tight to his body, and he was pacing in a precise three-stride formation that spanned the entire potted plant section. I noted he wasn't biting his nails.

"The sí-no says Dr. Chance has been coming and going from the FPMP," he told us, "but this building's off limits."

"Where's Lisa?"

"Somewhere safe." And apparently he wasn't going to be any more specific than that. Given the whole train yard scenario, I had no doubt there were several pre-planned hidey holes at his disposal. "I've got Richie and Laura hunkering down in the back room here 'til this all blows over, with Dr. Santiago 'treating' Richie to make sure he doesn't start acting too smart."

"But I thought you said the shop was a safe—"

"I'm not taking any chances. Richie's a mess, and the thought of someone else inside Laura…" Dreyfuss shuddered. "Your hunch about mediums being an easy target for possession was right on the mark. Theoretically, anyone but a Stiff is at risk, but mediums' subtle bodies are a hell of a lot easier to shove out of the way."

Right. And I'd need to shove out my own spirits if I wanted to escort Dr. Chance to the veil. I said, "We should try to make sure we don't expose too many Psychs to her. NPs too. With the mediumship test being as lame as it is, Laura's probably not the only one who scored a false negative."

"I'll start sending people home." Dreyfuss tapped his phone a few times, then said, "Shit. This is no piece of cake without Laura at the helm. Plus, what if the ghost rides home inside one of my agents? What then?"

"Distance shouldn't matter." Theoretically, anyway. I did my best to sound knowledgeable. "We'll flush her out. If Jacob and I amp up on psyactives—"

"Me too," Bly cut in. "I saw that thing, it was just for a second and it looked kinda…kinda jellied. But I saw it—and I want another crack at it. I know what it feels like, inside its head. If it slips into anyone, I'll know."

Before, it would have rankled to have Bly elbowing in on my territory. But now that I knew he was an ex-PsyCop, I was ecstatic to have his talent on board. I said, "Can you soften her up somehow to make her an easier target?"

"If you nudge people the wrong way, it can backfire. Some people need to be calmed down; it makes them complacent. Other people are easier to amp up. They start feeling overwhelmed. They get sloppy. That ghost thing was intense. It'll be more of a danger to itself if I crank that intensity up a few notches…but do you really want to make it more unpredictable than it already is?"

We all went quiet and considered whether or not it behooved us to face a new and intensified Jennifer Chance.

Jacob had been taking in the whole discussion with his own brand of intensity, analyzing, thinking. He had it all sorted out by the time he spoke. "It depends on how you plan to handle her. If you're going to coerce her into the proximity of this veil thing, then knocking her off-balance first might be helpful. But if you're going to haul her over there with a sheer force of will—with your talent—then we're better off discouraging her from struggling."

"Either one of those things could work," I said. "I won't know until I try. And I might even need to switch tactics midstream if it's not going the way I want it."

"Psyactives are no problem," Dreyfuss said, "but how will you find her? Using the psychic tuner as bait?"

"I figured if I was pumped up on psyactives, the TV would give me an edge."

Jacob said, "Her too, though. Right? The TV effects everyone in the range of its signal. You'll be stronger in its signal, but so will she."

I hadn't considered that. Plus, the GhosTV was Jennifer Chance's baby. She'd probably get more out of it than I did. Hoping to hone myself into a more precision tool, I turned to Bly. "Maybe you could take the edge off me. Y'know…so I don't panic."

"If the ghost phlegm didn't panic you, I can't imagine what would."

"Look, I know it's a mess in here." I pointed to my head. "Help a guy out."

"A certain level of anxiety is par for the course, Detective. For all of us. It keeps us from getting splattered like a bug on a windshield. If it ain't broke, I'm not gonna fix it."

And to think I'd been worried about him tinkering around inside my skull. Here he wouldn't even do it with an engraved invitation.

Dreyfuss' thumbs had been flying over his smartphone. He said, "Evacuation's underway, except for a couple of sturdy telepaths who can keep tabs on each other while they get the tuner in place. So the big question is, where do I tell them to put it?"

Surely one part of the building would hold a tactical advantage for us over another. I'd toured the whole place and it was fresh in my mind. We could set up in the boardroom. It was big enough to ensure we weren't tripping over each other, and I knew Jennifer Chance had access to the location since I'd seen her there before. But wouldn't it seem awfully suspicious for the four of us to be sitting in the boardroom in the lambent glow of the GhosTV static? Maybe we could set up in Dreyfuss' office among the repeaters, pretend we were doing something with the TV that was totally unrelated to Chance, then shove her through the veil when she came to check up on her cherished invention.

Great plan—provided we had access to the veil from Dreyfuss' office.

"This veil thing," I said to Jacob, hoping he could glean some insight from our conversation with Chekotah. "That's where we need to set up the ambush."

"Is it in a fixed physical position, or does it move around?"

Had me there. I turned my hands up empty.

"Maybe the veil is more of a concept than a temporal location," he surmised. "I think what you really need to worry about is the silver cord."

I glanced at Dreyfuss' busy thumbs as if I might see a psychic scar where the goopy jellyfish tethers had been attached, but there was nothing there. Nothing I could see without psychic enhancement, anyway. Could Jennifer Chance be tethered to one of her GhosTVs, and if so, which one? Or had she attached to Dr. K to keep him from winning her Nobel? Those possibilities were worth checking into, but it made sense to try the obvious solution first: Chance's killer. "Before all the Lexuses leave the hive," I said, "have your trigger-man stay behind."

Dreyfuss looked up from his phone. "My what?"

Here I thought the Regional Director and I understood each other. Now he was making me spell it all out. "Whichever agent shot Dr. Chance, they should stay. They're the most likely anchor."

He looked at me so funny I almost thought he was going to admit to being the shooter. So I was totally unprepared when what actually came out of his mouth was, "There is no 'trigger man.' Jennifer Chance killed herself."

He was lying—he must have been. People who shot themselves didn't leave neat holes in their own foreheads.

Unless the entry wound had been solely for my benefit.

"How?" I asked.

"Suffocated." Dreyfuss gave an entirely humorless laugh. "I put her in the world's safest room, and she turned away from the cameras, covered her nose and mouth with the plastic wrap from her fucking sandwich, laid down on her hands and died."

Something you believe to be true is revealed as false. Evidently that damn tarot card was going to haunt me for the rest of my life.

"No wonder you had me pegged for a ruthless sociopath," Dreyfuss said. "First Jennifer Chance makes it look like I sent my ex-wife to gun down Roger Burke, then she tells you I had her executed."

Well, there was the spying and the threat of strip-search, too. But he hadn't been exaggerating when he told me not to take the spying personally because we were all on Candid Camera. The investigation of Laura was proof of that. I could only hope he wouldn't have actually let TSA shine a light up my rectum. I might never feel chummy with Con Dreyfuss, but I desperately wanted to believe we were both on the same side.

"Although," Dreyfuss said, "come to think of it, it's possible I bear some responsibility for her death, in a roundabout kind of way. I was trying to get her to spill the location of the final TV, and I told her that I was going to find out from Roger Burke anyway once I got him out of prison, so she might as well tell me herself and start banking some favors. It didn't occur to me she wanted to keep that last TV to herself so badly she was willing to kill herself to do it." He pondered a ragged cuticle, but didn't bite it off. "Here's what I don't understand. If you thought I had Dr. Chance shot, didn't you wonder what happened to the bullet wound?"

"Not really." She'd done a realistic job with her post-mortem special effects. Probably had first-hand information on what the hole would look like, being an MD and all. "She wore it loud and proud. I could hardly miss it."

Dreyfuss eyebrows shot up. "I'm not talking about her ghost, Detective. I'm talking about her corpse."

CHAPTER 33

MY BREATH STREAMED FROM ME in a visible cloud—not because I was hot on the trail of a ghost, but because the temperature was a chilly fourteen degrees in Cold Storage. Fatigue, overwhelm, a gut feeling of aversion, or sheer stupidity...I may never know what to chalk up my negligence to. Now I was kicking myself for bailing when Dr. K tried to show it to me. A stainless steel wall held telltale cubbies, most with serial numbers on the front, and each with its own dual lock, part manual and part digital. I was surprised there was no thumbprint reader and retinal scan. Maybe that stuff's just in the movies. One door stood open. Dreyfuss stepped up to it, planted his feet, stuffed his hands in the pockets of his hoodie, and turned to me. "Anybody home in there?"

I forced myself up to the vault and peered in. It was empty. "I take it you're not talking about the body."

"I had it moved to the warming area. It's probably not quite ready—it takes half a week to thaw a twenty-pound turkey, so you can hardly expect a human being to melt in a few hours. But I figured we might need it, so I got the ball rolling. Just in case."

Although my gut was churning with dread, and although I was fighting back an impending puke reflex, what I said was, "Show me."

Dreyfuss keycarded us all through to yet another workroom. Cripes, how much important stuff had I missed on my initial survey? Unlike the rest of the lab, which was filled with stainless steel work surfaces and laminate cabinets covered in labels, this room crinkled with plastic. Floors, ceilings, carts and countertops, everything in it was covered in a disposable clear film. Plastic even hung from the ceiling in the center of the room, forming a hermetically sealed column. The change in air pressure when we opened the door caused the plastic column to flex as if it was breathing. This film was heavier than the rest, thick enough to appear translucent rather than clear, but despite the occlusion, my eyes sketched out the contents soon enough. A tank, maybe six feet long, filled with greenish fluid, resting on a waist-high table. And inside that tank, a body.

Dreyfuss handed out surgical gloves and masks, then slid a mask over his own face. "The lab's trying to keep as much bacteria off the body as possible. And the repeated freezing and thawing's not doing it any favors either. You can work through the gloves, right? Or should we make an exception for our star medium?"

Gloves were fine, but my hands went tacky the second I snapped them on. A bead of sweat rolled down my temple, and I realized that in contrast to the chilly morgue, the workroom was sauna-warm. I blotted my forehead with my sleeve, then grabbed my salt and my Florida Water from my pockets and slipped out of my overcoat—not much better—and my jacket, too. Before I could wonder what to do with them, Bly took them from me and hung them on plastic-covered hooks beside the door. "They're no protection against a ghost anyway," he said. "Might as well minimize your distractions."

That was one way of looking at it, though I felt skinny and vulnerable in my shirtsleeves, which clung to me where they were starting to wick sweat. It should have felt intrusive, that he intuited my apprehension. It didn't. Instead, it made me feel less alone.

"Do you need anything else?" Dreyfuss asked. "I've got Carl standing by in case you change your mind."

Nothing against Carl, but he'd been trained by Richie—and Richie's traditional prayer methodology was so foreign to me that I worried Carl's presence might be more of a liability than an asset. Plus, given how territorial he is, I didn't want to catch hell for dipping into his metaphysical supplies. No, Jacob had the candles and Bly had the incense, and I had my trusty pocket kit, though it felt woefully small in the plastic cavern of the workroom. But I'd been feeding it white light all day, and if that wasn't enough, then all the salt in Utah wouldn't help me. "I'm ready. Just as soon as the horse pills kick in."

"Any minute now," Dreyfuss said. He checked his phone, then added, "It's been fun, Detective. If we come out of this alive and intact, the drinks are on me."

"Hold on a second. You're not staying?"

"Unfortunately, my services are required elsewhere. Washington's heading over here for another round of snatch n' grab—and now they're after her body." It only made sense for her to try and keep the object that anchored her among the living as far away from me as possible. Who was the poor Psych she'd borrowed a body from to make the call—and was she still hiding inside it or not? "Lisa and I turned the problem upside down," Dreyfuss said, "and there was no way to stop the government thugs from crashing our party. But if anyone can stall them long enough for you to evacuate the ghost before they can grab the body…it's me."

Although it wasn't as if Con Dreyfuss would be able to do anything against a spirit, even taking his psychic ability into account, I was dismayed that he had to leave. "But it all works out," I said, "since you'll live to see tomorrow."

"I used to wonder if Lisa would ever lie to me about that when push came to shove, y'know, to make me feel better." I imagined that beneath the surgical mask there was a wry twist to his mouth. "Evidently not."

The door whispered shut behind Dreyfuss, then locked with a firm click. Jacob began stalking the perimeter like a caged beast, relentlessly scanning the surroundings as if he was worried he'd miss an important tactical advantage. Bly did a shoulder roll and glanced nervously around the room. "It's funny, the things you don't notice 'til they're gone," he said. "I've never been in the lab while it was empty. It doesn't feel right."

Jacob said, "Then you'll feel it when Chance gets here."

"I don't know. I mean, I didn't even realize it was a separate thing until I saw it turn to jelly. I just…I don't know."

"We're fine," I said. "Everything's fine. She's not here." Yet. I wasn't quite sure if I wanted her to make an appearance or not, though I supposed a showdown in the time and place of our choosing was preferable to the big ugly surprise we'd found at Richie's house. I shifted my stance, and a cramp seized my calf muscle. When I screwed up my face in pain, my jaw cramped too. "I forgot how much this hurts."

"It hurts?" Bly asked. I actually felt sorry for him.

"There's discomfort," Jacob said. Red veins ghosted his temples. They grew clearer, more pronounced, as I focused on them. I looked to Bly. Around his mask, thin-skin. Checked my own fingers. Tracers. And the parts where my subtle bodies weren't quite lined up with my physical, I realized, felt a lot less crampy than the limbs I was using to stand on. I was scared to shift my awareness to those bodies, though, for fear of coming apart.

"Jesus." Bly rolled his shoulders again.

"Are you picking up on anything?" I asked in hopes of distracting him from the very painful "discomfort."

"I'm not sure…."

"I have no idea what it would feel like to be empathic," I told him. "So however she registered back there in the kitchen—anger, desperation, obsession—look for that. 'Cos I guarantee everyone else is just plain scared."

Bly turned his focus outward, went still for a moment, then said, "No. I don't feel her."

"Okay, then. Jacob, fire up the candles and incense."

He seemed relieved to have a task, something he could do other than standing around and dreading the ghost's arrival. The cardinal points had been marked on the plastic with grease pencil prior to our arrival, so in no time flat, Jacob had a candle burning at each point. There were no pyrotechnics this time around, not like the hospital basement. No drop in temperature or change in pressure. Just another reminder that this ghost was whole different enchilada.

In the course of my police work, salting repeaters had become pretty routine. I saw now I'd let myself get soft by considering anything having to do with the spirit world routine. Fine. If I wasn't following a pattern, I'd be considering my every move, therefore I'd be less likely to get sloppy. I sent a haze of white light outward, feeling for the glow of the candles, the smoke of the myrrh. The room shone brighter, not as if the lights were turned up, but as if a special lens had slid across my vision that made all the plasticky highlights shine brighter. I squinted into the sparkle-vision and cast my gaze around the room.

"How can you be so calm?" Bly asked me. I think he meant it rhetorically. I figured it was best to treat it as if he did. I held up a gloved finger for silence, I gathered myself, and I parted the thick plastic sheeting.

Her blotchy, grayish forehead was clear. No bullet hole. None. Sonofabitch. Maybe on some level I'd still believed Con was conning me. But no amount of makeup could hide a bullet wound, not from this distance. It hadn't been Dreyfuss manipulating me—it was Jennifer Chance. Even from beyond the grave. It didn't seem fair. While Lydia had trouble making cigarettes appear, Chance's ghost was capable of generating special effects. I guess a lifetime of studying subtle bodies had its perks.

The physical body looked terrible, though. It wasn't the first corpse I'd ever seen, and it probably wouldn't be the last, but the fact that I'd had several conversations with her over the past few months must have led me to gloss over the fact that she was dead. Seeing the empty shell brought home her death with way more impact than chatting with her ghost. The body was half-submerged in the fluid, which smelled like the stuff they keep the combs in at the barber shop. It was covered by an opaque plastic sheet drawn up to its chest—to protect its modesty or spare us the shock of seeing both death and nudity? Since there was something distinctly brain-shaped in a Tupperware container beside her tank, I presumed they'd made a cranial incision. The cut was hidden by her lank blonde hair, combed straight back in a style in which she never would have worn it. The stitched ends of an autopsy Y-incision did show over each collarbone, angled out to her shoulders like grisly bra straps.

I considered the sheer deadness of the form on the table, and then I pulled down a fresh stream of white light, looking deeper. No one was home. The thing before us was nothing but thawed meat.

"This isn't the anchor," I said. "Jennifer Chance was pragmatic. What use would she have for a dead body—even one that used to be hers? We need to turn on the TV to get her attention."

"Let the psyactive kick in before you do that," Jacob suggested.

My seized up calf muscles were bringing tears to my eyes. "Oh, they're locked and loaded, believe you me."

Jacob looked at the TV and frowned. He was having cold feet about firing it up, but he didn't second-guess me. Not now, not in front of Bly, and not when we'd established that the two of them were going to follow my lead no matter what. If our roles were reversed, it would eat me up to watch him march head-first into danger too. But that's what we both signed up for—and that's what made us lousy partners for the sorts of regular people we were trying to protect.

I knelt before the TV and peered into the modified speaker well. I could twirl the settings, screw them up so that neither of us was at an advantage, but what if I ended up tipping the balance so the ghost got a better signal than I did? I should have been practicing all this time, gotten to know this thing inside and out, rather than deliberately ignoring it. Of course that was only dawning on me now, because when FPMP Washington got here I could kiss the GhosTV goodbye.

What was it anyway that made the goons decide to take another sweep? They'd been pretty damn thorough the first time around. Had they found something on one of the computers they took? There was nothing there they couldn't have seen ages ago from the servers. The only source of intel I could think of was Jennifer Chance herself. Dreyfuss must have mentioned having access to her body outside the flower shop, somewhere she was eavesdropping. She'd realized it was a liability and she prompted her flying monkeys to come and take it away.

But how?

Not through Richie or Laura, since they had Santiago watching their thought patterns. But it wasn't as if the three of us were the only mediums on the planet. I imagined Chance pushing against people to see if any subtle bodies were easy to jar loose, like an opportunistic criminal trying the doors on a line of parked cars to see if someone with a nice stereo might have neglected to lock up…like the dead guy down on Maxwell Street. If she was currently hunkered down in a living body, she could be anywhere by now, and how would I find her? Despair churned in my gut, despair and futility and a horrible sense of helplessness, because if I couldn't do this thing, then no one could.

Bly cleared his throat and said, "I could take the edge off that discouragement."

"Nah. I need all the edge I can get." I looked at him, the eyes showing above his mask round in their sockets of muscle beneath his transparent skin. And I looked to Jacob, with his bulging webwork of veins. These things were so visually clear that my talent was off the charts, and yet I couldn't do a damn thing about Jennifer Chance if she wasn't fucking there. I tried to stand and my cramped legs didn't comply. I cracked my knee on the plastic-covered tile and spun awkwardly on it to glare at the body.

And then I saw it. A glint. Hard to spot among the dangling plastic suffused with its white ambient glow, but when I cocked my head, when I squinted, I saw it again. A tether—hair thin, practically invisible—extending from the body's solar plexus.

When Bert Chekotah compared the connection to a spider's web, I'd figured it was more of his contrived Native American phraseology. But that was exactly what it looked like, one of those long, thin, single strands you don't notice until it brushes against your face. Bly gasped—he felt the revelation as acutely as I did. Jacob looked between us, gleaning some idea of what was going on in my head by body language alone. I nodded to him, and that was enough. I wasn't sure how sensitive this thin cord was to vibration, but in case it was the equivalent of a ghostly listening device, I opted to speak in our micro-expression language rather than give out any information.

White light. I pointed to the ceiling, then to my forehead, and then made a drawing down motion. Jacob nodded. Good. Bly nodded too. Excellent. We were as ready as we were ever going to be. I fixed the position of the slender cord in my mind, and then I closed my eyes and opened the faucet wide.

Although it's been explained to me, I can't claim I technically understand what the crampy psyactive does. I felt it, though, like my capacity for white light had been doubled, and my ability to draw it in reached farther and pulled harder. I flooded myself, checked to see if it felt okay, then sucked down even more. My inner vision went so bright that everything was white, and I could no longer tell if my eyes were open or closed. I opened them experimentally, and everything was white on white, and yet I could see it all with a vitreous clarity. Jacob, Bly, the plastic, the dormant TV, and the body. The spider's web blazed as if it was the most solid thing in the room, like anyone who walked through it would fall into two halves like a big, ripe cheese. I held up my hands to keep Bly and Jacob where they were—probably looking like a sweaty faith healer, kneeling there in my damp shirt with my arms outstretched—and the three of us went completely still.

The slender silver cord glittered.

I wasn't seeing an astral cord, I realized, but something that led to a different subtle body, the stuff that ghosts are made of. This cord could lead us to Jennifer Chance…though it would be a heck of a lot more convenient if it could reel her in. I looked at it, got a feel for it—sharp, yes, and strong too. But delicate, in a brittle way. Like glass, something that could cut just as easily as it could shatter. Maybe Chekotah was able to brush it away, but he'd had Hugo Cooper in the room with him while he did so. I couldn't risk severing the tie while Jennifer Chance was out and about. Because what if that left some poor medium huddled in the corner of their own mind while Chance ran the controls? Nope, I needed her here, where I could see her. So I stared hard at that cord, really fixed on it, and mentally, I pulled.

Nothing.

Nothing but a familiar throbbing in my skull, anyway. It was the Triple-Shot scene all over again. Me straining fit to burst a brain vein, and no reaction whatsoever in the spirit realm. Only now I was twice as hopped up. Probably twice as likely to rupture something important by pushing too hard in the wrong direction. The more I thought about it, the more I realized it felt exactly like Triple-Shot, and me sitting here mentally grasping at Jennifer Chance wasn't going to get us anywhere at all.

Bly cleared his throat again. I glanced over my shoulder. Between the thin-skin and the surgical mask, I couldn't read his expression. "Despair doesn't really give you an edge."

"I'm only going to say this once," I told him, enunciating each word very clearly, since he couldn't see my face. "If I don't suddenly feel like a crazy female egomaniac to you, then stop nosing around my head."

Jacob's eyebrows went up. Mine, too. I wasn't usually that direct. And what the hell happened to teamwork?

"Gotcha." Bly didn't sound particularly threatened, but I supposed I'd made my point. "And by the way, anger's a lot more useful than despair."

Oh. There was a reason I was suddenly so pissed off.

While at least he told me when he was tweaking my emotions, thanks to him shifting my despair into something more active, I wasn't particularly mollified by the full disclosure. I gave him a very nasty look, then turned back to glare at the silver strand, too. Attempting to think at it was getting me nowhere, so what did that leave me? I aimed some white light at it…but that was just a variation on pulling at it with my mind. What, then? Pluck it like a guitar string and see if I got an answer?

I reached toward it, fully expecting my finger to pass straight through, like it would any other ghost or repeater—and got the psychic equivalent a 110-volt shock. I pulled my hand away and shook it, expecting the tip of my latex glove to open up like a banana peel, but the glove was untouched. I shook my tingling hand again, and muttered, "Sonofa…."

The word escaped me in a cloud of frost. The surgical mask trapped it, mostly, but some shot out around the edges, blowing down the front of my neck and up my cheekbones, fogging the scene that was already sparkly white to my inner vision. Two gasps followed. Apparently I wasn't the only one who could see the frost. And then a spike of fear knifed at my chest…except a detached, pissed-off part of me knew I wasn't actually afraid. "Get a grip, Bly, you're leaking. Put a lid on it."

"Shit. Oh, shit." Not exactly the stalwart ex-PsyCop federal agent I'd come to know and tolerate. At least he figured out some way to stem the flow, leaving my gut reeling with the abrupt roller coaster of anger and fear that settled finally at a cool, clear lucidity. I looked for the strand again, and it was plainly visible now to my mind's eye, sharp and bright. Now that I'd touched the thing we were acquainted, and there was no squinting and searching required. Even though I was crawling with white light, I sucked down some extra, and I sent it toward my fingertips as I reached for the strand to give it a tug.

I'd braced for the contact, and this time the rush was different. Instead of the silver strand zapping me, I was the one who zapped. My white light raced down the strand like flame through a fuse. My gut screamed at me to stop, but I couldn't, not now. Chance was surely onto me, and if I hesitated, she'd ensure that the next thing FPMP Washington hauled away was my drugged carcass.

No hesitation, then—I couldn't afford it. I closed my eyes, opened up the top of my head, and let white light flood in to replenish whatever juice was getting pulled up the strand. It thundered through me, and my physical eyes snapped open. There was my physical hand, steady in its physical latex glove. And around that, another hand, oversized. And another, with longer fingers. Around those, still more. Multiple subtle bodies, all slightly off-kilter from the physical, like a stack of misaligned transparencies. I had no idea which body was required to reel in the ghost of Jennifer Chance, so I gathered up my will, and using every damn one of those hands, I pulled.

All the air whooshed out of the room—and the heat, and the light, too. The plastic around us went dusky blue, flexing in as if it was breathing. Jacob's breath gusted out around his mask in a visible puff. Bly's too.

And then I felt the impact.

Chance's ghost roared up the silver strand and slammed against me like lightning. She tried to slip into me like a coat, one arm, then the other, but my subtle bodies were too fortified for her to stay put. Every part of her that slid in slid right back out, while I was there jerking around like I'd just invented a new punk dance. It wasn't enough to resist her ghost, though. I needed to command it. To break it.

"Oh God," Bly called out, "she's here!"

I ignored him. "More light," I told Jacob, and held out my hand. He was there, right there, and without hesitation he locked fingers with me and squeezed—I'd feel it in my knuckles later, I realized, just like I'd feel my calf muscles later—but for now I was so much more than physical that I transcended mundane things like pain, and cold, and fear. I saw him as the Cro-Magnon Red Energy Super-Stiff with one of my subtle bodies, and with another, as Jacob, just Jacob, the man I loved with all my heart, and trusted with my life. As the universe fed white light energy through my head, he pushed tingly tactile energy up my arm. When the ghost of Jennifer Chance tried to slip into that arm, she yowled.

"More," I gasped, and the tingle became a buzz, and then a roar. I knocked away my surgical mask to try and catch my breath, and my words streamed out on a thick white cloud. "Keep gathering it while you—" I didn't need to explain. He was already doing it.

I didn't have the fine control to grab Chance with the proper subtle body, so I went at her with all of them in a big, ungainly sweep. Her arm was flailing near mine, trying to align, and I grabbed it by the wrist. It turned into jelly, which drooled to the floor. Somewhere behind us Bly was retching, but I shut him out, grateful he was at least keeping his terror out of my head, even if he couldn't keep his lunch in his gullet. The arm-gooping didn't seem to do Chance any damage. She pulled herself together and tried one more time to jump into me, but she bounced off as if an electrical force field was in place.

Her eyes glowed with rage—literally glowed, with a crackling silvery light—and then, since she couldn't get into me, she swung around and took a stab at getting into Jacob. It was a sight to behold. She dove in hard, and where she touched him, she dematerialized. It was like watching someone fling a human-shaped water balloon against him and seeing it explode. He rocked back, ectoplasm raining around us, and I squeezed his hand tight enough that he couldn't pull it away. "You're fine!" I called to him. "She can't do anything to you, not a damn thing."

Unfortunately, Chance could hear me as well as Jacob could. The ethers gathered, and the ghost re-formed yet again…and then those ghostly eyes lit on Jack Bly.

"Oh no you don't." Each word was a puff of frost as I lunged for her with my free hand. It went through her arm, splattering jelly, once, twice, and then I realize I'd been grabbing for the wrong spot. The ghostly shape of Jennifer Chance was just as much a shell as that mottled hunk of sutured meat stewing in the warming tank. I needed to grab her by the essence—by the soul, for lack of a better word. I pictured the place where the silver strand had connected her to her physical body's solar plexus, targeted the same spot on her ghost…and I grabbed.

It was like plunging my hand into a snowbank. An electrified snowbank. An electrified snowbank that was on fire, and was also full of razor blades and acid. I let out a huff in surprise and pain, and my breath was a great crystalline cloud. My fingers had closed on something, though, something solid, something throbbing and squirming and struggling to break free. It hurt like all getout, but no way in hell would I let go so she could take a crack at Bly. Now that I had a grip, though, what the heck did I do with her?

The veil, I was supposed to lead her to the veil. But I could hardly locate the damn veil while I was struggling to keep hold of her spirit. If only Jacob could hang on to her for a sec while I…my eyes fell to the corpse, and before I could second guess myself, I slammed my fist into its gut. My physical fist bounced off, but my other fists—astral, ethereal, whatever they were—those subtle fists kept on going. "Grab her," I gasped to Jacob, "grab the body—anywhere, both hands—just grab it!"

The spirit tried to slither out when it realized what we were doing, but Jacob dove at the body like a defensive lineman. The plastic tank buckled, spraying chemical fluid. The corpse was torn from my grasp, and now Jacob had it by one hip and one shoulder, with everything in between firmly pinned.

"That's it," I shouted, "that's perfect." I gathered my white light for a final push. "Hold her there while—"

"Jesus Christ," he blurbled into the chemical solution, "It's moving."

Bly made a strangled noise, then staggered out through the door, splattering vomit.

"Don't let go," I pleaded with Jacob.

"Then hurry!"

There was only so long I could expect him to wrestle an animated corpse without losing his marbles. After all, Zigler was never the same since the zombie basement, and all he'd done was look at the damn things. I got to work picturing the veil, death, the great hereafter. I tried to visualize all those locales, and I experienced a jab of panic. Would I even be able to find the afterlife, me, a card-carrying agnostic? What if I couldn't? What if, in the end, I failed us all, and Chance slid free, and Jacob ended up spending three nights a week on a psychiatrist's couch for the rest of his life…?

The workroom door flew open, and from it, a puke-covered Bly called out, "What are ya, scared? You…you…*homo!*"

Rage flooded me, sharp, sudden, and exhilarating. If he'd been any closer I would have clocked him one good, but along with the anger, I felt a frosty clarity descend. I'd be damned if I let Chance get away to wreak havoc with decent people for the sake of her fucking invention. I'd be damned.

Images flashed through my mind, of all the newly dead I'd seen turning toward the light, a light that looked a lot like the white light I'd been pulling down, only infinitely brighter. And as I pictured it, I realized it was there. Not that I'd summoned it, since a lowly mortal like me could never hope to change its course. But nonetheless, it was there, tugging at my awareness. Like a portal. Or a wormhole. Or a sun.

"On the count of three," I told Jacob, "let go of her. Got it?" He was face down on the twitching cadaver, so I went with the assumption that he was onboard. "One…two…three!"

Jacob flew backward, hands in the air, and I lunged. I saw the spirit try to roll out to one side, sneaky, like maybe she'd get away. But I also saw the core of her, the soul body, and I made a grab for that. It wasn't only my talent at play. Jennifer Chance wasn't supposed to be there. She'd been expected elsewhere ever since she made the decision to cover her face in plastic wrap and lay down to die. Between me pushing and the gleaming white portal pulling, her grip on physical reality began to erode.

She was a fighter, though, and ectoplasm flew as she battered me with her ghostly fists. We teetered at the brink of the veil, me pushing, her pushing back. I was all set for the final push when a wad of ghost goo came between the plastic-covered floor and the sole of my shoe. I slid, flailing, but I was determined to keep hold of her. But with which hand? My subtle bodies fanned apart, and suddenly the gentle tug of the veil was a strong, irresistible pull. A piece of me slid out—and yet in the face of this separation, I felt surprisingly calm. I decided that if it was my time to go, at least I'd take Dr. Chance with me, and I clamped onto her with everything I had.

And then there was light.

It was perfect. I was perfect. Everything was perfect—me, the world, and the universe. It was profoundly simple, this feeling of perfection. It was sublime. I was still me, maybe, but I was everything. Whatever Jennifer Chance was didn't cease to exist, yet it somehow ceased to matter, because she too was one with everything.

"Vic?"

I fell. Or maybe I'd been falling ever since I slid on the ectoplasm. Or maybe I wasn't falling, maybe I'd mistakenly swallowed one Seconal too many, and maybe I was in bed with an intense case of the spins. No, that wasn't it. There'd been a hard slam when I hit. The room was covered in plastic and the floor I was sprawled on was coated in chemicals and slime. And Jacob's face was hovering over mine as he shook me by the shoulders. "Vic!"

I blinked and said, "Yes." My recently-stretched consciousness thought this single word should encompass volumes of meaning, but my worldly sensibility was slowly coming back to me as well, and I realized that most physical people can't really communicate in sighs and glances and micro-expressions, as much as they might want to. So I added, "We did it. She's gone."

CHAPTER 34

MY PHONE RESTED ON THE dining room table amid the half-puzzled male dancers while I attempted to choose between my red tie and my other red tie. After an address and a time, the text from Dreyfuss had simply read, *Wear something nice.* That meant Jacob broke out the cufflinks, while I dug around until I found one of my special tall-guy jackets that actually fit me. It covered all the bumps and bruises I'd picked up flailing around the lab that morning, too.

"Celebratory dinner?" I suggested.

Jacob peered critically in the bathroom mirror, smoothed his eyebrows, stroked his goatee, then patted down the sides of his already-perfect hair. "It's never that simple with him."

Probably not, but it wasn't in me to feel sardonic about it. About ninety nine point nine percent of the kumbaya had fled me once I'd fallen out of the white light. But for now, I still remembered how it was to be inside the glow…and the mere memory of that sensation was enough to make me feel magnanimous toward everyone. Even Con Dreyfuss.

We were both eager to see Lisa again and ask her what really happened. Reassurances that Richie and Laura were okay would be in order too. I also wanted to hear how Dreyfuss fared against Washington, whose goons had swept in and relieved us of a slime-covered corpse without batting a G-man eyelash. There wasn't a doubt in my mind that they would've gladly scooped up the GhosTV too, had Jack Bly not summoned the presence of mind to turn it toward the wall, throw a plastic sheet over the top, and cover it with lab equipment so that it blended in passably with the cabinetry.

We found the restaurant and handed the car keys to the valet, while I wondered idly if there might be a tracking device hidden somewhere in the fob. It was a ritzy joint. Hopefully there'd be something identifiable on the menu.

We ran into Bly at the coat check. I can't speak for Jacob, but I was glad to see him. He wasn't as battered as Jacob and me, but given what we'd all seen in the lab morgue, he was probably donning a few fresh scars on the inside. "Listen," he murmured, once the coat check girl was out of range, "that *homo* thing I said before…."

I got it—he'd been trying to pull me out of an impending funk by pissing me off. It worked, too. "I know."

"I'm fine with it," he said. "Really. My favorite aunt is a lesbian."

The old me would have rankled at the idea that my personal life was anything for him to be "fine" with. But in my white light afterglow, I could tell he was attempting to stammer out an apology. And I appreciated it.

"And I've never yakked at a scene before," he told Jacob. "Never. But I could feel it, really feel it, inside the…body." He looked a bit green just scanning through the memory. While my deathly experience had been a moment in the light, Bly had absorbed the emotions of Jennifer Chance trapped inside her own corpse. On psyactives, no less. Poor sap.

"I've been meaning to tell you," I said, "the shaved head, the tan, the workout, it all looks great on you. But the colored contacts are a little over the top."

Jacob stopped walking and stared. The hardcore critique must've seemed like it came out of left field to him, but the empath got it. Bly let out a breath and gave his head a rueful shake. "How long have you known? Not long—I can feel it, not long."

"Known what?" Jacob said easily, picking up on the new camaraderie between Bly and me in that mundanely empathic way of his.

"Remember John Wembly?" I asked, while Bly made a small "shoosh" motion. I lowered my voice. "You know, the PsyCop, with the hair?" Recognition dawned on Jacob's face. "The one who went missing," I added.

Jacob checked Bly out unapologetically, scrutinizing him from head to toe, then said, "Your trainer's doing a great job."

Bly turned toward the dining room, smirking. "She's a tyrant," he threw back over his shoulder. "Made me give up soda. Cheese, too." Sheesh, that *was* pretty extreme. Good thing he actually liked chard.

Jacob watched the doorway where Bly had disappeared for a moment, then said, "Cheekbone implants. If it weren't for those, I would've spotted him."

"Yeah, yeah. Says you." I bumped him affably with my elbow. "Go find our seats—I'm hitting the can." You never knew how long these dull multi-course affairs might last, and I didn't want to navigate a dangerously upscale dinner with a full bladder. The lighting was elegantly subdued, meaning, the warren of hallways and private dining rooms was a confusing blur of linens, woodwork and candles. Right when I suspected I might have gone a full 360 and ended up back with Jacob, I saw Lisa flit past a doorway. She was looking pretty ripped, too. I guess all that yoga was starting to pay off.

"Lisa," I called after her. "Hey, Lisa, wait up." But when she turned to face me, it wasn't Lisa at all, just some other Hispanic girl with bigger hoop earrings and more makeup. "Oh. Sorry."

I backpedaled while the girl said, "No, it's—"

"Never mind." I ducked into the nearest room, aghast at the thought I'd nearly grabbed the poor stranger by her shoulder. Nothing ruins a nice dinner like getting maced on your way to the john…which, it appeared, I'd actually managed to stumble into. It was one of those toilets with a lounge, the type that usually had an attendant waiting to awkwardly hand you a towel, or a breath mint, or a comb. The lounge was full of fresh flowers, or maybe incredibly realistic fakes. I was about to double-check that I wasn't blundering into a public *ladies* room when I heard Crash's voice, and then my awkwardness fell away, and I charged in to grab him up and squash him against me to celebrate the fact that Ash Man was only his chat handle, and not his physical state of being.

But then another man's voice joined his, breathy, unfamiliar, and unabashedly gay. "She's perfect. Shakira and Mariah and Ashanti all rolled into one. Just a lil' more sparkle."

Crash again: "Whoa, cowboy. Easy on the fairy dust. This isn't a rave."

I rounded the corner into a restroom, but not the sink-and-stalls type I'd been expecting. The single opulent powder room was full of flowers, cushions, lights, and mirrors. Crash was there with his new-old boyfriend Red, each of them dressed to the nines, combs and attitudes poised, flanking a woman in a styling chair. Seated between them like a Hollywood diva, impeccably made up, hair piled high and sparkling with glitter, was Lisa. All three looked up, startled, and met my eyes in the various mirrors. "Uh…hey," I said. "What's going on?" Because it looked like Lisa was ready to star in a music video. Maybe with the dancers from the unfinished puzzle.

While Crash had his eyes on me, Red seized the opportunity to spritz Lisa with another layer of shimmery spray. Crash turned a warning look on him, and he replied with infuriating nonchalance, "Now, you listen to me, Curtis. I know what I'm doing. Every girl's a princess on her wedding day."

Beneath all the sparkles, I realized, Lisa's salsa video tango dress was white. Not simply because she favored neutral tones, either.

Wow.

Just…wow.

"Victor…" she attempted to pry herself from the chair, but she might have been glued there with glitter spray. Red gave her a hand up, patting her sparkly brown cascades of curls into place with his long-fingered hands as she turned toward me. "Constantine proposed this afternoon and I didn't have time to tell you—it was all really sudden."

"Oh." I forced a smile, not that I was angry or apprehensive or anything. Just blindsided. And cripplingly aware that this was one of those moments where I really didn't want to say the wrong thing, because if I tainted her special day, she'd be within her rights to hold it against me for the rest of our lives. It made sense, of course. When Con Dreyfuss had a woman in his sights, he slapped a ring on her before she got away. But even I knew Lisa wouldn't take kindly to that observation, so I decided to go with,

"Well, you look fantastic." I took her hands in mine and gazed into her eyes. I figured I'd better not make her cry or else a pretty spiffy makeup job would go to waste, so instead I quipped, "If you wanted a bigger tent, you should have said so."

She laughed, and the sentimental tears that had been threatening on the horizon receded, for now. "You're okay? The exorcism—everything went okay? Because the sí-no—"

Hopefully she hadn't been checking up on me while I was one with the light. I strongly suspect that for those few seconds, I was technically dead. It wasn't an unpleasant experience. Heck, it wasn't even all that frightening. Nonetheless, it was an act I didn't care to repeat. If that's what it took to command spirits—ejecting your etheric form and hoping you're stronger than the ghost you're attempting to wrangle—I'd just as soon stick to my Florida Water and salt. "Jennifer Chance has moved on, right? I'm here. And I take it Dreyfuss survived the Washington goons if he lived to sweep you off your feet."

She nodded.

"Then it's all good."

I'm not much of a hugger, and neither is Lisa, but at that moment it felt perfectly natural to pull her close and plant a kiss on the top of her head.

Even if it did leave me spitting glitter.

Once I'd found the real men's room and done my business, I was in the stall pulling a few singles out of my wallet to tip the attendant when a familiar voice spared me the effort. "Would you mind waiting outside for a few minutes?" Con Dreyfuss said to the attendant, undoubtedly slipping him an outrageous gratuity. "I wanted to have a private chat with my friend." I wasn't sure if he'd used his talent to find me alone, or if he'd been scoping out the facilities from the bar, but either way I didn't actually mind.

I tucked my wallet away and considered stepping out of the stall, but the fact that I couldn't see him made it easier to say what needed saying.

"Are we alone?" I asked.

"We are."

"Whatever it was you did to make Laura Kim dump you…don't even think about pulling it with Lisa."

"Sadly, you're correct in assuming that I was never the one to initiate the divorce proceedings. You probably figure it was some horrible excess on my part that scared them away. Drugs. Gambling. Cheating." Actually, I'd suspected he was a workaholic of epic proportions. "None of the above. Well, except a little toke once in a blue moon. No, it was the night terrors that drove 'em off. I don't dream like regular people dream. Instead, I see people die. Every night. Back in my salad days, I used to think that meant I had a few screws loose. Then something called the Internet came along, and I discovered all these people actually did kick the bucket. That confirmation only made it worse, knowing that real people were buying it left and right, and there wasn't a damn thing I could do but watch it happen. Not only that, but I started obsessing on the idea that one of those days, it was going to be me. I'd be the one drowning or choking or falling into a wood chipper. Poor Laura. She was determined to fix me…and I guess I thought if anyone could, it was her. You can imagine what a failure she felt like when nothing she said or did would stop me from waking up five times a night in a cold sweat, flailing in the bed and screaming bloody murder."

Fucking hell. "No wonder you never had Lisa sleep over."

"Ha, I came off as a real gentleman, too. Until things got past second base…then I had to come clean. Miss Lisa's seen some righteously fucked-up shit herself, though. She understood. Now, when I ask her if I'll live to see another day, she tells me, *Just you wait, buddy boy.* And, well…I believe her. Somehow, it does the trick. My nightly wanderings are nowhere near as frequent or violent as they used to be."

Silence stretched between us, and I chose to relinquish the safety and anonymity of my stall. Maybe I wasn't ready to hear any more personal details from him, or maybe I was worried I'd be lulled into sharing some of my own. But I did a startled double-take when I found some strange guy in a suit standing where I'd expected Dreyfuss to be waiting for me, a guy who'd recently stopped a few fists with his face.

And then I realized it was him.

He met my eyes in the mirror, then ran a washcloth under cold water and pressed it to his lip. "Not exactly the impression I'd been hoping to make on Lisa's big sister."

Sister? That explained the mistaken identity out in the hallway. Ironically enough, I probably would've walked right past Dreyfuss without knowing it was him. Wild corkscrew curls? Gone. A short haircut instead—trendy and flattering enough that I presumed Crash or Red had clipped it. Baggy sweats? Gone, too. His sleek black suit fit perfectly, and it turned out he'd been hiding a bantam-weight boxer's build under all those layers of fleece. The beating his face had recently taken was no doubt responsible for bringing the boxing comparison to mind. Between the split lip and the brand new shiner, he must've taken two punches, minimum, to buy me the time I needed with the body. Given that he had no reassurance of coming through his encounter with Washington at all, he must've counted himself lucky to escape with a couple of dings. But seeing them on the face of the Regional Director of the FPMP brought home that none of us were nearly as safe as we tended to believe.

"Since I have you alone..." he dropped the cloth in the basin and pulled an envelope from his pocket. "Here's your back pay. Plus a little extra for your trouble." He shook the envelope and pills rattled inside. "Don't take 'em all at once. That's what cyanide's for."

I took the envelope and squeezed it. Felt like a couple dozen capsules in there, easy. My inner neurotic rejoiced at the thought of a month's worth of deep, dreamless sleep. That joy was diminished, however, by thoughts of psychic jellyfish floating along behind me on their goopy tethers. I gave the envelope a final longing squeeze, then slid it back across the countertop. "I'm thinking I should renegotiate my terms."

"This late in the game?" Dreyfuss shook his head. "I'll do what I can, but no guarantees."

"I need to track down someone, a woman, a homeless woman. She was treated for alcohol poisoning in the emergency room at LaSalle Memorial Hospital—I don't know her name, but I can get you the dates."

"Doable. Give whatever details you can to The Fixer. I'll make sure she's expecting them."

"And my partner, Bob Zigler. His talent is wasted at the Fifth Precinct. I want him to have a job, a meaningful job where he can make a difference, something that doesn't eat his soul for lunch and shit it right back out. Something that pays decent, too."

"Zigler's a fine investigator. The FPMP can make him an offer. Whether he accepts it or not will be up to him."

Dare I ask for another pair of tickets behind the fifty-yard line? I supposed it couldn't hurt. "And one more thing. The last perp I brought in, a guy who stabbed his wife in the neck and threw her in the back of his truck…I need to make sure he doesn't walk."

"Is that so?" Dreyfuss raised an eyebrow. "Never thought I'd hear Mr. Fifth Amendment asking me to fix a trial. What happened?"

He knew damn well what happened. I'd go so far as to say he'd made sure the headline about the dog dish murderer had run somewhere I'd be likely to see it.

Dreyfuss turned toward the mirror and fiddled with the top of his new haircut, frowning, and said, "If it were within my power, I'd do it in a heartbeat. But a stunt like that would require a significant amount of favors. Unfortunately, I've burned all my favors in planning our honeymoon."

"Where the heck are you two going? Cuba?"

"Actually, Havana's not a bad idea. But, no. It's not the location that's expensive. It's the duration."

He eyed me via reflection while the actual meaning of what he was saying dawned on me. Dreyfuss and Lisa were about to redact themselves. "Not forever," I blurted out. "I mean…when things blow over with Washington…."

"Then it'll just be someone else lurking in the shadows. Think about it. We're the weapons that are too dangerous to fall into the wrong hands.

If someone twitchy gets wind of what either me or *mi novia* can do, it's game over."

"Unless Dr. K's research panned out, and Psych became so common that you weren't all that special anymore."

"People like us—Psychs with so much natural ability that we're completely over the top—don't have any chance of really blending in with the herd. Maybe someday, but not in this generation."

"But Dr. K said the field of Psych is like aeronautics and computers. We both remember typing on typewriters and looking stuff up in encyclopedias. You know how futuristic it felt to open up a browser window and type a search term for the first time—over a dial-up modem. Now we've got it on our damn phones. You just got finished telling me how the Internet helped you figure yourself out, so you can't deny that change can happen in leaps and bounds."

"Someone pinch me…either I'm dreaming, or Victor Bayne reveals himself to be a closet optimist."

He tucked the envelope of Seconal back into his pocket, and the thought of swallowing a familiar red capsule made my mouth water. If I asked for one, just one, he'd probably give it to me. Heck, he'd probably give me the whole envelope; Con Dreyfuss was nothing if not generous. But if I had a handful of reds in my pocket, no matter how hard I tried to resist, I'd end up taking one. Maybe two. And if I said or did anything loopy while I was under the influence, the sí-no would tattle on me and tell Lisa I got high at her wedding.

I exited the mens room before I did anything I'd end up regretting.

Maybe Lisa was fully prepared to take on the remote seer's night terrors. But Dreyfuss would need all the luck he could get to embark on his new life under the scrutiny of the sí-no.

CHAPTER 35

WHEN I GOT THE CALL, Jacob was dozing in the passenger seat while I played designated driver. The gears of the FPMP machine turn fast. I was still full of grilled snapper, wedding cake and squelched, bitter tears when the new Regional Director tapped me. I said I'd need to think about it, but really, I was deciding whether I'd do Jacob the courtesy of discussing my next step with him first. As I considered the offer, I found myself making a right where I'd normally turn left, heading south down streets that were post-midnight empty, over the river, through Greektown, and past U of I.

Although it was nearly two o'clock in the morning, Jim's Original was still open. Apparently they never close. A half dozen drunk frat boys were pooling their spare change to try and alleviate their munchies. It took me a moment to pick out the dead panhandler from the crowd. I watched for a few moments, and there he was, in all his spectral glory. Matted hair. Frayed trenchcoat. Hunched shoulders. Everything about him screamed out to my cop-sense that he was up to no good. He meandered through the group of college kids, between them, *in* them, trying them on for size, one, then another.

I'm told alcohol is a mild antipsyactive. But Jacob wasn't wasted, only exhausted. He'd do fine—we had the element of surprise on our side. I shook him by the knee and his head jerked up. "Where are we?"

"Maxwell Street."

"You're *hungry*?"

"Nope." I drummed my fingers on the steering wheel. "We're gonna do a salting."

That woke him up good. He straightened in his seat and squared his shoulders. "Did you bring candles? Should I clear the area?"

He pulled his wallet, but before he could storm out there and scare the frat boys half to death with his Fed badge, I caught him by the sleeve. "Relax. Take a deep breath. Focus on getting your vibration right."

Concentration furrowed his brow. "It's hard to…. I can't exactly feel it, not like before. With the psyactives."

"I know. Without the horse pills, it probably feels like you're making it all up. But trust me, you're not."

We sat there together, each attuning ourselves to our talent. As I sucked down white light, I considered what it meant to be an exorcist. I wasn't comfortable with the responsibility of being judge, jury and executioner… but these things were already dead, so the due process analogy didn't really hold up. Especially considering its track record in my own recent experience. I watched the panhandler eel in and out of a particular kid, a scrawny dweeb who just wanted a hot dog, and that was all the confirmation I needed that I was making the right move.

"So," I told Jacob. I didn't want to train him to require total silence and concentration to work on his vibe, after all. "I got a call from the FPMP. After the possession incident, Richie decided he was in way over his head. He quit." It seemed like a stunningly wise decision. Then again, Richie's sense of self-preservation was pretty well honed. "They asked me to be his replacement."

"And when you were through laughing, what did you say?"

"Nothing, yet."

The college kids sauntered away with their greasy bags of fries. The panhandler drifted into the hot dog stand…and probably into the fry cook. Jacob looked me over. "You're actually considering it."

I nodded once.

"Well," he said, overly casual, "whatever you think is best."

For all that he badmouthed Dreyfuss and complained about the surveillance on us, I knew that deep down, Jacob was ecstatic I'd had a change of heart. The moment my back was turned, he'd indulge in a little victory dance. The thing is, I didn't feel as if I was making a concession.

Why bother tracking down murderers when the biased jurors were only going to let them walk? And why settle for a two-man Spook Squad, just me and a single overtaxed NP, when I could be working with a whole team of experts?

Besides, if I didn't take the job, they'd offer it to my old Camp Hell nemesis…no, not Faun Windsong, I made peace with her. The other one, Dead Darla. Yep, she'd been flushed out of the woodwork earlier that day. She had the honor of being the medium Jennifer Chance wore to make her final phone call. Obviously I wasn't about to leave the FPMP in her care when all she could do was sense the occasional cold spot.

"You ready to salt this creep?" I asked.

"Almost. Gimme another minute."

Jacob was feeling it—what a relief. If I could help him trust his gut, he'd only get better…at whatever it is his talent actually does.

While he finished charging his psychic batteries, I pulled up the last call I received and hit the callback button. "Okay," I said. "I'll do it."

"Oh my God. Oh my *God*!" Laura Kim let out a very un-Director-like squeal of delight. "I promise you won't regret it." That sentiment was way too optimistic, but one can only adopt so many manatees, so I figured I should refrain from contradicting my new boss.

Change was in the air, and though I'd been tempted to stay the course and cling to my paper PsyCop license out of sheer stubbornness, I could see that someone needed to step in and take care of the repeaters, and the jellyfish, and the icky, grabby, self-entitled ghosts. That someone might as well be me.

ABOUT THIS STORY

IN THE LATE 80'S, I lived just south of Maxwell Street. It is an actual street, though the name also refers to the neighborhood around that street. It's all different now. U of I bought up the land and built stuff on it. But back then it was its own little world.

Maxwell is a small east-west street on the South Side that only runs a few blocks before being interrupted, and Halsted is the main artery that intersects it. Heading south of Maxwell down Halsted, you'd traverse a scary viaduct (a walkable distance, though one that I would never dare walk because of the gangs, only travel by car or bus) and then end up in the Mexican neighborhood Pilsen I called home for many years. To the north was the Kennedy, and across that forbidding bridge over the highway was Greektown, home to spectacular diners (Greek potatoes!) and bakeries (baklava!), and an esoteric shop called Athenian Candle Company (still there!) which is my visual and olfactory mental image for Sticks and Stones.

To the east, the old early 20th century garment district had a few shops left, specialty fabric stores that felt industrial and forbidding inside. People came from the far suburbs to find textiles there they couldn't get elsewhere. And the fabric was all jumbled up in big rolls with no attempt to display it enticingly. As a Fiber Arts student I spent plenty of time in these stores.

West of Halsted, six days a week, was a half-abandoned stretch of fields and parking lots scattered with a few crumbling warehouses. Until Sunday came. And on Sunday, sometime in the wee hours of the morning, a ragged bazaar sprang up—seemingly out of nowhere, like something from a dark fairy tale. People set up tables and stalls, and even sold things off the back of trucks. Cut-rate nicknacks and chachkies out the wazoo. Produce, yes, tons of produce, though it was never quite apparent what anything cost and you were taking your chances of getting ripped off just because the vendor didn't like the look of you. Bootleg? Oh yes, all kinds of bootleg. Subtly misprinted caps and T-shirts for the "licensed" goods, cassette tapes and VHS for the media. I'm not a sports fan so the jerseys didn't appeal to me, and I never bought any tapes, figuring I'd get home and find those tapes were either poorly dubbed, or altogether blank.

And the crowds. It was a milling throng of desperate, grim, crabby humanity. Then some dope would always be trying to drive his car through it and end up getting stuck in the pedestrian traffic. One time a car rolled over my foot…and then stopped right on it. I somehow found the presence of mind to yell, "Move, you're on my foot!" rather than just, "Aiiii!" Miraculously, nothing was broken.

Blanketing this entire scene was the smell of roasting sausage and grilled onions emanating from the hot dog shops on Maxwell Street itself. It didn't matter if it was the crack of dawn—and believe me, you had to show up early or everything would be picked over—and it didn't matter if you'd eaten breakfast. One whiff of a Maxwell Street Polish and it felt like you'd never eaten before in your life. They were dirt cheap, so of course it seemed economical to get at least two. The poppy seed buns were steamy and soft. The onions were grilled to the point of caramelization. And there was always a hot pickled pepper tucked into the bun. Shoot, I need one right now. And it's 7:30 on a Monday morning. In Wisconsin.

After I moved away, the area was cleaned up and the flea market relocated to a pavilion type thing to the east of Maxwell Street. I've never been there but I'm sure it's nowhere near as seedy, and nowhere near as fun.

Crash would have enjoyed the original Maxwell Street, but I think by the time he was able to drive himself there from Arlington Heights, the urban bazaar of my memories had been paved over long ago. I've got Crash on the mind because I'm eager to explore more of him in a standalone. When I looked at how much of his story belonged in

Spook Squad, I realized that I needed to limit him to a few key scenes that mirrored what was going on with Vic, otherwise Vic's story would become too difficult and cumbersome to follow. But it also seemed there was a whole iceberg under the surface that would be fun to tap. Crash will get his own story, but if you're curious about Red, his first mention is in an interview I ran in my newsletter a few years ago.

find the interview at http://psycop.com/extras

ABOUT THE AUTHOR

LIKE LISA, JORDAN CASTILLO PRICE buys her jewelry from spinner racks in stores like Target and Sears, or better yet, at garage sales. She'd feel anxious about wearing a real diamond tennis bracelet for fear of breaking it.

Since the writing of this novel, she was been rather leery of free smoothies. Though that hasn't stopped her from accepting them.

Connect with Jordan in the following online places:
jordancastilloprice.com
facebook.com/jordancastilloprice
twitter.com/jordancprice

THE PSYCOP SERIES

PAPERBACK

PsyCop Partners (contains Among the Living and Criss Cross)
PsyCop Property (contains Body & Soul and Secrets)
Camp Hell
GhosTV
Spook Squad

EBOOK

Among the Living - PsyCop 1
Criss Cross - PsyCop 2
Body & Soul - PsyCop 3
Secrets - PsyCop 4
Camp Hell - PsyCop 5
GhosTV - PsyCop 6
Spook Squad - PsyCop 7
Inside Out - PsyCop Short
Many Happy Returns - PsyCop Short
Mind Reader - PsyCop Short
Striking Sparks - PsyCop Short
Thaw - PsyCop Short
In the Dark - PsyCop Short
bonus flash fiction at PsyCop.com